# THE TORRENT

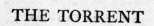

## BY THE SAME AUTHOR

THE FOUR HORSEMEN OF THE APOCALYPSE

MARE NOSTRUM (*Our Sea*)

BLOOD AND SAND

LA BODEGA (*The Fruit of the Vine*)

THE SHADOW OF THE CATHEDRAL

WOMAN TRIUMPHANT

THE ENEMIES OF WOMEN

MEXICO IN REVOLUTION

THE MAYFLOWER

E. P. DUTTON & COMPANY

# THE TORRENT

## (*ENTRE NARANJOS*)

BY

## VICENTE BLASCO IBAÑEZ

TRANSLATED FROM THE SPANISH BY

### ISAAC GOLDBERG

AND

### ARTHUR LIVINGSTON

NEW YORK
E. P. DUTTON & COMPANY
681 FIFTH AVENUE

# THE TORRENT

## PART ONE

### I

"Your friends are waiting for you at the Club. They saw you for a moment only, this morning; they'll be wanting to hear all your stories about life in Madrid."

Doña Bernarda fixed upon the young deputy a pair of deep, scrutinizing, severely maternal eyes that recalled to Rafael all the roguish anxieties of his childhood.

"Are you going directly to the Club? . . ." she added. "Andrés will be starting too, right away."

Rafael, in reply, wished a blunt "good-afternoon" to his mother and don Andrés, who were still at table sipping their coffee, and strode out of the dining-room.

Finding himself on the broad, red-marble staircase in the silence of that ancient mansion, of such princely magnificence, he experienced the sudden sense of comfort and wellbeing that a traveler feels on plunging into a bath after a tedious journey.

Ever since he had arrived, with the noisy reception at the station, the hurrahs, the deafening music, handshakes here, crowding there, the pushing and elbowing of more than a thousand people who had thronged the streets of Alcira to get a close look at him, this was the first moment he had found himself alone, his own master, able to do exactly as he pleased, without needing to smile automatically in all directions and welcome with demonstrations of affection persons whose faces he could scarcely recall.

What a deep breath of relief he drew as he went down the deserted staircase, which echoed his every footstep! How large and beautiful the *patio* was! How broad and lustrous the leaves of the plantains flourishing in their green boxes! There he had spent the best years of his childhood. The little boys who in those days used to be hiding behind the wide portal, waiting for a chance to play with the son of the powerful don Ramón Brull, were now the grown men, the sinewy orchard workers, who had been parading from the station to his house, waving their arms, and shouting *vivas* for their deputy—Alcira's "favorite son."

This contrast between the past and present flattered Rafael's conceit, though, in the background of his thoughts, the suspicion lurked that his mother had been not a little instrumental in the preparation of his noisy reception, not to mention don Andrés, and numerous other friends, ever loyal to anyone connected with the greatness of the Brulls, *caciques* —political bosses—and leading citizens of the district.

To enjoy these recollections of childhood and the pleasure of finding himself once more at home, after several months in Madrid, he stood for some time motionless in the *patio*, looking up at the balconies of the first story, then at the attic windows—from which in mischievous years gone by he had many a time withdrawn his head at the sound of his mother's scolding voice—and lastly, at the veil of luminous blue above—a patch of sky drenched in that Spanish sunlight which ripens the oranges to clusters of flaming gold.

He thought he could still see his father—the imposing, solemn don Ramón—sauntering about the *patio*, his hands behind his back, answering in a few impressive words the questions flung at him by his party adherents, who followed him about with idolatrous eyes. If the old man could only have come back to life that morning to see how his son had been acclaimed by the entire city! . . .

A barely perceptible sound like the buzzing of two flies broke the deep silence of the mansion. The deputy looked toward the only balcony window that was open, though but slightly. His mother and don Andrés were still talking in the dining-room—and of him, as usual, without a doubt! And, lest they should call him, and suddenly deprive him of his keen enjoyment at being alone, he left the *patio* and went out into the street.

It was only the month of March; but at two in the afternoon the air was almost uncomfortably hot. Accustomed to the cold wind of Madrid and to the winter rains, Rafael inhaled, with a sense of voluptuous pleasure, the warm breeze that wafted the perfume of the blossoming orchards through the narrow lanes of the ancient town.

Once, years before, he had been in Italy on a Catholic pilgrimage, entrusted by his mother to the care of a priest from Valencia, who would not think of returning to Spain without paying a visit to don Carlos. A memory of a Venetian *calle* now came back to Rafael's mind as he traversed the streets of old Alcira—shadowy, cramped, sunk deep as wells between rows of high houses. With all the economy of a city built on an island, Alcira rears its edifices higher and higher as its population grows, leaving just enough space free for the bare needs of traffic.

The streets were deserted. The noisy, orchard workers who had welcomed Rafael had gone back to the fields again. All the idlers had fled to the cafés, and as the deputy walked smartly by in front of these, warm waves of air came out upon him through the windows, with the clatter of poker chips, the noise of billiard balls, and the uproar of heated argument.

Rafael reached the Suburban Bridge, one of the two means of egress from the Old City  The Júcar was combing its muddy, reddish waters on the piles of the ancient structure. A number of row-boats, made fast to the houses on the shore, were tugging at their moorings. Rafael recognized among them the fine craft that he had once used for lonely trips on the river. It lay there quite forgotten, gradually shedding its coat of white paint out in the weather.

Then he looked at the bridge itself; the Gothic-arched gate, a relic of the old fortifications; the battlements of yellowish, chipped rock, which looked as if all the rats of the river had come at night to nibble at them; then two niches with a collection of mutilated, dust-laden images—San Bernardo, patron Saint of Alcira, and his estimable sisters. Dear old San Bernardo, *alias* Prince Hamete, son of the

Moorish king of Carlet, converted to Christ by the mystic poesy of the Christian cult,—and still wearing in his mangled forehead the nail of martyrdom!

As Rafael walked past the rude, disfigured statue he thought of all the stories his mother, an uncompromising clerical and a woman of credulous faith, had told him of the patron of Alcira, particularly the legend of the enmity and struggle between San Vicente and San Bernardo, an ingenuous fancy of popular superstition.

Saint Vincent, who was an eloquent preacher arrived at Alcira on one of his tours, and stopped at a blacksmith's shop near the bridge to get his donkey shod. When the work was done the horseshoer asked for the usual price for his labor; but San Vicente, accustomed to living on the bounty of the faithful, waxed indignant, and looking at the Júcar, exclaimed, vindictively:

"Some day folks will say: 'This is where Alcira used to be'."

"Not while Bernardo is here!" the statue of San Bernardo remarked from its pedestal.

And there the statue of the saint still stood, like an eternal sentinel, watching over the Júcar to exorcise the curse of the rancorous Saint Vincent! To be sure the river would rise and overflow its banks every year, reaching to the very feet of San Bernardo sometimes, and coming within an ace of pulling the wily saint down from his perch. It is also true that every five or six years the flood would shake houses loose from their foundations, destroy good farm land, drown people, and commit other horrible depredations—all in obedience to the curse of Valencia's patron; but the saint of Alcira was the better man

of the two for all of that! And, if you didn't believe it, there the city was, still planted firmly on its
feet and quite unscathed, except for a scratch here
and there from times when the rains were excep-
tionally heavy and the waters came down from Cuenca in a great roaring torrent!

With a smile and a nod to the powerful saint, as
to an old friend of childhood, Rafael crossed the
bridge and entered the *arrabal,* the "New City,"
ample, roomy, unobstructed, as if the close-packed
houses of the island, to get elbow-room and a breath
of air, had stampeded in a flock to the other bank
of the river, scattering hither and thither in the hilar-
ious disorder of children let loose from school.

The deputy paused at the head of the street on
which his club was located. Even from there he
could hear the talking and laughing of the many
members, who had gathered in much greater number
than usual because of his arrival. What would he
be in for down there? A speech, probably! A
speech on local politics! Or, if not a speech, idle
talk about the orange crop, or cock-fighting. He
would be expected to tell them what kind of a man
the Premier was—and then spend the afternoon ana-
lyzing the character of every minister! Then don
Andrés would be there, that boresome Mentor who,
at the instance of Rafael's mother, would never let
him out of sight for a moment. Bah! The Club
could wait! He would have plenty of time later in
the day to stifle in that smoke-filled parlor where,
the moment he showed his face, everybody would be
upon him and pester the life out of him with questions and wire-pulling!

And more and more yielding to the lure of the

southern sunshine and to those perfumes of May floating about him in wintertime, he turned off into a lane that led to the fields.

As he emerged from the ancient Ghetto and found himself in the open country, he drew a deep breath, as if to imprison in his lungs all the life, bloom and color of his native soil.

The orange orchards lined both banks of the stream with straight rows of green, round tree-tops. The sun glistened off the varnished leaves; the wheels of irrigating machines sounded from the distance like humming insects. The moisture rising from the canals, joined the clouds from the chimneys of the motors, to form a thin veil of mist over the country-side, that gave a pearly transparency to the golden light of the afternoon.

To one side rose the hill of San Salvador, its crest topped with the Hermitage, and the pines, the cypresses, and the prickly pears around that rough testimonial of popular piety. The sanctuary seemed to be talking to him like an indiscreet friend, betraying the real motive that had caused him to evade his appointment with his political friends and disobey his mother into the bargain.

Something more than the beauty of the fields had enticed him from the city. When the rays of the rising sun had awakened him that morning on the train, the first thing he had seen, before opening his eyes even, was an orange orchard, the bank of the Júcar, and a house painted blue,—the very one that was now in sight away off there, among the round tree-tops along the river.

How many times in past months his thoughts had lingered on the memory of that same scene!

Afternoons, in the Congress, while the Premier on the Blue Bench would be answering the interpellations of the Opposition in sharp incisive tones, Rafael's brain would begin to doze, reduced to jelly, as it were, by the incessant hammering of words, words, words! Before his closed eyes a dark veil would begin to unroll as if the moist, cellar-like gloom in which the Chamber is always plunged, had thickened suddenly, and against this curtain, like a cinema dream, rows of orange-trees would come into view, and a blue house with open windows; and pouring through the windows a stream of notes from a soft voice, ever so sweet, singing *lieder* and ballads as an accompaniment to the hard, sonorous paragraphs snapping from the Premier's teeth. Then applause and disorder! The moment for voting had arrived, and the fading outlines of the Blue House still hovering before his dreamy eyes, the member for Alcira would ask his neighbor:

"How do we vote? Yes or no?"

The same it was at night at the Opera, where music served only to remind him of a familiar voice winding like a thread of gold out across the orchards through the orange-trees; and the same again, after dinner with his colleagues on committees, when the deputies, their cigars tilted cockily upwards between their lips, and with all the voluptuous gaiety inspired by good digestions, would troop off to see the night out in some trustworthy house of assignation where their dignity as representatives of the country would not be compromised!

Now that blue house was actually before his eyes! And he was hurrying toward it,—not without some hesitation; a vague uneasiness he could not explain.

His heart was in his mouth, it seemed, and he found it hard to breathe.

Orchard workers came along the road, occasionally, stepping aside to make room for the famous man, though he answered their greeting absent-mindedly. What a nuisance! They would all be sure to tell where they had seen him! His mother would know all about it within half an hour! And, that evening, a scene in the dining-room! As Rafael walked on toward the Blue House, he thought bitterly of his situation. Why was he going there anyhow? Why insist on living in a stew all the time? He had had two or three short but violent scenes with his mother a few months before. What a fury that stern, pious, and puritanic woman became when she found out that her son had been calling down at the Blue House and was on friendly terms with a strange lady, an outsider, whom the respectable folk of the city would have nothing to do with, and of whom not a good word was ever heard except from the men at the Club, when they were sure their wives were not in hearing distance!

Tempestuous scenes they had been! He was running for Congress at the time. Was he trying—she wanted to know—to dishonor the family and compromise his political future? Was that what his poor father had lived for—a life of sacrifice and struggle, of service to "the Party," which, many a time, had meant shouldering a gun? And a loose woman was to be allowed to ruin the House of Brull, which for thirty years had been putting every cent it owned into politics, for the benefit of My Lords up in Madrid! And just when a Brull was about to reap the reward of so many sacrifices at last, and become a deputy—the means perhaps of clearing off the property, which was lousy with attachments and mortgages! . . .

Rafael had been no match for that energetic mother, the soul of "the Party." Meekly he had promised never to return to the Blue House, never to call again on that "loose woman"—doña Bernarda actually hissed as she said the word.

However, the upshot of it all had been that Rafael simply discovered how weak he was. Despite his promise, he returned to the Blue House often, but by round-about ways and over long detours, skulking from cover to cover, as he had done in childhood days when stealing oranges from the orchards. There he was, a man whose name was on the lips of the whole county, and who at any moment might be invested with authority from the people, thus realizing the life-long dream of his father! But the sight of a woman in the fields, a child, a beggar, would make him blanch with terror! And that was not the worst of it! Whenever he entered the Blue House now he had to pretend he came openly, without any fear whatever. And so things had gone on down to the very eve of his departure for Madrid.

As Rafael reached this point in his reminiscences, he asked himself what hope had led him to disobey his mother and brook her truly formidable wrath.

In that blue house he had found only frank, disinterested friendship,—a somewhat ironic comradeship, the condescending tolerance of a person compelled by solitude to choose as her comrade the least repulsive among a host of inferiors. Alas! How clearly he remembered and could again foresee the sceptical, cold smile with which his words were always received, though he was sure he had crammed them with burning passion! What a laugh she had given,—as insolent and as cutting as a lash,—the day he had dared to declare his love!

"Now the soft-pedal on slush, eh, Rafael- ito? . . . If you want us to go on being friends, all right, but it's on condition you treat me as a man. Comrades, eh, and nothing more."

And with a look at him through those green, luminous, devilish eyes of hers, she had taken her seat at the piano and begun one of her divine songs, as if she thought the magic of her art might raise a barrier between them.

On another occasion, she was irritable rather; Rafael's appealing eyes, his words of amorous adoration, seemed to provoke her, and she had said with brutal frankness:

"Don't waste your breath, please! I am through with love. I know men too well! But even if anyone were to upset me again, it would not be you, Rafaelito dear."

And yet he had persisted, insensible to the irony and the scorn of this terrible *amigo* in skirts, and indifferent as well to the conflicts that his blind passion might provoke at home if his mother knew.

He tried to free himself from his infatuation, but unsuccessfully. With that in view he fixed his attention on the woman's past; it was said that despite her beauty, her aristrocratic manners, the brilliancy of mind with which she had dazzled him—a poor country boy—she was only an adventuress who had made her way over half the globe from one pair of arms to another. Well, in that case, it would

be a great exploit to win a woman whom princes and
celebrated men had loved! But since that was impossible, why go on, why continue endangering his
career and having trouble with his mother all the
time?

To forget her, he stressed, before his own mind,
words and attitudes of hers that might be judged
defects; and he would taste the joy of duty well done
when, after such gymnastics of the will, he could
think of her without great emotion.

At the beginning of his life in Madrid he imagined he had recovered. New surroundings; continuous and petty satisfactions to vanity; the kow-
towing of doorkeepers in Congress; the flattery of
visitors from here, there and everywhere who came
with requests for passes to admit them to the galleries; the sense of being treated as a comrade by
celebrities, whose names his father had always mentioned with bated breath; the "honorable" always
written before his name; all Alcira speaking to him
with affectionate familiarity; this rubbing elbows, on
the benches of the conservative majority, with a
battalion of dukes, counts and marquises—young
men who had become deputies to round out the distinction conferred by beautiful sweethearts or winning thoroughbreds,—all this had intoxicated him,
filled his mind completely, crowding out all other
thoughts, and persuading him that he had been completely cured.

But as he grew familiar with his new life, and the
novelty of all this adulation wore off, tenacious recollections rose again in his memory. At night, when
sleep relaxed the will to forget, which his vigilance
kept at painful tension, that blue house, the green,

diabolical eyes of its principal denizen, that pair of fresh lips with their ironic smile that seemed to quiver between two rows of gleaming white teeth, would become the inevitable center of all his dreams.

Why resist any longer? He could think of her as much as he pleased—that, at least, his mother would never learn. And he gave himself up to the imagination of love, where distance lent an ever stronger enchantment to that woman.

He felt a vehement longing to return to his city. Absence seemed to do away with all the obstacles at home. His mother was not so formidable as he had thought. Who could tell whether, when he went back—changed as he felt himself to be by his new experiences—it would not be easier to continue the old relations? After so much isolation and solitude she might receive him in more cordial fashion!

The Cortes were about to adjourn, so, in obedience to repeated urging from his fellow-partisans, and from doña Bernarda, to *do something*—anything at all—to show interest in the home town—he took the floor one afternoon at the opening of the session, when only the president, the sergeant-at-arms, and a few reporters asleep in the press-gallery, were present, and, with his lunch rising in his throat from emotion, asked the Minister of Internal Affairs to show a little more despatch in the matter of flood protection at Alcira—a bill still in its infancy, though it had been pending some seventy years.

After this he was free to return with the halo of a "business-like" deputy shining about his head—"a zealous defender of the region's interests," the local weekly and party organ called him. And that

morning, as he stepped off the train, the deputy, deaf
to the Royal March and to the *vivas,* stood up on tip-
toe, trying to descry through the waving banners the
Blue House nestling in the distance among the orange-trees.

As he approached the place that afternoon he
was almost sick with nervousness and emotion. For
one last time he thought of his mother, so intent
upon maintaing her prestige and so fearful of hostile gossip; of the demagogues who had thronged the
doors of the cafés that morning, making fun of the
demonstration in his honor; but all his scruples vanished at sight of the hedge of tall rose-bays and
prickly hawthorns and of the two blue pillars supporting a barrier of green wooden bars. Resolutely
he pushed the gate open, and entered the garden.

Orange-trees stretched in rows along broad
straight walks of red earth. On either side of the
approach to the house was a tangle of tall rose-
bushes on which the first buds, heralds of an early
spring, were already beginning to appear.

Above the chattering of the sparrows and the
rustle of the wind in the trees, Rafael could hear
the sound of a piano—the keys barely touched by
the player's fingers—and a soft, timid voice, as if
the song were meant for the singer alone.

It was she. Rafael knew the music: a *Lied* by
Schubert—the favorite composer of the day; a master "whose best work was still unknown," as she
said in the cant she had learned from the critics,
alluding to the fact that only the least subtle of the
melancholy composer's works had thus far been pop-
ularized.

The young man advanced slowly, cautiously, as if

afraid lest the sound of his footsteps break in upon
that melody which seemed to be rocking the garden
lovingly to sleep in the afternoon's golden sunlight.

He reached the open space in front of the house
and once more found there the same murmuring
palms, the same rubblework benches with seats and
backs of flowered tile that he knew so well. There,
in fact, she had so often laughed at his feverish protestations.

The door was closed; but through a half-opened
window he could see a patch of silk; a woman's
back, bending slightly forward over the music.

As Rafael came up a dog began to bark at the
end of the garden. Some hens that had been scratching about in sand of the drive, scampered off cackling
with fright. The music stopped. A chair scraped as
it was pushed back. The lady was rising to her feet.

At the balcony a flowing gown of blue appeared;
but all that Rafael saw was a pair of eyes—green
eyes, that seemed to fill the entire window with a
flood of light.

"Beppa! Beppina!" cried a firm, a warm, a sonorous, soprano voice. *"Apri la porta.* Open the
door."

And with a slight inclination of her splendid head
of thick auburn hair that seemed to crown her with
a helmet of old gold, she smiled to him with a friendly, somewhat mocking, intimacy:

"Welcome, Rafaelito. I don't know why, but I
was expecting you this afternoon. We have heard
all about your triumphs; the music and the tumult
reached even to our desert. My congratulations to
the Honorable don Rafael Brull. Come right in,
*su señoría."*

## II

From Valencia to Játiva, in all that immense territory covered with rice-fields and orange groves which Valencians embrace under the general and rather vague designation of *La Ribera*, there was no one unfamiliar with the name of Brull and the political power it stood for.

As if national unity had not yet been effected and the country were still divided into *taifas* and *waliatos* as in the days when one Moorish King reigned over Carlet, another over Denia, and a third over Játiva, the election system maintained a sort of inviolable rulership in every district; and when the Administration people came to Alcira in forecasting their political prospects, they always said the same thing:

"We're all right there. We can rely on Brull."

The Brull dynasty had been bossing the district for thirty years, with ever-increasing power.

The founder of this sovereign house had been Rafael's grandfather, the shrewd don Jaime, who had established the family fortune by fifty years of slow exploitation of ignorance and poverty. He began life as a clerk in the *Ayuntamiento* of Alcira; then he became secretary to the municipal judge, then assistant to the city clerk, then assistant-registrar of deeds. There was not a subordinate position in those offices where the poor come in contact with the law that he did not get his hands on; and from such points of vantage, by selling justice as a favor and using power or adroitness to subdue the refractory, he felt his way along, appropriating parcel after parcel of that fertile soil which he adored with a miser's covetousness.

A brazen charlatan he was, every moment talking of "Article Number So-and-So" of the law that applied to the case. The poor orchard workers came to have as much awe for his learning as fear of his malice, and in all their controversies they sought his advice and paid for it, as if he were a lawyer.

When he had gotten a small fortune together, he continued holding his menial posts in the city administration to retain the superstitious respect which is inspired in peasant-folk by all who are on good terms with the law; but not content with playing the eternal beggar, dependent on the humble gratuities of the poor, he took to pulling them out of their financial difficulties, lending them money on the collateral of their future harvests.

But six per cent seemed too petty a profit for him. The real plight of these folk came when a horse died and they had to buy another. Don Jaime became a dealer in dray horses, buying more or less defective animals from gypsies in Valencia, praising their virtues to the skies, and reselling them as thoroughbreds. And no sale on the instalment plan! Cash down! The horses did not belong to him— as he vowed with his hand pressed solemnly to his bosom—and their owners wished to realize on their value at once. The best he could do in the circumstances—prompted by his greatness of heart, which always overflowed at the sight of poverty—was to borrow money for the purchase from a friend of his.

The peasant in his desperate need would fall into the snare, and carry off the horse after signing all kinds of notes and mortgages to cover the loan of money he had not seen! For the don Jaime who spoke for the unknown party in the deal transferred the cash to the same don Jaime who spoke for the owner of the horse. Result: the rustic bought an animal, without chaffering, at double its value, having in addition borrowed a lot of money at cut-throat interest. In every turn-over of this sort don Jaime doubled his principal. New straits inevitably developed for the dupe; the interest kept piling up; hence new concessions, still more ruinous than the first, that don Jaime might be placated and give the purchaser a month's reprieve.

Every Wednesday, which was market-day in Alcira and brought a great crowd of orchard-folk to town, the street where don Jaime lived was the busiest in the city. People came in droves to ask for renewal of their notes, each leaving a tip of several *pesetas* usually, not to be counted against the debt itself. Others, humbly, timidly, as if they had come to rob the grasping Shylock, would ask for loans; and the strange thing about it, as the malicious noted, was that all these people, after leaving everything they owned in don Jaime's hands, went off content, their faces beaming with satisfaction, as if they had just been rescued from a danger.

This was don Jaime's chief skill. He had the trick of making usury look like kindness; he always spoke of *those fellows,* those hidden owners of the money and the horses—heartless wretches who were "after him," holding him responsible for the shortcomings of all their debtors. The burdens he thus supposedly assumed won him a reputation as a kind-hearted soul, and such confidence was the wily old demon able to instill in his victims that when mortgages were foreclosed on homes or fields, many of the unfortunates despoiled, would say, resignedly:

"It's not his fault. What could the poor man do if they forced him to it? It's those *other fellows* who are sucking the blood of us poor folks."

And so, quietly, leisurely, tranquilly, don Jaime got possession of a field here, then another there, then a third between the two; and in a few years he had rounded out a beautiful orchard of orange-trees, with virtually no expenditure of capital at all. Thus his property went on increasing, and, with his radiant smile, his spectacles on his forehead and his paunch growing fatter and fatter, he could be seen surrounded by new victims, addressing them with the affectionate *tu,* patting them on the back, and vowing that this weakness he had for the doing of favors would some day bring him to dying like a dog in the gutter.

Thus he went on prospering. Nor was all the scoffing of city people of any avail in shaking the confidence reposed in him by that flock of rustics, who feared him as they feared the Law itself and believed in him as they believed in God.

A loan to a spendthrift eldest son made him the proprietor of the fine city mansion, which came to be known as "the Brull place." From that date he began to hob-nob with the large real-estate owners of the city, who, though they despised this upstart, made a small place for him in their midst with the instinctive solidarity that characterizes the freemasonry of money. To gain a little more standing for his name, he became a votary of San Bernardo, contributed to the funds for church festivals, and danced attendance on the *alcalde,* whoever that "mayor" might be. In his eyes now, the only people in Alcira were such as collected thousands of *duros,* whenever harvest time came around. The rest were rabble, rabble, sir!

Then, at last he resigned the petty offices he had been filling; and handing his usury business over to those who formerly had served him as go-betweens, he set himself to the task of marrying off his son and sole heir, Ramón, an idling ne'er-do-well, who was always getting into trouble and upsetting the tranquil comfort that surrounded old Brull as he rested from his plunderings.

The father felt the satisfaction of a bully in having such a tall, strong, daring and insolent son, a boy who compelled respect in cafés and clubs more with his fists than with the special privileges conferred in small towns by wealth. Let anyone dare make fun of the old usurer when he had such a fireeater to protect him!

Ramón had wanted to join the Army; but every time he referred to what he called his vocation, his father would fly into a rage. "Do you think that is what I've worked for all these years?" He could remember the time when, as a poor clerk, he had been forced to fawn on his superiors and listen humbly, cringingly, to their reprimands. He did not want a boy of his to be shoved about hither and thither like a mere machine. "Plenty of brass buttons," he exclaimed with the scorn of a man never to be taken in by external show, "and plenty of gold braid! But after all, a slave, a slave!"

No, he wanted to see his son free and influential, continuing the conquest of the city, completing the family greatness of which he had laid the foundations, getting power over people much as he himself had gotten power over money. Ramón must become a lawyer, the only career for a man destined to rule others. It was a passionate ambition the old pettifogger had, to see his scion enter through the front door and with head proudly erect, the precincts of the law, into which he had crawled so cautiously and at the risk, more than once, of being dragged out with a chain fastened to his ankle.

Ramón spent several years in Valencia without getting beyond the elementary courses in Common Law. The cursed classes were held in the morning, you see, and he had to go to bed at dawn—the hour when the lights in the pool-rooms went out. Besides, in his quarters at the hotel he had a magnificent shotgun—a present from his father; and homesickness for the orchards made him pass many an afternoon at the pigeon traps where he was far better known than at the University.

This fine specimen of masculine youth—tall, muscular, tanned, with a pair of domineering eyes to which thick eyebrows gave a touch of harshness—had been born for action, and excitement; Ramón simply couldn't concentrate on books!

Old Brull, who through niggardliness and prudence had placed his son on "half rations," as he put it, sent the boy just money enough to keep him going; but dupe, in turn, of the wiles he had formerly practiced on the rustics of Alcira, he was compelled to make frequent trips to Valencia, to come to some understanding with money lenders there, who had advanced loans to his son on such terms that insolvency might lead Ramón to a prison cell.

Home to Alcira came rumors of other exploits by the "Prince," as don Jaime called his boy in view of the latter's ability to run through money. In parties with friends of the family, don Ramón's doings were spoken of as scandalous actually—a duel after a quarrel at cards; then a father and a brother—common workingmen in flannel shirts!—who had sworn they would kill him if he didn't marry a certain girl he had been taking to her shop by day and to dance-halls by night.

Old Brull made up his mind to tolerate these escapades of his son no longer; and he made him give up his studies. Ramón would not be a lawyer; well, after all, one didn't have to have a degree to be a man of importance. Besides the father felt he was getting old; it was hard for him to look after the working of his orchards personally. He could make good use of that son who seemed to have been born to impose his will upon everybody around him.

For some time past don Jaime had had his eye on the daughter of a friend of his. The Brull house showed noticeable lack of a woman's presence. His wife had died shortly after his retirement from business, and the old codger stamped in rage at the slovenliness and laziness displayed by his servants. He would marry Ramón to Bernarda—an ugly, ill-humored, yellowish, skinny creature—but sole heiress to her father's three beautiful orchards. Besides, she was conspicuous for her industrious, economical ways, and a parsimony in her expenditures that came pretty close to stinginess.

Ramón did as his father bade him.  Brought up with all the ideas of a rural skinflint, he thought no decent person could object to marrying an ugly bad-tempered woman, so long as she had plenty of money.

The father-in-law and the daughter-in-law understood each other perfectly.  The old man's eyes would water at sight of that stern, long-faced puritan, who never had much to say in the house, but went into high dudgeon over the slightest waste on the part of the domestics, scolding the farmhands for the merest oversight in the orchards, haggling and wrangling with the orange drummers for a *centime* more or less per hundredweight.  That new daughter of his was to be the solace of his old age!

Meantime, the "prince" would be off hunting every morning in the nearby mountains and lounging every afternoon in the café; but he was no longer content with the admiration of the idlers hanging around a billiard table, nor was he taking part in the game upstairs.  He was frequenting the circles of "serious" people now, had made friends with the *alcalde* and was talking all the time of the great need for getting all "decent" folk together to take the "rabble" in hand!

"Ambition is pecking at him," the old man gleefully remarked to his daughter-in-law.  "Let him alone, woman; he'll get there, he'll get there . . . That's the way I like to see him."

Ramón began by winning a seat in the *Ayuntamiento,* and soon was an outstanding figure there.  The least objection to his views he regarded as a personal insult; he would transfer debates in session out into the streets and settle them there with

threats and fisticuffs. His greatest glory was to
have his enemies say of him:

"Look out for that Ramón . . . He's a tough
proposition."

Along with all this combativeness, he sought to
win friends by a lavish hand that was his father's
torment. He "did favors," assured a living, that
is, to every loafer and bully in town. He was
ready to be "touched" by anyone who could serve,
in tavern and café, as advertising agent of his rising fame.

And he rose rapidly, in fact. The old folks who
had pushed him forward with influence and counsel soon found themselves left far behind. In a
short time he had become *alcalde;* his prestige out-
grew the limits of the city, spread over the whole
district, and eventually reached the capital of the
province itself. He got able-bodied men exempted
from military service; he winked at corruption in
the city councils that backed him, although the per-
petrators deserved to go to prison; he saw to it that
the constabulary was not too energetic in running
down the *roders,* the "wanderers," who, for some
well-placed shot at election time, would be forced to
flee to the mountains. No one in the whole country dared make a move without the previous consent of don Ramón, whom his adherents always re-
spectfully called their *quefe,* their "chief."

Old Brull lived long enough to see Ramón reach
the zenith of his fame. That scallawag was realizing the old man's dream: the conquest of the city,
ruling over men where his father had gotten only
money! And, in addition don Jaime lived to see

the perpetuation of the Brull dynasty assured by
the birth of a grandson, Rafael, the child of a couple
who had never loved each other, but were united
only by avarice and ambition.

Old Brull died like a saint. He departed this
life with the consolation of all the last sacraments.
Every cleric in the city helped to waft his soul
heavenward with clouds of incense at the solemn
obsequies. And, though the rabble—the political
opponents of the son, that is—recalled those
Wednesdays long before when the flock from the
orchards would come to let itself be fleeced in the
old Shylock's office, all safe and sane people—people who had something in this world to lose—
mourned the death of so worthy and industrious a
man, a man who had risen from the lowest estate and
had finally been able to accumulate a fortune by
hard work, honest hard work!

In Rafael's father there still remained much of
the wild student who had caused so many tongues
to wag in his youthful days. But his doings with
peasant girls were hushed up now; fear of the
*cacique's* power stifled all gossip; and since, moreover, affairs with such lowly women cost very little
money, doña Bernarda pretended to know nothing
about them. She did not love her husband much.
She was leading that narrow, self-centered life of the
country woman, who feels that all her duties are fulfilled if she remains faithful to her mate and keeps
saving money.

By a noteworthy anomaly, she, who was so stingy,
so thrifty, ready to start a squabble on the public
square in defense of the family money against day-

laborers or middlemen, was tolerance itself toward
the lavish expenditures of her husband in maintain-
ing his political sovereignty over the region.

Every election opened a new breach in the family fortune. Don Ramón would receive orders to
carry his district for some non-resident, who might
not have lived there more than a day or two. So
those who governed yonder in Madrid had ordered
—and orders must be obeyed. In every town whole
muttons would be set turning over the fires. Tavern
wine would flow like water. Debts would be can-
celled and fistfulls of *pesetas* would be distributed
among the most recalcitrant, all at don Ramón's
expense of course. And his wife, who wore a calico
wrapper to save on clothes and stinted so much on
food that there was hardly anything left for the
servants to eat, would be arrayed in splendor when
the day for the contest came around, ready in her
excitement to help her husband throw the entire
house through the window, if need be.

This, however, was all pure speculation on her
part. The money that was being scattered so madly
broadcast was a "loan" simply. Some day she
would get it back with interest. Already her piercing eyes were caressing the tiny, dark-complexioned,
restless little creature that lay across her knees, seeing in him the privileged heir-apparent who would
one day reap the harvest from all such family sacrifices.

Doña Bernarda had taken refuge in religion as in
a cool, refreshing oasis in the desert of vulgarity
and monotony in her life. Her heart would swell
with pride every time a priest would say to her in
the church:

"Take good care of don Ramón. Thanks to him the wave of demagogy halts at the temple door and evil fails to triumph in the District. He is the bulwark of the Lord against the impious!"

And when, after such a declaration, which flattered her worldly vanity and assured her of a mansion in Heaven, she would pass through the streets of Alcira in her calico wrapper and a shawl not over-clean, greeted affectionately, effusively, by the leading citizens, she would pardon don Ramón all the infidelities she knew about and consider the sacrifice of her fortune a good investment.

"If it were not for what we do, what would happen to the District. . . . The lower scum would conquer—those wild-eyed mechanics and common laborers who read the Valencian newspapers and talk about equality all the time. And they would divide up the orchards, and demand that the product of the harvests—thousands and thousands of *duros* paid for oranges by the Englishmen and the French —should belong to all." But to stave off such a cataclysm, there stood don Ramón, the scourge of the wicked, the champion of "the cause" which he led to triumph, gun in hand, at election time; and just as he was able to send any rebellious trouble-maker off to the penal settlement, so he found it easy to keep at liberty all those who, despite the various murders that figured in their biographies, lent themselves to the service of the government in this support of "law and order!"

The patrimony of the House of Brull went down and down, but its prestige rose higher and higher. The sacks of money filled by the old man at the cost of so much roguery were shaken empty over all the

District; nor were several assaults upon the municipal treasury sufficient to bring them back to normal
roundness. Don Ramón contemplated this squan-
dering impassively, proud that people should be talking of his generosity as much as of his power.

The whole District worshipped as a sacred flag-
staff that bronzed, muscular, massive figure, which
floated a huge, flowing, gray-flecked mustache from
its upper end.

"Don Ramón, you ought to remove that bush,"
his clerical friends would say to him with a smile of
affectionate banter. "Why, man, you look just like
Victor Emmanuel himself, the Pope's jailer."

But though don Ramón was a fervent Catholic
(who never went to mass), and hated all the infidel
turnkeys of the Holy Father, he would grin and give
a satisfied twirl at the offending mouth-piece, quite
flattered at bottom to be likened to a king.

The *patio* of the Brull mansion was the throne of
his sovereignty. His partisans would find him there,
pacing up and down among the green boxes of plantain trees, his hands clasped behind his broad, strong,
but now somewhat stooping back—a majestic back
withal, capable of supporting hosts and hosts of
friends.

There he "administered justice," decided the fate
of families, settled the affairs of towns—all in a
few off-hand but short and decisive words, like one
of those ancient Moorish kings who, in that selfsame territory, centuries before, legislated for their
subjects under the open sky. On market-days the
*patio* would be thronged. Carts would stop in long
lines on either side of the door. All the hitching-
posts along the streets would have horses tied to

them, and inside, the house would be buzzing like a bee-hive with the chatter of that rustic gentry.

Don Ramón would give them all a hearing, frowning gravely meanwhile, his chin on his bosom and one hand on the head of the little Rafael at his side —a pose copied from a chromo of the Kaiser petting the Crown Prince.

On afternoons when the *Ayuntamiento* was in session, the chief could never leave his *patio*. Of course not a chair in the city hall could be dusted without his permission; but he preferred to remain invisible, like a god, knowing well that his power would seem more terrible if it spoke only from the pillar of fire or from the whirlwind.

All day long city councilors would go trotting back and forth from the City Hall to the Brull *patio*. The few enemies don Ramón had in the Council— meddlers, doña Bernarda called them—idiots who swallowed everything in print provided it were against the King and religion—attacked the *cacique* persistently, censuring everything he did. Don Ramón's henchmen would tremble with impotent rage. "That charge must be answered! Let's see now: somebody go and ask the boss!"

And a *regidor* would be off to don Ramón's like a greyhound; and arriving at the *patio* panting, out of breath, he would heave a sigh of relief and contentment at sight of "the chief" there, pacing up and down as usual, ready to get his friends out of their difficulties as if the limitless resources of Providence were at his command. "So-and-So said this-and-that!" Don Ramón would stop in his tracks, think a moment, and finally say, in an enigmatic oracular voice: "Very well, tell him to put this in his pipe and smoke it!" Whereupon the henchman, mouth agape, would rush back to the session like a racehorse. His companions would gather about him eager to know the reply that don Ramón's wisdom had deigned to suggest; and a quarrel would start then, each one anxious to have the privilege of annihilating the enemy with the magic words—all talking at the same time like magpies suddenly set chattering by the dawn of a new light.

If the opposition held its ground, again stupefaction would come over them. Another mad dash in quest of a new consultation. Thus the sessions would go by, to the great delight of the barber Cupido—the sharpest and meanest tongue in the city—who, whenever the Council met, would observe to his early morning shaves:

"Holiday today: the usual race of councilors bareback."

When party exigencies forced don Ramón to be out of town, it was his wife, the energetic doña Bernarda, who attended to the consultations, issuing statements on party policy, as wise and apt as those of "the chief" himself.

This collaboration in the upbuilding and the upholding of the family influence was the single bond of union between husband and wife. This cold woman, a complete stranger to tenderness, would flush with pleasure every time the chief approved her ideas. If only she were "boss" of "the Party!" . . . Don Andrés had often said as much himself!

This don Andrés was her husband's most intimate friend, one of those men who are born to be second everywhere and in everything. Loyal to the family to the point of sacrifice, he served, with the couple itself, to fill out the Holy Trinity of the Brull religion that was the faith of all the District. Where don Ramón could not go in person, don Andrés would be present for him, as the chief's *alter ego*. In the towns he was respected as the supreme vicar of that god whose throne was in the *patio* of the plantain trees; and people too shy to lay their supplications before the god himself, would seek out that jolly advocate,—a very approachable bachelor, who always had a smile on his tanned, wrinkled face, and a story under his stiff cigar-stained mustache.

Don Andrés had no relatives, and spent almost all his time at the Brull's. He was like a piece of furniture that seems always to be getting in the way at first; but when all were once accustomed to him, he became an indispensable fixture in the family. In the days when don Ramón had been a young subordinate of the *Ayuntamiento,* he had met and liked the man, and taking him into the ranks of his "heelers," had promoted him rapidly to be chief of staff. In the opinion of the "boss," there wasn't a cleverer, shrewder fellow in the world than don Andrés, nor one with a better memory for names and faces. Brull was the strategist who directed the campaign; don Andrés the tactician who commanded actual operations and cleaned up behind the lines when the enemy was divided and undone. Don Ramón was given to settling everything in a violent manner, and drew his gun at the slightest provocation. If his methods had been followed, "the Party" would have murdered someone every day. Don Andrés had a smooth tongue and a seraphic smile that simply wound *alcaldes* or rebellious electors around his little finger, and his specialty was the art of letting loose a rain of sealed documents over the District that started complicated and never-ending prosecutions against troublesome opponents.

He attended to "the chief's" correspondence, and was tutor and playmate to the little Rafael, taking the boy on long walks through the orchard country. To doña Bernarda he was confidential adviser.

That surly, severe woman showed her bare heart to no one in the world save don Andrés. Whenever he called her his "señora," or his "worthy mistress," she could not restrain a gesture of satisfaction; and it was to him that she poured out her complaints against her husband's misdeeds. Her affection for him was that of a dame of ancient chivalry for her private squire. Enthusiasm for the glory of the house united them in such intimacy that the opposition wagged its tongues, asserting that doña Bernarda was getting even for her husband's waywardness. But don Andrés, who smiled scornfully when accused of taking advantage of the chief's influence to drive hard bargains to his own advantage, was not the man to be trifled with if gossip ventured to smirch his friendship with the *señora*.

Their Trinity was most closely cemented, however, by their fondness for Rafael, the little tot destined to bring fame to the name of Brull and realize the ambitions of both his grandfather and his father.

Rafael was a quiet, morose little boy, whose gentleness of disposition seemed to irritate the hard-hearted doña Bernarda. He was always hanging on to her skirts. Every time she raised her eyes she would find the little fellow's gaze fixed upon her.

"Go out and play in the *patio*," the mother would say.

And the little fellow, moody and resigned, would leave the room, as if in obedience to a disagreeable command.

Don Andrés alone was successful in amusing the child, with his tales and his strolls through the orchards, picking flowers for him, making whistles for him out of reeds. It was don Andrés who took him to school, also, and who advertised the boy's fondness for study everywhere.

If don Rafael were a serious, melancholy lad, that defect was chargeable to his interest in books, and at the Casino, the "Party's" Club, he would say to his fellow-worshippers:

"You'll see something doing when Rafaelito grows up. That kid is going to be another Canovas."

And before all those rustic minds the vision of a Brull at the head of the Government would suddenly flash, filling the first page of the newspapers with speeches six columns long, and a *To Be Continued* at the end; and they could see themselves rolling in money and running all Spain, just as they now ran their District, to their own sweet wills.

Never did a Prince of Wales grow up amid the respect and the adulation heaped upon little Brull. At school, the children regarded him as a superior being who had condescended to come down among them for his education. A well-scribbled sheet, a lesson fluently repeated, were enough for the teacher, who belonged to "the Party" (just to collect his wages on time and without trouble,) to declare in prophetic tones:

"Go on working like that, señor de Brull. You are destined to great things."

At the *tertulias* his mother attended evenings in his company, it was enough for him to recite a fable or get off some piece of learning characteristic of a studious child eager to bring his school work into the conversation, for the women to rush upon him and smother him with kisses.

"But how much that child knows! . . . How brilliant he is!"

And some old woman would add, sententiously:

"Bernarda, take good care of the child; don't let him use his brain so much. It's bad for him. See how peaked he looks! . . ."

He finished his preparatory education with the Dominicans, taking the leading rôle in all the plays given in the tiny theatre of the friars, and always with a place in the first line on prize days. The Party organ dedicated an annual article to the scholastic prodigies of the "gifted son of our distinguished chief don Ramón Brull, the country's hope, who already merits title as the shining light of the future!"

When Rafael, escorted by his mother and half a dozen women who had witnessed the exercises, would come home, gleaming with medals and his arms full of diplomas, he would stoop and kiss his father's hard, bristly hand; and that claw would caress the boy's head and absent-mindedly sink into the old man's vest pocket—for don Ramón expected to pay for all welcome favors.

"Very good," the hoarse voice would murmur. "That's the way I like to see you do . . . Here's a *duro*."

And not till the following year would the boy
again know what a caress from his father meant.
On certain occasions, playing in the *patio,* he had
surprised the austere old man gazing at him fixedly,
as if trying to foresee his future.

Don Andrés took charge of settling Rafael in Valencia when he began his university studies. The
dream of old don Jaime, disillusioned in the son,
would be fulfilled in the third generation!

"This one at least will be a lawyer!" said doña
Bernarda, who in the old days had imbibed don
Jaime's eagerness for the university degree, which to
her seemed like a title of nobility for the family.

And lest the corruption of the city should lead
the son astray as it had done Ramón in his student
days, she would send don Andrés frequently to the
capital, and write letter after letter to her Valencian friends, particularly to a canon of her intimate acquaintance, asking them not to lose sight
of the boy.

But Rafael was good behavior itself; a model
boy, a "serious" young man, the good canon assured
the mother. The distinctions and the prizes that
came to him in Alcira continued to pursue him in
Valencia; and besides, don Ramón and his wife
learned from the papers of the triumphs achieved by
their son in the debating society, a nightly gathering
of law students in a university hall, where future
Solons wrangled on such themes as "Resolved: that
the French Revolution was more of a good than
an evil," or "Resolved, that Socialism is superior to
Christianity."

Some terrible youths, who had to get home before ten o'clock to escape a whipping, declared them-

selves rabid socialists and frightened the beadles
with curses on the institution of property—all rights
reserved, of course, to apply, as soon as they got
out of college, for some position under the government as registrar of deeds or secretary of prefec-
ture! But Rafael, ever sane and a congenital "mod-
erate," was not of those fire-brands; he sat on "the
Right" of the august assembly of Wranglers, main-
taining a "sound" attitude on all questions, thinking
what he thought "with" Saint Thomas and "with"
other orthodox sages whom his clerical Mentor
pointed out to him.

These triumphs were announced by telegraph in
the Party papers, which, to garnish the chief's glory
and avoid suspicion of "inspiration," always began
the article with: "According to a despatch printed
in the Metropolitan press . . ."

"What a boy!" the priests of Alcira would say
to doña Bernarda. "What a silver tongue! You'll
see; he'll be a second Manterola!"

And whenever Rafael came home for the holidays
or on vacation, each time taller than before, dressed
like a fashion-plate and with mannerisms that she
took for the height of distinction, the saintly mother
would say to herself with the satisfaction of a woman who knows what it means to be homely:

"What a handsome chap he's getting to be. All
the rich girls in town will be after him. He'll have
his pick of them."

Doña Bernarda felt proud of her Rafael, a tall
youth, with delicate yet powerful hands, large eyes,
an aquiline nose, a curly beard and a certain leisurely,
undulating grace of movement that suggested one of
those young Arabs of the white cloak and elegant

babooshes, who constitute the native aristocracy of Spain's African colonies.

Every time the student came home, his father gave him the same silent caress. In course of time the *duro* had been replaced by a hundred *peseta* note; but the rough claw that grazed his head was falling now with an energy ever weaker and seemed to grow lighter with the years.

Rafael, from long periods of absence, noted his father's condition better than the rest. The old man was ill, very ill. As tall as ever, as austere and imposing, and as little given to words. But he was growing thinner. His fierce eyes were sinking deeper into their sockets. There was little left to him now except his massive frame. His neck, once as sturdy as a bull's, showed the tendons and the arteries under the loose, wrinkled skin; and his mustache, once so arrogant, but now withering with each successive day, drooped dispiritedly like the banner of a defeated army wet with rain.

The boy was surprised at the gestures and tears of anger with which his mother welcomed expression of his fears.

"Well, I hope he'll die as soon as possible . . . Lot's of use he is to us ! . . . May the Lord be merciful and take him off right now."

Rafael said nothing, not caring to pry into the conjugal drama that was secretly and silently playing its last act before his eyes.

Don Ramón, that somber libertine of insatiable appetites, prey to a sinister, mysterious inebriation, was tossing in a last whirlwind of tempestuous desire, as though the blaze of sunset had set fire to what remained of his vitality.

With a deliberate, determined lustfulness, he went scouring the District like a wild satyr, and his brutish assaults, his terrorism and abuse of authority, were reported back by scurrilous tongues to the seignorial mansion, where his friend don Andrés was trying in vain to pacify the wife.

"That man!" doña Bernarda would stammer in her rage. "That man is going to ruin us! Doesn't he see he's compromising his son's future?"

His most enthusiastic adherents, without losing their traditional respect for him, would speak smilingly of his "weaknesses"; but at night, when don Ramón, exhausted by his struggle with the insatiable demon gnawing at his spirit, would be snoring painfully away, with a disgusting rattle that made it impossible for people in the house to sleep, doña Bernarda would sit up in her bed with her thin arms folded across her bosom, and pray to herself:

"My Lord, My God! May this man die as soon as possible! May all this come to an end soon, oh Lord!"

And Bernarda's God must have heard her prayer, for her husband got rapidly worse.

"Take care of yourself, don Ramón," his curate friends would say to him. They were the only ones who dared allude to his disorderly life. "You're getting old, and boyish pranks at your age are invitations to Death!"

The *cacique* would smile, proud, at bottom, that all men should know that such exploits were possible for a man at his age.

He had enough strength left for one more caress the day when, escorted by don Andrés, Rafael entered with his degree as a Doctor of Law. He gave the boy his shotgun—a veritable jewel, the admiration of the entire District—and a magnificent horse. And as if he had been waiting around just to see the realization of old Don Jaime's ambition, which he himself had not been able to fulfill, he passed away.

All the bells of the city tolled mournfully.

The Party weekly came out with a black border a palm wide; and from all over the District folks came in droves to see whether the powerful don Ramón Brull, who had been able to rain upon the just and unjust alike on this earth, could possibly have died the same as any other human being.

# III

When doña Bernarda found herself alone, and absolute mistress of her home, she could not conceal her satisfaction.

Now they would see what a woman could do.

She counted on the advice and experience of don Andrés, who was closer than ever to her now; and on the prestige of Rafael, the young lawyer, who bade fair to sustain the reputation of the Brulls.

The power of the family continued unchanged. Don Andrés, who, at the death of his master, had succeeded to the authority of a second father in the Brull house, saw to the maintenance of relations with the authorities at the provincial capital and with the still bigger fish in Madrid. Petitions were heard in the *patio* the same as ever. Loyal party adherents were received as cordially as before and the same favors were done, nor was there any decline of influence in places that don Andrés referred to as "the spheres of public administration."

There came an election for Parliament, and as usual, doña Bernarda secured the triumph of the individual whose nomination had been dictated from Madrid. Don Ramón had left the party machine in perfect condition; all it needed was enough "grease" to keep it running smoothly; and there his widow was besides, ever alert at the slightest suggestion of a creak in the gearing.

At provincial headquarters they spoke of the District with the usual confidence:

"It's ours. Brull's son is as powerful as the old man himself."

The truth was that Rafael took little interest in "the Party." He looked upon it as one of the family properties, the title to which no one could dispute. He confined his personal activities to obeying his mother. "Go to Riola with don Andrés. Our friends there will be happy to see you." And he would go on the trip, to suffer the torment of an interminable rally, a *paella,* during which his fellow partisans would bore him with their uncouth merriment and ill-mannered flattery. "You really ought to give your horse a couple of days' rest. Instead of going out for a ride, spend your afternoon at the Club! Our fellows are complaining they never get a sight of you." Whereupon Rafael would give up his rides—his sole pleasure practically—and plunge into a thick smoke-laden atmosphere of noise and shouting, where he would have to answer questions of the most illustrious members of the party. They would sit around, filling their coffee-saucers with cigar-ash, disputing as to which was the better orator, Castelar or Canovas, and, in case of a war between France and Germany, which of the two would win—idle subjects that always provoked disagreements and led to quarrels.

The only time he entered into voluntary relations with "the Party" was when he took his pen in hand and manufactured for the Brull weekly a series of articles on "Law and Morality" and "Liberty and Faith,"—the rehashings of a faithful, industrious plodder at school, prolix commonplaces seasoned with what metaphysical terminology he remembered, and which, from the very reason that nobody under stood them, excited the admiration of his fellow partisans. They would blink at the articles and say to don Andrés:

"What a pen, eh? Just let anyone dare to argue with him. . . . Deep, that noodle, I tell you!"

Nights, when his mother did not oblige him to visit the home of some influential voter who must be kept content, he would spend reading, no longer, however, as in Valencia, books lent him by the canon, but works that he bought himself, following the recommendations of the press, and that his mother respected with the veneration always inspired in her by printed paper sewed and bound, an awe comparable only to the scorn she felt for newspapers, dedicated, every one of them, as she averred, to the purpose of insulting holy things and stirring up the brutal passions of "the rabble."

These years of random reading, unrestrained by the scruples and the fears of a student, gradually and quietly shattered many of Rafael's firm beliefs. They broke the mould in which the friends of his mother had cast his mind and made him dream of a broader life than the one known to those about him. French novels transported him to a Paris that far outshone the Madrid he had known for a moment in his graduate days. Love stories awoke in his youthful imagination an ardor for adventure and involved passions in which there was something of the intense love of indulgence that had been his father's besetting sin. He came to dwell more and more in the fictitious world of his readings, where there were elegant, perfumed, clever women, practicing a certain art in the refinement of their vices.

The uncouth, sunburned orchard-girls inspired

him with revulsion as if they had been women of
another race, creatures of an inferior genus. The
young ladies of the city seemed to him peasants in
disguise, with the narrow, selfish, stingy instincts
of their parents. They knew the exact market price
of oranges and just how much land was owned by
each aspirant to their hand; and they adjusted their
love to the wealth of the pretender, believing it the
test of quality to appear implacable toward everything not fashioned to the mould of their petty life
of prejudice and tradition.

For that reason he was deeply bored by his colorless, humdrum existence, so far removed from that
other purely imaginative life which rose from the
pages of his books and enveloped him with an exotic,
exciting perfume.

Some day he would be free, and take flight on his
own wings; and that day of liberation would come
when he got to be deputy. He waited for his coming of age much as an heir-apparent waits for the
moment of his coronation.

From early boyhood he had been taught to look
forward to the great event which would cut his life
in two, opening out new pathways for a "forward
march" to fame and fortune.

"When my little boy gets to be deputy," his
mother would say in her rare moments of affectionate expansiveness, "the girls will fight for him because he is so handsome! And he'll marry a mil-
lionairess!"

Meanwhile, in long years of impatient anticipation, his life went on, with no special circumstance
to break its dull monotony—the life of an aspirant
certain of his lot, "killing time" till the call should

come to enter on his heritage. He was like those noble youngsters of bygone centuries who, graced in their cradles by the rank of colonel from the monarch, played around with hoop and top till they were old enough to join their regiments. He had been born a deputy, and a deputy he was sure to be: for the moment, he was waiting for his cue in the wings of the theatre of life.

His trip to Italy on a pilgrimage to see the Pope was the one event that had disturbed the dreary course of his existence. But in that country of marvels, with a pious canon for a guide, he visited churches rather than museums. Of theatres he saw only two—larks permitted by his tutor, whose austerity was somewhat mollified in those changing scenes. Indifferently they passed the famous artistic works of the Italian churches, but paused always to venerate some relic with miracles as famous as absurd. Even so, Rafael managed to catch a confused and passing glimpse of a world different from the one in which he was predestined to pass his life. From a distance he sensed something of the love of pleasure and romance he had drunk in like an intoxicating wine from his reading. In Milan he admired a gilded, adventurous bohemia of opera; in Rome, the splendor of a refined, artistic aristocracy in perpetual rivalry with that of Paris and London; and in Florence, an English nobility that had come in quest of sunlight and a chance to air its straw hats, show off the fair hair of its ladies, and chatter its own language in gardens where once upon a time the somber Dante dreamed and Boccaccio told his merry tales to drive fear of plague away.

That journey, of impressions as rapid and as

fleeting as a reel of moving-pictures, leaving in
Rafael's mind a maze of names, buildings, paintings
and cities, served to give greater breadth to his
thinking, as well as added stimulus to his imagination. Wider still became the gulf that separated
him from the people and ideas he met in his common everyday life. He felt a longing for the extraordinary, for the original, for the adventuresome-
ness of artistic youth; and political master of a
county, heir of a feudal dominion virtually, he nevertheless would read the name of any writer or painter
whatsoever with the superstitious respect of a rustic
churl. "A wretched, ruined lot who haven't even
a bed to die on," his mother viewed such people; but
Rafael nourished a secret envy for all who lived in
that ideal world, which he was certain must be filled
with pleasures and exciting things he had scarcely
dared to dream of. What would he not give to be
a bohemian like the personages he met in the books
of Murger, member of a merry band of "intellectuals," leading a life of joy and proud devotion to
higher things in a bourgeois age that knew only
thirst for money and prejudice of class! Talent for
saying pretty things, for writing winged verses that
soared like larks to heaven! A garret underneath
the roof, off there in Paris, in the Latin Quarter!
A Mimí poor but spiritual, who would love him,
and—between one kiss and another—be able to discuss—not the price of oranges, like the girls who
followed him with tender eyes at home—but serious
"elevated" things! In exchange for all that he
would gladly have given his future deputyship and
all the orchards he had inherited, which, though en-
cumbered by mortgages not to mention moral debts

left by the rascality of his father and grandfather—
still would bring him a tidy annuity for realizing
his bohemian dreams.

Such preoccupations made life as a party leader,
tied down to the petty interests of a constituency,
quite unthinkable! At the risk of angering his
mother, he fled the Club, to court the solitude of
the hills and fields. There his imagination could
range in greater freedom, peopling the roads, the
meadows, the orange groves with creatures of his
fancy, often conversing aloud with the heroines of
some "grand passion," carried on along the lines
laid down by the latest novel he had read.

One afternoon toward the close of summer Rafael
climbed the little mountain of San Salvador, which
lies close to the city. From the eminence he was
fond of looking out over the vast domains of his
family. For all the inhabitants of that fertile plain
were—as don Andrés said whenever he wished to
emphasize the party's greatness—like so many cattle
branded with the name of Brull.

As he went up the winding, stony trail, Rafael
thought of the mountains of Assisi, which he had
visited with his friend the canon, a great admirer
of the Saint of Umbria. It was a landscape that
suggested asceticism. Crags of bluish or reddish
rock lined the roadway on either side, with pines
and cypresses rising from the hollows, and extending
black, winding, snaky roots out over the fallow soil.
At intervals, white shrines with tiny roofs harbored
mosaics of glazed tiles depicting the Stations on the
*Via Dolorosa.* The pointed green caps of the cypresses, as they waved, seemed bent on frightening
away the white butterflies that were fluttering about

over the rosemary and the nettles. The parasol-pines projected patches of shade across the burning road, where the sun-baked earth crackled and crumbled to dead dust under every foot-step.

Reaching the little square in front of the Hermitage, he rested from the ascent, stretching out full length on the crescent of rubblework that formed a bench near the sanctuary. There silence reigned, the silence of high hill-tops. From below, the noises of the restless life and labor of the plain came weakened, softened, by the wind, like the murmuring of waves breaking on a distant shore. Among the prickly-pears that grew in close thicket behind the bench, insects were buzzing about, shining in the sun like buds of gold. Some hens, belonging to the Hermitage, were pecking away in one corner of the square, clucking, and dusting their feathers in the gravel.

Rafael surrendered to the charm of the exquisite scene. With reason had it been called "Paradise" by its ancient owners, Moors from the magic gardens of Bagdad, accustomed to the splendors of *The Thousand and One Nights*, but who went into ecstacies nevertheless on beholding for the first time the wondrous *ribera* of Valencia!

Throughout the great valley, orange groves, extending like shimmering waves of velvet; hedges and enclosures of lighter green, cutting the crimson earth into geometric figures; clumps of palms spurting like jets of verdure upward toward the sky, and falling off again in languorous swoons; villas blue and rose-colored, nestling in flowering gardens; white farmhouses half concealed behind green swirls of forest; spindling smokestacks of irrigation engines, with yellow sooty tops; Alcira, its houses clustered on the island and overflowing to the opposite bank, all of whitish, bony hue, pock-marked with tiny windows; beyond, Carcagente, the rival city, girdled in its belt of leafy orchards; off toward the sea, sharp, angular mountains, with outlines that from afar suggested the fantastic castles imagined by Doré; and inland, the towns of the upper *ribera* floating in an emerald lake of orchard, the distant mountains taking on a violet hue from the setting sun that was creeping like a bristly porcupine of gold into the hot vapors of the horizon.

Behind the Hermitage all the lower *ribera* stretched, one expanse of rice-fields drowned under an artificial flood; then, Sueca and Cullera, their white houses perched on those fecund lagoons like towns in landscapes of India; then, Albufera, with its lake, a sheet of silver glistening in the sunlight; then, Valencia, like a cloud of smoke drifting along the base of a mountain range of hazy blue; and, at last, in the background, the halo, as it were, of this apotheosis of light and color, the Mediterranean— the palpitant azure Gulf bounded by the cape of San Antonio and the peaks of Sagunto and Almenara, that jutted up against the sky-line like the black fins of giant whales.

As Rafael looked down upon the towers of the crumbling convent of La Murta, almost hidden in its pine-groves, he thought of all the tragedy of the Reconquest; and almost mourned the fate of those farmer-warriors whose white cloaks he could imagine as still floating among the groves of those magic trees of Asia's paradise. It was the influence of the Moor in his Spanish ancestry. Christian, clerical even, though he was, he had inherited a melancholy, dreamy turn of mind from the very Arabs who had created all that Eden.

He pictured to himself the tiny kingdoms of those old *walis*; vassal districts very like the one his family ruled. But instead of resting on influence, bribery, intimidation, and the abuse of law, they lived by the lances of horsemen as apt at tilling the soil as at capering in tournaments with an elegance never equalled by any chevaliers of the North. He could see the court of Valencia, with the romantic gardens of Ruzafa, where poets sang mournful strophes over the wane of the Valencian Moor, while beautiful maidens listened from behind the blossoming rose-bushes. And then the catastrophe came. In a torrent of steel, barbarians swept down from the arid hills of Aragon to appease their hunger in the bounty of the plain—the *almogávares*—naked, wild, bloodthirsty savages, who never washed. And as allies of this horde, bankrupt Christian noblemen, their worn-out lands mortgaged to the Israelite, but good cavalrymen, withal, armored, and with dragon-wings on their helmets; and among the Christians, adventurers of various tongues, soldiers of fortune out for plunder and booty in the name of the Cross —the "black sheep" of every Christian family. And they seized the great garden of Valencia, installed themselves in the Moorish palaces, called themselves counts and marquises, and with their swords held that privileged country for the King of Aragon, while the conquered Saracens continued to fertilize it with their toil.

"Valencia, Valencia, Valencia! Thy walls are ruins, thy gardens grave-yards, thy sons slaves unto the Christian . . . " groaned the poet, covering his eyes with his cloak. And Rafael could see, passing like phantoms before his eyes, leaning forward on the necks of small, sleek, sinewy horses, that seemed to fly over the ground, their legs horizontal, their nostrils belching smoke, the Moors, the real people of Valencia, conquered, degenerated by the very abundance of their soil, abandoning their gardens before the onrush of brutal, primitive invaders, speeding on their way toward the unending night of African barbarism. At this eternal exile of the first Valencians who left to oblivion and decay a civilization, the last vestiges of which today survive in the universities of Fez, Rafael felt the sorrow he would have experienced had it all been a disaster to his family or his party.

While he was thinking of all these dead things, life in its feverish agitation surrounded him. A cloud of sparrows was darting about the roof of the Hermitage. On the mountain side a flock of dark-fleeced sheep was grazing; and when any of them discovered a blade of grass among the rocks, they would begin calling to one another with a melancholy bleating.

Rafael could hear the voices of some women who seemed to be climbing the road, and from his reclining position he finally made out two parasols that were gradually rising to view over the edge of his bench. One was of flaming red silk, skilfully embroidered and suggesting the filigreed dome of a mosque; the second, of flowered calico, was apparently keeping at a respectful distance behind the first.

Two women entered the little square, and as

Rafael sat up and removed his hat, the taller, who seemed to be the mistress, acknowledged his courtesy with a slight bow, went on to the other end of the esplanade, and stood, with her back turned toward him, looking at the view. The other sat down some distance off, breathing laboriously from the exertion of the climb.

Who were those women? . . . Rafael knew the whole city, and had never seen them.

The one seated near him was doubtless the servant of the other—her maid or her companion. She was dressed in black, simply but with a certain charm, like the French soubrettes he had seen in illustrated novels. But rustic origin and lack of cultivation were evident from the stains on the backs of her unshapely hands; from her broad, flat, finger-nails; and from her large ungainly feet, quite out of harmony with the pair of stylish boots she was wearing —cast-off articles, doubtless, of the lady. She was pretty, nevertheless, with a fresh exuberance of youth. Her large, gray, credulous eyes were those of a stupid but playful lamb; her hair, straight, and a very light blond, hung loosely here and there over a freckled face, dark with sunburn. She handled her closed parasol somewhat awkwardly and kept looking anxiously at the doubled gold chain that drooped from her neck to her waist, as if to reassure herself that a gift long-coveted had not been lost.

Rafael's interest drifted to the lady. His eyes rested on the back of a head of tightly-gathered golden hair, as luminous as a burnished helmet; on a white neck, plump, rounded; on a pair of broad, lithe shoulders, hidden under a blue silk blouse, the

lines tapering rapidly, gracefully toward the waist;
on a gray skirt, finally, falling in harmonious folds
like the draping of a statue, and under the hem the
solid heels of two shoes of English style encasing
feet that must have been as agile and as strong as
they were tiny.

The lady called to her maid in a voice that was
sonorous, vibrant, velvety, though Rafael could
catch only the accented syllables of her words, that
seemed to melt together in the melodious silence of
the mountain top. The young man was sure she
had not spoken Spanish. A foreigner, almost certainly! . . .

She was expressing admiration and enthusiasm
for the view, talking rapidly, pointing out the principal towns that could be seen, calling them by their
names,—the only words that Rafael could make out
clearly. Who was this woman whom he had never
seen, who spoke a foreign language and yet knew
the *ribera* well? Perhaps the wife of one of the
French or English orange-dealers established in the
city! Meanwhile his eyes were devouring that
superb, that opulent, that elegant beauty which
seemed to be challenging him with its indifference
to his presence.

The keeper of the Hermitage issued cautiously
from the house—a peasant who made his living from
visitors to the heights. Attracted by the promising appearance of the strange lady, the hermit came
forward to greet her, offering to fetch water from
the cistern, and to unveil the image of the miraculous
virgin, in her honor.

The woman turned around to answer the man,
and that gave Rafael an opportunity to study her at

his leisure. She was tall, ever so tall, as tall as he perhaps. But the impression her height of stature made was softened by a grace of figure that revealed strength allied to elegance. A strong bust, sculpturesque, supporting a head that engaged the young man's wrapt attention. A hot mist of emotion seemed to cloud his vision as he looked into her large eyes, so green, so luminous! The golden hair fell forward upon a forehead of pearly whiteness, veined at the temples with delicate lines of blue. Viewed in profile her gracefully moulded nose, quivering with vitality at the nostrils, filled out a beauty that was distinctly modern, piquantly charming. In those lineaments, Rafael thought he could recognize any number of famous actresses. He had seen her before. Where? . . . He did not know. Perhaps in some illustrated weekly! Perhaps in some album of stage celebrities! Or maybe on the cover of some match-box—a common medium of publicity for famous European belles. Of one thing he was certain: at sight of that wonderful face he felt as though he were meeting an old friend after a long absence.

The recluse, in hopes of a perquisite, led the two women toward the door of the hermitage, where his wife and daughter had appeared, to feast their eyes on the huge diamonds sparkling at the ears of the strange lady.

"Enter, *siñorita*," the rustic invited. "I'll show you the Virgin, the Virgin *del Lluch,* you understand, the only genuine one. She came here alone all the way from Majorca. People down in Palma claim they have the real Virgin. But what can they say for themselves? They are jealous because our Lady chose Alcira; and here we have her, proving that she's the real one by the miracles she works."

He opened the door of the tiny church, which was as cool and gloomy as a cellar. At the rear, on a baroque altar of tarnished gold, stood the little statue with its hollow cloak and its black face.

Rapidly, by rote almost, the good man recited the history of the image. The Virgin *del Lluch* was the patroness of Majorca. A hermit had been compelled to flee from there, for a reason no one had been able to discover—perhaps to get away from some Saracen girl of those exciting, war-like days! And to rescue the Virgin from profanation he brought her to Alcira, and built this sanctuary for her. Later people from Majorca came to return her to their island. But the celestial lady had taken a liking to Alcira and its inhabitants. Over the water, and without even wetting her feet, she came gliding back. Then the Majorcans, to keep what had happened quiet, counterfeited a new statue that looked just like the first. All this was gospel truth, and as proof, there lay the original hermit buried at the foot of the altar; and there was the Virgin, too, her face blackened by the sun and the salt wind on her miraculous voyage over the sea.

The beautiful lady smiled slightly, as she listened. The maid was all ears, not to lose a word of a language she but half understood, her credulous peasant eyes traveling from the Virgin to the hermit and from the hermit to the Virgin, plainly expressing the wonder she was feeling at such a portentous miracle. Rafael had followed the party into the shrine and taken a position near the fascinating stranger. She, however, pretended not to see him.

"That is only a legend," he ventured to remark,

when the rustic had finished his story. "You understand, of course, that nobody hereabouts accepts such tales as true."

"I suppose so," the lady answered coldly.

"Legend or no legend, don Rafael," the recluse grumbled, somewhat peeved, "that's what my grandfather and all the folk of his day used to say; and that's what people still believe. If the story has been handed down so long, there must be something to it."

The patch of sunlight that shone through the doorway upon the flagstones was darkened by the shadow of a woman. It was a poorly clad orchard worker, young, it seemed, but with a face pale, and as rough as wrinkled paper, all the crevices and hollows of her cranium showing, her eyes sunken and dull, her unkempt hair escaping from beneath her knotted kerchief. She was barefoot, carrying her shoes in her hand. She stood with her legs wide apart, as if in an effort to keep her balance. She seemed to feel intense pain whenever she stepped upon the ground. Illness and poverty were written on every feature of her person.

The recluse knew her well; and as the unfortunate creature, panting with the effort of the climb, sank upon a little bench to rest her feet, he told her story briefly to the visitors.

She was ill, very, very ill. With no faith in doctors, who, according to her, "treated her with nothing but words"; she believed that the Virgin *del Lluch* would ultimately cure her. And, though at home she could scarcely move from her chair and was always being scolded by her husband for neglecting the housework, every week she would climb the steep mountain-side, barefoot, her shoes in her hand.

The hermit approached the sick woman, accepting a copper coin she offered. A few couplets to the Virgin, as usual, he supposed!

"Visanteta, a few *gochos!*" shouted the rustic, going to the door. And his daughter came into the chapel—a dirty, dark-skinned creature with African eyes, who might just have escaped from a gipsy band.

She took a seat upon a bench, turning her back upon the Virgin with the bored ill-humored expression of a person compelled to do a dull task day after day; and in a hoarse, harsh, almost frantic voice, which echoed deafeningly in that small enclosure, she began a drawling chant that rehearsed the story of the statue and the portentous miracles it had wrought.

The sick woman, kneeling before the altar without releasing her hold upon her shoes, the heels of her feet, which were bruised and bleeding from the stones, showing from under her skirts, repeated a refrain at the end of each stanza, imploring the protection of the Virgin. Her voice had a weak and hollow sound, like the wail of a child. Her sunken eyes, misty with tears, were fixed upon the Virgin with a dolorous expression of supplication. Her words came more tremulous and more distant at each couplet.

The beautiful stranger was plainly affected at the pitiful sight. Her maid had knelt and was following the sing-song rhythm of the chant, with prayers in a language that Rafael recognized at last. It was Italian.

"What a great thing faith is!" the lady murmured with a sigh.

"Yes, *señora;* a beautiful thing!"

Rafael tried to think of something "brilliant" on the grandeur of faith, from Saint Thomas, or one of the other "sound" authors he had studied. But he ransacked his memory in vain. Nothing! That charming woman had filled his mind with thoughts far other than quotations from the Fathers!

The couplets to the Virgin came to an end. With the last stanza the wild singer disappeared; and the sick woman, after several abortive efforts, rose painfully to her feet. The recluse approached her with the solicitude of a shopkeeper concerned for the quality of his wares. Were things going any better? Were the visits to the Virgin doing good? . . . The unfortunate woman did not dare to answer, for fear of offending the miraculous Lady. She did not know! . . . Yes . . . she really must be a little better . . . But that climb! . . . This offering had not had such good results as the previous ones, she thought; but she had faith: the Virgin would be good to her and cure her in the end. At the church door she collapsed from pain. The recluse placed her on his chair and ran to the cistern to get a glass of water. The Italian maid, her eyes bulging with fright, leaned over the poor woman, petting her:

"*Poverina! Poverina! . . . Coraggio!*" The invalid, rallying from her swoon, opened her eyes and gazed vacantly at the stranger, not understanding her words but guessing their kindly intention.

The lady stepped out to the *plazoleta*, deeply moved, it seemed, by what she had been witnessing.

Rafael followed, with affected absent-mindedness, somewhat ashamed of his insistence, yet at the same time looking for an opportunity to renew their conversation.

On finding herself once more in the presence of that wonderful panorama, where the eye ran unobstructed to the very limit of the horizon, the charming creature seemed to breathe more freely.

"Good God!" she exclaimed, as if speaking to herself. "How sad and yet how wonderful! This view is ever so beautiful. But that woman! . . . That poor woman!"

"She's been that way for years, to my personal knowledge," Rafael remarked, pretending to have known the invalid for a long time, though he had scarcely ever deigned to notice her before. "Our peasants are queer people. They despise doctors, and refuse their help, preferring to kill themselves with these barbarous prayers and devotions, which they expect will do them good."

"But they may be right, after all!" the lady replied. "Disease is often incurable, and science can do for it about as much as faith—sometimes, even less. . . . But here we are laughing and enjoying ourselves while suffering passes us by, rubs elbows with us even, without our noticing!" . . .

Rafael was at a loss for reply. What sort of woman was this? What a way she had of talking! Accustomed as he was to the commonplace chatter of his mother's friends, and still under the influence of this meeting, which had so deeply disturbed him, the poor boy imagined himself in the presence of a sage in skirts—a philosopher under the disguise of female beauty come from beyond the Pyrenees, from some gloomy German alehouse perhaps, to upset his peace of mind.

The stranger was silent for a time, her gaze fixed upon the horizon. Then around her attractive sensuous lips, through which two rows of shining, dazzling teeth were gleaming, the suggestion of a smile began to play, a smile of joy at the landscape.

"How beautiful this all is!" she exclaimed, without turning toward her companion. "How I have longed to see it again!"

At last the opportunity had come to ask the question he had been so eager to put: and she herself had offered the opportunity!

"Do you come from here?" he asked, in a tremulous voice, fearing lest his inquisitiveness be scornfully repelled.

"Yes," the lady replied, curtly.

"Well, that's strange. I have never seen you. . . ."

"There's nothing strange about that. I arrived only yesterday."

"Just as I said! . . . I know everyone in the city. My name is Rafael Brull. I'm the son of don Ramón, who was mayor of Alcira many times."

At last he had let it out! The poor fellow had been dying to reveal his name, tell who he was, pronounce that magic word so influential in the District, certain it would be the "Open Sesame" to that wonderful stranger's grace! After that, perhaps, she would tell him who she was! But the lady commented on his declaration with an "Ah!" of cold indifference. She did not show that his name was even known to her, though she did sweep him with a rapid, scrutinizing, half-mocking glance that seemed to betray a hidden thought:

"Not bad-looking, but what a dunce!"

Rafael blushed, feeling he had made a false step in volunteering his name with the pompousness he would have used toward some bumpkin of the region.

A painful silence followed. Rafael was anxious to get out of his plight. That glacial indifference, that disdainful courtesy, which, without a trace of rudeness, still kept him at a distance, hurt his vanity to the quick. But since there was no stopping now, he ventured a second question:

"And are you thinking of remaining in Alcira very long? . . ."

Rafael thought the ground was giving way beneath his feet. Another glance from those green eyes! But, alas, this time it was cold and menacing, a livid flash of lightning refracted from a mirror of ice.

"I don't know . . ." she answered, with a deliberateness intended to accentuate unmistakable scorn. "I usually leave places the moment they begin to bore me." And looking Rafael squarely in the face she added, with freezing formality, after a pause:

"Good afternoon, sir."

Rafael was crushed. He saw her turn toward the doorway of the sanctuary and call her maid. Every step of hers, every movement of her proud figure, seemed to raise a barrier in front of him. He saw her bend affectionately over the sick orchard-woman, open a little pink bag that her maid handed her, and, rummaging about among some sparkling trinkets and embroidered handkerchiefs, draw out a hand filled with shining silver coins. She emptied the money into the apron of the astonished peasant girl, gave something as well to the recluse, who was no less astounded, and then, opening her red parasol, walked off, followed by her maid.

As she passed Rafael, she answered the doffing of his hat with a barely perceptible inclination of her head; and, without looking at him, started on her way down the stony mountain path.

The young man stood gazing after her through the pines and the cypresses as her proud athletic figure grew smaller in the distance.

The perfume of her presence seemed to linger about him when she had gone, obsessing him with the atmosphere of superiority and exotic elegance that emanated from her whole being.

Rafael noticed finally that the recluse was approaching, unable to restrain a desire to communicate his admiration to someone.

"What a woman!" the man cried, rolling his eyes to express his full enthusiasm.

She had given him a *duro*, one of those white discs which, in that atheistic age, so rarely ascended that mountain trail! And there the poor invalid sat at the door of the Hermitage, staring into her apron blankly, hypnotized by the glitter of all that wealth! *Duros, pesetas*, two-*pesetas*, dimes! All the money the lady had brought! Even a gold button, which must have come from her glove!

Rafael shared in the general astonishment. But who the devil was that woman?

"How do I know!" the rustic answered. "But judging from the language of the maid," he went on with great conviction: "I should say she was some

Frenchwoman . . . some Frenchwoman . . . with a pile of money!"

Rafael turned once more in the direction of the two parasols that were slowly winding down the slope. They were barely visible now. The larger of the two, a mere speck of red, was already blending into the green of the first orchards on the plain . . . At last it had disappeared completely.

Left alone, Rafael burst into rage! The place where he had made such a sorry exhibition of himself seemed odious to him now. He fumed with vexation at the memory of that cold glance, which had checked any advance toward familiarity, repelled him, crushed him! The thought of his stupid questions filled him with hot shame.

Without replying to the "good-evening" from the recluse and his family, he started down the mountain, in hopes of meeting the woman again, somewhere, some time, he knew not when nor how. The heir of don Ramón, the hope of the District, strode furiously on, his arms aquiver with a nervous tremor. And aggressively, menacingly, addressing his own ego as though it were a henchman cringing terror-stricken in front of him, he muttered:

"You imbecile! . . . You lout! . . . You peasant! You provincial ass! You . . . rube!"

## IV

Doña Bernarda did not suspect the reason why her son rose on the following morning pale, and with dark rings under his eyes, as if he had spent a bad night. Nor could his political friends guess, that afternoon, why in such fine weather, Rafael should come and shut himself up in the stifling atmosphere of the Club.

When he came in, a crowd of noisy henchmen gathered round him to discuss all over again the great news that had been keeping "the Party" in feverish excitement for a week past: the Cortes were to be dissolved! The newspapers had been talking of nothing else. Within two or three months, before the close of the year at the latest, there would be a new election, and therewith, as all averred, a landslide for don Rafael Brull. The intimate friend and lieutenant of the House of Brull was the best informed. If the elections took place on the date indicated by the newspapers, Rafael would still be five or six months short of his twenty-fifth birth-day. But don Andrés had written to Madrid to consult the Party leaders. The prime minister was agreeable—"there were precedents!" —and even though Rafael should be a few weeks short of the legal age, the seat would go to him just the same. They would send no more "foundlings" from Madrid! Alcira would have no more "unknowns" foisted upon her! And the whole Tribe

of Brull dependents was preparing for the contest
with the enthusiasm of a prize-fighter sure of victory
beforehand.

All this bustling expectation left Rafael cold. For
years he had been looking forward to that election
time, when the chance would come for his free life
in Madrid. Now that it was at hand he was completely indifferent to the whole matter, as if he were
the last person in the world concerned.

He looked impatiently at the table where don
Andrés, with three other leading citizens, was having his daily hand at cards before coming to sit
down at Rafael's side. That was a canny habit of
don Andrés. He liked to be seen in his capacity
of Regent, sheltering the heir-apparent under the
wing of his prestige and experienced wisdom.

Well along in the afternoon, when the Club parlor
was less crowded with members, the atmosphere
freer of smoke, and the ivory balls less noisy on the
green cloth, don Andrés considered his game at an
end, and took a chair in his disciple's circle, where
as usual Rafael was sitting with the most parasitic
and adulatory of his partisans.

The boy pretended to be listening to their conversation, but all the while he was preparing mentally a question he had decided to put to don Andrés
the day before.

At last he made up his mind.

"You know everybody, don Andrés. Well, yesterday, up on San Salvador, I met a fine-looking
woman who seems to be a foreigner. She says she's
living here. Who is she?"

The old man burst into a loud laugh, and pushed

his chair back from the table, so that his big paunch would have room to shake in.

"So you've seen her, too!" he exclaimed between one guffaw and another. "Well, sir, what a city this is! That woman got in the day before yesterday, and everybody's seen her already. She's the talk of the town. You were the only one who hadn't asked me about her so far. And now you've bitten! . . . Ho! Ho! Ho! What a place this is!"

When he had had his laugh out—Rafael, meanwhile, did not see the joke—he continued in more measured style:

"That 'foreign woman,' as you call her, boy, comes from Alcira. In fact, she was born about two doors from you. Don't you know doña Pepa, 'the doctor's woman,' they call her—a little lady who has an orchard close by the river and lives in the Blue House, that's always under water when the Júcar floods? She once owned the place you have just beyond where you live, and she's the one who sold it to your father—the only property don Ramón ever bought, so far as I know. Don't you remember?"

Rafael thought he did. As he went back in his memory, the picture of an old wrinkled woman rose before his mind, a woman round-shouldered, bent with age, but with a kindly face smiling with simple-mindedness and good nature. He could see her now, with a rosary usually in her hand, a camp-stool under her arm, and her *mantilla* drawn down over her face. As she passed the Brull door on her way to church, she would greet his mother; and doña Bernarda would remark in a patronizing way: "Doña

Pepa is a very fine woman; one of God's own souls.
. . . The only decent person in her family."

"Yes; I remember; I remember doña Pepa," said
Rafael.

"Well, your 'foreigner,'" don Andrés continued,
"is doña Pepa's niece, daughter of her brother, the
doctor. The girl has been all over the world singing grand opera. You were probably too young to
remember Doctor Moreno, who was the scandal of
the province in those days. . . ."

But Rafael certainly did remember Doctor
Moreno! That name was one of the freshest of
his childhood recollections, the bugaboo of many
nights of terror and alarm, when he would hide his
trembling head under the clothes. If he cried about
going to bed so early, his mother would say to him
in a mysterious voice:

"If you don't keep quiet and go right to sleep
I'll send for Doctor Moreno!"

A weird, a formidable personage, the Doctor!
Rafael could see him as clearly as if he were sitting
there in front of him; with that huge, black, curly
beard; those large, burning eyes that always shone
with an inner fire; and that tall, angular figure that
seemed taller than ever as young Brull evoked it
from the hazes of his early years. Perhaps the
Doctor had been a good fellow, who knows! At
any rate Rafael thought so, as his mind now reverted
to that distant period of his life; but he could still
remember the fright he had felt as a child, when
once in a narrow street he met the terrible Doctor,
who had looked at him through those glowing pupils
and caressed his cheeks gently and kindly with a

hand that seemed to the youngster as hot as a live
coal! He had fled in terror, as almost all good boys
did when the Doctor petted them.

What a horrible reputation Doctor Moreno had!
The curates of the town spoke of him in terms of
hair-raising horror. An infidel! A man cut off
from Mother Church! Nobody knew for certain
just what high authority had excommunicated him,
but he was, no doubt, outside the pale of decent,
Christian folks. Proof of that there was, a-plenty.
His whole attic was filled with mysterious books in
foreign languages, all containing horrible doctrines
against God and the authority of His representatives
on earth. He defended a certain fellow by the
name of Darwin, who claimed than men were related
to monkeys, a view that gave much amusement to
the indignant doña Bernarda, who repeated all the
jokes on the crazy notion her favorite preacher
cracked of a Sunday in the pulpit. And such a
sorcerer! Hardly a disease could resist Doctor
Moreno. He worked wonders in the suburbs, among
the lower scum; and those laborers adored him with
as much fear as affection. He succeeded with people
who had been given up by the older doctors, wiseacres in long frocks and with gold-headed canes,
who trusted more in God than in science, as Rafael's
mother would say in praise of them. That devil of
a physician used new and unheard-of treatments he
learned from atheistic reviews and suspicious books
he imported from abroad. His competitors grumbled also because the Doctor had a mania for treating poor folk gratis, actually leaving money, sometimes, into the bargain; and he often refused to at-

tend wealthy people of "sound principles" who had been obliged to get their confessor's permission before placing themselves in his hands.

"Rascal! . . . Heretic! . . . Lower scum! . . ." doña Bernarda would exclaim.

But she said such things in a very low voice and with a certain fear, for those days were bad ones for the House of Brull. Rafael remembered how gloomy his father had been about that time, hardly even leaving the *patio*. Had it not been for the respect his hairy claws and his frowning eye-brows inspired, the rabble would have eaten him alive. "Others" were in command, . . . "others" . . . everybody, in fact, except the House of Brull.

The monarchy had been treasonably overturned; the men of the Revolution of September were legislating in Madrid. The petty tradesmen of the city, ever rebellious against the tyranny of don Ramón, had taken guns in their hands and formed a little militia, ready to send a fusilade into the *cacique* who had formerly trodden them under foot. In the streets people were singing the *Marseillaise*, waving tricolored bunting, and hurrahing for the Republic. Candles were being burned before pictures af Castelar. And meantime that fanatical Doctor, a Republican, was preaching on the public squares, explaining the "rights of man" at daytime meetings in the country and at night meetings in town. Wild with enthusiasm he repeated, in different words, the orations of the portentous Tribune who in those days was traveling from one end of Spain to the other, administering to the people the sacrament of democracy to the music of his eloquence, which raised all the grandeurs of History from the tomb.

Rafael's mother, shutting all the doors and windows, would lift her angry eyes toward heaven every time the crowd, returning from a meeting, would pass through her street with banners flying and halt two doors away, in front of the Doctor's house, where they would cheer, and cheer. "How long, oh Lord, how long?" And though nobody insulted her nor asked her for so much as a pin, she talked of moving to some other country. Those people demanded a Republic—they belonged, as she said, to the "Dividing-up" gang. The way things were going, they'd soon be winning; and then they would plunder the house, and perhaps cut her throat and strangle the baby!

"Never mind them, never mind them!" the fallen *cacique* would reply, with a condescending smile. "They aren't so bad as you imagine. They'll sing their *Marseillaise* for a time and shout themselves hoarse. Why shouldn't they, if they're content with so little? Other days are coming. The Carlists will see to it that our cause triumphs."

In don Ramón's judgment, the Doctor was a good sort, though his head may have been a bit turned by books. He knew him very well: they had been schoolmates together, and Rafael's father had never cared to join the hue and cry against Doctor Moreno. The one thing that seemed to bother him was that, as soon as the Republic was proclaimed, the Doctor's friends were eager to send him as a deputy to the Constituent Assembly of '73. That lunatic a deputy! Whereas he, the friend and agent of so many Conservative ministries, had never dared think of the

office for himself, because of the fairly superstitious
awe in which he held it! The end of the world
was surely coming!

But the Doctor had refused the nomination. If
he were to go to Madrid, what would become of the
poor people who depended on him for health and
protection? Besides, he liked a quiet, sedentary
life, with his books and his studies, where he could
satisfy his desires without quarrels and fighting. His
deep convictions impelled him to mingle with the
masses, and speak in public places—where he proved
to be a successful agitator, but he refused to join
party organizations; and after a lecture or an oration, he would spend days and days with his books
and magazines, alone save for his sister—a docile,
pious woman who worshipped him, though she be-
wailed his irreligion—and for his little daughter, a
blonde girl whom Rafael could scarcely remember,
because her father's unpopularity with the "best
people" kept the little child away from "good society."

The Doctor had one passion—music; and everybody admired his talent for that art. What didn't
the man know, anyhow? According to doña Bernarda and her friends, that remarkable skill had
been acquired through "evil arts." It was another
fruit of his impiety! But that did not prevent
crowds from thronging the streets at night, cautioning pedestrians to walk more softly as they approached his house; nor from opening their windows
to hear better when that devil of a doctor would be
playing his violoncello. This he did when certain
friends of his came up from Valencia to spend a few
days with him—a queer, long-haired crew that talked

a strange language and referred to a fellow called
Beethoven with as much respect as if he were San
Bernardo himself.

"Yes, don Andrés," said Rafael. "I remember
Doctor Moreno very well." And his ears seemed
to tingle again with the diabolical melodies that had
floated in to the side of his little bed on terrible
nights still fresh in his memory.

"Very well," continued the old man. "That lady
is the Doctor's daughter. What a man he was!
How he made your father and me fume in the days
of '73! Now that all that is so far in the past, I'll
say he was a fine fellow. His brain had gone somewhat bad from reading too much, like don Quixote;
and he was crazy over music. Most charming manners he had, however. He married a beautiful
orchard-girl, who happened to be very poor. He
said the marriage was . . . for the purpose of per-
petuating the species—those were his very words—
of having strong, sound, healthy children. For that
he didn't need to bother about his wife's social position. What he was looking for was health. So he
picked out that Teresa of his, as strong as an ox,
and as fresh as an apple. But little good it did the
poor woman. She had one baby and died a few
days afterward, despite the science and the desperate
efforts of her husband. They had lived together
less than a year."

Rafael's companions were listening with as much
attention as he; for morbid curiosity is the characteristic of the people of small places, where the keenest
pleasure available is that of knowing the private
affairs of others intimately.

"And now comes the good part," don Andrés

continued. "The mad Doctor had two saints: Castelar and Beethoven. The pictures of those fellows were scattered in every room of the house, even in the attic. This Beethoven (in case you don't know it), was an Italian or an Englishman, I'm not sure which—one of those fellows who makes music up out of his head for people to play in theatres or for lunatics like Moreno to amuse themselves with. Well, when his daughter was born the Doctor wondered what name to give her. As a tribute to Emilio Castelar, his idol, he felt he ought to call her Emilia: but he liked the sound of Leonora better (no, not Lenor, but Leonora!). According to what he told us, that was the title of the only opera Beethoven ever wrote—an opera he could read, for that matter, the way I read the paper. Anyhow, the foreigner won out; and the Doctor packed the child off to church with his sister, who took a few neighbors of the poorer sort along to see Leonora baptized.

"You can imagine what the priest said after he had looked in vain through the catalogue of saints for that name. At the time I was employed in the municipal offices, and I had to intervene. This was all before the Revolution; Gonzalez Brabo was boss in those days—and good old days they were! Let an enemy of law and order or sound religion just raise his voice and he was off on his way to Fernando Pio in no time. Well, what a racket the Doctor raised! He sat himself down in that church—first time he'd ever been in the place—and insisted that his daughter be labeled as he directed. Later he thought he would take her home without any baptism at all, saying he had no use for the ceremony anyhow, and that he put up with it only to please his sister. During the argument, he called all the curates and acolytes assembled in the sacristy there, a pack of 'brahmans.'"

"He must have said Brahmins," interrupted Rafael.

"Yes, that's it: and Bonzes, too—just joking, of course—I remember very well. But finally he compromised and let her be baptized with the orthodox name of 'Leonor.' Not that he cared what they called her in the church. As he went out he said to the priest: "She will be 'Leonora' for reasons that please her father, and which you wouldn't understand even if I were to explain them to you." What a hubbub followed! Don Ramón and I had to interfere to calm the good curates; they were for sending him up for sacrilege, insult to religion, what not! We had to go some to quiet things down. In those days, boy, a matter of that sort was more serious than killing a man."

"Which name did she keep?" asked a friend of Rafael.

"Leonora, as her father wished. That girl always took after the old man. Just as queer as he was. The Doctor all over again! I haven't seen her yet. They say she's a stunning beauty, like her mother, who was a blonde, and the handsomest girl in all these parts. When the Doctor had dressed his wife up like a lady, she wasn't much for manners, but she certainly was something to look at. . . ."

"And what became of Moreno?" asked another. "Is it true, as they said years ago, that he shot himself?"

"Oh, some say one thing, some another. Perhaps it's all a lie. Who knows! It all happened so far away. . . . After the Republic fell, it was the turn of decent people again. Poor Moreno took it all harder than he did the death of his Teresa, and kept himself locked up in his house day in, day out. Your father was stronger than before and we ran things in a way that was a sight for sore eyes! Don Antonio up in Madrid gave orders to the Governors to give us a free hand in cleaning up everything that was left of the Revolution. The people who before had been cheering for the Doctor all the time, now kept away from him for fear we should catch them. Some afternoons he would go for a walk in the suburbs, or a stroll over to his sister's orchard, near the river—always with Leonora at his side. She was now about eleven years old. All his affection was centered on her. Poor Doctor! How things had changed from the days when his mobs would meet the troops shot for shot in the streets of Alcira, shouting *vivas* for the Federal Republic! . . . In his solitude and in all the dejection coming from the defeat of his perverted ideas, he took more than ever to music. He had but one joy left him. Leonora loved music as much as he. She learned her lessons rapidly; and soon could accompany her father's violoncello on the piano. They would spend the days playing together, going through the whole pile of music sheets they kept stored in the attic along with those accursed medical books. Besides, the little girl showed she had a voice, and it seemed to grow fuller and more beautiful every day. 'She will be a singer, a great singer,' her father proclaimed enthusiastically. And when some tenant of his or one of his dependents came into the house and could hardly believe his ears at the sweetness of the little angel's voice, the Doctor would rub his hands and gleefully exclaim: 'What do you think of the little lady, eh? . . . Some day people in Alcira will be proud she was born here.' "

Don Andrés paused to sift his recollections, and after a long silence added:

"The truth is, I can't tell you any more. At that time, we were in power again, and I had very little to do with the Doctor. We gradually lost sight of him, forgot him, practically. The music we heard when going by the house was all there was to remind us of him. We learned one day, through his sister, doña Pepa, that he had gone way off with the little girl somewhere—what was that city you visited, Rafael?—Milan, yes, Milan, that's it! I've been told that's the market for singers. He wanted his Leonora to become a prima donna. He never came back, poor fellow! . . . Things must have gone badly with them. Every year he would write home to his sister to sell another piece of land. It is known that over there they lived in real poverty. In a few years the little fortune the Doctor got from his parents was gone. Poor doña Pepa, kind old soul, even disposed of the house—which belonged half to the Doctor and half to her—sent him every cent of the money, and moved to the orchard. Ever since then she's been coming in to mass and to Forty Hours in all sorts of weather. I could learn nothing for certain after that. People lie so, you see. Some say poor Moreno shot himself because his daughter left him when she got placed on the stage; others say that he died like a dog in a poorhouse. The only sure thing is that he died and that his daughter went on having a great time all over those countries

over there. The way she went it! They even
say she had a king or two. As for money! Say,
boys, there are ways and ways of earning it, and
ways and ways of spending it! The fellow who
knows all about that side of her is the barber Cupido.
He imagines he's an artist, because he plays the
guitar; and besides he has a Republican grouch, and
was a great admirer of her father's. He's the only
one in town who followed all she was up to, in the
papers. They say she doesn't sing under her own
name, but uses some prettier sounding one—foreign,
I believe. Cupido is a regular busybody and you
can get all the latest news in his barbershop. Only
yesterday he went to doña Pepa's farmhouse to
greet the '*eminent artist,*' as he calls her. There's
no end to what he tells. Trunks in every corner,
enough to pack a house-full of things into, and silk
dresses . . . shopfuls of them! Hats, I can't say
how many; jewelry-boxes on every table with diamonds that strike you blind. And she told Cupido
to have the station-agent get a move on and send
what was still missing—the heavier luggage—boxes
and boxes that come from way off somewhere—the
other end of the world, and that cost a fortune just
to ship . . . There you are! . . . And why not?
The way she earned it!"

Don Andrés winking maliciously and laughing
like an old faun, gave a sly nudge at Rafael, who was
listening in deep abstraction to the story.

"But is she going to live on here?" asked the
young man. "Accustomed as she is to flitting about
the world, do you think she'll be able to stand this
place?"

"Nobody can tell," don Andrés replied. "Not even Cupido can find that out. She'll stay until she gets bored, he says. And to be in less danger of that, she has brought her whole establishment along on her back, like a snail."

"Well, she'll be bored soon enough," one of Rafael's friends observed. "I suppose she thinks she's going to be admired and stared at as she was abroad! Moreno's girl! Did you ever hear of such a family? . . . Daughter of that *descamisado*, as my father calls him because he died without a stitch on his back! And all people say of them! Last night her arrival was the subject of conversation in every decent home in town, and there wasn't a man who did not promise to fight shy of her. If she thinks Alcira is anything like the places where they dance the razzle-dazzle and there's no shame, she'll be sadly disappointed."

Don Andrés laughed slyly.

"Yes, boys! She'll be disappointed. There's a plenty of morality in this town, and much wholesome fear of scandal. We're probably as bad as people in other places, but we don't want anybody to find us out. I'm afraid this Leonora is going to spend most of her time with her aunt—a silly old thing, whatever her many virtues may be. They say she's brought a French maid along . . . But she's beginning to cry 'sour grapes' already. Do you know what she said to Cupido yesterday? That she had come here with the idea of living all by herself, just to get away from people; and when the barber spoke to her of society in Alcira, she made a wry face, as much as to say the place was filled with no-accounts.

That's what the women were talking most about last night.  You can see why!  She has always been the favorite of so many big guns!"

An idea seemed to flit across the wrinkled forehead of don Andrés, tracing a wicked smile around his lips:

"You know what I think, Rafael?  You're young and you're handsome, and you've been abroad.  Why don't you make a try for her, if only to prick the bubble of her conceit and show her there are people here, too.  They say she's mighty good-looking, and, what the deuce!  It wouldn't be so hard.  When she finds out who you are! . . ."

The old man said this with the idea of flattering Rafael, certain that the prestige of his "prince" was such that no woman could resist him.  But Rafael had lived through the previous afternoon, and the words seemed very bitter pills.  Don Andrés at once grew serious, as if a frightful vision had suddenly passed before his eyes; and he added in a respectful tone:

"But no: that was only a jest.  Don't pay any attention to what I say.  Your mother would be terribly provoked."

The thought of doña Bernarda, the personification of austere, uncompromising virtue, chased the mirth from every face in the company.

"The strange thing about all this," said Rafael, who was anxious to turn the conversation in a different direction, "is that now everybody remembers the Doctor's daughter.  But years and years went by without her name being mentioned, in my hearing at least."

"Well, it's a question of District matters, you

see," the old man answered. "All I've been telling you boys, happened long before your day, and your parents, who knew the Doctor and his daughter, have always been careful not to bring this woman into their conversation; for, as Rafael's mother says, she's the disgrace of Alcira. From time to time we got a bit of news; something that Cupido fished out of the newspapers and spread all over town, or something that that silly doña Pepa would let drop, while telling inquisitive people about the glories her niece was winning abroad; anyhow, all a heap of lies that were invented I don't know where or by whom. They kept all that quiet, banking the fire, so to speak. If it hadn't got into the girl's head to come back to Alcira, you would never have heard of her probably. But now she's here, and they're telling all they know, or think they know, about her life, digging up tales of things that happened years and years ago. You take my word for it, boys, I've always considered her a high-flyer myself, but, just the same, people here do tell awful whoppers . . . and swear to them. She can't be as bad as they say . . . If one were to swallow everything one hears! Wasn't poor don Ramón the greatest man the District ever produced? Well, what don't they say about him? . . ."

And the conversation drifted away from Doctor Moreno's daughter. Rafael had learned all he wished to know. That woman had been born within a few hundred yards of his own birthplace. They had passed their childhood years almost side by side; and yet, on meeting for the first time in their lives, they had felt themselves complete strangers to each other.

This separation would increase with time. She made fun of the city, lived outside its circle of influence, in the open country; she would not meet the town halfway, and the town would not go to her.

How get to know her better, then? . . . Rafael was tempted as he walked aimlessly about the streets, to look up the barber Cupido in his shop that very afternoon. That merry rogue was the only person in all Alcira who entered her house. But Brull did not dare, for fear of gossip. His dignity as a party leader forbade his entering that barbershop where the walls were papered with copies of "Revolution" and where a picture of Pi y Margall reigned in place of the King's. How could he justify his presence in a place he had never visited before? How explain to Cupido his interest in that woman, without having the whole city know about it before sundown?

Twice he walked up and down in front of the striped window-panes of the barbershop, without mustering the courage to raise the latch. Finally he sauntered off toward the orchards, following the riverbank slowly along, with his gaze fixed on that blue house, which had never before attracted his attention, but which now seemed the most beautiful detail in that ample paradise of orange-trees.

Through the groves he could see the balcony of the house, and on it a woman unfolding shining gowns of delicate colors. She was shaking the prima donna's skirts to straighten out the wrinkles and the folds caused by the packing in the trunks.

It was the Italian maid—that Beppa of the reddish hair whom he had seen the previous afternoon with her mistress.

He thought the girl was looking at him, and that she even recognized him through the foliage, despite the distance. He felt a sudden timorousness, like a child caught redhanded doing something wrong. He turned in his tracks and strode rapidly off toward the city.

But later, he felt quite comforted. Merely to have approached the Blue House seemed like progress toward acquaintance with the beautiful Leonora.

All work had stopped on the rich farm lands of
the *ribera*.

The first winter rains were falling over the entire
District. Day after day the gray sky, heavy with
clouds, seemed to reach down and touch the very
tops of the trees. The reddish soil of the fields
grew dark under the continuous downpour; the
roads, winding deep between the mudwalls and the
fences of the orchards, were changed to rushing
streams. The weeping orange-trees seemed to
shrink and cringe under the deluge, as if in aggrieved
protest at the sudden anger of that kindly, friendly
land of sunshine.

The Júcar was rising. The waters, turned to so
much liquid clay, lashed red and slimy against the
buttresses of the bridges. People living along the
banks followed the swelling of the river with anxious eyes, studying the markers placed along the
shores to note how the water was coming up.

"*Munta?*" . . . asked the people from the interior,
in their quaint dialect.

"*Munta!*" answered the river dwellers.

And the water was indeed slowly rising, already
threatening the city that had so audaciously taken
root in the very middle of its bed.

But despite the danger, the townspeople seemed
to be feeling nothing more than uneasy curiosity.
No one thought of moving across the bridges to take

refuge on the high land.  Nonsense!  The Júcar was always flooding.  You had to expect something of the sort every once in a while.  Thank heaven there was something to break the monotony of life in that sleepy town!  Why complain at a week's vacation?  It was hard to disturb the placid complacency of those descendants of the Moors.  Floods had been coming since the days of their fathers, their grandfathers and their great-grandfathers, and never had the town been carried off.  A few houses at the worst.  Why suppose the catastrophe would be due now? . . . The Júcar was a sort of husband to Alcira.  As happens in any decent family, there would be a quarrel now and then—a thrashing followed by kisses and reconciliation.  Just imagine—living seven or eight centuries together!  Besides,—and this the lesser people thought—there was Father San Bernardo, as powerful as God Himself in all that concerned Alcira.  He was able, single-handed, to tame the writhing monster that wound its coiling way underneath the bridges.

It rained day and night; and yet the city, from its animation, seemed to be having a holiday.  The young ones, sent home from school because of the bad weather, were all on the bridges throwing branches into the water to see how swift the current was, or playing along the lanes close to the river, planting sticks in the banks and waiting for the ever-broadening torrent to reach them.

Under the shelter of the projecting eaves, whence broken water-spouts were belching streams as thick as a man's arm, loungers in the cafés would slip along the streets toward the river-front; and after glancing at the flood from the scant protection of their umbrellas, would make their way proudly back, stopping in every drinking place to offer their opinions on the rise that had taken place since their previous inspection.

The city from end to end was one seething storm of heated, typically "Southern" argument and prophecy. Friendships were being made and broken, over questions as to whether the river had risen four inches the past hour, or only one, and as to whether this freshet were more important than the one five years before.

Meantime the sky kept on weeping through its countless eyes; the river, roaring more wrathful every moment, was now licking at the ends of the low-lying streets near the bank, creeping up into the gardens on the shore, stealing in between the orange-trees, opening holes in the hedges and the mud-walls.

The main concern of the populace was whether it were raining also in the mountains of Cuenca. If much water came down from there, the flood would become serious. And experienced eyes studied the color of the waters carefully. If there was any black in them, it meant they came from the upper provinces.

The cloud-burst lasted for two whole days. The night of the second day closed, and the roar of the river sounded forebodingly in the darkness. On its black surface lights could be seen reflected like restless flashes of flame—candles from the shore houses and lanterns of watchmen on guard along the banks.

In the lower streets the water was coming under the doors into the houses. Women and children were taking refuge in the garrets while the men, with their trousers rolled up to their knees, were splashing about in the liquid silt, carrying their farming tools to places of safety, or tugging at some donkey who would be balking at going too deep into the water.

All these people of the suburbs, on finding their houses flooded in the darkness of night, lost the jesting calm which they had so boastfully displayed during the daytime. Now fear of the supernatural came over them, and with childish anxiety they sought protection of some Higher Power to avert the danger. Perhaps this freshet was the final one! Perhaps they were the victims destined to perish in the final downfall of the city! . . . Women began to shriek with terror on seeing their wretched lanes converted into deep canals.

"*El pare San Bernat! . . . Que traguen al pare San Bernat!* Father Saint Bernard! . . . Let them fetch father Saint Bernard!"

The men looked at each other uneasily. Nobody could handle a matter like this so well as the glorious patron. It was now high time to have recourse to him, as had so often been done before, and get him to perform his miracle.

They ought to go to the City Council, and compel the big guns there, in spite of their scepticism, to bring the saint out for the consolation of the poor.

In an hour a veritable army was formed. Mobs issued from the dark lanes, paddling in the water like frogs, and raising their war-cry: "*San Bernat! San Bernat!*"; the men, with their sleeves and trousers rolled up, or even entirely naked save for the sash that is never removed from the skin of a Valencian peasant; the women, with their skirts raised

over their heads for protection, sinking their tanned,
skinny, over-worked legs into the slime, and all
drenched from head to foot, the wet clothes stick-
ing to their bodies; and at the head, a number of
strong young men with four-wicked tapers lighted,
sputtering and crackling in the rain and casting a
weird flickering radiance back over the clamoring
multitude.

"*San Bernat! San Bernat! . . . Viva el pare
San Bernat!* Father Saint Bernard, *viva!*"

Under the drizzle pouring from the sky and the
streams tumbling from the eavespouts, the mob
rushed along through the streets in a wild riot.
Doors and windows flew open, and new voices were
added to the delirious uproar, while at every crossing recruits would come to swell the on-rushing
avalanche headed for the *Ayuntamiento*. Muskets,
ancient blunderbusses, and horse-pistols as big as
guns, could be seen in the menacing throng, as
though those wild forms were to compel the grant-
ing of a petition that might be denied, or to slay
the river, perhaps.

The *alcalde*, with all the members of the council,
was waiting at the door of the City Hall. They
had come running to the place, marshalling the
*alguacils* and the patrols, to face and quell the mu-
tiny.

"What do you want?" the Mayor asked the
crowd.

What did they want! They wanted the one
remedy, the one salvation, for the city: they wanted
to take the omnipotent saint to the bank of the river
that he might awe it with his presence, just as their

ancestors had been doing for centuries and centuries, and thanks to which the city was still standing!

Some of the city people, whom the peasants regarded as atheists, began to smile at the strange request. Wouldn't it be better to spend the time getting all the valuables out of the houses on the bank? A tempest of protests followed this proposal. "Out with the saint! Out with *San Bernat!* We want the miracle! The miracle!" Those simple people were thinking of the wonders they had learned in their childhood at their mothers' knees; times in former centuries, when it had been enough for San Bernardo to appear on a river road, to start the flood down again, draining off from the orchard lands as water leaks from a broken pitcher.

The *alcalde*, a liegeman of the Brull dynasty, was in a quandary. He was afraid of that ugly mob and was anxious to yield, as usual; but it would be a serious breach of etiquette not to consult "the chief." Fortunately, just as the huge, dark mass of human beings was beginning to surge in indignation at his silence, and hisses and shouts of anger were being raised, Rafael appeared.

Doña Bernarda had sent him out at the first sign of uneasiness in the populace. It was in circumstances such as these that her husband used to shine, taking the helm in every crisis, giving orders and settling questions, though to no avail at all. But when the river returned to its normal level, and danger was past, the peasant would remember don Ramón's "sacrifices" and call him the father of the poor. If the miraculous saint must come out, let Rafael be the one to produce him! The elections were at hand. The flood could not have come in better time. There must be no false steps, no frightening opportunity away. Something rather must be done to get people to talking about him as they used to talk about his father on similar occasions.

So Rafael, after having the purpose of this demonstration explained to him by the most ardent of the leaders, gave a magnificent gesture of consent:

"Granted; have *San Bernat* brought out!"

With a thunder of applause and *vivas* for young Brull, the black avalanche headed rumbling for the church.

They must now persuade the curate to take the saint out, and that good priest—a fat, kindly, but rather shrewd fellow—always objected to what he called a bit of old-fashioned mummery. The truth was he looked forward with little pleasure to a tramp out in the rain at the head of a procession, trying to keep dry under an umbrella, with his *soutane* rolled up to his knees, and his shoes coming off at every step in the mire. Besides, some day, in the very face of San Bernardo, the river might carry half the city off, and then what a fix, what a fix, religion would be in, all on account of those disturbers of the peace!

Rafael and his henchmen of the *Ayuntamiento* tried their hardest to convince the curate; but his only reply was to ask whether water was coming down from Cuenca.

"I believe it is," said the *alcalde*. "You can see that makes the danger worse. It's more than ever necessary to bring out the saint."

"Well, if there's water coming down from Cuenca," the priest answered, "we'd better let it come, and San Bernardo also had better keep indoors, at home. Matters concerning saints must be treated with great discretion, take my word for that. . . . And, if you don't agree with me, just remember that freshet when the river got above the bridges. We brought the saint out, and the river almost carried him off downstream."

The crowd, growing restless at the delay, began to shout against the priest. The good sense of that canny churchman was powerless in the face of superstitions instilled by centuries of fanaticism.

"Since you will it so, so let it be," he said gravely. "Let the Saint come forth, and may the Lord have mercy on us!"

A frenzied acclamation burst from the crowd, which now filled the whole square in front of the church. The rain continued falling, and above the serried ranks of heads covered with skirts, cloaks, and an occasional umbrella, the flames of the tapers flickered, staining the wet faces red.

The people smiled happily in all their discomfort from the downpour. Confident of success, they were foretasting gleefully the terror of the stream at sight of the blessed image entering its waters. What could not San Bernardo do? His marvelous history, a blend of Moorish and Christian romance, flamed in all those credulous imaginations. He was a saint native to that region—the second son of the Moorish king of Carlet. Through his talent, courtesy and beauty he won such success at court in Valencia, that he rose to the post of prime minister.

Once when his sovereign had to have some dealings with the king of Aragon, he sent San Bernardo, who at that time was called Prince Hamete, to Bar-

celona. During his journey he drew up one night
at the portal of the monastery of Poblet. The chants
of the Cistercians, drifting mystical and vague
through the Gothic arches, moved the Saracen youth
to the bottom of his soul. He felt drawn to the
religion of his enemies by the magic of its poetry.
He received baptism, assumed the white habit of
Saint Bernard of Clairvaux, and later returned to
the kingdom of Valencia to preach Christianity.
There he enjoyed the tolerance Saracen monarchs
always had for new religious doctrines. He converted his two sisters—beautiful Mooresses they
were—and they took the names of Gracia and
Maria, and aflame in turn with pious fervor, they
chose to go with their brother on his tour of preach-
ment.

But the old king of Carlet had died, and his first-
born—the arrogant Almanzor, a brutal, vainglori-
ous Moor—succeeded to the rulership of the tiny
state—a sort of military satrapy. This haughty
potentate, offended in his magnificence to see members of his family traveling over the roads dressed
like vagabonds and preaching a religion of beggars,
called a troop of horse and set out in pursuit of his
brother and sisters. He came upon them near
Alcira, hiding on the riverbank. With one slash
of his sword he cut the heads off both his sisters;
San Bernardo he crucified and drove a big nail
through his forehead. Thus the sacred preacher
perished, but all the humble continued to adore him;
for here was a handsome prince, who had turned to
a poor man, become a wandering mendicant even—
a sacrifice that endeared him to the poorest of his
votaries. Of all this that crowd of peasants was

thinking as it shouted *vivas* to San Bernardo, now, surely, prime minister of God, as he had been of the pagan king of Valencia.

The procession was rapidly organized. Along the narrow lanes of the island where the rain coursed in streams, people kept coming in droves. They were barefoot for the most part, but some were sinking shoes indifferently into the water. Most of them had tapers or shotguns. The women did their best to shelter little ones under the skirts they had gathered about their heads. The musicians, all barefoot, were in regular uniform—gold braided jackets and plumed hats—looking for all the world like Malay chiefs who beautify their nakedness with castoff coats and three-cornered hats the missionaries give them.

In front of the church the lights of the tapers blended into one great flare. Through the wide doorway the candles on the altars gleamed like a distant constellation.

The whole neighborhood, almost, had assembled in the square, despite the increasing rain. Many had come to scoff. What a farce it all would be! They did well, however, to wait two days! The rain was almost over. It would probably stop by the time they got the Saint out!

In double file of tapers the procession began to move between two lines of tightly jammed spectators.

"*Vitol el pare San Bernat!* Hurrah for father San Bernardo!" a multitude of hoarse voices cried.

"*Vitol les chermanetes!* Hurrah for his sisters!" others added, to correct the lack of gallantry displayed by the most enthusiastic of the idolators in putting ladies last.

For the sisters, the holy martyrs, Gracia and Maria, also figured in the procession. San Bernardo never went anywhere alone. As even children in baby-school knew, not a power on earth, not all the men and horses in the orchards put together, could lift the saint from his altar unless his sisters went first. That was one of his miracles long accredited by tradition. He had very little confidence in women—less pious commentators said—and not willing to trust his sisters out of sight, he insisted that they precede him whenever he left his pedestal.

The holy sisters appeared in the church doorway, swaying on their litters above the heads of the worshippers.

"*Vitol les chermanetes!*"

And the poor *chermanetes,* dripping from every fold of their vestments, came out into that dark, tempestuous, rain-soaked atmosphere that was rent by sheaves of crude light from the tapers.

The musicians tuned their instruments, ready to break into the Royal March! In the brilliantly lighted doorway something shining could be seen laboriously advancing, swaying this way and that, as if the waves of an angry sea were rocking it.

The crowd again began to cheer, and the music sounded.

"*Vitol el pare San Bernat!*"

But the music and the acclamations were drowned by a deafening crash, as if the island had suddenly burst into a thousand pieces, dragging the city to the depths of the Abyss. The square was shooting a fusillade of lightning flashes, a veritable cannonade. Those ancient arms, blunderbusses, muzzle-loaders, pistols, crammed full of powder, could roar like artillery. All the guns in the neighborhood were saluting the appearance of the Saint. And the crowd, drunk with the smell of powder, began to shout and gesticulate in the presence of that bronze image, whose round, kindly face—that of a healthy well-fed friar—seemed to quiver with life in the light of the torches.

Eight strong men, almost naked, came forward staggering under the weight of the metal saint. The crowd surged against them, threatening to upset the statue. But two bare-breasted strong-armed boys, devotees of the patron, were marching on either side, and they fought the multitude back.

The women, shoved hither and thither and almost suffocated in the jam, burst into tears as their gaze fell upon the miraculous image.

"*Ay,* father San Bernardo! Father San Bernardo! Save us! Save us!"

Others dragged children out from the folds of their skirts, and held them out above their heads toward the powerful guards.

"Lift him up! Let him kiss the Saint!"

And those muscular peasants would pick the children up like dolls, now by an arm, now by a leg, now by the nape of the neck, raise them to a level with the saint, that they might kiss the bronze face, and then toss them back into the arms of their mothers, working like automatons, dropping one child to seize another, with the regularity of machines in action. Many times the impact was too rough; the noses of the children would flatten against the folds of the metallic garb; but the fervor of the crowd seemed to infect the little ones. They were the future adorers of the Moorish monk. Rubbing their bruises with their soft little hands they would swallow their tears and return to their snug places in their mothers' skirts.

Behind the glorious saint marched Rafael and the gentlemen of the *Ayuntamiento* with long wax tapers; and after them the curate, grumbling as he heard the first dashes of rain beat on the large red silk umbrella which the sacristan held over him, and felt the impact of the crowd of orchard-folk, that was mixed at random with the musicians. The latter, paying more attention to where they stepped than to their instruments, played a rather discordant march. Guns, meanwhile, continued to blaze away. The wild cheering for San Bernardo and his sisters went on; and, framed in a red nimbus of torch-light, greeted at every street-corner by a new fusillade, the image sailed along over that sea of heads, pelted by the rain, which, in the light of the candles, looked like a maze of transparent crystal threads. Around the saint the arms of the athletes kept ever moving, lifting children up to bump their drooling noses on the bronze of father San Bernardo. Balconies and windows along the way were filled with women, their heads protected by their skirts.

Sighs, wails, exclamations of entreaty welcomed the passing saint in a chorus of despair and hope.

"Save us, father San Bernardo! . . . Save us! . . ."

The procession reached the river, crossing and recrossing the bridges that led to the suburbs. The flickering torches were mirrored in the dark edges of the stream, which was growing momentarily more terrifying and clamorous. The water had not yet

reached the railing, as at other times.   Miracle!
San Bernardo was at work already!

Then the procession marched to points where the
river had flooded the lanes near the bank, and
turned them to virtual ponds.  The more fanatical of the devotees, lifting their tapers above their
heads, went out fearlessly neck high into the water:
for surely the Saint must not go in alone.

One old man, shaking with malaria, caught in the
rice-fields, and hardly able to hold the taper in his
trembling hands, hesitated at the brink of the stream.

"Go on in, *agüelo!*" the women encouraged affectionately.  "Father San Bernardo will cure you.
Don't lose such a chance!"

When the saint was out performing miracles, he
might remember the old man, too.  So *agüelo*—
"grandaddy"—shivering in his drenched clothes and
his teeth chattering, walked resolutely in.

The statue was making its way very slowly along
the inundated streets, for the feet of the bearers
sank deep into the water under their load; and they
could advance at all only with the aid of the faithful, who gathered about the litter on all sides to
help.  A writhing mass of bare, sinewy arms rose
from the water like tentacles of a human octo-
pus to carry the Saint along.

Just behind the image came the curate and the
political dignitaries, riding astride the shoulders of
some enthusiasts who, for the greater pomp of the
ceremony, were willing to serve as mounts, though
the tapers of their riders kept getting into their
faces.

The curate began to feel the cold water creeping
up his back, and ordered the Saint inshore again.   In

fact San Bernardo was already at the end of the
lane, and actually in the river itself.  His guards of
honor were having a time of it to keep their feet in
the face of the current, but they were still willing to
go on, believing that the farther the statue went into
the stream, the sooner the waters would go down.
At last, however, the most foolhardy withdrew.
The Saint came back.  Though the procession at
once went on to the next road and to the next,
repeating the same performance.

And suddenly it stopped raining.

A wild cheer, a shout of joy and triumph, shook
the multitude.

*"Vitol el pare San Bernat! . . ."*  Now would
the people of the neighboring towns dare dispute his
immense power? . . . There was the proof!  Two
days of incessant downpour, and then, the moment
the Saint showed his face out of doors—fair weather!  Excuse me!

In fervent thanksgiving weeping women rushed
upon the saint and began to kiss whatever part of the
image was within reach—the handles of the litter,
the decorations of the pedestal, the bronze body itself.  The tottering structure of wood and metal
began to stagger and reel like a frail bark tossing
over a sea of shrieking heads and extended arms
that trembled with exaltation.

The procession marched on for more than an
hour still along the river.  Then the priest, who
was dripping wet and had exhausted more than a
dozen "horses" under him, forbade it to continue.
Leave it to those peasants, and the nonsense would
go on till dawn!  So the curate observed that the

Saint had already done what was required of him. Now it was time to go home!

Rafael handed his taper to one of his henchmen and stopped on the bridge with a number of experienced observers, who were lamenting the damage done by the flood. At every moment, no one could say just how, alarming reports of the destruction wrought by the river were coming in. Now a mill had been isolated by the waters, and the people there had taken refuge on the roof, firing their shotguns as signals of distress. Many orchards had been completely submerged. The few boats available in the city were doing the best they could in the work of rescue. The valley had become one vast lake. Rowboats caught in the shifting currents were in danger of smashing against hidden obstructions; and it was practically impossible to push a punt upstream with oars.

Yet the people spoke with relative calmness. They were accustomed to this almost annual visitation, and accepted it resignedly as an inevitable evil. Besides, they referred hopefully to telegrams received by the *alcalde*. By dawn help would be coming in. The governor in Valencia was sending a detachment of marines, and the lagoon would be filled with navy boats. Everything would be all right in a few hours. But if the water got much higher meanwhile. . . !

They consulted stakes and other water marks along the river, and violent disputes arose. Rafael, for his part, could see the flood was still rising, though but slowly.

The peasants refused to believe it. How could

the river rise after Father San Bernardo had gone into it? No, sir! it was *not* rising. That was all a lie intended to discredit the patron. And a sturdy youth with flashing eyes threatened to disembowel with one stroke of his knife—like that!—a certain scoffer who maintained that the river would go on rising if only for the pleasure of refuting that charlatan of a friar.

Rafael approached the brawlers, and by the dim lantern light recognized Cupido—the barber—a sarcastic fellow, with curly side-whiskers and an aquiline nose, who took great pleasure in poking fun at the barbarous, unshakable faith of the illiterate peasants.

Brull knew the barber very well. The man was one of his childhood favorites. Fear of his mother was the only thing that had kept him from frequenting Cupido's shop—the rendezvous of the city's gayest set, a hotbed of gossip and practical jokes, a school of guitar playing and love songs that kept the whole neighborhood astir. Besides, Cupido was the freak of the city, the sharp-tongued but irresponsible practical joker, who was forgiven everything in advance, and could enjoy his idiosyncrasies and speak his mind about people without starting a riot against him. He was, for instance, the one person in Alcira who scoffed at the tyranny of the Brulls without thereby losing entrance to the Party Club, where the young men admired his wit and his eccentric way of dressing.

Rafael was still fond of Cupido, though not very intimate with him. In all the sedate, conservative world around him, the barber seemed the only person really worth while talking with. Cupido was almost an artist. In winter he would go to Valencia to hear the operas praised by the newspapers, and in one corner of his shop he had heaps of novels and illustrated magazines, much mildewed and softened by the damp, and their leaves worn through from continual thumbing by customers.

He had very little to do with Rafael, guessing that the youth's mother would not regard such a friendship with any too much favor; but he displayed a certain liking for the boy; and addressed him familiarly, having known him as a child. Of Rafael he said everywhere:

"He's the best one in the family; the only Brull with more brains than crookedness."

Nothing too small for Cupido to notice ever happened in Alcira. Every weakness, every foible of the city's celebrities was made public by him in his barbershop, to the delight of the Opposition, whose members gathered there to read their party organ. The gentlemen of the *Ayuntamiento* feared the barber more than any ten newspapers combined, and whenever some famous Conservative minister referred in parliament to a "revolutionary hydra" or a "hotbed of anarchy," they pictured to themselves a barbershop like that of Cupido, but much larger perhaps, scattering a poisonous atmosphere of cruel gibe and perverse effrontery all through the nation.

The barber was inevitably on hand where anything was going on. It might be at the very end of the suburbs, or away out in the country. In a few moments Cupido would put in an appearance to learn all about it, give advice to those who might need it, arbitrate between disputants and afterward tell the whole story with a thousand embellishments.

He had plenty of time on his hands for leading such a life. Two young fellows, as crazy as their employer, tended shop. Cupido paid them with music-lessons and meals—better or worse these latter, according to the day's receipts, which were divided fraternally among the three. And if the "boss" sometimes astonished the city by going out for a walk in midwinter in a suit of white duck, they, not to be outdone, would shave off their hair and eyebrows and show heads as smooth as billiard-balls behind the shop windows, to the great commotion of the city, which would flock *en masse* to see "Cupido's Chinamen."

A flood was always a great day for the barber. He closed shop and planted himself out on a bridge, oblivious to wind and rain, haranguing the crowds of spectators, terrifying the stupid with his exaggerations and inventions, and announcing hair-raising news which he asserted he had just received from the Governor by telegraph, and according to which, in two hours, there would not be a cellar-hole left of the place. Even the miracle-working San Bernardo would be washed into the sea!

When Rafael found him upon the bridge that night, after the procession, Cupido was on the point of coming to blows with several rustics, who had grown indignant at his heresies.

Stepping aside from the crowd, the two began a conversation about the dangers of the flood. Cupido, as usual, was well-informed. He had been told a poor old man had been cut off in an orchard and drowned. That was probably not the only accident that had taken place. Horses and pigs in large numbers had drifted past under the bridge, early in the afternoon.

The barber talked earnestly and with some sadness, it seemed. Rafael listened in silence, scanning his face anxiously, as if looking for a chance to speak of something which he dared not broach.

"And how about the Blue House," he ventured finally. "that farm of doña Pepa's where you go sometimes? Will anything be wrong down there?"

"It's a good solid place," the barber replied, "and this isn't the first flood it's been through. . . . But it's right on the river, and by this time the garden must be a lake; the water will surely be up to the second story. I'll bet doña Pepa's poor niece is scared out of her wits. . . . Just imagine—coming from so far away and from such pretty places, and running into a mess like this. . . ."

Rafael seemed to meditate for a moment. Then as if an idea that had been dancing about in his head all day had just occurred to him, he said:

"Suppose we take a run down there! . . . What do you say, Cupido?"

"Down there! . . . And how'll we get there?"

But the proposal, from its very rashness, was bound to appeal to a man like the barber, who at length began to laugh, as if the adventure were a highly amusing one.

"You're right! We could get through! It will look funny, all right! Us two paddling up like a couple of Venetian gondoliers to serenade a celebrated prima donna in her fright. . . . I've a good mind to run home and fetch my guitar along. . . ."

"What the devil, Cupido! No guitar business!

What a josher you are! Our job is to get those women out of there. They'll get drowned if we don't."

The barber, insisting on his romantic idea, fixed a pair of shrewd eyes on Rafael.

"I see! So you're interested in the illustrious *artiste,* too. . . . You rascal! You're smitten on her reputation for good looks. . . . But no. . . . I remember . . . you've seen her; she told me so herself."

"She! . . . She spoke to you about me?"

"Oh, nothing important! She told me she saw you one afternoon up at the Hermitage."

Cupido kept the rest to himself. He did not say that Leonora, on mentioning Rafael's name, had added that he looked like an "idiot."

Rafael's heart leaped with joy! She had talked of him! She had not forgotten that meeting which had left such a painful memory in him! . . . What was he doing, then, standing like a fool there on that bridge, when down at the Blue House they might be needing a man's help?

"Listen, Cupido; I have my boat right handy here; you know, the boat father had made to order in Valencia as a present for me. Steel frame; hard wood; safe as a warship. You know the river. . . . I've seen you handle an oar more than once; and I've got a pair of arms myself. . . . What do you say?"

"I say, let's go," the barber answered resolutely.

They asked for a torch, and with the help of several men dragged Rafael's boat toward a stairway on the riverbank.

Above, through the crowds on the bridge, the

news of the expedition flashed, but exaggerated and much idealized by the curious. The men were going to save a poor family that had taken refuge on the roof of a house—poor devils in danger of being swept off at any moment. Rafael had learned of their plight, and he was starting to save them at the risk of his own skin. And a wealthy, powerful man like him, with so much to live for! Damn it, those Brulls were all men, anyhow! . . . And yet see how people talked against them! What a heart! And the peasants followed the blood-red glow of the torch in the boat as it mirrored across the waters, gazing adoringly at Rafael, who was sitting in the stern. Out of the dark entreating voices called. Many loyal followers of the Brulls were eager to go with the chief—drown with him, if need be.

Cupido protested. No; for a job like that, the fewer the better; the boat had to be light; he would do for the oars and Rafael could steer.

"Let her go! Let her go!" called Rafael.

And the boat, after hesitating a second, shot off on the current.

In the narrow gorge between the Old City and the New, the swollen torrent swept them along like lightning. The barber used his oars just to keep the boat away from the shore. Submerged rocks sent great whirlpools to the surface and pulled the boat this way and that. The light of the torch cast a dull reddish glow out over the muddy eddies. Tree trunks, refuse, dead animals, went floating by, shapeless masses with only a few dark points visible above the surface, as though some dead man covered with mud were swimming under water. Out on that swirling current, with the slimy vapors of the river rising to his nostrils and the eddies sucking and boiling all around, Rafael thought himself the victim of a weird nightmare and began even to repent of his rashness. Cries kept coming from houses close to the river; windows were suddenly lighted up; and from them great shadowy arms like the wings of a windmill waved in greeting to that red flame which people saw gliding past along the river, bringing the outlines of the boat and the two men into distinct view. The news of their expedition had spread throughout the city and people were on the watch for them as they sped by: *"Viva* don Rafael! *Viva* Brull!"

But the hero who was risking his life to save a family of poor folks out there in the darkness of that sticky, murky, sepulchral night, had in mind only one thing—a blue house, into which he was to penetrate at last, in so strange and romantic a fashion.

From time to time a scraping sound or a jolt of the boat would bring him back to reality.

"Your tiller there!" Cupido would shout, without, however, taking his eyes from the water ahead. "Look out, Rafaelito, or we'll get smashed!"

The boat was indeed a good one, for any other, would long before have come to grief in those rapids jammed with rocks and debris.

They were around the city in no time. Few lighted windows were now to be seen. High, steep banks of slippery mud—quite unscalable—crested with walls, were slipping past on either hand, with an occasional palisade, the piles just emerging from the water. Somewhat ahead, the open river, where the two arms that girt the Old City reunited in what was now a vast lake!

The two men went on blindly. All normal landmarks were gone. The banks had disappeared, and in the blackness, beyond the red circle of torch light, they could make out only water and then more water—an immense incessantly rolling sheet that was taking them they knew not where. From time to time a black spot would show above the muddy surface; the crest of some submerged canebrake; the top of a tree; a strange, fantastic vegetation that seemed to be writhing in the gloom. The river, free now from the gorges and shallows around the city, had ceased its roaring. It seethed and swirled along in absolute silence, effacing all trace of the land. The two men felt like a couple of shipwrecked sailors adrift on a shoreless, sunless ocean, alone save for the reddish flame flickering at the prow, and the submerged treetops that appeared and vanished rapidly.

"Better begin to row, Cupido," said Rafael. "The current is very strong. We must be still in the river. Let's turn to the right and see if we can get into the orchards."

The barber bent to the oars, and the boat, slowly, on account of the current, came around and headed for a line of tree-tops that peered above the surface of the flood like seaweed floating on the ocean. Shortly the bottom began to scrape on invisible obstacles. Entanglements below were clutching at the keel, and it took some effort occasionally to get free. The lake was still dark and apparently shoreless, but the current was not so strong and the surface had stopped rolling. The two men knew they had reached dead water. What looked like dark, gigantic mushrooms, huge umbrellas, or lustrous domes, caught the reflection of the torch, at times. Those were orange-trees. The rescuers were in the orchards. But in which? How find the way in the darkness? Here and there the branches were too thick to break through and the boat would tip as if it were going over. They would back water, make a detour, or try another route.

They were going very slowly for fear of striking something, zig-zagging meanwhile to avoid snags. As a result they lost direction altogether, and could no longer say which way the river lay. Darkness and water everywhere! The submerged orange-trees, all alike, formed complicated lanes over the inundation, a labyrinth in which they grew momentarily more confused. They were now rowing about quite aimlessly.

Cupido was perspiring freely, under the hard work. The boat was moving slower and slower because of the branches catching at the keel.

"This is worse than the river," he murmured. "Rafael, you're facing forward. Can't you make out any light ahead?"

"Not a one!"

The torch would throw some huge clump of leaves into relief for a moment. When that was gone, the light would be swallowed up into damp, thick, empty space.

Thus they wandered about and about the flooded countryside. The barber's strength had given out and he passed the oars over to Rafael, who was also nearly exhausted.

How long had they been gone? Were they to stay there forever? And their minds dulled by fatigue and the sense of being lost, they imagined the night would never end—that the torch would go out and leave the boat a black coffin, for their corpses to float in eternally.

Rafael, who was now facing astern suddenly noticed a light on his left. They were going away from it; perhaps that was the house they had been so painfully searching for.

"It may be," Cupido agreed. "Perhaps we went by without seeing it, and now we're downstream, toward the sea. . . . But even if it is not the Blue House, what of it? The main thing is to find someone there. That's far better than wandering around here in the dark. Give me the oars, again Rafael. If that isn't doña Pepita's place, at least we'll find out where we are."

He pulled the boat around, and gradually they made their way through the treetops toward the light. They struck several snags, orchard fences, perhaps, or submerged walls—but the light kept growing brighter. Finally it had become a large red square across which dark forms were moving. Over the waters a golden, shimmering wake of light was streaming.

The torch from the boat brought out the lines of a broad house with a low roof that seemed to be floating on the water. It was the upper story of a building that had been swamped by the inundation. The lower story was under water. The flood, indeed, was getting closer to the upper rooms. The balconies and windows looked like landings of a pier in an immense lake.

"Seems to me as if we'd struck the place," the barber said.

A warm, resonant voice, that of a woman, vibrant, but with a deep, melodious softness, broke the silence.

"Hey, you in the boat there! . . . Here, here!"

The voice betrayed no fear. It showed not a trace of emotion.

"Didn't I tell you so! . . ." the barber exclaimed. "The very place we were looking for. Doña Leonora! . . . It's I! It's I!"

A rippling laugh came out into gloom.

"Why, it's Cupido! It's Cupido! . . . I can tell him by his voice. Auntie, auntie! Don't cry any more. Don't be afraid; and stop your praying, please! Here comes the God of Love in a pearl shallop to rescue us!"

Rafael shrank at the sound of that somewhat mocking voice, which seemed to people the darkness with brilliantly colored butterflies.

Now in the luminous square of a window he could make out the haughty profile of a woman among other black forms that were going to and fro past the light inside, in agreeable surprise at the unexpected visit.

The craft drew up to the balcony. The men rose to their feet and were able to reach an iron railing. The barber, from the prow, was looking for something strong where he could make the boat fast.

Leonora was leaning over the balustrade while the light from the torch lit up the golden helmet of her thick, luxuriant hair. She was trying to identify that other man down there who had bashfully sat down again in the stern.

"You're a real friend, Cupido! . . . Thank you, thank you, ever and ever so much. This is one of the favors we never forget. . . . But who has come along with you? . . ."

The barber was already fastening the boat to the iron railing.

"It's don Rafael Brull," he answered slowly. "A gentleman you have met already, I believe. You must thank him for this visit. The boat is his, and it was he who got me out on this adventure."

"Oh, thank you, Señor Brull," said Leonora, greeting the man with the wave of a hand that flashed blue and red from the rings on its fingers. "I must repeat what I said to our friend Cupido. Come right in, and I hope you'll excuse my introducing you through a second-story window."

Rafael had jumped to his feet and was answering her greeting with an awkward bow, clasping the iron railing in order not to fall. Cupido jumped into the house and was followed by the young man, who took pains to make the climb gracefully and sprightly.

He was not sure how well he succeeded. That had been too much excitement for a single night: first the wild trip through the gorges near the city; then those hours of desperate aimless rowing over the winding lanes of the flooded countryside; and now, all at once, a solid floor under his feet, a roof over his head, warmth, and the society of that madly beautiful woman, who seemed to intoxicate him with her perfume, and whose eyes he did not dare meet with his own for fear of fainting from embarrassment.

"Come right in, *caballero*," she said to him. "You surely need something after this escapade of yours.

You are sopping wet, both of you. . . . Poor boys!
Just look at them! . . . Beppa! . . . Auntie!
But do come in, sir!"

And she fairly pushed Rafael forward with a
sort of maternal authoritativeness, much as a kindly
woman might take her child in hand after he has
done some naughty prank of which she is secretly
proud.

The rooms were in disorder. Clothes everywhere
and heaps of rustic furniture that contrasted with
the other pieces arranged along the walls! The
household belongings of the gardener had been
brought upstairs as soon as the flood started. An
old farmer, his wife—who was beside herself with
fear—and several children, who were slinking in the
corners, had taken refuge in the upper story with
the ladies, as soon as the water began seeping into
their humble home.

Rafael entered the dining-room, and there sat
doña Pepita, poor old woman, heaped in an armchair, the wrinkles of her features moistened with
tears and her two hands clutching a rosary. Cupido
was trying vainly to cheer her with jokes about the
inundation.

"Look, auntie! This gentleman is the son of your
friend, doña Bernarda. He came over here in a boat
to help us out. It was very nice of him, wasn't it?"

The old woman seemed quite to have lost her
mind from terror. She looked vacantly at the new
arrivals, as if they had been there all their lives.
At last she seemed to realize what they were saying.

"Why, it's Rafael!" she exclaimed in surprise.
"Rafaelito. . . . And you came to see us in such

weather! Suppose you get drowned? What will your mother say? . . . Lord, how crazy of you! Lord!"

But it was not madness, and even if it were, it was very sweet of him! That, at least, was what Rafael seemed to read in those clear, luminous eyes of the golden sparkles that caressed him with their velvety touch every time he dared to look at them. Leonora was staring at him: studying him in the lamplight, as if trying to understand the difference between the man in front of her and the boy she had met on her walk to the Hermitage.

Doña Pepa's spirits rallied now that men were in the house; and with a supreme effort of will, the old lady decided to leave her armchair for a look at the flood, which had stopped rising, if, indeed, it were not actually receding.

"How much water, oh Lord our God! . . . How many terrible things we'll learn of tomorrow! This must be a punishment from Heaven . . . a warning to us to think of our many sins."

Leonora meanwhile was bustling busily about, hurrying the refreshments. Those gentlemen couldn't be left like that—she kept cautioning to her maid and the peasant woman. Just imagine, with their clothes wet through! How tired they must be after that all night struggle! Poor fellows! It was enough just to look at them! And she set biscuits on the table, cakes, a bottle of rum—everything, including a box of Russian cigarettes with gilded tips—to the shocked surprise of the gardener's wife.

"Let them come here, auntie," she said to the old lady. "Don't make them talk any more now. . . . They need to eat and drink a little, and get warm.

. . . I'm sorry I have so little to offer you. What in the world can I get for them? Let's see! Let's see!"

And while the two men were being forced, by that somewhat despotic attentiveness, to take seats at the table, Leonora and her maid went into the adjoining room, where keys began to rattle and tops of chests to rise and fall.

Rafael, in his deep emotion, could scarcely manage a few drops of rum; but the barber chewed away for all he was worth, downing glass after glass of liquor, and talking on and on through a mouth crammed with food while his face grew redder and redder.

When Leonora reappeared, her maid was following her with a great bundle of clothes in her arms.

"You understand, of course, we haven't a stitch of men's clothes in the house. But in war-time we get along as best we can, eh? We're in what you might call a state of siege here."

Rafael noted the dimples that a charming smile traced in those wonderful cheeks! And what perfect teeth—jewels in a casket of red velvet!

"Now, Cupido; off with those wet things of yours; you're not going to catch pneumonia on my account, and thus deprive the city of its one bright spot. Here's something to put on while we are drying your clothes."

And she offered the barber a magnificent gown of blue velvet, with veritable cascades of lace at the breast and on the sleeves.

Cupido nearly fell off his chair. . . . Was he going to dress in top style for once in his life? And with those side-whiskers? . . . How the people in

Alcira would howl if they could only see him now!
And entering at once into the fun of the situation,
he hastened into the next room to don his gown.

"For you," Leonora said to Rafael with a motherly smile, "I could find only this fur cloak. Come,
now, take off that jacket of yours; it's dripping wet."

With a blush, the young man refused. No, he
was all right! Nothing would happen to him! He
had been wetter than that many times.

Leonora without losing her smile, seemed to grow
impatient. No one in that house ever talked back
to her.

"Come, Rafael, don't be so silly. We'll have to
treat you like a child."

And taking him by a sleeve, as if he were a refractory baby, she began to pull at his jacket.

The young man, in his confusion, was hardly
aware of what was taking place. He seemed to be
traveling along on an endless horizon, at greater
speed than he had been swept down the river just
before. She had called him by his first name; he was
a pampered guest in a house he had for months been
trying in vain to enter, and she, Leonora, was calling him "child" and treating him like a child, as if
they had been friends all their lives. What sort of
woman was this? Was he not lost in some strange
world? The women of the city—the girls he met
at the parties at his home, seemed to be creatures
of another race, living far, ever so far, away, at
the other end of the earth, cut off from him forever
by that immense sheet of water.

"Come, Mr. Obstinate, or we'll have to undress
you like a doll."

She was bending over him; he could feel her breath

upon his cheeks, and the touch of her delicate, agile hands; and a sense of delicious intoxication swept over him.

The fur coat was drawn snugly about his shoulders. It was a rare garment; a cloak of blue fox as soft as silk, thick, yet light as the plumes of some fantastic bird. Though Rafael passed for a tall man, its edges touched the floor. The young man realized that thousands of francs had suddenly been thrown over his back, and tremblingly he gathered the bottom up, lest he should step upon it.

Leonora laughed at his embarrassment.

"Don't be afraid; no matter if you do tread on it. One would think you were wearing a sacred veil from the respect you show that coat. It isn't worth much. I use it only to travel in. A grandduke gave it to me in Saint Petersburg."

And to show more clearly how little she prized the princely gift, she wrapped it closer around the boy, patting at his shoulders to fit it more tightly to him.

Slowly they walked back into the front room. Meanwhile, the appearance of the barber, dressed in his luxuriant gown, was greeted with shouts of laughter in the dining-room. Cupido was taking full advantage of the occasion. The train in one hand and stroking his side-whiskers with the other, he was writhing about like a prima donna in her big scene and singing in a falsetto soprano voice. The peasant family laughed like mad, forgetting the disaster that had overtaken their home; Beppa opened her eyes wide, surprised at the elegant figure of the man, and the grace with which he pronounced the Italian verses. Even poor doña Pepa hitched

around in her armchair and applauded. The barber, according to her, was the most charming devil
in the world.

Rafael was standing on the balcony, at Leonora's
side, his gaze lost in the darkness, his spirit lulled
by the music of her sweet voice, his body snug and
comfortable in that elegant garment which seemed
to have retained something of the warmth and perfume of her shoulders. With marks of very real interest, she was questioning him about the desperate
trip down the river.

Rafael answered her inquiries with bated breath.

"What you have done," the prima donna was
saying, "deserves my deep, deep gratitude! It is
a chivalrous act worthy of ancient times. Lohengrin, arriving in his little boat to save Elsa! Only
the swan is lacking . . . unless you want to call
Cupido a swan. . . ."

"And suppose you had been carried off—
drowned! . . ." the youth exclaimed in justifica-
tion of his rashness.

"Drowned! . . . I must confess that at first I
was somewhat afraid. Not so much of dying, for
I'm somewhat tired of life—as you will realize after
you've known me a little longer. But a death like
that, suffocated in that mud, that filthy, dirty water
that smells so bad, doesn't at all appeal to me. If it
were some green, transparent Swiss lake! . . . I
want beauty even in death; I'm concerned with the
'final posture,' like the Romans, and I was afraid
of perishing here like a rat in a sewer . . . . And
nevertheless, I couldn't help laughing at my aunt
and our poor servants to see the fright they were
in! . . . Now the water is no longer rising, and the

house is strong. Our only trouble is that we're
cut off, and I'm waiting for daylight to come so that
we can see where we are. The sight of all this
country changed into a lake must be very beautiful,
isn't it, Rafael?"

"You've probably seen far more interesting
things," the young man replied.

"I don't deny that; but I'm always most impressed by the sensation of the moment."

And she fell silent, showing by her sudden seri-
ousness the vexation that his distant allusion to her
past had caused.

For some moments neither of them spoke; and
it was Leonora who finally broke the silence.

"The truth is, if the water had gone on rising,
we would have owed our lives to you. . . . Let's
see, now, frankly: why did you come? What kind
inspiration made you think of me. You hardly know
me!"

Rafael blushed with embarrassment, and trembled
from head to foot, as if she had asked him for a
mortal confession. He was on the point of uttering
the great truth, baring in one great explosion all his
thoughts and dreams and dreads of past days. But
he restrained himself and grasped wildly for an
answer.

"My enthusiasm for the artist," he replied timidly.
"I admire your talent very much."

Leonora burst into a noisy laugh.

"But you don't know me! You've never heard me
sing! . . . What do you know about my "talent,"
as they call it? If it weren't for that chatterbox of
a Cupido, Alcira would never dream that I am a

singer and that I'm somewhat well-known—except in my own country."

Rafael was crushed by the reply; he did not dare protest.

"Come, Rafael," the woman continued affectionately, "don't be a child and try to pass off the fibs boys use to deceive mama with. I know why you came here. Do you imagine you haven't been seen from this very balcony hovering about here every afternoon, lurking in the road like a spy? You are discovered, sir."

The shy Rafael thought the balcony was collapsing underneath his feet. He shivered in abject terror, drew the fur cloak tighter around him, without knowing what he was about, and shook his head in energetic denial.

"So it's not true, you fraud?" she said, with comic indignation. "You deny that since we met up at the Hermitage you have been taking all your walks in this neighborhood? *Dios mío!* What a monster of falsehood have we here? And how brazenly he lies."

And Rafael, vanquished by her frank merriment, had finally to smile, confessing his crime with a loud laugh.

"You're probably surprised at what I do and say," continued Leonora drawing closer to him, leaning a shoulder against his with unaffected carelessness, as if she were with a girl friend. "I'm not like most women. A fine thing it would be for me, with the life I lead, to play the hypocrite! . . . My poor aunt thinks I'm crazy because I say just what I feel; in my time I've been much liked and much disliked on account of the mania I have for not concealing anything. . . . Do you want me to tell you the real truth? . . . Very well; you've come here because you love me, or, at least, because you think you love me: a failing all boys of your age have, as soon as they find a woman different from the others they know."

Rafael bowed his head and said nothing; he did not dare look up. He felt the gaze of those green eyes upon the back of his head and they seemed to reach right into his soul.

"Let's see your face. Raise that head of yours a little. Why don't you say it isn't so, as you did before? Am I right or not?"

"And supposing you were right? . . ." Rafael ventured to murmur, finding himself thus suddenly discovered.

"Since I know I am, I thought it best to provoke this explanation, so as to avoid any misunderstandings. After what has happened to-night, I want to have you for a friend; friend you understand, and nothing more; a comradeship based on gratitude. We ought to know in advance exactly where we stand. We'll be friends, won't we? . . . You must feel quite at home here; and I'm sure I shall find you a very agreeable chum. What you've done to-night has given you a greater hold on my affection than you could ever have gained in any ordinary social way; but you're going to promise me that you won't drift into any of that silly love-making that has always been the bane of my existence."

"And if I can't help myself?" murmured Rafael.

"'And if I can't help myself'," said Leonora,

laughing and mimicking the voice of the young man and the expression on his face. " 'And if I can't help myself'! That's what they all say! And why can't you help yourself? How can one take seriously a love for a woman you are now seeing for the second time? These sudden passions are all inventions of you men. They're not genuine. You get them out of the novels you read, or out of the operas we sing. Nonsense that poets write and callow boys swallow like so many boobies and try to transplant into real life! The trouble is we singers are in the secret, and laugh at such bosh. Well, now you know—good friends, and the soft pedal on sentiment and drama, eh? In that way we'll get along very well and the house will be yours."

Leonora paused and, threatening him playfully with her forefinger, added:

"Otherwise, you may consider me just as ungrateful and cruel as you please, but your gallant conduct of to-night won't count. You'll not be permitted to enter this place again. I want no adorers; I have come here looking for rest, friendship, peace . . . Love! A beautiful, cruel hoax! . . ."

She was speaking very earnestly, without moving, her gaze lost on that immense sheet of water.

Rafael dared to look at her squarely now. He had raised his head and was studying her as she stood there thinking. Her beautiful face was tinted with a bluish light, that seemed to surround her with a halo of romance. Morning was coming on, and the leaden curtains of the sky were rent in the direction of the sea, allowing a livid light to filter through.

Leonora shivered as if from cold, and snuggled instinctively against Rafael. With a shake of her head she seemed to rout a troop of painful thoughts, and stretching out a hand to him she said:

"Which shall it be? Friends, or distant acquaintances? Do you promise to be good, be a real comrade?"

Rafael eagerly clasped that soft, muscular hand, and felt her rings cut deliciously into his fingers.

"Very well—friends then! . . . I'll resign myself, since there's no help for it."

"In that case you will find what you now believe a sacrifice something quite tolerable and quite consoling; you don't know me, but I know myself. Believe me, even should I come to love you—as I never shall—you would be the loser by it. I am worth much more as a friend than as a lover. And more than one man in the world has found that out."

"I will be a friend, ready to do much more for you than I've done to-night. I hope you will come to know me too."

"No promises now! What more can you do for me? The river doesn't flood every day. You can't expect to be a hero every other moment. No, I'm satisfied with to-night's exploit. You can't imagine how grateful I am. It has made a very deep impression on my—friendly—heart. . . . May I be quite frank? Well, when I met you there at the Hermitage, I took you for one of these local *señoritos* who have such an easy time of it in town, and so, look upon every woman they meet as their property for the asking. Afterwards, when I saw you lurking about the house, my scorn increased. 'Who does that little dandy think he is?' I said to myself.

And how Beppa and I laughed over it! I hadn't
even noticed your face and your figure: I hadn't
realized how handsome you were. . . ."

Leonora laughed at the thought of how angry
she had been, and Rafael, overwhelmed by such
candor, likewise smiled to conceal his embarrassment.

"But after what happened to-night I am fond of
you . . . as people are fond of friends. I am alone
here: the friendship of a good and noble boy like
yourself, capable of sacrifice for a woman whom
he hardly knows, is a very comforting thing to have.
Besides, that much doesn't compromise me. I am a
bird of passage, you see; I have alighted here because I'm tired, ill—I don't just know what's the
matter, but deeply broken in spirit anyhow. I need
rest, just plain existence—a plunge into sweet noth-
ingness, where I can forget everything; and I gratefully accept your friendship. Later on, when you
least expect it, probably, I'll fly away. The very
first morning when I wake up, feel quite myself
again—and hear inside my head the song of the mischievous bird that has advised me to do so many
foolish things in my life—I'll pack up my trunk and
take flight! I'll drop you a line of course; I'll send
you newspaper clippings that speak of me, and you'll
see you have a friend who does not forget you and
who sends you greetings from London, Saint Petersburg, or New York—any one of the corners of this
world which many believe so large yet where I am
unable to stir without encountering things that bore
me."

"May that moment be long delayed!" said Rafael. "May it never come!"

"Rash boy!" Leonora exclaimed. "You don't know me. If I were to stay here very long, we'd finish by quarreling and coming to blows. At bottom I hate men: I have always been their most terrible enemy."

Behind their backs they heard the rustle of the gown that Cupido was dragging along behind him with absurd antics. He was coming to the balcony with doña Pepita to see the sunrise.

Through its dense clouds the sky was beginning to shed a gray, wan light, under which the vast, watery plain took on the whitish color of absinthe. Down the stream the debris of the inundation was floating, sweepings of wretched poverty, uprooted trees, clumps of reeds, thatched roofs from huts, all dirty, slimy, nauseating. Bits of flotsam and jetsam became entangled between the orange-trees and formed dams that little by little grew with the new spoils brought along by the current.

In the distance at the very end of the lake, a number of black points could be seen in regular rhythmic motion, stirring their legs like aquatic flies around some roofs barely protruding above the immense field of water. The rescuers had arrived from Valencia—with whale-boats of the Fleet, brought overland by rail to the scene of the flood.

The provincial authorities would soon be arriving in Alcira; and the presence of Rafael was indispensable. Cupido himself, with sudden gravity, advised him to go and meet those boats.

While the barber was putting on his own clothes, Rafael, with intense regret, removed his fur cloak. It seemed that in taking it off he was losing the warmth of that night of sweet intimacy, the contact of that soft shoulder that had for hours long been leaning against him.

Leonora meanwhile looked at him fixedly.

"We understand each other, don't we?" she asked, slowly. "Friends, with no hope of anything more than that. If you break the pact, you'll not enter this place again, not even by the second-story window, as you did last night."

"Yes, friends and nothing more," Rafael murmured with a tone of sincere sadness, that seemed to move Leonora.

Her green eyes lighted up: her pupils seemed to glitter with spangles of gold. She stepped nearer and held out her hand.

"You're a good boy; that's the way I like you: resignation and obedience. For this time, and in reward for your good sense, we'll make just one exception. Let's not part thus coldly. . . . So,—you may kiss me,—as they do it on the stage—here!"

And she raised her hand up toward his lips. Rafael seized it hungrily and kissed it over and over again, until Leonora, tearing it away with a violence that showed extraordinary strength, reprimanded him sharply.

"You rogue! . . . Up to mischief so soon! What an abuse of confidence? Good-bye! Cupido is calling you. . . . Good-bye."

And she pushed him toward the balcony, where the barber was already holding the boat against the railing.

"Hop in, Rafael," said Cupido. "Better lean on me; the water's going down and the boat's very low."

Rafael jumped into his white craft, which was now dirty and stained from the red water. The barber took the oars. They began to move away.

"Good-bye! Good-bye! Many thanks!" cried doña Pepa. The maid and the whole family of the gardener had come out on the balcony.

Rafael let go the tiller, and turned toward the house. He could see nothing, however, but that proud beauty, who was waving her handkerchief to them. He watched her for a long time, and when the crests of the submerged trees hid the balcony from view, he bowed his head, giving himself up entirely to the silent pleasure of tasting the sweetness that he could still feel upon his burning lips.

# CHAPTER VI

The elections set the whole District agog. The crucial moment for the House of Brull had come, and all its loyal henchmen, as though still uncertain of the Party's omnipotence, and fearing the sudden appearance of hidden enemies, were running this way and that about the city and the outlying towns, shouting Rafael's name as a clarion call to victory.

The inundation was something of the forgotten past. The beneficent sun had dried the fields. The orchards fertilized by the silt of the recent flood looked more beautiful than ever. A magnificent harvest was forecasted, and, as sole reminders of the catastrophe, there remained only a shattered enclosure here, a fallen fence there, or some sunken road with the banks washed away. Most of the damage had been repaired in a few days, and people were quite content, referring to the past danger jokingly. Until next time!

Besides, plenty of relief money had been given out. Help had come from Valencia, from Madrid, from every corner of Spain, thanks to the whimpering publicity given the inundation in the local press; and since the pious believer must attribute all his boons to the protection of some patron saint, the peasants thanked Rafael and his mother for this alms, resolving to be more faithful than ever to the powerful family. So—long live the Father of the Poor!

Doña Bernarda's ambitious dreams were on the point of realization, and she could not give herself a moment's rest. Her son's cool indifference was something she could not understand for the life of her! The District was his all right, but was that a reason for falling asleep on the job? Who could tell what the "enemies of law and order"—there was more than one of them in the city—might spring at the very last moment? No, he must wake up— go and make a speech—now at this town, now at that—and say a few words of encouragement to the people of property, especially. And why not visit the *alcalde,* down in X——, just to show that poor devil he was being taken seriously. Rafael must show himself in public, keep everybody talking about him and thinking about him!

And Rafael obeyed, but taking good care to avoid the company of don Andrés on such trips, in order to spend a few hours at the Blue House on the way out or back, or else, to cut his engagement altogether and pass the day with Leonora, trembling to return home lest his mother should have learned what he had been up to.

Doña Bernarda, in fact, had not been slow in detecting her son's new friendship. To begin with, her one concern in life was Rafael's health and conduct. And in that gossipy inquisitive country-town, her son could do virtually nothing which she did not know all about in the course of a few hours. An indiscreet remark of Cupido had even brought her to the bottom of that mysterious and perilous night trip down the flooded river—not to rescue a "poor

family," but to call on that *comica*—that "chorus
girl"—as doña Bernarda called Leonora in a furious
burst of scorn.  Stormy scenes occurred that were
to leave a strong undercurrent of bitterness and fear
in Rafael's character.  Doña Bernarda's harshness
of disposition broke the young man's spirit, making him realize with what good reason he had always feared his mother.  That uncompromising
pietist, with her armorplate of impeccable virtue and
"sound principles" about her, crushed him flat with
her very first words.  What in the world was he
thinking of?  Was he bound to dishonor the name
of Brull?  Now after so many, many years of
family sacrifice, was he going to make a fool of himself, and give his enemies a hold on him, just because of the first ballet-skirt that came along?  And
in her rage she did not hesitate to rend the veil of
reticence behind which her conjugal fury and her
conjugal unhappiness had run their parallel courses.

"The same as your father!" doña Bernarda exclaimed.  "There's no escaping blood: a woman-
chaser, a friend of low-lives, ready to drive me out
of house and home for the sake of any one of them
. . . and I, big fool that I am, work for men like
that!  Forgetting the salvation of my soul in the
next world to see you get farther along in this than
your father did! . . . And how do you repay me?
Just as he did; with one disappointment, one irri-
tation, after another!"

Then softening somewhat and feeling the need of
imparting her great plans for the future, she would
pass from anger to friendly confidence, and give Rafael insight into the condition of the family.  He
was so busy with Party affairs, and thumbing his big

books upstairs, that he did not know how things were going at home. And he didn't need to know for that matter: she was there to take care of that. But Rafael must realize the gaps that had been opened in their fortune by his father's wild conduct just before he died. She was performing miracles of economy. Thanks to her efficient administration of affairs, and to the loyal aid of don Andrés, many debts had already been paid off, and she had redeemed several mortgages. But the burden was a heavy one and it would still be many years before she could call herself quite free of it.

Besides—and as doña Bernarda came to this part of her talk she grew tenderer and more insinuating still—he was now the leading man of the District and so he must be the wealthiest. Now that wouldn't be a difficult thing to manage. All he had to do was be a good son, and follow the advice of his mama, who loved him more than anything else in the world . . . A deputy now, and later on, when he came back from Madrid, marry! There were plenty of good girls around—well brought up, educated in the fear of the Lord—and millionairesses besides—who would be more than glad to be his wife.

Rafael smiled faintly at this harangue. He knew whom his mother had in mind—Remedios, the daughter of the richest man in town—a rustic, the latter, with more luck than brains, who flooded the English markets with oranges and made enormous profits, circumventing by instinctive shrewdness all the commercial combinations made against him.

That was why Rafael's mother was always insistently urging her son to visit the house of Remedios, inventing all sorts of pretexts to get him there.

Besides, doña Bernarda invited Remedios to the Brull place frequently, and rarely indeed did Rafael come home of an afternoon without finding that timid maiden there—a dull, handsomish sort of girl, dressed up in clothes that did cruel injustice to a peasant beauty rapidly transformed, by her father's good luck, into a young "society" girl.

"But, mama," said Rafael, smiling. "I'm not thinking of marriage! . . . And when I do, I'll have to consider my own feelings."

After that interview a moral gulf had opened between mother and son. As a child, Rafael had known his mother to frown and sulk after some mischievous prank of his. But now, her aggressive, menacing, uncommunicative glumness was prolonged for days and days.

On returning home at night he would find himself subjected to a searching cross-examination that would last all during supper. Don Andrés would usually be present, though he did not dare raise his head when that masterful woman spoke. Where had he been? Whom had he seen? . . . Rafael felt himself surrounded by a system of espionage that followed him wherever he went in the city or in the country.

"No sir, today you were at the chorus-girl's house again! . . . Take care, Rafael! Mark my word! You're killing me, you're killing me . . . !"

And then those absurd clandestine trips to the Blue House began, the leading man of the district, the advocate of Alcira's fortunes, creeping on his stomach, skulking from bush to bush, in order not to be seen by telltale observers!

Don Andrés did his best to console the irate

woman. It was just a passing whim of Rafael's!
Boys will be boys! You've got to let them have a
good time now and then! What do you expect with
a handsome fellow like that and from the best family in the region! And the cynical old man, accustomed to easy conquests in the suburbs, blinked maliciously, taking it for granted that Rafael had won
a complete triumph down at the Blue House. How
else explain the youth's assiduity in his visits there,
and his timid though tenacious rebelliousness against
his mother's authority?

"Such affairs, oh you enjoy them—what's the
use! But in the end they weary a fellow, doña Bernarda," the old man said sententiously. "She'll be
clearing out some fine day. Besides, just let Rafael
go to Madrid as deputy, and see the society there!
When he comes back he'll have forgotten this woman ever existed!"

The faithful lieutenant of the Brulls would have
been astonished to know how little Rafael was pro-
gressing with his suit.

Leonora was not the woman that she had shown
herself on the night of the flood. With the fascination of danger gone, the novelty of the adventure,
and the extraordinary circumstances of their second
interview, she treated Rafael with a kindly indifference like any other of the adorers who had flocked
about her in her day. She had come to look upon
him as a new piece of furniture that she found in
place in front of her every afternoon; an automaton, who appeared as regularly as a clock strikes,
to spend hours and hours staring at her, pale, shrinking with an absurd consciousness of inferiority, and

often answering her questions with stupid phrases that made her laugh.

Her irony and deliberate frankness wounded Rafael cruelly. "Hello, Rafaelito," she would say sometimes as he came in. "You here again? Better look out! People will be talking about us before long. Then what will mama say to you?" And Rafael would be stung to the quick. What a disgrace, to be tied to a mother's apron-strings, and have to stoop to all those subterfuges to visit this place without raising a rumpus at home!

But try as he would, meanwhile, he could not shake off the spell that Leonora was exercising over him.

Besides, what wonderful afternoons when she deigned to be good! Sometimes, wearied with walks about the open country, and bored, as might have been expected of a frivolous, fickle character like hers, with the monotony of the landscape of orange-trees and palms, she would take refuge in her parlor, and sit down at the piano! With the hushed awe of a pious worshipper, Rafael would take a chair in a corner, and gluing his eyes upon those two majestic shoulders over which curly tresses fell like golden plumes, he would listen to her rich, sweet, mellow voice as it blended with the languishing chords of the piano; while through the open windows the breath of the murmurous orchard made its way drenched in the golden light of autumn, saturated with the seasoned perfume of the ripe oranges that peered with faces of fire through the festoons of leaves.

Shubert, with his moody romances, was her favorite composer. The melancholy of that sad music had a peculiar fascination for her in her solitude. Her passionate, tumultuous soul seemed to fall into a languorous enervation under the fragrance of the orange blossoms. At times, she would be assailed by sudden recollections of triumphs on the stage, and on such occasions, setting the piano ringing with the sublime fury of the Valkyries' Ride, she would begin to shout Brunhilde's "Hojotojo," the impetuous, savage war-cry of Wotan's daughter—a melodious scream with which she had brought many an audience to its feet, and which, in that deserted paradise, made Rafael shudder and admire, as if the singer were some strange divinity—a blond goddess with green eyes, wont to charge across the ice-fields through whirlwinds of driving snow, but who, there, in a land of sunshine, had deigned to become a simple, an entrancing woman!

And then again, throwing her beautiful body back in her chair, as if in her mind's eye she could see some old palatial hall festooned with roses, and in it a maze of hoop skirts, powdered wigs, and red heels, whirling in the dance, she would brush the keys with a minuet by Mozart, as subtly fragrant as priceless perfume, as seductive as the smile of a painted princess with beauty-patches and false dimples!

Rafael had not forgotten the first night of their friendship, nor the fingers that had been offered to his lips in that selfsame parlor. Once he was moved to repeat the scene, and bending low over the keys, had tried to kiss Leonora's hand.

The actress started, as if awakening from a dream. Her eyes flashed angrily, though her lips did not lose their smile; and she raised her hand threateningly, with all its fantastic glitter of jewelry, and pretended to strike at him:

"Take care, Rafael; you're a child and I'll treat you as such. You already know that I don't like to be annoyed. I won't send you away this time, but if you do it again, you'll get a good cuffing. Don't forget that when I want my hand kissed I begin by giving it voluntarily. What a nuisance! Such a thing happens only once in a life-time. . . . But, I understand: no more music for today; it's all over! I'll have to entertain the little boy so's he won't fuss."

And she began to tell him stories of her professional career, which Rafael at once appraised as new progress toward intimacy with the divine beauty.

He looked over her pictures for the various operas in which she had sung; a rich collection of beautiful photographs, with studio signatures in almost every European tongue, some of them in strange alphabets that Rafael could not identify. That pale, mystic Elizabeth of *Tannhäuser* had been taken in Milan; that ideal, romantic Elsa of *Lohengrin,* in Munich; here was a wide-eyed, bourgeois Eva from *die Meistersinger,* photographed in Vienna; there a proud arrogant Brunhilde, with hostile, flashing eyes, that bore the imprint of St. Petersburg. And there were other souvenirs of seasons at Covent Garden, at the San Carlos of Lisbon, the Scala of Milan, and opera houses of New York and Rio de Janeiro.

As Rafael handled the large pasteboard mountings, he felt much like a boy watching strange steamers entering a harbor and scattering the perfumes of distant, mysterious lands all around. Each picture seemed to wrap him in the atmosphere of its country, and from that peaceful salon, murmuring with the breathing of the silent orchard, he seemed to be traveling all over the earth.

The photographs were all of the same characters—heroines of Wagner. Leonora, a fanatic worshipper of the German genius, was ever speaking of him in terms of intimate familiarity, as if she had known him personally, and wished to sing no operas but his. And in her eager desire to compass all the Master's work, she did not hesitate to compromise her reputation for power and vigor by attempting rôles of lighter or tenderer vein.

Rafael gazed at the portraits one by one; here she seemed emaciated, wan, as if she had just recovered from an illness; there, she was strong and proud, as if challenging the world with her beauty.

"Oh, Rafael!" she murmured pensively. "Life isn't all gaiety. I have had my stormy times like everybody else. I have lived centuries, it seems, and these strips of cardboard are chapters of my life-story."

And while she surrendered to a dreamy re-living of the past, Rafael would go into ecstasies over a picture of Brunhilde, a beautiful photograph which he had more than once thought of stealing.

That Brunhilde was Leonora herself; the arrogant Valkyrie, the strong, the valiant Amazon, capable of trying to beat him for the slightest unwarranted liberty he took—and of doing it besides. Beneath the helmet of polished steel, with its two wings of white plumes, her blond locks fell, while a savage flash glittered in her green eyes, and her nostrils seemed to palpitate with indomitable fierceness. A cloak fell from her shoulders that were round, muscular, powerful. A steel coat of mail curved outward around her magnificent bust, and her bare arms, one holding the lance, and the other resting on a burnished shield, as shining and luminous as a sheet of crystal, showed vigor and strength under feminine grace of line. There she was in all her goddess-like majesty—the Pallas of a mythology of the North, as beautiful as heroism, as terrible as war. Rafael could understand the mad enthusiasm, the electrified commotion of her audiences as they saw her stepping out among the rocks of painted canvas, setting the boards a-tremble with her lithe footsteps, rudely raising her lance and shield above the white wings of her helmet and shouting the cry of the Valkyries—*"Hojotoho!"* which, repeated in the green tranquility of that Valencian orchard, seemed to make the lanes of foliage quiver with a tremor of admiring ecstasy.

Across the whole world, and everywhere in triumph, that whimsical, adventuresome, madcap woman, of whose life as an actress so many stories were told, had carried the arrogance of the virgin warrior-maid conceived by the master Wagner. In a bulky book, of uneven irregular pages, where the singer with the minute conscientiousness of a child, had preserved everything the newspapers of the globe had written about her, Rafael found echos of her stormy ovations. Many of the printed clippings were yellow with age, but they could still evoke before his dazzled eyes, visions of theaters packed with elegant, sensuous women, as beautiful as Wotan's daughter in the coat-of-mail; atmospheres hot

with light and enthusiasm, a-glitter with sparkling
jewels and sparkling eyes; and in the background,
with her helmet and her lance, the dominating Valkyrie herself greeted with frantic applause and limitless admiration.

In the collection were newspaper reproductions of
the singer's photographs, biographical notices, criti-
cal articles relating to the triumphs of the celebrated
*diva* Leonora Brunna—for such was the stage name
adopted by Doctor Moreno's daughter—clipping
after clipping printed in Castilian or South American
Spanish; columns of the clear, close print of English
papers; paragraphs on the coarse, thin paper of
the French and Italian press; compact masses of
Gothic characters, which troubled Rafael's eyes, and
unintelligible Russian letters, that, to him, looked
like whimsical scrawls of a childish hand. And all
in praise of Leonora, one universal tribute to the
talent of that woman, who was looked upon so scornfully by the citified peasants of the boy's native town.
A divinity, indeed! And Rafael felt a growing
hatred and contempt for the gross, uncouth virtue of
those who had left her in a social vacuum. Why had
she come to Alcira, anyway? What could possibly
have led her to abandon a world of triumphs, where
she was admired by everyone, for the life, virtually,
of a barnyard?

Later she showed him some of her more personal
mementoes; jewels of rare beauty, expensive bau-
bles, "testimonials," reminiscent of "evenings of
honor," when admirers had surprised her in the
green room while outside the audience was applauding wildly, and she, lowering her lance, and surrounded by ushers with huge bouquets, would step

forward to the footlights and make her bow of acknowledgment, under a deluge of tinsel and flowers. One medallion bore the portrait of the venerable don Pedro of Brazil, the artist-emperor, who paid tribute to the singer in a greeting written in diamonds. Gem-incrusted frames of gold spoke of enthusiasts who perhaps had begun by desiring the woman to resign themselves in the end to admiration for the artist. Here was a collection of illuminated diplomas from charitable societies thanking her for assistance at benefits. Queen Victoria of England had given her a fan with an autograph dated from a concert at Windsor Castle. From Isabel II came a royal bracelet, as a souvenir of various evenings at the Castilla Palace in Paris. Millionaires, princes, grand-dukes, presidents of Spanish-American republics, had left a whole museum of costly trinkets at her feet. Characteristic of adorers from the United States, where people always temper enthusiasm with usefulness, were a number of portfolios, their bindings much worn by time, containing railroad shares, land titles, stocks in enterprises of varying stability, suggesting the rambles of the American promotor from the prairies of Canada to the pampas of the Argentine.

In the presence of all the trophies that the arrogant Valkyrie had gathered in on her triumphal passage through the world, Rafael felt pride, first of all, at being friends with such a woman; but at the same time a sense of his own insignificance, exaggerating, if anything, the difference that separated them. How in the world had he ever dared make love to a person like Leonora Brunna?

Finally came the most interesting, the most intimate of all her treasures—an album which she allowed him hurriedly to glimpse through, forbidding him, however, even to look at certain of the pages. It was a volume modestly bound in dark leather with silver clasps; but Rafael gazed upon it as on a wonderful fetish, and with all the awe-struck adoration inspired by great names. Kings and emperors were the least among the celebrities who had knelt in homage before the goddess. The overshadowing geniuses of art were there, dedicating a word of affection, a line of verse, a bar of music, to the beautiful songstress. Rafael stared in open-mouthed wonderment at the signatures of the old Verdi and of Boito. Then came the younger masters, of the new Italian school, noisy and triumphant with the clamor of art brought within range of the mob. In gallant phrases the Frenchmen, Massenet and Saint-Saens, paid their respects to the greatest interpreter of the greatest of composers; Rafael could decipher what was in Italian, scenting the sweet perfume of Latin adulation despite the fact that he scarcely knew the language. A sonnet by Illica moved him actually to tears. Other inscriptions were meaningless to him—the lines from Hans Keller, especially, the great orchestral conductor, disciple and confidant of Wagner, the artistic executor charged with watching over the master's glory— that Hans Keller of whom Leonora was speaking all the time with the fondness of a woman and the admiration of an artist—all of which did not prevent her from adding that he was "a barbarian." Stanzas in German, in Russian and in English, which, as the singer re-read them brought a contented smile

to her features, Rafael, to his great despair, could
not induce her to translate.

"Those are matters you wouldn't understand. Go
on to the next page. I mustn't make you blush."

And that was the only explanation she would
give—as though he were a child.

Some Italian verses, written in a tremulous hand
and in crooked lines, attracted Rafael's attention.
He could half make their meaning out, but Leonora
would never let him finish reading them. It was
an amorous, desperate lament; a cry of racking passion condemned to disappointment, writhing in isolation like a wild beast in its cage: Luigi Macchia.

"And who is Luigi Macchia?" asked Rafael.
"Why such despair?"

"He was a young fellow from Naples," Leonora
answered, at last, one afternoon, in a sad voice,
and turning her head, as if to conceal the tears that
had come to her eyes. "One day they found him
under the pine trees of Posilipo, with a bullet through
his head. He wanted to die, you see, and he killed
himself. . . . But put all this aside and let's go
down to the garden. I need a breath of air."

They sauntered along the avenue that was bordered with rose-bushes, and several minutes went
by before either of them spoke. Leonora seemed
quite absorbed in her thoughts. Her brows were
knitted and her lips pressed tightly together, as if
she were suffering the sting of painful recollections.

"Suicide!" she said at last. "Doesn't that seem
a silly thing to do, Rafael? Kill yourself for a
woman? Just as if we women were obliged to love
every man who thinks he's in love with us! . . .

How stupid men are! We have to be their servants, love them willy-nilly. And if we don't, they kill themselves just to spite us."

And she was silent for a time.

"Poor Macchia! He was a good boy, and deserved to be happy. But if I were to surrender to every desperate protestation made to me! . . . However, he went and did just what he said he would do. . . . How crazy they get! And the worst of it is, I have found others like him in my travels."

She explained no farther. Rafael gazed at her, but respected her silence, trying in vain to guess the thoughts that were stirring behind her shining eyes, as green and golden as the sea under a noonday sun. What a wealth of romance must be hidden in that woman's past! What tragedies must have been woven into the checkered fabric of her wonderful career! . . .

So the days went by, and election time came around. Rafael, in passive rebellion against his mother, who rarely spoke a word to him now, had completely neglected the campaign. But on the decisive Sunday he triumphed completely, and Rafael Brull, Deputy from Alcira, spent the night shaking hands, receiving congratulations, listening to serenades, waiting for morning to come that he might run to the Blue House and receive Leonora's ironic good wishes.

"I'm very glad to hear it," the actress said. "Now you'll be leaving very soon and I'll lose sight of you. It was high time really! You know, my dear child, you were beginning to get tiresome with your assiduous worship, that mute, persistent, tenacious adoration of yours. But up in Madrid you'll get over it all. Tut, tut, now . . . don't say you won't. No need to perjure yourself. I guess I know what young men are like! And you're a young man. The next time we meet, you'll have other things in your head. I'll be a friend, just a friend; and that's what—and all—I want to be."

"But will I find you here when I come back?" Rafael asked, anxiously.

"You want to know more things than anybody I ever knew! How can I say whether I'll be here or not? Nobody in the world was ever sure of holding me. I don't know where I'll be tomorrow myself. . . . But, no," she continued, gravely, "if you come back by next spring, you'll find me here. I'm thinking of staying surely until then. I want to see the orange-trees in bloom, go back to my early childhood—the only memories of my past that have followed me everywhere. Many a time I have gone to Nice, spending a fortune and crossing half the world to get there—and just to see a handful of puny orange-trees in bloom; now I want to take one great, deep, plunge into the deluge of orange blossoms that inundates these fields every year. It's the one thing that keeps me in Alcira. . . . I'm sure. So if you come back about that season, you will find me; and we will meet for one last time; for that will be the limit of my endurance. I shall simply have to fly away, however hard poor auntie takes it. . . . For the present, however, I am quite comfortable. You see I was so tired! I find this solitude a welcome refuge after a stormy voyage. Only something very important indeed could persuade me to leave it at once."

But they saw each other on many another afternoon in the garden, there. It was saturated now with the fragrance of ripe oranges. The vast valley lay blue beneath the winter sun. Oranges, oranges, everywhere, reaching out, it seemed, through the foliage, to the industrious hands that were plucking them from the branches. Carts were creaking all along the roads, trundling heaps of golden fruit over the ruts. The large shipping houses rang again with the voices of girls singing at their work as they selected and wrapped the oranges in paper. Hammers were pounding at the wooden crates, and off toward France and England in great golden waves those daughters of the South rolled—capsules of golden skin, filled with sweet juice—the quintessence of Spanish sunshine.

Leonora, standing on tiptoe under an old tree, with her back toward Rafael, was looking for a particularly choice orange among the dense branches. As she swayed this way and that, the proud, graceful curves of her vigorous slenderness became more beautiful than ever.

"I'm leaving tomorrow," the young man said, dispiritedly.

Leonora turned around. She had found her orange and was peeling it with her long pink nails.

"Tomorrow?" she said, smiling. "Everything comes if you wait long enough! . . . The best of success to you, señor deputy."

And bringing the fragrant fruit to her lips, she sank her white, glistening teeth into the golden pulp, closing her eyes rapturously, to sense the full warm sweetness of the juice.

Rafael stood there pale and trembling, as if something desperate were in his mind.

"Leonora! Leonora! . . . Surely you are not going to send me away like this?"

And then suddenly, carried away by a passion so long restrained, so long crushed under timidity and fear, he ran up to her, seized her hands and hungrily sought her lips.

"Oh! What in the world are you up to, Rafael? . . . How dare you!" she cried. And with one thrust of her powerful arms she threw him back, staggering, against the orange-tree. The young man stood there with lowered head, humiliation and shame written on every line of his face.

"You see, I'm a strong woman," said Leonora, in a voice quivering with anger. "None of your foolish tricks, or you'll be sorry!"

She glared at him for a long time; but then gradually recovered her equanimity, and began to laugh at the pitable spectacle before her.

"But what a child you are, Rafael! . . . Is that what you call a friendly good-bye? . . . How little you know me, silly! You force matters, you do, I see. Well just understand, I'm impregnable, unless I choose to be otherwise. Why, men have died without being able to kiss so much as the tip of my fingers. It's time you were going, Rafael. We'll still be friends, of course. . . . But in case we are to see each other again, don't forget what I tell you. We are through with such nonsense once and for all. Don't waste your time. I cannot be yours. I'm tired of men; perhaps I hate them. I have known the handsomest, the most elegant, the most famous of them all. I have been almost a queen; queen 'on the left hand side,' as the French say, but so much mistress of the situation that, had I cared to get mixed up in such vulgarity, I could have changed ministries and overturned thrones. Men renowned in Europe for their elegance—and their follies— have grovelled at my feet, and I have treated them worse than I have treated you. The most celebrated women have envied me and hated me—copying my dresses and my poses. And when, tired of all that brilliancy and noise, I said 'Good-bye' and came to this retreat, do you think it was to give myself to a village *señorito*, though a few hundred country bumpkins think he is a wonder? . . . Oh, say, Rafael, really. . . ."

And she laughed a cruel, mocking laugh—that cut Rafael to the quick. The young man bowed his head and his chest heaved painfully, as if the tears that could not find issue through his eyes were stifling, choking him. He seemed on the point of utter collapse.

Leonora repented of her cruelty.

She stepped up to the boy until she was almost touching him. Then taking his chin in her two hands, she made him raise his head.

"Oh, I have hurt you, haven't I! What mean things I said to the poor child! Let me see now. Lift that head up! Look me straight in the eye! Say that you forgive me. . . . That cursed habit I have of never holding my tongue! I have offended you; but please, don't pay any attention to that! I was joking! What a fine way of repaying you for what you did that night! . . . No; Rafael, you are a very handsome chap indeed . . .

and very distinguished . . . and you will make a great name for yourself, up in Madrid! . . . You'll be what they call a 'personage,' and you'll marry— oh my—a very stylish, elegant, society girl! I can see all that. . . . But, meanwhile, my dear boy, don't depend on me. We are going to be friends, and nothing more than friends, ever! Why, there are tears in your eyes! Well, here. Come . . . kiss my hand, I will let you . . . as you did that night —there, like that! I could be yours only if I loved you; but alas! I shall never fall in love with the dashing Rafaelito! I'm an old woman, already, and I've been so lavish with my heart, spent it so freely, I'm afraid I have none left. . . . Poor, poor little Rafael! I'm so sorry . . . but, you see, you came so late . . . so late . . .!"

# PART TWO

## I

Hidden in the tall, thick rose-bushes that bounded the *plazoleta* in front of the Blue House, and under four old dead palms that drooped their branches dry and melancholy under the vigorous tufts of younger trees, were two rubblework benches, white-washed, the backs and armrests of ancient Valencian tiles, the glazed surfaces flecked with arabesques and varicolored fancies inherited from days of Saracen rule—sturdy, but comfortable seats, with the graceful lines of the sofas of the Eighteenth Century; and in them Leonora liked to spend her time in late afternoons especially, when the palm trees covered the little square with a cool, delightful shade.

On that warm March day, doña Pepa was sitting in one of them, her silver-rimmed spectacles on her nose, reading the "Life" of the day's saint. At her side was the maid. A true daughter of the *campagna* of Rome, Beppa had been trained to piety from her earliest years; and she was listening attentively so as not to miss a word.

On the other bench were Leonora and Rafael. The actress, with lowered head, was following the movements of her hands, busily engaged on some embroidery.

Rafael found Leonora much changed after his months of absence.

She was dressed simply, like any young lady of the city; her face and hands, so white and marble-like before, had taken on the golden transparency of ripened grain under the continued caress of the Valencian sun. Her slender fingers were bare of all rings, and her pink ears were not, as formerly, a-gleam with thick clusters of diamonds.

"I've become a regular peasant, haven't I?" she said, as if she could read in Rafael's eyes his astonishment at the transformation she had undergone. "It's life in the open that works such miracles: today one frill, tomorrow another, and a woman eventually gets rid of everything that was once a part of her body almost. I feel better this way. . . . Would you believe it? I've actually deserted my dressing-table, and the perfume I used lies all forsaken and forlorn. Fresh water, plenty of fresh water . . . that's what I like. I'm a long way from the Leonora who had to paint herself every night like a clown before she could appear before an audience. Take a good look at me! Well . . . what do you think? You might mistake me for one of your vassals almost, eh? I'll bet that if I had gone out this morning to join your demonstration at the station you wouldn't have recognized me in the crowd."

Rafael was going to say—and quite seriously, too—that he thought her more beautiful than ever. Leonora seemed to have descended from her height and drawn closer to him. But she guessed what was coming, and to forestall any compliments, hastened to resume control of the conversation.

"Now don't say you like me better this way. What nonsense! Remember, you come from

Madrid, from real elegance, a world you did not know before! . . . But, to tell the truth, I like this simplicity; and the important thing in life is to please yourself, isn't it? It was a slow transformation, but an irresistible one; this country life gradually filled me with its peace and calm; it went to my head like a bland delicious wine. I just sleep and sleep, living the life of a human animal, free from every emotion, and quite willing never to wake up again. Why, Rafaelito! If nothing extraordinary happens and the devil doesn't give an unexpected tug at my sleeve, I can conceive of staying on here forever. I think of the outer world as a sailor must of the sea, when he finds himself all cosy at home after a voyage of continuous tempest."

"That's right, do stay," said Rafael. "You can't imagine how I worried up in Madrid wondering whether or not I'd find you here on my return."

"Don't go telling any fibs," said Leonora, gently, smiling with just a suggestion of gratification. "Do you think we haven't been following your doings in Madrid? Though you never were a friend, exactly, of good old Cupido, you've been writing him frequently—and all sorts of nonsense; just as a pretext for the really important thing—the postscript, with your regards to the 'illustrious artist,' sure to provoke the consoling reply that the 'illustrious artist' was still here. How those letters made me laugh!"

"Anyway, that will prove I wasn't lying that day when I assured you I would not forget, in Madrid. Well, Leonora; I didn't! The separation has made me worse, much worse, in fact."

"Thanks, Rafael," Leonora answered, quite seriously, as if she had lost mastery over the irony of former days. "I know you're telling the truth. And it saddens me, because it really is too bad. You understand, of course, that I can't love you. . . . So—if you don't mind—let's talk of something else."

And hastily, to shift the conversation from such dangerous ground, she began to chat about her rustic pleasures.

"I have a hen-coop that's too charming for anything. If you could only see me mornings, in a circle of cackling feathers, throwing fusillades of corn about to keep the roosters away. You see they get under my skirts and peck at my feet. It's hard to realize I can be the same woman who, just a few months ago, was brandishing a stage lance and interpreting Wagner's dreams, no less, as finely as you please! You'll soon see *my* vassals. I have the most astonishing layers you ever saw; and every morning I rummage around in the straw like a thief to get the eggs, and when I find them, they are still warm. . . . I've forgotten the piano. I hadn't opened it for more than a week, but this afternoon— I don't know why—I just felt like spending a little while in the society of the geniuses. I was thirsty for music . . . one of those moody whims of the olden days. Perhaps the presentiment that you were coming: the thought of those afternoons when you were upstairs, sitting like a booby in the corner, listening to me. . . . But don't jump to the conclusion, my dear deputy, that everything here is mere play—just chickens and the simple life. No, sir! I have turned my leisure to serious account. I have done big things to the house. You would never guess! A bathroom, if you please! And it just scandalizes poor auntie; while Beppa says it's a sin to give so much thought to matters of the body. I could give up many of my old habits, but not my bath; it's the one luxury I have kept, and I sent to Valencia for the plumbers, the marble, and the wood and . . . well . . . it's a gem. I'll show it to you, by and by. If some fine day I should suddenly take it into my head to fly away, that bath will remain here, for my poor aunt to preach about and show how her madcap niece squandered a mint of money on sinful folly, as she calls it."

And she laughed, with a glance at the innocent doña Pepa, who, there on the other bench, was for the hundredth time explaining to the Italian maid the prodigious miracles wrought by the patron of Alcira, and trying to persuade the "foreigner" to transfer her faith to that saint, and waste no more time on the second or third raters of Italy.

"Don't imagine," the actress continued, "that I forgot you during all this time. I am a real friend, you see, and take an interest! I learned through Cupido, who ferrets out everything, just what you were doing in Madrid. I, too, figured among your admirers. That proves what friendship can do! . . . I don't know why, but when señor Brull is concerned, I swallow the biggest whoppers, though I know they're lies. When you made your speech in the Chambers on that matter of flood protection, I sent to Alcira for the paper and read the story through I don't know how many times, believing blindly everything said in praise of you. I once met Gladstone at a concert given by the Queen at Windsor Castle; I have known men who got to be presidents of their countries on sheer eloquence—

not to mention the politicians of Spain. The majority of them I've had, one time or another, as hangers-on in my dressing-room—once I had sung at the 'Real.' Well, despite all that, I took the exaggerations your party friends printed about you quite seriously for some days, putting you on a level with all the solemn top-notchers I have known. And why, do you suppose? Perhaps from my isolation and tranquillity here, which do make you lose perspective; or perhaps it was the influence of environment! It is impossible to live in this region without being a subject of the Brulls! . . . Can I be falling in love with you unawares?"

And once more she laughed the gleeful, candid, mocking laugh of other days. At first she had received him seriously, simply, under the influence still of solitude, country life and the longing for rest and quiet. But once in actual contact with him again, the sight, again, of that lovesick expression in eyes which now, however, showed a trace of self-possession, the old teaser had reappeared in her; and her irony cut into the youth's flesh like a steel blade.

"Stranger things than that have happened," Rafael snapped boldly, and imitating her sarcastic smile. "It's humanly conceivable that even you should wind up by falling in love with even me—out of pity, of course!"

"No," answered Leonora bluntly. "It's not even humanly conceivable. I'll never fall in love with you. . . . And even if I should," she continued in a gentle, almost mothering tone, "you would never know about it. I should keep it jolly well to myself—so as to prevent your going crazy on finding

your affections returned.    All afternoon I have been
trying to evade this explanation.    I have brought up
a thousand subjects, I have inquired about your life
in Madrid—even going into details that haven't
the slightest interest for me—all to keep the talk
off love.    But with you, that's impossible; you always come back to that sooner or later.    Very well,
so be it. . . . But I'll never love you—I must not
love you.    If I had made your acquaintance somewhere else, but under the same romantic circumstances, I don't say it mightn't have happened. But
here! . . . My scruples may make you laugh, but I
feel as though I'd be committing a crime to love you.
It would be like entering a home and repaying the
hospitality by purloining the silverware."

"That's a new kind of nonsense you are talking,"
Rafael exclaimed.    "Just what do you mean? I
don't think I understand, exactly."

"Well, you live here, you see, and you hardly
realize what it's all like.    Love for love's sake
alone!    That may happen in the world where I
come from.    There folks aren't scandalized at
things.    Virtue is broad-minded and tolerant; and
people, through a selfish desire to have their own
weaknesses condoned, are careful not to censure
others too harshly.    But here! . . . Here love is
the straight and narrow path that leads to marriage.
Now let's see how good a liar you are!    Would you
be capable of saying that you would marry me? . . ."

She gazed straight at the youth out of her green,
luminous, mocking eyes, and with such frankness
that Rafael bowed his head, stuttering as he started
to speak.

"Exactly," she went on.    "You wouldn't, and

you are right. For that would be a piece of solemn, deliberate barbarity. I'm not one of the women who are made for such things. Many men have proposed marriage to me in my time, to prove what fools they were, I suppose. More than once they've offered me their ducal crowns or the prestige of their marquisates, with the idea that title and social position would hold me back when I got bored and tried to fly away. But imagine me married! Could anything be more absurd?"

She laughed hysterically, almost, but with an undertone that hurt Rafael deeply. There was a ring of sarcasm, of unspeakable scorn in it, which reminded the young man of Mephisto's mirth during his infernal serenade to Marguerite.

"Moreover," continued Leonora, recovering her composure, "you don't seem to realize just how I stand in this community. Don't imagine what's said about me in town escapes me. . . . I just have to notice the way the women look at me the few times I go in there. And I know also what happened to you before you left for Madrid. We find out everything here, Rafaelito. The gossip of these people carries—it reaches even this solitary spot. I know perfectly well how your mother hates me, and I've even heard about the squabbles you've had at home over coming here. Well, we must put a stop to all that! I am going to ask you not to visit me any more. I will always be your friend; but if we stop seeing each other it will be to the advantage of us both."

That was a painful thrust for Rafael. So she knew! But to escape from what he felt to be a ridiculous position, he affected an air of independence.

"Don't you believe such bosh! It's just election gossip spread by my enemies. I am of age, and I daresay I can go where I please, without asking mamma."

"Very well; keep on coming, if you really want to; but all the same, it shows how people feel toward me—a declaration of war, virtually. And if I should ever fall in love with you . . . heavens! What would they say then? They'd be sure I had come here for the sole purpose of capturing their don Rafael! You can see how far such a thing is from my mind. It would be the end of the peace and quiet I came here to find. If they talk that way now, when I'm as innocent as a lamb, imagine how their tongues would wag then! . . . No, I'm not looking for excitement! Let them snap at me as much as they please; but I mustn't be to blame. It must be out of pure envy on their part. I wouldn't stoop to provoking them!"

And with a turn of her head in the direction of the city that was hidden from view behind the rows of orange-trees, she laughed disdainfully.

Then her gleeful frankness returned once more—a candor of which she was always ready to make herself the first victim—and in a low, confidential, affectionate tone she continued:

"Besides, Rafaelito, you haven't had a good look at me. Why, I'm almost an old woman! . . . Oh, I know it, I know it. You don't have to tell me. You and I are of the same age; but you are a man; and I'm a woman. And the way I've lived has added considerably to my years. You are still on the very threshold of life. I've been knocking about the world since I was sixteen, from one theatre to another. And my accursed disposition, my mania for concealing nothing, for refusing to lie, has helped make me worse than I really am. I have many enemies in this world who are just gloating, I am sure, because I have suddenly disappeared. You can't advance a step on the stage without rousing the jealousy of someone; and that kind of jealousy is the most bloodthirsty of human passions. Can you imagine what my kind colleagues say about me? That I've gotten along as a woman of the *demi-monde* rather than as an artist—that I'm a *cocotte,* using my voice and the stage for soliciting, as it were."

"Damn the liars!" cried Rafael hotly. "I'd like to have someone say that in my hearing."

"Bah! Don't be a child. Liars, yes, but what they say has a grain of truth in it. I have been something of the sort, really; though the blame had not been wholly mine. . . . I've done crazy foolish things—giving a loose rein to my whims, for the fun of the thing. Sometimes it would be wealth, magnificence, luxury; then again bravery; then again just plain, ordinary, good looks! And I would be off the moment the excitement, the novelty, was gone, without a thought for the desperation of my lovers at finding their dreams shattered. And from all this wild career of mine—it has taken in a good part of Europe—I have come to one conclusion: either that what the poets call love is a lie, a pleasant lie, if you wish; or else that I was not born to love, that I am immune; for as I go back over my exciting and variegated past, I have to recognize that in my life love has not amounted to this!"

And she gave a sharp snap with her pink fingers.

"I am telling you everything, you see," she continued. "During your long absence I thought of you often. Somehow I want you to know me thoroughly, once and for all. In that way perhaps we can get along together better. I can understand now why it is a peasant woman will walk miles and miles, under a scorching sun or a pouring rain, to have a priest listen to her confession. I am in that mood this afternoon. I feel as though I must tell everything. Even if I tried not to, I should not succeed. There's a little demon inside me here urging me, compelling me, to unveil all my past."

"Please feel quite free to do so. To be a confessor even, to deserve your confidence, is some progress for me, at any rate."

"Progress? But why should you care to progress . . . into my heart! My heart is only an empty shell! Do you think you'd be getting much if you got me? I'm absolutely, absolutely worthless! Don't laugh, please! I mean it! Absolutely worthless. Here in this solitude I have been able to study myself at leisure, see myself as I really am. I recognize it plain as day: I am nothing, nothing. Good looking? . . . Well, yes; I confess I am not what you'd call ugly. Even if, with a ridiculous false modesty, I were to say I was, there's my past history to prove that plenty of men have found me beautiful. But, alas, Rafaelito! That's only the outside, my façade, so to speak. A few winter rains will wash the paint off and show the mould that's underneath. Inside, believe me, Rafael,

I am a ruin. The walls are crumbling, the floors are giving way. I have burned my life out in gaiety. I have singed my wings in a headlong rush into the candle-flame of life. Do you know what I am? I am one of those old hulks drawn up on the beach. From a distance their paint seems to have all the color of their first voyages; but when you get closer you see that all they ask for is to be let alone to grow old and crumble away on the sand in peace. And you, who are setting out on your life voyage, come gaily asking for a berth on a wreck that will go to the bottom as soon as it strikes deep water, and carry you down with it! . . . Rafael, my dear boy, don't be foolish. I am all right to have as a friend; but it's too late for me to be anything more . . . even if I were to love you. We are of a different breed. I have been studying you, and I see that you are a sensible, honest, plodding sort of fellow. Whereas I—I belong to the butterflies, to the opposite of all you are. I am a conscript under the banner of Bohemia, and I cannot desert the colors. Each of us on his own road then. You'll easily find a woman to make you happy. . . . The sillier she is, the better. . . . You were born to be a family man."

It occurred to Rafael that she might be poking fun at him, as she so often did. But no; there was a ring of sincerity in her voice. The forced smile had vanished from her face. She was speaking tenderly, affectionately, as if in motherly counsel to a son in danger of going wrong.

"And don't make yourself over, Rafael. If the world were made up of people like me, life would be impossible. I too have moments when I should like to become a different person entirely—a fowl, a

cow, or something, like the folks around me, thinking of money all the time, and of what I'll eat tomorrow; buying land, haggling with farmers on the
market, studying fertilizers, having children who'd
keep me busy with their colds and the shoes they'd
tear, my widest vision limited to getting a good
price for the fall crop. There are times when I
envy a hen. How good it must be, to be a hen!
A fence around me to mark the boundaries of my
world, my meals for the trouble of pecking at them,
my life-work to sit hour after hour in the sun, bal-
anced on a roost. . . . You laugh? Well, I've made
a good start already toward becoming a hen, and
the career suits me to a 't.' Every Wednesday I go
to market, to buy a pullet and some eggs; and I
haggle with the vendors just for the fun of it, finally
giving them the price they ask for; I invite the
peasant women to have a cup of chocolate with me,
and come home escorted by a whole crowd of them;
and they listen in astonishment when I talk to Beppa
in Italian! If you could only see how fond they are
of me! . . . They can hardly believe their eyes when
they see the *siñorita* isn't half so black as the city
people paint her. You remember that poor woman
we saw up at the Hermitage that afternoon? Well,
she's a frequent visitor, and I always give her something. She, too, is fond of me. . . . Now all that
is agreeable, isn't it? Peace; the affection of the
humble; an innocent old woman, my poor aunt, who
seems to have grown younger since I came here!
Nevertheless, some fine day, this shell, this rustic
bark that has formed around me in the sun and the
air of the orchards, will burst, and the woman of
old—the Valkyrie—will step out of it again. And

then, to horse, to horse! Off on another gallop around the world, in a tempest of pleasure, acclaimed by a chorus of brutal libertines! . . . I am sure that is bound to happen. I swore to remain here until Spring. Well, Spring is almost here! Look at those rose-bushes! Look at those orange-trees! Bursting with life! Oh, Rafael, I'm afraid of Springtime. Spring has always been a season of disaster for me."

And she was lost in thought for a moment. Doña Pepa and the Italian maid had gone into the house. The good old woman could never keep away from the kitchen long.

Leonora had dropped her embroidery upon the bench and was looking upward, her head thrown back, the muscles of her arching neck tense and drawn. She seemed wrapt in ecstacy, as if visions of the past were filing by in front of her. Suddenly she shuddered and sat up.

"I'm afraid I'm ill, Rafael. I don't know what's the matter with me today. Perhaps it's the surprise of seeing you; this talk of ours that has called me back to the past, after so many months of tranquillity. . . . Please don't speak! No, not a word, please. You have the rare skill, though you don't know it, of making me talk, of reminding me of things I was determined to forget. . . . Come, give me your arm; let's walk out through the garden; it will do me good."

They arose, and began to saunter along over the broad avenue that led from the gate to the little square. The house was soon behind them, lost in the thick crests of the orange-trees. Leonora smiled mischievously and lifted a forefinger in warning.

"I took it for granted you had returned from your trip a more serious, a more well-behaved person. No nonsense, no familiarities, eh? Besides, you know already that I'm strong, and can fight—if I have to."

# II

Rafael spent a sleepless night tossing about in his bed.

Party admirers had honored him with a serenade that had lasted beyond midnight. The "prominents" among them had shown some pique at having cooled their heels all afternoon at the Club waiting for the deputy in vain. He put in an appearance well on towards evening, and after shaking hands once more all around and responding to speeches of congratulation, as he had done that morning, he went straight home.

He had not dared raise his head in Doña Bernarda's presence. He was afraid of those glowering eyes, where he could read, unmistakably, the detailed story of everything he had done that afternoon. At the same time he was nursing a resolve to disobey his mother, meet her domineering, overbearing aggressiveness with glacial disregard.

The serenade over, he had hurried to his room, to avoid any chance of an accounting.

Snug in his bed, with the light out, he gave way to an intense, a rapturous recollection of all that had taken place that afternoon. For all the fatigue of the journey and the bad night spent in a sleeping-car, he lay there with his eyes open in the dark, going over and over again in his feverish mind all that Leonora told him during that final hour of their walk through the garden. Her whole, her real life's story it had been, recorded in a disordered, a disconnected way—as if she must unburden herself of the whole thing all at once—with gaps and leaps that Rafael now filled in from his own lurid imagination.

Italy, the Italy of his trip abroad, came back to him now, vivid, palpitant, vitalized, glorified by Leonora's revelations.

The shadowy majestic Gallery of Victor Emmanuel at Milan! The immense triumphal arch, a gigantic mouth protended to swallow up the Cathedral! The double arcade, cross-shaped, its walls covered with columns, set with a double row of windows under a vast crystal roof. Hardly a trace of masonry on the lower stories; nothing but plate glass—the windows of book-shops, music shops, cafés, restaurants, jewelry stores, haberdasheries, expensive tailoring establishments.

At one end, the Duomo, bristling with a forest of statues and perforated spires; at the other, the monument to Leonardo da Vinci, and the famous *Teatro de la Scala*! Within the four arms of the Gallery, a continuous bustle of people, an incessant going and coming of merging, dissolving crowds: a quadruple avalanche flowing toward the grand square at the center of the cross, where the Café Biffi, known to actors and singers the world over, spreads its rows of marble tables! A hubbub of cries, greetings, conversations, footsteps, echoing in the galleries as in an immense cloister, the lofty skylight quivering with the hum of busy human ants, forever, day and night, crawling, darting this way and that, underneath it!

Such is the world's market of song-birds; the

world's Rialto of Music; the world's recruiting office
for its army of voices. From that center, march
forth to glory or to the poorhouse, all those who
one fine day have touched their throats and believed
they have some talent for singing. In Milan, from
every corner of the earth, all the unhappy aspirants
of art, casting aside their needles, their tools or
their pens, foregather to eat the macaroni of the
*trattoria*, trusting that the world will some day do
them justice by strewing their paths with millions.
Beginners, in the first place, who, to make their
start, will accept contracts in any obscure municipal
theatre of the Milan district, in hopes of a paragraph in a musical weekly to send to the folks at
home as evidence of promise and success; and with
them, overwhelming them with the importance of
their past, the veterans of art—the celebrities of a
vanished generation: tenors with gray hair and false
teeth; strong, proud, old men who cough and clear
their throats to show they still preserve their sonorous baritone; retired singers who, with incredible
niggardliness, lend their savings at usury or turn
shopkeepers after dragging silks and velvets over
world famous "boards."

Whenever the two dozen "stars," the stars of
first magnitude that shine in the leading operas of
the globe, pass through the Gallery, they attract as
much admiring attention as monarchs appearing before their subjects. The *pariahs*, still waiting for a
contract, bow their heads in veneration; and tell, in
bated breath, of the castle on Lake Como that the
great tenor has bought, of the dazzling jewels owned
by the eminent soprano, of the graceful tilt at which
the applauded baritone wears his hat; and in their

voices there is a tingle of jealousy, of bitterness against destiny—the feeling that they are just as worthy of such splendor—the protest against "bad luck," to which they attribute failure. Hope forever flutters before these unfortunates, blinding them with the flash of its golden mail, keeping them in a wretched despondent inactivity. They wait and they trust, without any clear idea of how they are to attain glory and wealth, wasting their lives in impotence, to die ultimately "with their boots on," on some bench of the Gallery.

Then, there is another flock, a flock of girls, victims of the Chimera, walking with a nimble, a prancing step, with music scores under their arms, on the way to the *maestro's*; slender, light-haired English *misses*, who want to become prima donnas of comic opera; fair-skinned, buxom Russian *parishnas* who greet their acquaintances with the sweeping bow of a dramatic soprano; Spanish *señoritas* of bold faces and free manners, preparing for stage careers as Bizet's cigarette-girl—frivolous, sonorous song-birds nesting hundreds of leagues away, and who have flown hither dazzled by the tinsel of glory.

At the close of the Carnival season, singers who have been abroad for the winter season appear in the Gallery. They come from London, St. Petersburg, New York, Melbourne, Buenos Aires, looking for new contracts. They have trotted about the globe as though the whole world were home to them. They have spent a week in a train or a month on a steamer, to get back to their corner in the Gallery. Nothing has changed, for all of their distant rambles. They take their usual table. They renew their old intrigues, their old gossip, their old jealousies, as if they had been gone a day. They stand around in front of the show-windows with an air of proud disdain, like princes traveling incognito, but unable quite to conceal their exalted station. They tell about the ovations accorded them by foreign audiences. They exhibit the diamonds on their fingers and in their neckties. They hint at affairs with great ladies who offered to leave home and husband to follow them to Milan. They exaggerate the salaries they received on their trip, and frown haughtily when some unfortunate "colleague" solicits a drink at the nearby Biffi. And when the new contracts come in, the mercenary nightingales again take wing, indifferently, they care not whither. Once more, trains and steamers distribute them, with their conceits and their petulances, all over the globe, to gather them in again some months later and bring them back to the Gallery, their real home—the spot to which they are really tied, and on which they are fated to drag out their old age.

Meantime, the *pariahs*, those who never arrive, the "bohemians" of Milan—when they are left alone console themselves with tales of famous comrades, of contracts they themselves refused to accept, pretending uncompromising hauteur toward impresarios and composers to justify their idleness; and wrapped in fur coats that almost sweep the ground, with their "garibaldis" on the backs of their heads, they hover around Biffi's, defying the cold draughts that blow at the crossing of the Gallery, talking and talking away to quiet the hunger that is gnawing at their stomachs; despising the humble toil of those who make their living by their hands, continuing undaunted in their poverty, content with their genius as artists, facing misfortune with a candor and an endurance as heroic as it is pathetic, their dark lives illumined by Hope, who keeps them company till she closes their eyes.

Of that strange world, Rafael had caught a glimpse, barely, during the few days he had spent in Milan. His companion, the canon, had run across a former chorister from the cathedral of Valencia, who could find nothing to do but loiter night and day about the Gallery. Through him Brull had learned of the life led by these journeymen of art, always on hand in the "marketplace," waiting for the employer who never comes.

He tried to picture the early days of Leonora in that great city, as one of the girls who trot gracefully over the sidewalks with music sheets under their arms, or enliven the narrow side streets with all those trills and cadences that come streaming out through the windows.

He could see her walking through the Gallery at Doctor Moreno's side: a blonde beauty, svelte, somewhat thin, over-grown, taller than her years, gazing with astonishment through those large green eyes of hers at the cold, bustling city, so different from the warm orchards of her childhood home; the father, bearded, wrinkled, nervous, still irritated at the ruin of his Republican hopes; a veritable ogre to strangers who did not know his lamb-like gentleness. Like exiles who had found a refuge in art, they two went their way through that life of emptiness, of void, a world of greedy teachers anxious to prolong the period of study, and of singers incapable of speaking kindly even of themselves.

They lived on a fourth floor on the *Via Passarella* —a narrow, gloomy thoroughfare with high houses, like the streets of old Alcira, preempted by music publishers, theatrical agencies and retired artists. Their janitor was a former chorus leader; the main floor was rented by an agency exclusively engaged from sun to sun in testing voices. The others were occupied by singers who began their vocal exercises the moment they got out of bed, setting the house ringing like a huge music-box from roof to cellar. The Doctor and his daughter had two rooms in the house of *Signora Isabella*, a former ballet-dancer who had achieved notorious "triumphs" in the principal courts of Europe, but was now a skeleton wrapped in wrinkled skin, groping her way through the corridors, quarreling over money in foul-mouthed language with the servants, and with no other vestiges of her past than the gowns of rustling silk, and the diamonds, emeralds and pearls that took their turns in her stiff, shrivelled ears. This harpy had loved Leonora with the fondness of the veteran for the new recruit.

Every day Doctor Moreno went to a café of the Gallery, where he would meet a group of old musicians who had fought under Garibaldi, and young men who wrote *libretti* for the stage, and articles for Republican and Socialist newspapers. That was his world: the only thing that helped him endure his stay in Milan. After a lonely life back there in his native land, this corner of the smoke-filled café seemed like Paradise to him. There, in a labored Italian, sprinkled with Spanish interjections, he could talk of Beethoven and of the hero of Marsala; and for hour after hour he would sit wrapt in ecstasy, gazing, through the dense atmosphere, at the red shirt and the blond, grayish locks of the great Giuseppe, while his comrades told stories of this, the most romantic, of adventurers.

During such absences of her father, Leonora would remain in charge of *Signora Isabella*; and bashful, shrinking, half bewildered, would spend the day in the salon of the former ballet-dancer, with its coterie of the latter's friends, also ruins surviving from the past, burned-out "flames" of great personages long since dead. And these witches, smoking their cigarettes, and looking their jewels over every other moment to be sure they had not been stolen, would size up "the little girl," as they called her, to conclude that she would "go very far" if she learned how to "play the game."

"I had excellent teachers," said Leonora, in speaking of that period of her youth. "They were good souls at bottom, but they had very little still to learn about life. I don't remember just when I began to see through them. I don't believe I was ever what they call an 'innocent' child."

Some evenings the Doctor would take her to his group in the café, or to some second balcony seat under the roof of *La Scala,* if a couple of complimentary tickets happened to come his way. Thus she was introduced to her father's friends, bohemians with whom music went hand in hand with the ideas and the ideals of revolution, curious mixtures of artist and conspirator; aged, bald-headed, nearsighted "professors," their backs bent by a lifetime spent leaning over music stands; and swarthy youths with fiery eyes, stiff, long hair and red neckties, always talking about overthrowing the social order because their operas had not been accepted at *La Scala* or because no *maestro* could be found to take their musical dramas seriously. One of them attracted Leonora. Leaning back on a side-seat in the café, she would sit and watch him for hours and hours. He was a fair-haired, extremely delicate boy. His tapering goatee and his fine, silky hair, covered by a sweeping, soft felt hat, made her think of Van Dyck's portrait of Charles I of England that she had seen in print somewhere. They called him "the poet" at the café, and gossip had it that an old woman, a retired "star," was paying for his keep—and his amusements—until his verses should bring him fame. "Well," said Leonora, simply, with a smile, "he was my first love—a calf-and-puppy love, a schoolgirl's infatuation which nobody ever knew about"; for though the Doctor's daughter spent hours with her green golden eyes fixed upon the poet, the latter never suspected his good fortune; doubtless because the beauty of his patroness, the superannuated *díva*, had so obsessed him that the attractions of other women left him quite unmoved.

How vividly Leonora remembered those days of poverty and dreams! . . . Little by little the modest capital the Doctor owned in Alcira vanished, what with living expenses and music lessons. Doña Pepa, at her brother's instance, sold one piece of land after another; but even such remittances were often long delayed; and then, instead of eating in the *trattoria*, near *la Scala*, with dancing students and the more successful of the young singers, they would stay at home; and Leonora would lay aside her scores and take a turn at cooking, learning mysterious recipes from the old *danseuse*. For weeks at a time they would live on nothing but macaroni and rice served *al burro*, a diet that her father abhorred, the Doctor, meanwhile, pretending illness to justify his absence from the café. But these periods of want and poverty were endured by father and daughter in silence. Before their friends, they still maintained the pose of well-to-do people with plenty of income from property in Spain.

Leonora underwent a rapid transformation. She had already passed her period of growth—that preadolescent "awkward age" when the features are in constant change before settling down to their definitive forms and the limbs seem to grow longer and longer and thinner and thinner. The long-legged spindling "flapper," who was never quite sure where to stow her legs, became the reserved, well-proportioned girl with the mysterious gleam of puberty in her eyes. Her clothes seemed, naturally, willingly, to curve to her fuller, rounding outlines. Her skirts went down to her feet and covered the skinny, colt-like appendages that had formerly made the denizens of the Gallery repress a smile.

Her singing master was struck with the beauty of his pupil. As a tenor, Signor Boldini had had his hour of success back in the days of the *Statuto*, when Victor Emmanuel was still king of Piedmont and the Austrians were in Milan. Convinced that he could rise no higher, he had come to earth, stepping aside to let those behind him pass on, turning his stage experience to the advantage of a large class of girl-students whom he fondled with an affectionate, fatherly kindliness. His white goatee would quiver with admiring enthusiasm, as, playfully, lightly, he would touch his fingers to those virgin

throats, which, as he said, were his "property."
"All for art, and art for all!" And this motto, the
ideal of his life, he called it, had quite endeared him
to Doctor Moreno.

"That fellow Boldini could not be fonder of my
Leonora if she were his own daughter," the Doctor
would say every time the *maestro* praised the beauty
and the talent of his pupil and prophesied great triumphs for her.

And Leonora went on with her lessons, accepting
the light, the playful, the innocent caresses of the
old singer; until one afternoon, in the midst of a
romanza, there was a hateful scene: the *maestro,*
despite her horrified struggling, claimed a feudal
right—the first fruits of her initiation into theatrical
life.

Through fear of her father Leonora kept silent.
What might he not do on finding his blind confidence
in the *maestro* so betrayed? She sank into resigned
passivity at last, and continued to visit Boldini's
house daily, learning ultimately to accept, as a matter of professional course, the repulsive flattery of
refined vice.

Poor Leonora entered on a life of wrong through
the open door, learning, at a single stroke, all the
turpitude acquired by that shrivelled *maestro* during
his long career back-stage. Boldini would have kept
her a pupil forever. He could never find her just
well enough prepared to make her début. But
hardly any money was coming from Spain now. Poor
doña Pepa had sold everything her brother owned
and a good deal of her own land besides. Only at
the cost of painful stinting could she send him anything at all. The Doctor, through connections with

Itinerant directors and impresarios *à l'aventure,* "launched" his daughter finally. Leonora began to sing in the small theatres of the Milan district—two or three night engagements at country fairs. Such companies were formed at random in the Gallery, on the very day of the performance sometimes,— troupes like the strolling players of old, leaving at a venture in a third-class compartment on the train with the prospect of returning on foot if the impresario made off with the money.

Leonora began to know what applause was, what it meant to give *encore* after *encore* before crowds of rustic landowners, dressed in their Sunday clothes, and ladies with false rings and plated chains; and she had her first thrills of feminine vanity on receiving bouquets and sonnets from subalterns and cadets in small garrison towns. Boldini followed her everywhere, neglecting his lessons, in pursuit of this, his last depraved infatuation. "All for art, art for all!" He must enjoy the fruits of his creation, be present at the triumphs of his star pupil! So he said to Doctor Moreno; and that unsuspecting gentleman, thankful for this added courtesy of the master, would leave her more and more to the old satyr's care.

The escape from that life came when she secured a contract for a whole winter in Padua. There she met the tenor Salvatti, a high and mighty *divo*, who looked down upon all his associates, though tolerated himself, by the public, only out of consideration for his past.

For years now he had been holding his own on the opera stage, less for his voice than for his dashing appearance, slightly repaired with pencil and

rouge, and the legend of romantic love affairs that
floated like a rainbow around his name—noble dames
fighting a clandestine warfare for him; queens scan-
dalizing their subjects by blind passions he inspired;
eminent divas selling their diamonds for the money
to hold him faithful by lavish gifts. The jealousy
of Salvatti's comrades tended to perpetuate and exaggerate this legend; and the tenor, worn out, poor,
and a wreck virtually for all of his pose of grandeur,
was able to make a living still from provincial publics, who charitably applauded him with the self-
conceit of climbers pampering a dethroned prince.

Leonora, playing opposite that famous man, "star-
ring," singing duets with him, clasping hands that
had been kissed by the queens of art, was deeply
stirred. This, at last, was the world she had
dreamed of in her dingy garret in Milan. Salvatti's
presence gave her just the illusion of aristocratic
grandeur she had longed for. Nor was he slow in
perceiving the impression he had made upon that
promising young woman. With a cold calculating
selfishness, he determined to profit by her naïve
admiration. Was it love that thrust her toward
him? As, so long afterwards, she analyzed her
passion to Rafael, she was vehemently certain it
had not been love: Salvatti could never have inspired
a genuine feeling in anyone. His egotism, his moral
corruptness, were too close to the surface. No, he
was a philanderer simply, an exploiter of women.
But for her it had been a blinding hallucination
nevertheless, fraught, during the first days, at least,
with the delicious exhiliration, the voluptuous abandonment of true love. She became the slave of the
decrepit tenor, voluntarily, just as she had become

her *maestro's* slave through fear. And so complete had her infatuation been, so overpowering its intoxication, that, in obedience to Salvatti, she fled with him at the end of the season, and deserted her father, who had objected to the intimacy.

Then came the black page in her life, that filled her eyes with anguished tears as she went on with her story. What folks said about her father's end was not true. Poor Doctor Moreno had not committed suicide. He was altogether too proud to confess in that way the deep grief that her ingratitude had caused him.

"Don't talk to me about that woman," he would say fiercely to his landlady at Milan whenever the old *danseuse* would mention Leonora. "I have no daughter: it was all a mistake."

Unbeknown to Salvatti, who became terribly grasping as he saw his power waning, Leonora would send her father a few hundred francs from London, from Naples, from Paris. The Doctor, though in direst poverty, would at once return the checks "to the sender" and, without writing a word; whereupon Leonora paid an allowance every month to the housekeeper, begging her not to abandon the old man.

The unhappy Doctor needed, indeed, all the care the landlady and her old friends could give him. The *povero signor spagnuolo*—the poor Spanish gentleman—spent his days locked up in his room, his violoncello between his knees, reading Beethoven, the only one "in his family"—as he said—"who had never played him false." When old Isabella, tired of his music, would literally put him out of the house to get a breath of air, he would wander like a phantom through the Gallery, distantly greeted by former friends, who avoided closer contact with that black despondency and feared the explosions of rage with which he received news of his daughter's rising fame.

A rapid rise she was making in very truth! The worldly old women who foregathered in the ballet-dancer's little parlor, could not contain their admiration for their "little girl's" success; and even grew indignant at the father for not accepting things "as things had to be." Salvatti? Just the support she needed! An expert pilot, who knew the chart of the opera world, who would steer her straight and keep her off the rocks.

The tenor had skilfully organized a world wide publicity for his young singer. Leonora's beauty and her artistic verve conquered every public. She had contracts with the leading theatres of Europe, and though critics found defects in her singing, her beauty helped them to forget these, and one and all they contributed loyally to the deification of the young goddess. Salvatti, sheltering his old age under this prestige which he so religiously fostered, was keeping in harness to the very end, and taking leave of life under the protecting shadow of that woman, the last to believe in him and tolerate his exploitation.

Applauded by select publics, courted in her dressing-room by celebrated men and women, Leonora began to find Salvatti's tyranny unbearable. She now saw him as he really was: miserly, petulant, spoiled by praise. Every bit of her money that came into his hands disappeared, she knew not where. Eager for revenge, though really answering the lure of the elegant world she glimpsed in the distance but was not yet a part of, she began to deceive Salvatti in passing adventures, taking a diabolical pleasure in the deceit. But no; as she looked back on that part of her life with the sober eye of experience, she understood that she had really been the one deceived. Salvatti, she remembered, would always retire at the opportune moment, facilitating her infidelities. She understood now that the man had carefully prepared such adventures for her with influential men whom he himself introduced to make certain profits out of the meeting—profits that he never declared.

After three years of this sort of life, when Leonora had reached the full splendor of her beauty, she chanced to become the favorite of fashion for one whole summer at Nice. Parisian newspapers, in their "society columns" referred, in veiled language, to the passion of an aged king, a democratic monarch, who had left his throne, much as a manufacturer of London or a stockbroker of Paris would leave his office, for a vacation on the Blue Coast. This tall, robust gentleman with a patriarchal beard —the very type of the good king in fairy tales—had not hesitated to be seen in public with a beautiful *artiste*.

That conquest, fleeting though it had been, put the finishing touch on Leonora's eminence! "Ah! La Brunna!" people would declare enthusiastically. "The favorite of king Ernesto. . . . Our greatest artist." And troops of adorers began to besiege her under the keen, mercenary eyes of the tenor Salvatti.

About this time her father died in a hospital at

Milan—a very sad end, as Signora Isabella, the former ballet-dancer, explained in her letters. Of what had he died? . . . The old lady could not say, as the physicians had differed; but her own view of the matter was that the *povero signor spagnuolo* had simply grown tired of living—a general collapse of that wonderful constitution, so strong, so powerful, in a way, yet strangely susceptible to moral and emotional influences. He was almost blind when admitted to the hospital. He seemed quite to have lost his mind—sunk in an unbreakable silence. Isabella had not dared to keep him in her house after he had fallen into that coma. But the strange thing was, that as death drew near, his memory of the past suddenly cleared, and the nurses would hear him groan for nights at a time, murmuring in Spanish with tenacious persistency:

"Leonora! My darling! Where are you? . . . Little girl, where are you?"

Leonora wept and wept, and did not leave her hotel for more than a week, to the great disgust of Salvatti, who observed, in addition, that tears were not good for her complexion.

Alone in the world! . . . Her own wrong-doing had killed her poor father! No one was left now except her good old aunt, who was "existing" far away in Spain, like a vegetable in a garden, her stupid mind entirely on her prayer-book. Leonora vented her anguish in a burst of hatred for Salvatti. He was responsible for her abandonment of her father! She deserted him, taking up with a certain count Selivestroff, a handsome and wealthy Russian, captain in the Imperial Guard.

So she had found her destiny! Her life would

always be like that!   She would pass from stage to
stage, from song to song, belonging to everybody—
and to nobody!

That fair Russian, so strong, so manly, so thoroughly a gentleman, had loved her truly, with a passionate humble adoration.

He would kneel submissively at her feet, like
Hercules in the presence of Adriadne, resting his
chin on her knees, looking up into her face with his
gray, kindly, caressing eyes.   Timidly, doubtfully,
he would approach her every day as if he were meeting her for the first time and feared a repulse.   He
would kiss her softly, delicately, with hushed reserve,
as if she were a fragile jewel that might break beneath his tenderest caress.     Poor Selivestroff!
Leonora had wept at the thought of him.   In Russia
and with princely Russian sumptuousness, they had
lived for a year in his castle, in the country, among
a population of sodden *moujiks* who worshipped that
beautiful woman in the white and blue furs as de-
votedly as if she had been a Virgin stepping forth
from the gilded background of an ikon.

But Leonora could not live away from stageland:
the ladies of the rural aristocracy avoided her, and
she needed applause and admiration.   She induced
Selivestroff to move to St. Petersburg, and for a
whole winter she sang at the Opera there, like a
grand dame turned opera singer out of love for the
work.

Once more she became the reigning *belle*.   All the
young Russian aristocrats who held commissions in
the Imperial Guard, or high posts in the Government, spoke enthusiastically of the great Spanish
beauty; and they envied Selivestroff.   The count

yearned moodily for the solitude of his castle, which
held so many loving memories for him. In the
bustling, competitive life of the capital, he grew jealous, sad, melancholy, irritable at the necessity of
defending his love. He could sense the underground
warfare that was being waged against him by
Leonora's countless admirers.

One morning she was rudely awakened and leapt
out of bed to find the count stretched out on a divan,
pale, his shirt stained with blood. A number of
gentlemen dressed in black were standing around
him. They had just brought him in from a carriage.
He had been wounded in the chest. The evening
before, on leaving the theatre, the count had gone
up for a moment to his Club. He had caught an
allusion to Leonora and himself in some words of a
friend. There had been blows—then hasty ar-
rangements for a duel, which had been fought at
sunrise, with pistols. Selivestroff died in the arms
of his mistress, smiling, seeking those delicate, powerful, pearly hands for one last time with his bleeding lips. Leonora mourned him deeply, truly. The
land where she had been so happy with the first man
she had really loved became intolerable to her, and
abandoning most of the riches that the count had
given her, she went forth into the world again,
storming the great theatres in a new fever of travel
and adventure.

She was then just twenty-three, but already felt
herself an old woman. How she had changed! . . .
More affairs? As she went over that period of her
life in her talk with Rafael, Leonora closed her
eyes with a shudder of modesty and remorse. Drunk
with fame and power she had rushed about the

world lavishing her beauty on anyone who interested her for the moment. The property of everybody and of nobody! She could not remember the names, even, of all the men who had loved her during that era of madness, so many had been caught in the wake of her stormy flight across the world! She had returned to Russia once, and been expelled by the Czar for compromising the prestige of the Imperial Family, through an affair with a grand duke who had wanted to marry her. In Rome she had posed in the nude for a young and unknown sculptor out of pure compassion for his silent admiration; and she herself made his "Venus" public, hoping that the world-wide scandal would bring fame to the work and to its author. In Genoa she found Salvatti again, now "retired," and living on usury from his savings. She received him with an amiable smile, lunched with him, treated him as an old comrade; and at dessert, when he had become hopelessly drunk, she seized a whip and avenged the blows she had received in her time of slavery to him, beating him with a ferocity that stained the apartment with gore and brought the police to the hotel. Another scandal! And this time her name bandied about in a criminal court! But she, a fugitive from justice, and proud of her exploit, sang in the United States, wildly acclaimed by the American public, which admired the combative Amazon even more than the artist.

There she made the acquaintance of Hans Keller, the famous orchestra conductor, and a pupil and friend of Wagner. The German *maestro* became her second love. With stiff, reddish hair, thick-rimmed eyeglasses, an enormous mustache that drooped over either side of his mouth and framed his chin, he was certainly not so handsome as Selive-stroff. But he had one irresistible charm, the charm of Art. With the tragic Russian in her mind and on her conscience, she felt the need of burning herself in the immortal flame of the ideal; and she adored the famous musician for the artistic associations that hovered about him. For the first time, the much-courted Leonora descended from her lofty heights to seek a man's attention and came with her amorous advances to disturb the placid calm of that artist so wholly engrossed in the cult of the sublime Master.

Hans Keller noticed the smile that fell like a sunbeam upon his music scrolls. He closed them and let himself be drawn off on the by-paths of love. Leonora's life with the *maestro* was an absolute rupture with all her past. Her one wish was to love and be loved—to throw a cloak of mystery over her real self, ashamed as she now was of her previous wild career. Her passion enthralled the musician and she in turn felt at once stirred and transfigured by the atmosphere of artistic fervor that haloed the illustrious pupil of Wagner.

The spirit of Him, the Master, as Hans Keller called Wagner with pious adoration, flashed before the singer's eyes like the revealing glory that converted Paul on the road to Damascus. Music, as she now saw clearly for the first time, was not a means of pleasing crowds, displaying physical beauty, and attracting men. It was a religion—the mysterious power that brings the infinite within us into contact with the infinite that surrounds us. She became the sinner awakening to repentance, and yearning for

the atoning peace of the cloister, a Magdalen of
Art, touched on the high road of worldliness and
frivolity by the mystic sublimity of the Beautiful;
and she cast herself at the feet of Him, the supreme
Master, as the most victorious of men, lord of the
mystery that moves all souls.

"Tell me more about Him," Leonora would say.
"How much I would give to have known him as you
did! . . . I did see him once in Venice: during his
last days . . . he was already dying."

And that meeting was, indeed, one of her most
vivid and lasting memories. The declining afternoon enlivening the dark waters of the Grand Canal
with its opalescent spangles; a gondola passing hers
in the opposite direction; and inside, a pair of blue,
imperious eyes, shining, under thick eyebrows, with
the cold glint of steel—eyes that could never be mistaken for common eyes, for the divine fire of the
Elect, of the demi-God, was bright within them!
And they seemed to envelop her in a flash of cerulean
light. It was He—ill, and about to die. His heart
was wounded, bleeding, pierced, perhaps, by the
shafts of mysterious melody, as hearts of the Virgin
sometimes bleed on altars bristling with swords.

Leonora could still see him as if he were there
in front of her. He looked smaller than he really
was, dwarfed, apparently, by illness, and by the
wrack of pain. His huge head, the head of a genius,
was bent low over the bosom of his wife Cosima.
He had removed the black felt hat so as to catch
the afternoon breeze full upon his loose gray locks.
His broad, high curved forehead, seemed to weigh
down upon his body like an ivory chest laden full of
unseen jewels. His arrogant nose, as strong as the

beak of a bird of prey, seemed to be reaching across
the sunken mouth toward the sensuous, powerful jaw.
A gray beard ran down along the neck, that was
wrinkled, wasted with age. A hasty vision it had
been, to be sure; but she had seen him; and his
venerable figure remained in her memory like a
landscape glimpsed at the flare of a lightning-flash.
She had witnessed his arrival in Venice to die in the
peace of those canals, in that silence which is broken
only by the stroke of the oar—where many years
before he had thought himself dying as he wrote his
*Tristan*—that hymn to the Death that is pure, to
the Death that liberates! She saw him stretched
out in the dark boat; and the splash of the water
against the marble of the palaces echoed in her
imagination like the wailing, thrilling trumpets at
the burial of Siegfried—the hero of Poetry marching to the Valhalla of immortality and glory upon
a shield of ebony—motionless, inert as the young
hero of the Germanic legend—and followed by the
lamentations of that poor prisoner of life, Human-
ity, that ever eagerly seeks a crack, a chink, in the
wall about it, through which the inspiriting, comforting ray of beauty may penetrate.

And the singer gazed with tearful eyes at the
broad *boina* of black velvet, the lock of gray hair,
two broken, rusty steel pens—souvenirs of the Master, that Hans Keller had piously preserved in a
glass case.

"You knew him—tell me how he lived. Tell me
everything: talk to me about the Poet . . . the
Hero."

And the musician, no less moved, described the
Master as he had seen him in the best of health; a

small man, tightly wrapped in an overcoat—with a powerful, heavy frame, however, despite his slight stature—as restless as a nervous woman, as vibrant as a steel spring, with a smile that lightly touched with bitterness his thin, colorless lips. Then came his "genialities," as people said, the caprices of his genius, that figure so largely in the Wagner legend: his smoker, a jacket of gold satin with pearl flowers for buttons; the precious cloths that rolled about like waves of light in his study, velvets and silks, of flaming reds and greens and blues, thrown across the furniture and the tables haphazard, with no reference to usefulness—for their sheer beauty only— to stimulate the eye with the goad of color, satisfy the Master's passion for brightness; and perfumes, as well, with which his garments—always of oriental splendor—were literally saturated; phials of rose emptied at random, filling the neighborhood with the fragrance of a fabulous garden, strong enough to overcome the hardiest uninitiate, but strangely exciting to that Prodigy in his struggle with the Unknown.

And then Hans Keller described the man himself, never relaxed, always quivering with mysterious thrills, incapable of sitting still, except at the piano, or at table for his meals; receiving visitors standing, pacing back and forth in his salon, his hands twitching in nervous uncertainty; changing the position of the armchairs, rearranging the furniture, suddenly stopping to hunt about his person for a snuffbox or a pair of glasses that he never found; turning his pockets inside out, pulling his velvet house-cap now down over one eye, now back over the crown of his head, or again, throwing it into the air with a shout of joy or crumpling it in his hand, as he became excited in the course of a discussion!

And Keller would close his eyes, imagining that he could still hear in the silence, the faint but commanding voice of the Master. Oh, where was he now? On some star, doubtless, eagerly following the infinite song of the spheres, a divine music that only his ears had been attuned to hear! And to choke his emotion, the musician would sit down at the piano, while Leonora, responsive to his mood, would approach him, and standing as rigid as a statue, with her hands lost in the musician's head of rough tangled hair, sing a fragment from the immortal *Tetralogy*.

Worship of Wagner transformed the butterfly into a new woman. Leonora adored Keller as a ray of light gone astray from the glowing star now extinguished forever; she felt the joy of humbleness, the sweetness of sacrifice, seeing in him not the man, but the chosen representative of the Divinity. Leonora could have grovelled at Keller's feet, let him trample on her—make a carpet of her beauty. She willed to become a slave to that lover who was the repository of the Master's thoughts; and who seemed to be magnified to gigantic proportions by the custody of such a treasure.

She tended him with the exquisite watchfulness of an enamored servant, following him, on his trips in the summer, the season of the great concerts, to Leipzig, Geneva, Paris; and she, the most famous living prima donna, would stay behind the scenes, with no jealousy for the applause she heard, waiting for Hans, perspiring and tired, to drop the baton amid the acclamations of the audience and come back-stage to have her dry his forehead with an almost filial caress.

And thus they traveled about Europe, spreading the light of the Master; Leonora, voluntarily in the background, like a patrician of old, dressed as a slave and following the Apostle in the name of the New Word.

The German musician let himself be adored, receiving all her caresses of enthusiasm and love with the absent-mindedness of an artist so preoccupied with sounds that at last he comes to hate words. He taught his language to Leonora that she might some day realize a dream of hers and sing in Bayreuth; and he grounded her in the principles that had guided the Master in the creation of his great characters. And so, when Leonora made her appearance on the stage one winter with the winged helmet and the lance of the Valkyrie, she attained an eminence in Wagnerian interpretation that was to follow her for the remainder of her career. Hans himself was carried away by her power, and could never recover from his astonishment at Leonora's complete assimilation of the spirit of the Master.

"If only He could hear you!" he would say with conviction. "I am sure He would be content."

And the pair traveled about the world together. Every springtime she, as spectator, would watch him directing Wagnerian choruses in the "Mystic Abyss" at Bayreuth. Winters it was he who went into ecstasies under her tremendous *"Hojotoho!"*—the fierce cry of a Valkyrie afraid of the austere father Wotan; or at sight of her awakening among the flames for the spirited Siegfried, the hero who feared nothing in the world, but trembled at the first glance of love!

But artists' passions are like flowers, fragrant, but quickly languishing. The rough German musician was a simple person, unstable, fickle, ready to be amused at any new plaything. Leonora admitted to Rafael that she could have lived to old age submissively at Keller's side, pampering his whims and selfish caprices. But one day Keller deserted her, as she had deserted others, to take up with a sickly, languid contralto, whose best charms could have been hardly comparable to the morbid delicacy of a hot-house flower. Leonora, mad with love and jealousy, pursued him, knocking at his door like a servant. For the first time she felt the voluptuous bitterness of being scorned, discarded, until reaction from despair brought her back to her former pride and self-control!

Love was over. She had had enough of artists; though an interesting sort of folk they were in their way. Far preferable were the ordinary, normal men she had known before Keller's time! The foolisher—the more commonplace—the better! She would never fall in love again!

Wearied, broken in spirit, disillusioned, she went back into her old world. But now the legend of her past beset her. Again men came, passionately besieging her, offering her wealth in return for a little love. They talked of killing themselves if she resisted, as if it were her duty to surrender, as if refusal on her part were treachery. The gloomy Macchia committed suicide in Naples. Why? Because she did not capitulate to his melancholy sonnets! In Vienna there had been a duel, in which one of her admirers was slain. An eccentric Englishman followed her about, looming in her pathway everywhere like the shadow of a fatal Destiny, vowing to kill anybody she should prefer to him. . . . She had had enough at last! She was wearied of such a life, disgusted at the male voracity that dogged her every step. She longed to fall out of sight, disappear, find rest and quiet in a complete surrender to some boundless dream. And the thought—a comforting, soothing thought, it had been—of the distant land of her childhood came back to her, the thought of her simple, pious aunt, the sole survivor of her family, who wrote to her twice every year, urging her to reconcile her soul with God—to which end the good old Doña Pepa was herself aiding with prayer!

She felt, too, somehow, without knowing just why, that a visit to her native soil would soften the painful memory of the ingratitude that had cost her father's life. She would care for the poor old woman! Her presence would bring a note of cheer into that gray, monotonous existence that had gone on without the slightest change, ever. And suddenly, one night, after an "Isolde" in Florence, she ordered Beppa, the loyal and silent companion of her wandering life, to pack her things!

Home! Home! Off for her native land! And might she find there something to keep her ever from returning to the troubled stirring world she was leaving!

She was the princess of the fairy tales longing to become a shepherdess. There she meant to stay, dozing in the shade of her orange-trees, now and then fondling a memory of her old life, perhaps, but wishing eternally to enjoy that tranquillity, fiercely repelling Rafael, therefore, because he had tried to awaken her, as Siegfried rouses Brunhilde, braving the flames to reach her side.

No; friends, friends, nothing else! She wanted no more of love. She already knew what that was. Besides, he had come too late. . . .

And Rafael tossed sleeplessly in his bed, rehearsing in the darkness the story he had been told. He felt dwarfed, annihilated, by the grandeur of the men who had preceded him in their adoration of that woman. A king, great artists, handsome and aristocratic paladins, Russian counts, potentates with vast wealth at their command! And he, a humble country boy, an obscure junior deputy, as submissive as a child to his mother's despotic ways, forced to beg for the money for his personal expenses even— he was trying to succeed them!

He laughed with bitter irony at his own presumptuousness. Now he understood Leonora's mocking tone, and the violence she had used in repulsing all boorish liberties he had tried to take. But despite the contempt he began to feel for himself, he lacked the strength to withdraw now. He had been caught up in the wake of seduction, the maelstrom of love that followed the actress everywhere, enslaving men, casting them, broken in spirit and in will, to earth, like so many slaves of Beauty.

# III

"Good morning, Rafaelito . . . we are seeing
each other betimes today. . . . I am up so early
not to miss the marketing. I remember that
Wednesday was always a great event in my life, as
a child. What a crowd! . . ."

And Leonora, with the great swarming cities far
from her mind, was really impressed at the numbers
of bustling people crowding the little square, called
*del Prado*, where every Wednesday the "grand market" of the Alcira region was held.

Their sashes bulging with money bags, peasants
were coming into town to buy supplies for the whole
week out in the orange country. Orchard women
were going from one stall to the next, as slender of
body and as neatly dressed as the peasant girls of
an opera ballet, their hair in *señorita* style, their
skirts of bright batiste gathered up to hold their
purchases and showing fine stockings and tight-
fitting shoes underneath. Tanned faces and rough
hands were the only signs to betray the rustic origin
of the girls; because those were prosperous days
for the orange growers of the District.

Along the walls hens were clucking, ranged in
piles and tied together by the feet. Here and there
were pyramids of eggs, vegetables, fruit. In "shops"
that were set up in the morning and taken down at
night, drygoods dealers were selling colored sashes,
strips of cotton cloth and calico, and black woolsey,

the eternal garb of every native of the Júcar valley. Beyond the Prado, in *El Alborchí*, was the hog market; and then came the *Hostal Gran* where horses were tried out. On Wednesdays all the business of the neighborhood was transacted—money borrowed or paid back, poultry stocks replenished, hogs bought to fatten on the farms, whole families anxiously following their progress; and new cart-horses, especially, the matter of greatest concern to the farmers, secured on mortgage, usually, or with cash saved up by desperate hoarding.

Though the sun had barely risen, the crowd, smelling of sweat and soil, already filled the market place with busy going and coming. The orchard-women embraced as they met, and with their heavy baskets propped on their hips, went into the chocolate shops to celebrate the encounter. The men gathered in groups; and from time to time, to "buck up" a little, would go off in parties to swallow a glass of sweet brandy. In and out among the rustics walked the city people: "petty bourgeois" of set manners, with old capes, and huge hempen baskets, where they would place the provisions they had bought after tenacious hagglings; *señoritas,* who found in these Wednesday markets a welcome relief from the monotony of their secluded life at home; idlers who spent hour after hour at the stall of some vendor friend, prying into what each marketer carried in his basket, grumbling at the stinginess of some and praising the generosity of others.

Rafael gazed at his friend in sheer astonishment. What a beauty she was! Who could ever have taken her, in that costume, for a world-famous prima donna!

Leonora looked the living picture of an orchard girl: a plain cotton dress, in anticipation of spring; a red kerchief around her neck; her blond hair uncovered, combed back with artful carelessness and hastily knotted low on the back of her head. Not a jewel, not a flower! Only her height and her striking comeliness marked her off from the other girls. Under the curious, devouring glances of the whole market throng, Rafael smilingly greeted her, feasting his eyes on her fresh, pink skin, still radiant from the morning bath, inhaling the subtle, indefinable fragrance that hovered about that strong, healthy, youthful person.

She was constantly smiling, as if bent on dazzling the bumpkins, who were gaping at her from a distance, with the pearly flash of her teeth. The market-place began to buzz with admiring curiosity, or the thrill of scandal. There, face to face, in view of the whole city, the deputy and the opera singer were talking and laughing together like the best of friends!

Rafael's supporters—the chief officials in the city government—who were loitering about the square, could not conceal their satisfaction. Even the humblest of the constables felt a certain pride. That beautiful fairy was talking with "the Chief," smiling at him, even. What an honor for "the Party!" But after all, why not? Everything considered, don Rafael Brull deserved all that, and more! And those men, who were very careful to keep silent when their wives spoke indignantly of the "stranger," admired her with the instinctive fervor that beauty inspires, and envied the deputy his good fortune. The old orchard-women wrapped the couple in caressing glances of approval. There was a handsome pair! What a fine match!

The town ladies in passing by would draw up full height and pretend not to see them. On meeting acquaintances they would make wry faces and say ironically: "Did you see? . . . here she is, in full sight of everybody, casting her fly for doña Bernarda's son!" What a disgrace! It was getting so a decent woman hardly dared go out of doors!

Leonora, quite unconscious of the interest she was arousing, chattered on about her shopping. Beppa, you see, had decided to stay at home with her aunt that morning; so she had come with her gardener's wife and another woman—there they were over there with the large baskets. She had no end of things to get—and she laughed as she read off the list. A regular housewife she had become, yes, sir! She knew the price of everything and could tell down to a *centime* just what it was costing her to live. It was like those hard times back in Milan, when she had gone with her music roll under her arm to get macaroni, butter or coffee at the grocer's. And what fun it all was! . . . However, Leonora observed that, without a doubt, her audience was interpreting her cordial offhand way with Rafael in the worst light possible. She gave him her hand and took leave. It was growing late! If she stood there much longer the best of the market would be carried off by others—if she found anything at all left! "Down to business, then! Good-bye!"

And the young man saw her make her way, followed by the two country women, through the crowds, pausing at the booths, welcomed by the vendors with their best smiles, as a customer who never haggled; interrupting her purchases to fondle the filthy, whining children the poor women were carrying in their arms, and taking the best fruits out of her basket to give to the little ones.

And everywhere general admiration! *"Así, siñorita!*—Here, my dear young lady!" *"Vinga, doña Leonor!*—This way, doña Leonora!" the huckstresses cried, calling her by name to show greater intimacy. And she would smile, with a familiar intimate word for everybody, her hand frequently visiting the purse of Russian leather that hung from her wrist. Cripples, blind beggars, men with missing arms or legs, all had learned of the generosity of that woman who scattered small change by the fistful.

Rafael gazed after her, smiling indifferently in acknowledgment of the congratulations the town notables were heaping on him. The *alcalde*—the most hen-pecked husband in Alcira, according to his enemies—affirmed with sparkling eyes that for a woman like that he was capable of doing almost any crazy thing. And they all joined in a chorus of invidious praise, taking it for granted that Rafael was the *artiste's* accepted lover; though the youth himself smiled bitterly at the thought of his real status with that wonderful woman.

And she vanished, finally, into the sea of heads at the other end of the market-place; though Rafael, from time to time, thought he could still make out a mass of golden hair rising above the *chevelures* of the other girls. Willingly he would have followed; but Don Matías was at his side—don Matías, the wealthy orange exporter, father of the wistful Remedios who was spending her days obediently at doña Bernarda's side.

That gentleman, heavy of speech and heavier still of thought, was pestering Rafael with a lot of nonsense about the orange business, giving the young man advice on a new bill he had drawn up and wanted to have introduced in Congress—a protectionist measure for Spanish oranges. "Why, it will be the making of the city, boy! Every mother's son of us swimming in money!" as he guaranteed with his hand upon his heart.

But Rafael's gaze was lost in the distant reaches of the Prado, to catch one more fleeting glimpse of a golden head of hair—proof of Leonora's presence still! He found it hard to be courteous, even, to this man who, according to authentic rumor, was destined to be his father-in-law. Of all the drawling trickling words only a few reached his ears, beating on his brain like monotonous hammer blows. "Glasgow . . . Liverpool . . . new markets . . . lower railroad rates . . . The English agents are a set of thieves . . ."

"Very well, let them go hang," Rafael answered mentally. And giving a mechanical "yes, yes!" to propositions he was not even hearing, he gazed away more intently than ever, fearing lest Leonora should already have gone. He felt relieved, however, when a gap opened in the crowd and he could see the actress seated in a chair that had been offered her by a huckstress. She was holding a child upon her knees, and talking with a tiny, wretched, sickly creature who looked to Rafael like the orchard-woman they had met at the hermitage.

"Well, what do you think of my plan?" don Matías asked.

"Excellent, magnificent, and well worthy of a man like you, who knows the question from top to bottom. We'll discuss the matter thoroughly when I return to the Cortes."

And to avoid a second exposition, he patted the wealthy boor on the back, and wondered why in the world Fortune should have picked such a disgusting man to smile on.

The whole city had known don Matías when he went around in peasant's clogs and worked a tiny orchard he had secured on lease. His son, a virtual half-wit, who took advantage of every opportunity to rifle the old man's pockets and spend the money in Valencia with bull-fighters, gamblers and horse-dealers, went barefoot in those days, scampering about the roads with the children of the gipsies encamped in *El Alborchí*. His daughter—the now well-behaved, the now modest, Remedios, who was passing day after day at complicated needlework under the tutelage of doña Bernarda—had grown up like a wild rabbit of the fields, repeating with shocking fidelity all the oaths and vile language she heard from the carters her father drank with.

"But you have to be an ox to get rich these days!" the barber Cupido would say when don Matías came up for discussion.

Little by little the man had worked his way into the orange export business—to England especially. His first stock he bought on credit; and at once Fortune began to blow upon him with bloated cheeks, and she was still puffing and puffing! His wealth had been accumulated in a few years. In crises where the most powerful vessels foundered, that rude and heavy bark, sailing on without chart or compass, suffered not the slightest harm. His shipments always arrived at the psychological moment. The fancy, carefully-selected oranges of other merchants would land at Liverpool or London when the markets were glutted and prices were falling scandalously. The lucky dolt would send anything at all along, whatever was available, cheap; and circumstances always seemed to favor him with an empty market and prices sky-high regardless of quality. He realized fabulous profits. He had nothing but scorn for all the wiseacres who subscribed to the English papers, received daily bulletins and compared market quotations from year to year, getting, for all their pains, results that made them tear their hair. He was an ignoramus and he was proud of it! He trusted to his lucky star. Whenever he thought it best, he would ship his produce off from the port of Valencia, and—there you are! —it would always turn out that his oranges found no competition on arrival and brought the highest prices. More than once it had happened that rough weather held his vessel up. Well—the market would sell out, and his shipment would have a clear field just the same!

Within two years he had a place in town and had become a "personage." He would smilingly declare that he wouldn't "go to the wall for under eighty thousand *duros*." Later, ever on the wing, his fortune reached dizzy heights. Folks whispered in superstitious awe the figures he made in net profits at the end of every sailing. He owned warehouses as large as churches in the vicinity of Alcira, employing armies of girls to wrap the oranges and regiments of carpenters to make the crates. He would buy the crop of an entire orchard at a single glance and never be more than a few pounds off. As for the pay he gave, the city was proud of its millionaire. Not even the Bank of Spain enjoyed the respect and confidence his firm had won. No clerks and cashiers! No mahogany furniture! Everything above board! Ask for a hundred thousand; and if don Matías said "yes," he just went in to his bedroom and, God knows from where, he would draw out a roll of bank-notes the size of your body!

And this lucky rustic, this upstart lout, rich without deserving it for any competence he had, was giving himself the airs of an intelligent dealer, presuming to approach Rafael, "his deputy," with a proposal for a freight-rate bill to promote the shipping of oranges into the interior of Spain! As if a little thing like a bill in Congress would make any difference to his way of getting money!

Of his wretched past don Matías preserved but a single trait: his respect for the house of Brull. The rest of the city he treated with a certain uppishness; but he could not conceal the awe which doña Bernarda inspired in him—a feeling that was strengthened by gratitude for her kindness in singling him out (after he had become rich), and for the interest she showed in his "little girl." He cherished a vivid memory of Rafael's father, the "greatest man" he had known in all his life. It seemed as though he could still see don Ramón stopping on his big horse in front of his humble farmhouse and, with the air of a grand lord, leaving orders for what don

Matías was to do in the coming elections. He knew the bad state in which the great man had left his affairs upon his death; and more than once he had given money to doña Bernarda outright, proud that she should do him the honor of appealing to him in her straits. But in his eyes, the House of Brull, poor or rich, was always the House of Brull, the cradle of a dynasty whose authority no power could shake. He had money. But those *others*, the Brulls—ah!—they had, up there in Madrid, friends, influence! If they wanted to they could get the ear of the Throne itself. They were people with a "pull," and if anyone suggested in his presence that Rafael's mother was thinking of Remedios as a daughter-in-law, don Matías would redden with satisfaction and modestly reply:

"I don't know; I imagine it's all talk. My Remedios is only a town girl, you see. The señor deputy is probably thinking of someone from the 'upper crust' in Madrid."

Rafael had for some time been aware of his mother's plans. But he had no use for "that crowd." The old man, despite his boresome habit of suggesting "new bills," he could stand on account of his touching loyalty to the Brull family. But the girl was an utterly insignificant creature, pretty, to be sure, but only as any ordinary young girl is pretty. And underneath that servile gentleness of hers lay an intelligence even more obtuse than her father's, a mind filled with nothing but piety and the religious phrases in which she had been educated.

That morning, followed by an aged servant, and with all the gravity of an orphan who must busy herself with the affairs of her household and act as head of the home, Remedios had walked by Rafael twice. She scarcely looked at him. The submissive smile of the future slave with which she usually greeted him had disappeared. She was quite pale, and her colorless lips were pressed tight together. Without a doubt in the world she had seen him, from a distance, talking and laughing with "the chorus girl." His mother would know all about it within an hour! Really, that young female seemed to think he was her private property! And the angry expression on her face was that of a jealous wife taking notes for a curtain-lecture!

Scenting a danger Rafael took hasty leave of don Matías and his other friends, and left the market place to avoid another meeting with Remedios. Leonora was still there. He would wait for her on the road to the orchard. He must take advantage of the early hour!

The orange country seemed to be quivering under the first kisses of spring. The lithe poplars bordering the road were covered with tender leaves. In the orchards the buds on the orange-trees, filling with the new sap, were ready to burst, as in one grand explosion of perfume, into white fragrant bloom. In the matted herbage on the river-banks the first flowers were growing. Rafael felt the cool caress of the sod as he sat down on the edge of the road. How sweet everything smelled! What a beautiful day it was!

The timorous, odorous violet must be sprouting on the damp ground yonder under the alders! And he went looking along the stream for those little purple flowers that bring dreams of love with their fragrance! He would make a bouquet to offer Leonora as she came by.

He felt thrilled with a boldness he had never known before. His hands burned feverishly. Perhaps it was the emotion from his own sense of daring. He had resolved to settle things that very morning. The fatuity of the man who feels himself ridiculous and is determined to raise himself in the eyes of his admirers, excited him, filling him with a cynical rashness.

What would his friends, who envied him as Leonora's lover, say if they knew she was treating him as an insignificant friend, a good little boy who helped her while away the hours in the solitude of her voluntary exile?

A few kisses—on her hand; a few kind words; many many cruel jests, such as come from a chum conscious of superiority . . . that was all he had won after months and months and months of assiduous courtship, months of disobedience to his mother, in whose house he had been living like a stranger, without affection, at daggers' points; months of exposure to the criticism of his enemies, who suspected him of a liaison with the "chorus girl" and were raising their brows, horror-stricken, in the name of morality. How they would scoff, if they knew the truth! Those addlepates down at the Club were always boasting of their amorous adventures, which began inevitably with the sudden physical attack and ended in easy triumph.

With the Spaniard's mortal dread of looking ridiculous, Rafael began to assure himself that those brutes were right—that such was the road to a woman's heart. He had been too respectful, too humble, gazing at Leonora, timidly, submissively, from afar, as an idolator might look at an ikon. Bosh! Wasn't he a man, and isn't the man the stronger? Some show of a male authority, that was what she needed! He liked her! Well, that was the end of it! His she must be! Besides, since she treated him so kindly, she surely loved him! A few scruples perhaps! But that would be nothing, before a show of real manhood!

Just as this valorous decision had emerged in the full splendor of its dignity from the mess of vacillation in his weak, irresolute character, Rafael heard voices down the road. He jumped to his feet. Leonora was approaching, followed by the two peasant women, who were bent low under their heavily laden baskets.

"Here, too!" the actress exclaimed with a laugh that rippled charmingly under the white skin of her throat. "You are getting to be my shadow. In the market place, on the road, everywhere! I find you every time I look around!"

She accepted the bouquet of violets from the young man's hand, inhaling their fragrance with evidence of keen enjoyment.

"Thanks, Rafael, they are the first I have seen this season. My beautiful, faithful old friend! Springtime! You have brought her to me this year, though I felt her coming days before! I am so happy—can't you see? I feel as though I'd been a silkworm all winter, coiled up in a cocoon, and had now suddenly grown my wings! And I'm going to fly out over this great green carpet, so sweet with its first perfumes! Don't you feel as I do, Rafael? . . ."

Rafael, gravely, said he did. He, too, felt a seething in his blood, the nip of life in every one of his pores! And his eyes ran over the bare neck in front of him, a neck of such tempting smoothness, its white beauty set off by the red kerchief; and over the violets resting on that strong, robust bosom. The two orchard women exchanged a shrewd smile, a meaningful wink, at sight of Rafael, and went on ahead of their mistress, with the evident design of not disturbing the couple by their presence; but Leonora caught the look on their faces.

"Yes, go right on," she said. "We'll take our time, but we'll be there soon!"

And when they were out of hearing she resumed, pointing to the women with her closed parasol:

"Did you see that? Didn't you notice their smiles and the winks they exchanged when they saw you on the road? . . . Oh, Rafael! You are blind as a bat! And no good is going to come of it! If I had any reputation to lose, I'd be mighty careful with a friend like you! What do you suppose they are thinking?"

And she laughed with a pout of condescension, as though for her part, she did not care what people might be saying about her friendship with Rafael.

"On the market-place all the huckstresses talk to me about you, with the idea of flattering me. They assure me we'd make a wonderful couple. My kitchen woman seizes every opportunity to tell me how handsome you are. You ought to thank her. . . . Even my aunt, my poor aunt, with one leg in

the grave, drew it out the other day to say to me:
'Do you notice that Rafael visits us quite frequently?
Do you think he wants to marry you?' Marry, you
see! Ha, ha, ha! Marry! That's all poor auntie
can see in the world for a woman!"

And she went on gaily chattering like a wild bird
escaped from a cage and happy at its liberty, though
her frank, mocking laughter was in strange contrast
with the expression of sinister determination on Rafael's face.

"But how glum and queer you look today! Are
you ill? . . . What's the matter?"

Rafael took advantage of this opening. Ill, yes!
Sick with love! He knew the whole place was
gossiping about them. But it wasn't his fault. He
simply couldn't hide his feelings. If she only realized what that mute adoration was costing him!
He had tried to root the thought of her out of his
mind, but that had been impossible. He must see
her, hear her! He lived for her alone. Study? Impossible! Play, with his friends? They had all
become obnoxious to him! His house was a cave,
a cellar, a place to eat in and sleep in. He left it
the moment he got out of bed, and kept away from
the city, too, which seemed stuffy, oppressive, like a
jail to him. Off to the fields; to the orchards, to
the Blue House where she lived! He would wait
and wait for afternoon to come—the time when, by
a tacit arrangement neither of them had proposed,
he might enter her orchard and find her on the bench
under the four dead palms! . . . Well, he could
not go on living that way. Poor folks envied him
his power, because he was a deputy, at twenty-five!
And yet his one purpose in life was to be . . . well,

she could guess what . . . that garden bench, for instance, gently, deliciously burdened with her weight for whole afternoons; or that needlework which played about in her soft fingers; or one of her servants, Beppa, perhaps, who could waken her in the morning, bend low over her sleeping head, and smooth the loose tresses spread like rivulets of gold over the white pillow. A slave, an animal, a thing even, provided it should be in continuous contact with her person—that was what he longed to be; not to find himself obliged, at nightfall, to leave her after a parting absurdly prolonged by childish pretexts, and return to his irritating, common, vulgar life at home, to the solitude of his room, where he imagined he could see a pair of green eyes staring at him from every dark corner, tempting him.

Leonora was not laughing. Her gold-spotted eyes had opened wide; her nostrils were quivering with emotion. She seemed deeply moved by the young man's eloquent sincerity.

"Poor Rafael! My poor dear boy! . . . And what are we going to do?"

Down at the Blue House, Rafael had never dared speak so openly. The presence of Leonora's servants; the nonchalant, mocking air with which she welcomed him at the door; the irony with which she met his every hint at a declaration had always crushed, humiliated him. But there, on the open highway, it was different somehow. He felt free. He would empty his whole heart out.

What anguish! Every day he went to the Blue House trembling with hope, enthralled in his dream of love! "Perhaps it will be today," he would say to himself each time. And his legs would give way at the knees, and he would choke as he swallowed! Then, hours later, at nightfall, he would slink home, downcast, dispirited, desperate, staggering along the road under the star-light as if he were drunk, repressing the tears burning in his eyes, longing for the peace of death, like a weary explorer who must go on and on breaking his way over one ice-field after another. She must have noticed, surely! She must have seen the untiring efforts he made to please her! . . . Ignorant, humble, recognizing the vast gulf that separated them because of the different lives they had led, how he had worked to raise himself to a level with the men who had loved and won her! If she spoke of the Russian count—a model of stylish elegance—the next day, to the great astonishment of his mother, Rafael would take out his best clothes and, all sweating in the hot sun and nearly strangled by a high collar, he would set out along that same road—his Road to Calvary—walking on his toes like a boarding-school girl in order not to get his shoes dirty. If Hans Keller had come to Leonora's mind, he would run through his histories of music, and dressing up like some artist he had read about in novels, would come to her house fully intending to deliver an oration on the immortal Master, Wagner, whom he knew nothing at all about, but whom he adored as a member of his family. . . . Good God! All that was ridiculous, he knew very well; it would have been far better to present himself just as he was, undisguised, in all his littleness. He knew that this pretending to equality with the thousand or more figures flitting in Leonora's memory, was grotesque. But there was nothing, absolutely nothing he would not do to stir her

heart a little, be loved for a day, a minute, a second
—and then die! . . .

There was a note of such real feeling in the
youth's confession that Leonora, more and more
deeply moved, unconsciously drew closer to him,
almost grazing him as they walked along; and she
smiled slightly, as she repeated her previous phrase
—a blend of motherly affection and compassion:

"Poor Rafael! . . . My poor dear boy!"

They had reached the gate to the orchard. The
walk inside was deserted. In the little square some
hens were scratching about.

Overwhelmed by the strain of that confession, in
which he had vented the anguish and dreams of many
months, Rafael leaned against the trunk of an old
orange-tree. Leonora stood in front of him, listening to his words, with head lowered, making marks
on the ground with the tip of her red parasol.

Die, yes; he had often read in novels about people dying for love. And he had always laughed
at the absurdity of such a thing. But he understood
now. Many a night, tossing in his delirium, he had
thought of ending his misery in some tragic manner.
The violent, domineering blood of his father seethed
in his veins. Once firmly convinced she could never
be his, he would kill her, to keep her from belonging
to anybody . . . and then stab himself! They
would fall together to the blood-soaked ground, and
lie there as on a bed of red damask, and he would
kiss her cold lips, without fear of being disturbed;
kiss her and kiss her, till the last breath of his life
exhaled upon her livid mouth.

He seemed to be saying all that with deadly earn-
estness. The muscles of his strong face quivered,

and his eyes—Moorish eyes—glowed like live coals. Leonora was looking at him passionately now, as if a man were in front of her. She shuddered with a strange fascination as she pictured his barbarous dreams, fraught with blood and death. This was something new! This boy, when he saw that his love was vain, would not gloomily and prosaically slay himself as Macchia, the Italian poet, had done. He would die, but asserting himself, killing the woman, destroying his idol when it would not harken to his entreaties!

And, pleasantly excited by Rafael's tragic demeanor, she gave way to the thrill of it, letting herself be carried along by his anguished rapture. He had taken her arm and was drawing her off the path, out among the low-hanging branches of the orange-trees.

For some time they were both silent. Leonora seemed to be drinking in the virile perfume of that savage passionate adoration.

Rafael thought he had offended her, and was sorry for his violent words.

She must pardon him; he was beside himself, exasperated beyond bounds at her strange resistance. Leonora! Leonora! Why persist in spoiling a perfectly beautiful thing? He was not wholly a matter of indifference in her eyes. She did not dislike him. Otherwise she would not have let him be a friend and have permitted his frequent visits. Love?. . . Of course she did not love him—poor unhappy wretch that he was, incapable of inspiring passion in a woman like her. But let her just accept him. He would teach her to love him in time, win her by the sheer beauty of his own tenderness and worship. His love alone, alas, was great enough for both of them and for all the famous lovers in history put together! He would be her slave; a carpet for her to tread underfoot; a dog, always at her feet, his eyes burning with the fire of eternal fidelity! She would finally learn to be fond of him, if not out of passion, at least out of gratitude and pity!

And as he spoke, he brought his face close to Leonora's, looking for his own image in the depths of her green eyes; and he pressed her arm in a fever of passion.

"Careful, Rafael. . . . That hurts! Let go of me."

And as if suddenly sensing a danger in the full of a sweet dream, she. shuddered and pulled herself free with a nervous violence.

Then, quite recovered from the intoxication into which she had been led by Rafael's passionate appeal, she began to speak calmly, composedly.

No; what he asked was impossible. Her fate was ordained; she did not want love any more. . . . Friendship had carried them a bit astray. It was her fault, but she would find a way to remedy that. If she had known him years before—perhaps! She might have learned to love him. He was more worthy of being loved than many of the men she had accepted. But he had come too late. Now she was content with just living. Besides, what a horror! Imagine a "grand passion" in a petty environment such as they were in, a tiny world of gossip-mongers and evil tongues! Imagine having to hide like a criminal to express a noble emotion! No, when she loved, she loved in the open, with the sublime immodesty of the masterpiece that scandalizes bumpkins with its naked beauty! How impossible it would be, finding herself nibbled at constantly by gossiping fools, quite beneath her contempt. She would feel the scorn and the indignation of a whole town about her. They would accuse her of leading an innocent boy astray, alienating him from his own mother. "No, Rafael; a thousand times no; I have a little conscience left! I'm not the irresponsible siren I used to be."

"But what about me?" cried the youth, seizing her arm again with a boyish petulance. "You think of yourself and of other people, but never of me. What am I going to do all along with my suffering?"

"Oh, you? Why . . . you will forget," said Leonora gravely. "I have just realized this very moment that it is impossible for me to stay here any longer. We two must separate. I will leave before Spring is over; I'll go . . . I don't know where, back to the world at any rate, take up my singing again, where I'll not find men of just your kind. Time, and my absence, will attend to the curing of you."

Leonora winced before the flash of savage desire that gleamed in Rafael's eyes. On her face she felt the ardent breath of lips that were seeking her own, and she heard him murmur with a stifled roar of passion:

"No. You shall not go; I refuse to let you go!"

And she felt his strong arms close about her, swaying her from head to foot, in a clasp to which madness added strength. Her feet left the ground, and a brutal thrust threw her to her side at the foot of an orange-tree.

But, in a flash, the Valkyrie reappeared in Leonora. With a supreme effort, she struggled free from the encircling vise, sat up, threw Rafael violently to his back, got to her feet, and stamped a foot brutally and mercilessly down upon the young man's chest, using her whole weight as though bent on crushing the very framework of his body.

Her face was an inspiring thing to look upon. She seemed to have gone mad! Her blond hair had fallen awry and was flecked with leaves and grass and bark. Her green eyes flashed with metallic glints, like daggers. Her lips were pale from emotion. And in that wild posture, whether through force of habit, or the suggestiveness of the effort she had made, she raised her warcry—a piercing, savage *"Hojotoho!"* that rent the calm of the orchard, frightening the hens and sending them scampering off over the paths. Her parasol she brandished as if it were the lance of Wotan's daughter, and several times she aimed it at Rafael's eyes, as if she intended to spear him blind.

The youth seemed to have collapsed less from the violence of the struggle than from an overpowering sense of shame. He lay motionless on the ground, without protesting, and as if not caring ever to rise again—longing to die under the pressure of that foot which was so heavily weighing down upon him, taking away his breath.

Leonora regained her composure, and slowly stepped back. Rafael sat up, and reached for his hat.

It was a painful moment. They stood there cold, as if the sun had gone out and a glacial wind were blowing through the orchard.

Rafael kept his eyes to the ground, afraid to look up and meet her gaze, ashamed at the thought of his disordered clothes, which were soiled with dirt; humiliated at having been beaten and pummeled like a robber caught by a victim he had expected to find powerless.

He heard Leonora's voice addressing him with the scornful *"tu"* a lady might use toward her lowest inferiors.

"Go!"

He raised his head and found Leonora looking at him, her eyes ablaze with anger and offended dignity.

"I'm never taken by force," she said coldly. "I give myself . . . if I feel like it."

And in the gesture of scorn and rage with which she dismissed him, Rafael thought he caught a trace of loathing at some memory of Boldini—that repugnant lecher, who had been the only person in the world to win her by violence.

Rafael tried to stammer an excuse, but that hateful association of the brutal scene rendered her implacable.

"Go! Go, or I'll beat you again! . . . And never come back!"

And to emphasize the words, as Rafael, humiliated and covered with dirt, was leaving the garden, she shut the gate behind him with such a violent slam that the bars almost went flying.

## IV

Doña Bernarda was much pleased with Rafael. The angry glances, the gestures of impatience, the wordless arguments between mother and son, which the household had formerly witnessed in such terror, had come to an end.

The boy had not been visiting the Blue House for some time. She knew that with absolute certainty, thanks to the gratuitous espionage conducted for her by persons attached to the Brull family. He scarcely ever left the house; a few moments at the Club after lunch; and the rest of the day in the dining-room, with her and family friends; or else, shut up in his room, with his books, probably, which the austere señora revered with the superstitious awe of ignorance.

Don Andrés, her advisor, commented upon the change with a gloating "I told you so." What had he always said, when doña Bernarda, in the confiding intimacies of that friendship which amounted almost to a senile, a tranquil, a distantly respectful passion, would complain of Rafael's contrariness? That it would all pass; that it was a young man's whim; that youth must have its fling! What was the use? Rafael hadn't studied to be a monk! Many boys his age, and even older ones, were far worse! . . . And the old gentleman smiled, for he was thinking of his own easy conquests with the

214

wretched flock of dirty, unkempt peasant girls who
wrapped the oranges in the shipping houses of Alcira. "You see, doña Bernarda, you suffered too
much with don Ramón. You are a bit too exact-
ing with Rafael. Let him have a good time! Let
him enjoy himself! He'll get tired of that chorus
girl soon enough, pretty as she is. Then you can
take hold and start him right!"

Doña Bernarda once again had reason to ap-
preciate the talent of her counsellor. His predic-
tions, made with a cynicism that always caused the
pious lady to blush, had been fulfilled to the letter!

She, too, was sure it was all over. Her son was
not so blind as his father had been. He had soon
wearied of a "lost woman" like Leonora; he had decided it was not worth while to quarrel with his
mamma over so trifling a matter, and have his enemies discredit him on that account. He was returning to the path of duty; and to express her un-
bounded joy, the good woman could not pamper
him enough.

"And how about . . . that?" her friends would
ask her, mysteriously.

"Nothing," she would answer, with a proud smile.
"Three weeks have gone by and he hasn't shown
the slightest inclination to go back. No, Rafael is
a good boy. All that was just a young one's notion. If you could only see him keeping me company in the parlor every afternoon! An angel!
Good as pie! He spends hour after hour chatting
with me and Matías's daughter."

And then, broadening her smile and winking cunningly, she would add:

"I think there's something doing in that direction."

And indeed something was "doing"; at least, to judge by appearances. Bored with wandering from room to room through the house, sick of his books, with which he would spend hours and hours turning pages without really seeing a word that was printed on them, Rafael had taken refuge in the sitting-room where his mother did her sewing, supervising a complicated piece of embroidery that Remedios was making.

The girl's submissive simplicity appealed to Rafael. Her ingenuousness gave him a sense of freshness and repose. She was a cosy secluded refuge where he might sleep after a tempest. His mother's satisfied smile was there to encourage him in this feeling. Never had he seen her so kind and so communicative. The pleasure of having him once more safe and obedient in her hands had mollified that disposition so stern by nature as to verge on rudeness.

Remedios, with her head bowed low over her embroidery, would blush deep red whenever Rafael praised her work or told her she was the prettiest girl in all Alcira. He would help her thread her needles, and hold his hands out to make a winding frame for the skeins; and more than once, with the familiarity of an old playmate, he would pinch her mischievously through the embroidery hoop. And she would never miss the chance to scream scandal.

"Rafael, don't be crazy," his mother would say, threatening him indulgently with her withered fore-finger. "Let Remedios work; if you carry on so I won't let you come into the parlor."

And at night, alone in the dining-room with don Andrés, when the hour of confidences came, doña Bernarda would forget the affairs of "the House" and of "the Party," to say with satisfaction:

"It's going better."

"Is Rafael taking to her?"

"More and more every day. We're getting there, we're getting there! That boy is the living image of his father when it comes to matters like this. Believe me, you can't let one of that tribe out of your sight a minute. If I didn't keep my eye peeled, that young devil would be doing something that would discredit the House forever."

And the good woman was sure that Doctor Moreno's daughter—that abominable creature whose good looks had been her nightmare for some months past—no longer existed for Rafael.

She knew, from her spies, that on one market morning the two had met on the street in town. Rafael had looked the other way, as if trying to avoid her; the "*comica*" had turned pale and walked straight ahead pretending not to see him. What did that mean? . . . A break for good of course! The impudent hussy was livid with rage, you see, perhaps because she could not trap her Rafael again; for he, weary of such uncleanliness, had abandoned her forever. Ah, the lost soul, the indecent gadabout! Excuse me! Was a woman to educate a son in the soundest and most virtuous principles, make a somebody of him, and then have an adventuress come along, a thousand times worse than a common street-woman, and carry him off, as nice as you please, in her filthy hands? What had the daughter of that scamp of a doctor thought? . . .

Let her fume! "You're sore just because you see
he's dumped you for good!"

In the joy of her triumph doña Bernarda was
thinking anxiously of her son's marriage to Remedios, and, coming down one peg on the ladder of her
dignity toward don Matías, she began to treat the
exporter as a member of the family, commenting con-
tentedly upon the growing affection that united their
two children.

"Well, if they're fond of each other," said the
rustic magnate, "the wedding can take place tomorrow so far as I'm concerned. Remedios means
a good deal to me; hard to find a girl like her for
running a house; but that needn't interfere with
the marriage. I'm mighty well satisfied, doña Bernarda, that we should be related through our children. I'm only sorry that don Ramón isn't here to
see it all."

And that was true. The one thing lacking to the
millionaire's perfect joy was that he would never
have the chance to treat the tall, imposing Don
Ramón on equal terms for once,—the crowning
triumph of a self-made man.

Doña Bernarda, too, saw in this union the realization of her fondest dreams: money joined to
power; the millions of a business, whose marvelous
successes seemed like deliberate tricks of Chance,
coming to revivify with their sap of gold the Brull
family tree, which was showing the signs of age and
long years of struggle!

Spring had come on apace. Some afternoons doña
Bernarda would take "the children" to her own
orchards or to the wealthy holdings of don Matías.
It was a sight worth seeing—the kindly shrewdness

with which she chaperoned the young couple, shouting with shocked alarm if they disappeared behind
the orange-trees for a moment or two in their frolics.

"That Rafael of ours," she would say to don Andrés, mimicking the long face he used to put on when
bringing up her troubles with her husband, "what a
rascal he is! I'll bet he's got both arms around her
by this time!"

"Let 'em alone, let 'em alone, doña Bernarda! The
deeper in he gets with this one, the less likely he'll
be to go back to the other."

Back to her? . . . There was no fear of that. It
was enough to watch Rafael picking flowers and
weaving them into the girl's hair while she pretended
to fight him off, blushing like a rose, and quite moved
at such homage.

"Now be good, Rafaelito," Remedios would murmur in a sort of entreating bleat, "don't touch me;
don't be so bold."

But her emotion would so betray her that you
could see the thing she most wanted in the world was
for Rafael to place upon her body once again those
hands that made her tingle from the tips of her toes
to the roots of her hair. She resisted only because
such was the duty of a well-educated Christian girl.
Like a young she-goat she would dash off with graceful, tripping bounds between the rows of orange-
trees, and *su señoria,* the member from Alcira,
would give chase with all his might, his nostrils quivering and his eyes ablaze.

"Let's see if he can catch you!" the mother would
call, with a laugh. "Run and let him try to catch
you!"

Don Andrés would roll up his wrinkled face into

the smile of an old faun. Such play made him
feel young again.

"Huh, *señora!* I believe you. This is getting on
—on, and then some. I'd say, marry them off pretty
quick; for, if you don't, mark my word, there'll soon
be something for Alcira to laugh about."

And they were both mistaken. Neither the mother nor don Andrés was present to note the expression of dejection and despair on Rafael's face when
he was alone, shut up in his room, where, in the
dark corners, he could still see a pair of green, mysterious eyes gleaming at him and tempting him.

Go back to her? Never! He still felt the shame,
the humiliation of that morning. He could see himself in all his tragic ridiculousnes, in a heap on the
ground, trampled under foot by that Amazon, covered with dirt, as humble and abashed as a criminal
caught redhanded and with no excuse. And then that
word, that had cut like the lash of a whip: "Go!"
As if he were a lackey who had dared approach a
Duchess! And then that gate slamming behind him,
falling like a slab over a tomb, setting up an eternal
barrier between him and the love of his life!

No, he would never go back! He was not brave
enough to face her again. That morning when he
had met her by chance near the market-place, he
thought he would die of shame; his legs sagged under him, and the street turned black as if night had
suddenly fallen. She had disappeared; but there
was a ringing in his ears; and he had had to take
hold of something, as if the earth were swaying under
his feet, and he would fall.

He needed to forget that unutterable disgrace—
a recollection as tenacious as remorse itself. That

was why he had plunged into the affair with his mother's protegée—as a sort of anaesthetic. She was a woman! And his hands, which seemed to have been unbound since that painful morning, went out toward her; his tongue, free after his vehement confession of love at the orchard-gate, spoke glibly now expressing an adoration that seemed to go beyond the inexpressive features of Remedios, and reach far, far away, to the Blue House, where the other woman was, offended and in hiding.

With Remedios he would feel some sign of life, only to relapse into torpid gloom the moment he was left alone. It was a foamy, frothy intoxication he felt when with the girl, an effervescence that all evaporated in solitude. He thought of Remedios as a piece of green fruit—sound, free of cut or stain, and with all the color of maturity, but lacking the taste that satisfies and the perfume that enthralls.

In his strange situation, spending days in childish games with a young girl who aroused in him nothing more than the bland sense of fraternal comradeship, and nights in sad and sleepless recollection, the one thing that pleased him was intimacy with his mother. Peace had been restored to the home. He could come and go without being conscious of a pair of eyes glaring upon him and without hearing words of indignation stifled between grating teeth.

Don Andrés and his friends at the Club kept asking him when the wedding would take place. In presence of "the children" doña Bernarda would speak of alterations that would have to be made in the house. She and the servants would occupy the ground floor. The whole first story would be for the couple, with new rooms that would be the talk of the city—they would get the best decorators in Valencia! Don Matías treated him familiarly, just as he had in the old days when he came to the *patio* to get his orders from don Ramón and found Rafael, as a child, playing at his father's feet.

"Everything I have will be for you two. Remedios is an angel, and the day I die, she will get more than my rascal of a son. All I ask of you is not to take her off to Madrid. Since she is leaving my roof, at least let me be able to see her every day."

And Rafael would listen to all these things as in a dream. In reality he had not expressed the slightest desire to marry; but there was his mother, taking everything for granted, arranging everything, imposing her will, accelerating his sluggish affection, literally forcing Remedios into his arms! His wedding was a foregone conclusion, the topic of conversation for the entire city.

Sunk in this sadness, in the clutch of the tranquillity which now surrounded him and which he was afraid to break; weak, as a matter of character, and without will power, he sought consolation in the reflection that the solution his mother was preparing was perhaps for the best.

His friendship with Leonora had been broken forever. Any day she might take flight! She had said so very often. She would be going very soon—when the blossoms were off the orange-trees! What would be left for him then . . . except to obey his mother? He would marry, and perhaps that would serve as a distraction. Little by little his affection for Remedios might grow. Perhaps in time he would even come to love her.

Such meditations brought him a little calm, lulling

him into an attitude of agreeable irresponsibility. He would turn child again, as he once had been, have his mother take charge of everything; let himself be drawn along, passive, unresisting, by the current of destiny.

But at times this resignation boiled up into hot, seething ebullitions of angry protest, of raging passion. At night Rafael could not sleep. The orange-trees were beginning to bloom. The blossoms, like an odorous snow, covered the orchards and shed their perfume as far even as the city streets. The air was heavy with fragrance. To breathe was to scent a nosegay. Through the window-gratings under the doors, through the walls, the virginal perfume of the vast orchards filtered—an intoxicating breath, that Rafael, in his impassioned restlessness, imagined as wafted from the Blue House, caressing Leonora's lovely figure, and catching something of the divine fragrance of her redolent beauty. And he would roll furiously between the sheets, biting the pillow and moaning.

"Leonora! Leonora!"

One night, toward the end of April, Rafael drew back in front of the door to his room, with the tremor he would have felt on the threshold of a place of horror. He could not endure the thought of the night that awaited him. The whole city seemed to have sunk into languor, in that atmosphere so heavily charged with perfume. The lash of spring was stirring all the impulses of life with its exciting caress, and goading every feeling to new intensity. Not the slightest breeze was blowing. The orchards saturated the calm atmosphere with their odorous respiration. The lungs expanded as if there were no air, and all space were being inhaled in each single breath.    A voluptuous shudder was stirring the countryside as it lay dozing under the light of the moon.

Hardly realizing what he was doing, Rafael went down into the street.    Soon he found himself upon the bridge, where a few strollers, hat in hand, were breathing the night air eagerly, looking at the clusters of broken light that the moon was scattering over the river like fragments of a mirror.

He went on through the silent, deserted streets of the suburbs, his footsteps echoing from the sidewalks.    One row of houses lay white and gleaming under the moon.    The other was plunged in shadow. He was drawn on and on into the mysterious silence of the fields.

His mother was asleep, he suddenly reflected.    She would know nothing.    He would be free till dawn. He yielded further to the attraction of the roads that wound in and out through the orchards, where so many times he had dreamed and hoped.

The spectacle was not new to Rafael.    Every year he had watched that fertile plain come to life at the touch of Springtime, cover itself with flowers, fill the air with perfumes; and yet, that night, as he beheld the vast mantle of orange-blossoms that had settled over the fields, and was gleaming in the moonlight like a fall of snow, he felt himself completely in control of an infinitely sweet emotion.

The orange-trees, covered from trunk to crown with white, ivory-smooth flowerets, seemed like webs of spun glass, the vegetation of one of those fantastic snow-mantled landscapes that quiver sometimes in the glass spheres of paper-weights.    The perfume came in continuous, successive waves, rolling out upon the infinite with a mysterious palpitation, transfiguring the country, imparting to it a feeling of supernaturalness—the vision of a better world, of a distant planet where men feed on perfume and live in eternal poetry. Everything was changed in this spacious love-nest softly lighted by a great lantern of mother-of-pearl. The sharp crackling of the branches sounded in the deep silence like so many kisses; the murmur of the river became the distant echo of passionate love-making, hushed voices whispering close to the loved one's ears words tremulous with adoration. From the canebrake a nightingale was singing softly, as if the beauty of the night had subdued its plaintive song.

How good it was to be alive! The blood tingled more rapidly, more hotly, through the body! Every sense seemed sharper, more acute; though that landscape imposed silence with its pale wan beauty, just as certain emotions of intense joy are tasted with a sense of mystic shrinking!

Rafael followed the usual path. He had turned instinctively toward the Blue House.

The shame of his disgrace still smarted raw within him. Had he met Leonora now in the middle of the road he would have recoiled in childish terror; but he would not meet her at such an hour. That reflection gave him strength to walk on. Behind him, over the roofs of the city, the tolling of a clock rolled. Midnight! He would go as far as the wall of her orchard, enter if that were possible, stand there a few moments in silent humility before the house, looking up adoringly at the windows behind which Leonora lay sleeping.

It would be his farewell! The whim had occurred to him as he left the city and saw the first
orange-trees laden with the blossoms whose perfume had for many months been holding the songstress there in patient expectation. Leonora would
never know he had been near her in the silent
orchard bathed in moonlight, taking leave of her
with the unspoken anguish of an eternal farewell,
as to a dream vanishing on the horizon of life!

The gate with the green wooden bars came into
view among the trees—the gate that had been
slammed behind him in insulting dismissal. Among
the thorns of the hedge he looked for an opening
he had discovered in the days when he used to hover
about the house. He went through, and his feet
sank into the fine, sandy soil of the orange-groves.
Above the tops of the trees, the house itself could
be seen, white in the moonlight. The rain-troughs
of the roof and the balustrades of the balconies
shone like silver. The windows were all closed.
Everything was asleep.

He was about to step forward, when a dark form
shot out from between two orange-trees and stopped
near him with a muffled growl. It was the house
dog, an ugly, ill-tempered animal trained to bite
before it barked.

Rafael recoiled instinctively from the warm
breath of that panting, furious muzzle which was
reaching for his leg; but the dog, after a second's
hesitation, began to wag its tail with pleasure; and
was content merely to sniff at the boy's trousers
so as to make absolutely sure of an old friend's identity. Rafael patted him on the head, as he had done

so many times, distractedly, in conversations with Leonora on the bench in the *plazoleta*. A good omen this encounter seemed! And he walked on, while the dog resumed his watch in the darkness.

Timidly he made his way forward in the shelter of a large patch of shadow cast by the orange-trees, dragging himself along, almost, like a thief afraid of an ambuscade.

He reached the walk leading to the *plazoleta* and was surprised to find the gate half open. Suddenly he heard a suppressed cry near by.

He turned around, and there on the tile bench, wrapped in the shadow of the palm-trees and the rose-bushes, he saw a white form—a woman. As she rose from her seat the moonlight fell squarely on her features.

"Leonora!"

The youth would have gladly sunk into the earth. "Rafael! You here? . . ."

And the two stood there in silence, face to face. He kept his eyes fixed on the ground, ashamed. She looked at him with a certain indecision.

"You've given me a scare that I'll never forgive you for," she said at last. "What are you doing here? . . ."

Rafael was at a loss for a reply. He stammered with an embarrassment that quite impressed Leonora; but despite his agitation, he noticed a strange glitter in the girl's eyes, and a mysterious veiling of her voice that seemed to transfigure her.

"Come, now," said Leonora gently, "don't hunt up any far-fetched excuses. . . . You were coming to bid me good-bye—and without trying to see

me! What a lot of nonsense! Why don't you say
right out that you are a victim of this dangerous
night—as I am, too?"

And her eyes, glittering with a tearful gleam,
swept the *plazoleta,* which lay white in the moonlight; and the snowy orange-blossoms, the rose-
bushes, the palm-trees, that stood out black against
the blue sky where the stars were twinkling like
grains of luminous sand. Her voice trembled with
a soft huskiness, as caressing as velvet.

Rafael, quite encouraged by this unexpected reception, tried to beg forgiveness for the madness that
had caused his expulsion from the place; but the
actress cut him short.

"Let's not discuss that unpleasant thing! It hurts
me just to think of it. You're forgiven; and since
you've fallen on this spot as though heaven had
dropped you here, you may stay a moment. But
. . . no liberties. You know me now."

And straightening up to her full height as an
Amazon sure of herself, she turned to the bench,
motioning to Rafael to take a seat at the other end.

"What a night! . . . I feel a strange intoxication
without wine! The orange-trees seem to inebriate
me with their very breath. An hour ago my room
was whirling round and round, as though I were
going to faint. My bed was like a frail bark tossing in a tempest. So I came down as I often do;
and here you can have me until sleep proves more
powerful than the beauty of this beautiful night."

She spoke with a languid abandonment; her voice
quivering, and tremors rippling across her shoulders,
as if all the perfume were hurting her, oppressing

her powerful vitality. Rafael sat looking at her over the length of the bench—a white, sepulchral figure, wrapped in the hooded cape of a dressing-gown—the first thing she had laid hands upon when she had thought of going out into the garden.

"I was frightened when I saw you," she continued, in a slow, faint voice. "A little fright, nothing more! A natural surprise, I suppose; and yet, I was thinking of you that very moment. I confess it. I was saying to myself: 'What can that crazy boy be doing, at this hour, I wonder?' And suddenly you appeared, like a ghost. You couldn't sleep; you were excited by all this fragrance; and you have come to try your luck anew, with the hope that brought you here at other times."

She spoke without her usual irony, softly, simply, as if she were talking to herself. Her body was thrown limply back against the bench, one arm resting behind her head.

Rafael started to speak once more of his repentance, of his desire to kneel in front of the house there in mute entreaty for pardon, while she would be sleeping in the room above. But Leonora interrupted him again.

"Hush! Your voice is very loud. They might hear you. My aunt's room is in the other wing of the house, but she's not a heavy sleeper. . . . Besides, I don't care to listen to talk about remorse, pardon, and such things. It makes me think of that morning. The mere fact that I am letting you stay here ought to be enough, oughtn't it? I want to forget all that. . . . Hush, Rafael! Silence makes the beauty of the night more wonderful. The fields seem to be talking with the moon, and these waves of perfume that are sweeping over us are echoes of their passionate words."

And she fell silent, keeping absolutely still, her eyes turned upward, catching the moonbeams in their tear-like moisture. From time to time Rafael saw her quiver with a mysterious tremor; then extend her arms and cross them behind her head of golden hair, in a voluptuous stretch that made her white robe rustle, while her limbs grew taut in a delicious tension. She seemed upset, ill almost; at times her panting breath was like a sob. Her head drooped over a shoulder and her breast heaved with countless sighs.

The youth was obediently silent, fearing lest the remembrance of his base audacity should again come up in the conversation; and not venturing to reduce the distance that separated them on the bench. She seemed to divine what he was thinking and began to speak, slowly, of the abnormal state of mind in which she found herself.

"I don't know what's the matter with me to-night. I feel like crying, without knowing why. I am filled with a strange inexplicable happiness, and yet I could just weep and weep. Oh, I know—it's the Springtime; all this fragrance that whips my nerves like a lash. I really believe I'm crazy. . . ., Springtime! My best friend—though she has done me only wrong! If ever I have been guilty of any foolish thing in my life, Spring was at the bottom of it. . . . It's youth reborn in us—madness paying us its annual visit. . . . And I—ever faithful to her, adoring her; waiting in this out-of-the-way spot almost a year for her to come, to see her once more in her best clothes, crowned with orange-blossoms like a virgin—a wicked virgin who pays me back for my devotion with betrayal! . . . Just see what I've come to! I am ill—I don't know why—with excess of life, perhaps. She drives me on I don't know where, but certainly where I ought not to go. . . . If it weren't for sheer will-power on my part, I'd collapse in a heap on this bench here. I'm just like a drunken man bending every effort to keep his feet and walk straight."

It was true; she was really ill. Her eyes grew more and more tearful; her body was quivering, shrinking, collapsing, as if life were overflowing within her and escaping through all her pores.

Again she was silent, for a long time, her eyes gazing vacantly into space; then, she murmured, as if in answer to a thought of her own.

"No one ever understood as well as He. He knew everything, felt as nobody ever felt the mysterious hidden workings of Nature; and He sang of Springtime as a god would sing. Hans used to remark that many a time; and it's so."

Without turning her head she added, in a dreamy musing voice.

"Rafael, you don't know *Die Walküre,* do you? You've never heard the Spring Song?"

He shook his head. And Leonora, with her eyes still gazing moonward, her head resting back against her arms, which escaped in all their round, pearly strength from her drooping sleeves, spoke slowly, collecting her memories, recreating in her mind's eye that Wagnerian scene of such intense poetry—the glorification and the triumph of Nature and Love.

Hunding's hut, a barbaric dwelling, hung with

savage trophies of the chase, suggesting the brutish existence of man scarcely yet possessed of the world, in perpetual strife with the elements and with wild animals. The eternal fugitive, forgotten of his father,—Sigmund by name, though he calls himself "Despair," wandering years and years through the forests, harrassed by beasts of prey who take him for one of themselves in his covering of skins, rests at last at the foot of the giant oak that sustains the hut; and as he drinks the hidromel in the horn offered to him by the sweet Siglinda, he gazes into her pure eyes and for the first time becomes aware that Love exists.

The husband, Hunding, the wild huntsman, takes leave of him at the end of the rustic supper: "Your father was the Wolf, and I am of the race of Hunters. Until the break of day, my house protects you; you are my guest; but as soon as the sun rises in the heavens you become my enemy, and we will fight. . . . Woman, prepare the night's drink; and let us be off to bed."

And the exile sits alone beside the fireplace, thinking of his immense loneliness. No home, no family, not even the magic sword promised him by his father the Wolf. And at daybreak, out of the hut that shelters him the enemy will come to slay him. The thought of the woman who allayed his thirst, the sparkle of those pure eyes wrapping him in a gaze of pity and love, is the one thing that sustains him. . . . She comes to him when her wild consort has fallen asleep. She shows him the hilt of the sword plunged into the oak by the god Wotan; nobody can pull it out: it will obey only the hand of him to whom it has been destined by the god.

As she speaks the wandering savage gazes at her in ecstasy, as if she were a white vision revealing to him the existence of something more than might and struggle in the world. It is the voice of Love. Slowly he draws near; embraces her; clasps her to his heart, while the door is pushed open by the breeze and the green forest appears, odorous in the moonlight—nocturnal Springtime, radiant and glorious, wrapped in a mantle of music and perfume.

Siglinda shudders. "Who has come in?" No one—and yet, a Stranger has entered the hovel, opening the door with an invisible hand. And Sigmund, at the inspiration of Love, divines the identity of the visitant. "It is Springtime laughing in the air about your tresses. The storms are gone; gone is the dark solitude. The radiant month of May, a young warrior in an armor of flowers, has come to give chase to bleak Winter, and in all this festival of rejoicing Nature, seeks his sweetheart: Youth. This night, which has brought you to me, is the unending night of Spring and Youth."

And, Leonora was thrilled as she heard in her memory the murmur of the orchestra accompanying the song of tenderness inspired by Spring; the rustle of the forest branches benumbed by the winter, now swaying with the new sap that had flowed into them like a torrent of vitality; and out on the brightly lighted *plazoleta* she could almost see Sigmund and Siglinda clasping in an eternal unseverable embrace, as she had seen them from the wings of the opera, where she would be waiting as a Valkyrie to step out and set an audience wild with her mighty *"Hojotoho!"*

She was feeling the same loneliness and yearning

that Sigmund felt in Hunding's hovel. Without a
family, without a home, wandering over the world,
she longed for someone to lean on, someone to clasp
tenderly to her heart! And it was she who unconsciously, instinctively, had drawn closer to Rafael,
and placed her hand in his.

She was ill. She sighed softly with the appealing entreaty of a child, as if the intense poetry of
that memory of music had shattered the frail rem-
nant of will that had kept her mistress of herself.

"I don't know what's the matter with me to-night.
I feel as though I were dying. . . . But such a sweet
death! So sweet! . . . What madness, Rafael!
How rash it was of us to have seen each other on
such a night! . . ."

And with supplicating eyes, as if entreating forgiveness, she gazed out into the majestic moonlight,
where the silence seemed to be stirring with the palpitation of a new life. She could divine that something was dying within her, that her will lay pros-
trate on the ground, without strength to defend itself.

Rafael, too, was overwhelmed. He held her
clasped against his breast, one of her hands in his.
She was weak, languid, will-less, incapable of resistance; yet he did not feel the brutal passion of
the previous meeting; he did not dare to move.
A sense of infinite tenderness came over him. All he
yearned for was to sit there hour after hour in
contact with that beautiful form, clasping her tightly
to him, making her one with him, as a jewel-case
might guard a jewel.

He whispered mysteriously into her ear, hardly
knowing what he was saying; tender words that

seemed to be coming from someone within him, thrilling him with a tingling, suffocating passion as they
left his lips.

Yes, it was true; that night was the night dreamed
of by the immortal Poet; the wedding night of smiling Youth and of martial May in his armor of flowers.   The fields were quivering voluptuously under
the rays of the moon; and they, two young hearts,
feeling the flutter of Love's wings about their hair,
why should they sit unresponsive there, blind to the
beauty of the night, deaf to the infinite caress that
was echoing from all around?

"Leonora!  Leonora!" moaned Rafael.

He had slipped down from the bench.  Before he
was aware of it, he found himself kneeling at her
feet, clutching her hands, and thrusting his face upward without daring to reach her lips.

She drew weakly back, protesting feebly, with
a girlish plaint:

"No, no; it would hurt me. . . .  I feel that I'm
dying."

"You belong to me," the youth continued with an
exaltation ill-suppressed.  "You belong to me forever; to gaze into your dear eyes, and to murmur
in your ear, your sweet, beautiful, name, and die, if
need be, here.  What do we care for the world and
its opinions?"

And Leonora with weakening resistance, continued to refuse:

"No, no. . . . I must not.  It's a feeling I can't
explain."

And that was so.  The gentle quiver of Nature
under the kiss of Springtime, the intense perfume of
the flower that is the emblem of virginity, had trans-

figured that madcap singer, that adventuress of a career so checkered, who had been violently thrust into her first experience of passion, and now for the first time felt the blush of modesty in the arms of a man. Nature, intoxicating her, shattering her will, seemed to have created a strange virginity in that body so familiar with the call of passion.

"Oh, Rafael, what is happening to me? . . . What's happening to me? It must be love; a new love that I did not think I should ever know. . . . Rafael . . . Rafael, my own boy!"

And weeping softly, she took his head in her hands, pressed her lips to his, and then fell back in her seat with eyes distended, maddened with the joy of that kiss.

"I belong to you, Rafael! Yours . . . but forever. I have always loved you from the first, but now . . . I adore you. . . . For the first time in my life I say that with all my soul."

Hardly able to realize his good fortune, Rafael was thrilled by a deeply generous sentiment. There was nothing he would not give to that woman. . . .

"Yes; you belong to me forever. . . . I will marry you."

But in his dreamy, wild intoxication he saw the artiste's eyes open wide in surprise, as a sad smile flitted across her lips.

"Marry me And why? . . . That's well enough for other women; but me you must love, my darling child, ever so much, as much as you can. . . . Just love me! . . . I believe only in Love!"

# V

"But my dear child, when are we getting to this island of yours? . . . It bores me to be here sitting on this seat, so far away from my little boy, watching his arms get tired from all that rowing. I must kiss him . . even if he says no! It will rest him, I am sure."

And rising to her feet, Leonora took two steps forward in the white boat, though threatening to upset it, and kissed Rafael several times. He lay aside the oars and laughingly defended himself.

"Madcap! We'll never get there at this rate. With rests like this we make very little progress, and I've promised to take you to my island."

Once again he bent to the oars, heading out toward midstream over the moonlit water, as if to vouchsafe the groves on either bank an equal pleasure in the romantic escapade.

It had been one of her caprices—a desire repeated during his visits to the Blue House on some afternoons, in the presence of doña Pepa and the maid, and on every night, as he passed through the opening in the hedge where Leonora's bare arms were waiting for him in the darkness.

For more than a week Rafael had been living in a sweet dream. Never had he imagined that life could be so beautiful. It was a mood of delicious abstraction. The city no longer existed for him. The people that moved about him seemed like so many spectres: his mother and Remedios were invisible beings. Their words he would hear and answer without taking the trouble to look up.

He spent his days in feverish impatience for night to come—that the family might finish supper and leave him free to go to his room, whence he would cautiously tip-toe, as soon as the house was silent and everybody was asleep.

Indifferent to everything foreign to his love, he did not realize the effect his conduct was having on his mother. She had noticed that his door was locked all morning while he slept off the fatigue of a sleepless night. She had already tired of asking him whether he was ill, and of getting the same reply:

"No, mama; I've been working nights; an important study I'm preparing."

It was all his mother could do on such occasions to restrain herself from shouting "Liar!" Two nights she had gone up to his room, to find the door locked and the keyhole dark. Her son was not inside. She would lie awake for him now; and every morning, somewhat before dawn, she would hear him softly open the outside door and tip-toe up the stairs, perhaps in his stocking-feet.

The female Spartan said nothing however, hoarding her indignation in silence, complaining only to don Andrés of the recrudescence of a madness that was upsetting all her plans. Through his numerous henchmen the counselor kept watch upon the young man. His spies followed Rafael cautiously through the night, up to the gate of the Blue House.

"What a scandal!" exclaimed doña Bernarda.

·'At night, too! He'll wind up by bringing her into this house! Can it be that that simpleton of a doña Pepita is blind to all this?"

And there was Rafael, unaware of the storm that was gathering about his head, no longer deigning even to speak to Remedios, or look at her, as with her head bowed like a sulky goat, she went around stifling her tears at the memory of those happy strolls in the orchard under doña Bernarda's surveillance.

The deputy had eyes for nothing outside of the Blue House; his happiness had blinded him. The one thing that annoyed him was the necessity of hiding his joy—his inability to make his good fortune public, so that all his admirers might learn of it.

He would willingly have gone back to the days of the Roman decadence, when the love affairs of the powerful became matters of national adoration.

"What do I care for their gossip" he once said to Leonora. "I love you so much that I'd like to see the whole city worship you in public. I'd like to snatch you up in my arms, and appear upon the bridge at high noon, before a concourse stupefied by your beauty: 'Am I or am I not your *"quefe"?*' I'd ask. 'Well, if I am, adore this woman, who is my very soul and without whom I could not live. The affection which you have for me you must have also for her.' And I'd do just as I say if it were possible."

"Silly boy . . . adorable child," she had replied, showering him with kisses, brushing his dark beard with her soft, quivering lips.

And it was during one of their meetings—when

their words were broken by sudden impulses of affection, and their lips were tightly pressed together
—that Leonora had expressed her capricious desire.

"I'm stifling in this house. I hate to caress you
inside four walls, as if you were only a passing whim.
This is unworthy of you. You are Love, who came
to seek me out on the most beautiful of nights. I like
you better in the open air. You look more handsome
to me then, and I feel younger."

And recalling those trips down the river about
which Rafael had told her so many times when they
were only friends—that islet with its curtains of
reeds, the willows bending over the water and the
nightingale singing from its hiding-place—she had
asked him, eagerly:

"What night are you going to take me there? It's
a whim of mine, a wild idea; but, what does love
exist for, if not to make people do the foolish things
that sweeten life? . . . Carry me off in your boat!
The bark that bore you there will transport the two
of us to your enchanted island; we will spend the
whole night in the open air."

And Rafael, who was flattered by the idea of taking his love publicly down the river, through the
slumbering countryside, unfastened his boat at midnight under the bridge and rowed it to a canebrake
near Leonora's orchard.

An hour later they emerged through the opening
in the hedge, arm in arm, laughing at the mischievous escapade, disturbing the majestic silence of the
landscape with noisy, insolent kisses.

They got into the boat, and with a favoring current, began to descend the Júcar, lulled by the murmur of the river as it glided between the high mud-banks covered with reeds that bent low over the water and formed mysterious hiding places.

Leonora clapped her hands with delight. She threw over her neck the silk shawl with which she had covered her head. She unbuttoned her light traveling coat, and inhaled with deep enjoyment the moist, somewhat muggy breeze that was curling along the surface of the river. Her hand trembled as it dipped into the water from time to time.

How beautiful it was! All by themselves, and wandering about, as if the world did not exist; as if all Nature belonged to them, to them alone! Here they were, slipping past clusters of slumbering houses, leaving the city far behind. And nobody had suspected that passion, which in its enthusiasm had broken its chains and left its mysterious lair to have the heavens and the fields for sympathetic witnesses. Leonora would have wished that the night should never end; that the waning moon, which seemed to have been slashed by a sword, should stop eternally in the sky to wrap them forever in its feeble, dying light; that the river should be endless, and the boat float on and on until, overwhelmed by so much love, they should breathe the last gasp of life away in a kiss as tenuous as a sigh.

"If you could only know how grateful I am to you for this excursion, Rafael! . . . I'm happy, so happy. Never have I had such a night as this. But where is the island? Have we gone astray, as you did the night of the flood?"

No! At last they reached the place. There Rafael had spent many an afternoon hidden in the bushes, cut off by the encircling waters, dreaming that he was an adventurer on the virgin prairies or the vast rivers of America, performing exploits he had read about in the novels of Fenimore Cooper and Mayne Reid.

A tributary joined the Júcar at this point, emptying gently into the main stream from under a thicket of reeds and trees that formed a triumphal arch of foliage. At the confluence rose the island—a tiny piece of land almost level with the water, but as fresh as green and fragrant as an aquatic bouquet. The banks were lined with dense clumps of cane, and a few willows that bent their hairy foliage low over the water, forming dark vaults through which the boat could make its way.

The two lovers entered the shade. The curtain of branches concealed them from the river; a bare tear of moonlight managed to filter through the mane of willows.

Leonora felt a first sense of uneasiness in this dark, damp, cave-like haunt. Invisible animals took to the water with dull splashes as they heard the boat's bow touch the mud of the bank. The actress clutched her lover's arm with nervous pleasure.

"Here we are," murmured Rafael. "Hold on to something and get out . . Careful, careful! Don't you want to hear the nightingale? Here we have him. Listen."

It was true. In one of the willows, at the other side of the island, the mysterious bird was trilling from his hiding place, a dizzying shower of notes, which broke at the crescendo of the musical whirlpool into a plaint as soft and long-sustained as a golden thread stretched in the silence of the night across the river, that seemed to be applauding with its hushed murmur. To get nearer, the lovers went up through the rushes, stopping, bending over at each step, to keep the branches from crackling underneath their feet.

Favoring moisture had covered the islet with an exuberant undergrowth. Leonora repressed exclamations of glee as she found her feet caught in meshes of reeds or received the rude caresses of the branches that snapped back, as Rafael went ahead, and brushed against her face. She called for help in a muffled voice; and Rafael, laughing also, would hold out his hand to her, taking her finally to the very foot of the tree where the nightingale was singing.

The bird, divining the presence of intruders, ceased his song. Doubtless he had heard the rustle of their clothing as they sat down at the foot of the tree, or the tender words they were murmuring into each other's ear.

Over all, the silence of slumbering Nature reigned —that silence made up of a thousand sounds, harmonizing and blending in one majestic calm; the murmur of the water, the stirring of the foliage, the mysterious movements of unseen creatures crawling along under the leaves or patiently boring their winding galleries in the creaking trunks.

The nightingale began again to sing, timidly, like an artist afraid of an impending interruption. He uttered a few disconnected notes with anxious rests between them—love sighs they seemed, broken by sobs of passion. Then gradually he took courage, regained self-confidence, and entered on his full song, just as a soft breeze rose, swept over the island, and set all the trees and reeds rustling in mysterious accompaniment.

The bird gradually grew intoxicated with the sound of his own trilling, cadenced, voice; one could almost see him up there in the thick darkness, panting, ardent, in the spasm of his musical inspiration, utterly engrossed in his own beautiful little world of song, overwhelmed by the charm of his own artistry.

But the bird had ceased his music when the two lovers awoke in a tight embrace, still in ecstasy from the song of love to which they had fallen asleep. Leonora was resting a dishevelled head on Rafael's shoulder, caressing his neck with an eager, wearied breathing, whispering in his ear, random, incoherent words that still were vibrant with emotion.

How happy she was there! Everything comes for true love! Many a time, during the days of her unkindness to him, she had looked out from her balcony upon the river winding down through the slumbering countryside; and she had thought with rapture of a stroll some day through that immense garden on Rafael's arm—of gliding, gliding down the Júcar, to that very island.

"My love is an ancient thing," she murmured. "Do you suppose, I have been loving you only since the other night? No, I have loved you for a long, long time . . . But don't you go and get conceited on that account, *su señoria!* I don't know how it began: It must have been when you were away in Madrid. When I saw you again I knew that I was lost. If I still resisted, it was because I was a wise woman; because I saw things clearly. Now I'm mad and I've thrown my better judgment to the winds. God knows what will become of us . . . But come what may, love me, Rafael, love me. Swear that you'll love me always. It would be cruel to desert me after awakening a passion like this."

And, in an impulse of dread, she nestled closer against his breast, sank her hands into his hair, lifted her head back to kiss him avidly on the face, the forehead, the eyes, the lips, nibbling playfully, tenderly at his nose and chin, yet with an affectionate vehemence that drew cries of mock protest from Rafael.

"Madcap!" he muttered, smiling. "You're hurting me."

Leonora looked steadily at him out of her two great eyes that were a-gleam with love.

"I could eat you up," she murmured. "I feel like devouring you, my heaven, my king, my god . . . What have you given me, tell me, little boy? How have you been able to fascinate me, make me feel a passion that I never, never felt before?"

And again they fell asleep.

Rafael stirred in his lover's arms, and suddenly sat up.

"It must be late. How many hours have we been here, do you suppose?"

"Many, many hours," Leonora answered sadly. "Hours of happiness always go so fast."

It was still dark. The moon had set. They arose and, hand in hand, groping their way along, they reached the boat. The splash of the oars began again to sound along the dark stream.

Suddenly the nightingale again piped gloomily in the willow wood, as if in farewell to a departing dream.

"Listen, my darling," said Leonora. "The poor little fellow is bidding us good-bye. Just hear how plaintively he says farewell."

And in the strange exhiliration that comes from fatigue, Leonora felt the flames of art flaring up within her, seething through her organism from head to foot.

A melody from *Die Meistersinger* came to her mind, the hymn that the good people of Nüremberg sing when Hans Sachs, their favorite singer, as bounteous and gentle as the Eternal Father, steps out on the platform for the contest in poetry. It was the song that the poet-minstrel, the friend of Albrecht Dürer, wrote in honor of Luther when the great Reformation broke; and the prima donna, rising to her feet in the stern, and returning the greeting of the nightingale began:

> *"Sorgiam, che spunta il dolce albor,*
> *cantar ascolto in mezzo ai fior*
> *voluttuoso un usignol*
> *spiegando a noi l'amante vol! . . ."*

Her ardent, powerful voice seemed to make the dark surface of the river tremble; it rolled in harmonious waves across the fields, and died away in the foliage of the distant island, whence the nightingale trilled an answer that was like a fainting sigh. Leonora tried to reproduce with her lips the majestic sonorousness of the Wagnerian chorus, mimicking the rumbling accompaniment of the orchestra,

while Rafael beat the water with his oars in time
with the pious, exalted melody with which the great
Master had turned to popular poetry adequately to
greet the outbreak of Reform.

They went on and on up the river against the current, Leonora singing, Rafael bending over the oars,
moving his sinewy arms like steel springs. He kept
the boat inshore, where the current was not so strong.
At times low branches brushed the heads of the
lovers, and drops of dew fell on their faces. Many
a time the boat glided through one of the verdant
archways of foliage, making its way slowly through
the lily-pads; and the green overhead would tremble
with the harmonious violence of that wonderful
voice, as vibrant and as resonant as a great silver
bell.

Day had not yet dawned—the *dolce albor* of
Hans Sachs' song—but at any moment the rosy rim
of sunrise would begin to climb the sky.

Rafael was hurrying to get back as soon as possible. Her sonorous voice of such tremendous range
seemed to be awakening the whole countryside. In
one cottage a window lighted up. Several times
along the river-bank, as they rowed past the reeds,
Rafael thought he heard the noise of snapping
branches, the cautious footsteps of spies who were
following them.

"Hush, my darling. You had better stop singing; they'll recognize you. They'll guess who you
are."

They reached the bank where they had embarked.
Leonora leaped ashore. They must separate there;
for she insisted on going home alone. And their
parting was sweet, slow, endless.

"Good-bye, my love; one kiss. Until tomorrow . . . no, later—today."

She walked a few steps up the bank, and then suddenly ran back to snuggle again in her lover's arms.

"Another, my prince . . . the last."

Day was breaking, announced not by the song of the lark, as in the garden of Shakespere's lovers at Verona, but by the sound of carts, creaking over country roads in the distance, and by a languid, sleepy melody of an orchard boy.

"Good-bye, Rafael . . . Now I must really go. They'll discover us."

Wrapping her coat about her she hurried away, waving a final farewell to him with her handkerchief.

Rafael rowed upstream toward the city. That part of the trip—he reflected—alone, tired, and struggling against the current, was the one bad part of the wonderful night. When he moored his boat near the bridge it was already broad day. The windows of the river houses were opening. Over the bridge carts laden with produce for the market were rumbling, and orchard women were going by with huge baskets on their heads. All these people looked down with interest on their deputy. He must have spent the night fishing. And this news passed from one to the other, though not a trace of fishing tackle was visible in the boat. How they envied rich folks, who could sleep all day and spend their time just as they pleased!

Rafael jumped ashore. All that curiosity he was attracting annoyed him. His mother would know everything by the time he got home!

As he climbed slowly and wearily, his arms numb from rowing, to the bridge, he heard his name called.

Don Andrés was standing there, gazing at him out of those yellow eyes of his, scowling through his wrinkles with an expression of stern authority.

"You've given me a fine night, Rafael. I know where you've been. I saw you row off last night with that woman; and plenty of my friends were on hand to follow you and find out just where you went. You've been on the island all night; that woman was singing away like a lunatic. . . . God of Gods, boy! Aren't there any houses in the world? Do you have to play the band when you're having an affair, so that everybody in the Kingdom can come and look?"

The old man was truly riled; all the more because he was himself the secretive, the dexterous, libertine, adopting every precaution not to be discovered in his "weaknesses." Was it anger or envy that he felt on seeing a couple enough in love with each other to be fearless of gossip and indifferent to danger, to throw prudence to the winds, and flaunt their passion before the world with the reckless insolence of happiness?

"Besides, your mother knows everything. She's discovered what you've been up to, these nights past. She knows you haven't been in your room. You're going to break that woman's heart!"

And with paternal severity he went on to speak of doña Bernarda's despair, of the danger to the future of the House, of the obligations they were under to don Matías, of the solemn promise given, of that poor girl waiting to be married!

Rafael walked along in silence and like an automaton. That old man's chatter brought down around his head, like a swarm of pestering mosquitoes, all the provoking, irritating obligations of his life. He felt like a man rudely awakened by a tactless servant in the middle of a sweet dream. His lips were still tingling with Leonora's kisses! His whole body was aglow with her gentle warmth! And here was this old curmudgeon coming along with a sermon on "duty," "family," "what they would say"—as if love amounted to nothing in this life! It was a plot against his happiness, and he felt stirred to the depths with a sense of outrage and revolt.

They had reached the entrance to the Brull mansion. Rafael was fumbling about for the key-hole with his key.

"Well," growled the old man. "What have you got to say to all this? What do you propose to do? Answer me! Haven't you got a tongue in your head?"

"I," replied the young man energetically—"will do as I please."

Don Andrés jumped as though he had been stung. My, how this Rafael had changed! . . . Never before had he seen that gleam of aggressiveness, arrogance, belligerency in the eye of the boy!

"Rafael, is that the way you answer me,—a man who has known you since you were born? Is that the tone of voice you use toward one who loves you as your own father loved you?"

"I'm of age, if you don't mind my saying so!" Rafael replied. "I'm not going to put up any longer with this comedy of being a somebody on the street and a baby in my own house. Henceforth just keep your advice to yourself until I ask for it. Good day, sir!"

As he went up the stairs he saw his mother on the first landing, in the semi-darkness of the closed house, illumined only by the light that entered through the window gratings. She stood there, erect, frowning, tempestuous, like a statue of Avenging Justice.

But Rafael did not waver. He went straight on up the stairs, fearless and without a tremor, like a proprietor who had been away from home for some time and strides arrogantly back into a house that is all his own.

# VI

"You're right, don Andrés. Rafael is not my son. He has changed. That wanton woman has made another man of him. Worse, a thousand times worse, than his father! Crazy over the huzzy! Capable of trampling on me if I should step between him and her. You complain of his lack of respect to you! Well, what about me? . . . You wouldn't have thought it possible! The other morning, when he came into the house, he treated me just as he treated you. Only a few words, but plain enough! He'll do just as he pleases, or—what amounts to the same thing—he'll keep up his affair with that woman until he wearies of her, or else blows up in one grand debauch, like his father. . . . My God! And that's what I've suffered for all these years. That's what I get for sacrificing myself, day in day out, trying to make somebody out of him!"

The austere doña Bernarda, dethroned by her son's resolute rebelliousness, wept as she said this. In her tears of a mother's grief there was something also of the chagrin of the authoritarian on finding in her own home a will rebellious to hers and stronger than hers.

Between sobs she told don Andrés how her son had been carrying on since his declaration of independence. He was no longer cautious about spend-

ing the night away from home. He was coming
in now in broad daylight; and, afternoons, with his
meals "still in his mouth" as she said, he would take
the road to the Blue House, on the run almost, as
if he could not get to perdition soon enough. The
dead hand of his father was upon him!

All you had to do was look at him. His face
discolored, yellow, pale; his skin drawn tight over
his cheekbones; and—the only sign of life—the
fire that gleamed in his eyes like a spark of wild
joy! Oh, a curse was on the family! They were
all alike . . .!

The mother did her best to conceal the truth
from Remedios. Poor girl! She was going about
crestfallen and in deep dejection, unable to explain
Rafael's sudden withdrawal.

The matter had to be kept secret; and that was
what held doña Bernarda's rage within bounds during her rapid, heated exchanges with her son.

Perhaps everything would come out all right in
the end—something unforeseen would turn up to
undo the evil spell that had been cast over Rafael.
And in this hope she used every effort to keep
Remedios and her father from learning what had
happened. She feigned contentment in their presence, and invented a thousand pretexts—studies,
work, even illness—to justify her son's neglect of
his "fiancée." At the same time, the disconsolate
mother feared the people around her—the gossip of
a small town, bored with itself, ever on the alert,
hunting for something interesting to talk about and
get scandalized about.

The news of Rafael's affair spread like wildfire
meanwhile, considerably magnified as it passed from

mouth to mouth. People told hair-raising tales of
that expedition down the river, of walks through the
orange groves, of nights spent at doña Pepa's house,
Rafael entering in the dark, in his stocking feet,
like a thief; of silhouettes of the lovers outlined in
suggestive poses against the bedroom curtain; of
their appearing in windows their arms about each
other's waists, looking at the stars—everything
sworn to by voluntary spies, who could say "I saw
it with my own eyes"—persons who had spent whole
nights, on the river-bank, behind some fence, in some
clump of bushes, to surprise the deputy on his way
to or from his assignations.

In the cafés or at the Casino, the men openly
envied Rafael, commenting with eyes a-glitter on
his good fortune. That fellow had been born under
a lucky star! But later at home they would add
their stern voices to the chorus of indignant women.
What a scandal! A deputy, a public man, a "personage" who ought to set an example for others!
That was a disgrace to the constituency! And
when the murmur of general protest reached the ears
of doña Bernarda, she lifted her hands to heaven
in despair. Where would it all end! Where would
it all end! That son of hers was bent on ruining
himself!

Don Matías, the rustic millionaire, said nothing;
and, in the presence of doña Bernarda, at least,
pretended to know nothing. His interest in a marriage connection with the Brull family counselled
prudence. He, too, hoped that it would all blow
over, prove to be the blind infatuation of a young
man. Feeling himself a father, more or less, to
the boy, he thought of giving Rafael just a bit of

advice when he came upon him in the street one
day. But he desisted after a word or two. A proud
glance of the youth completely floored him, making
him feel like the poor orange-grower of former
days, who had cringed before the majestic, gran-
diose don Ramón!

Rafael was intrenched in haughty silence. He
needed no advice. But alas! When at night he
reached his beloved's house—it seemed to be redolent with the very perfume of her, as if the furniture,
the curtains, the very walls about her had absorbed
the essence of her spirit—he felt the strain of that
insistent gossip, of the persecution of an entire city
that had fixed its eyes upon his love.

Two against a multitude! With the serene immodesty of the ancient idylls, they had abandoned
themselves to passion in a stupid, narrow environment, where sprightly gossip was the most appre-
ciated of the moral talents!

Leonora grew sad. She smiled as usual; she
flattered him with the same worship, as if he were
an idol; she was playful and gay; but in moments
of distraction, when she did not notice that he was
watching, Rafael would surprise a cast of bitterness
about her lips—and a sinister light in her eyes, the
reflection of painful thoughts.

She referred with acrid mirth one night to what
people were saying about them. Everything was
found out sooner or later in that city! The gossip
had gotten even to the Blue House! Her kitchen
woman had hinted that she had better not walk
so much along the river front—she might catch
malaria. On the market place the sole topic of
conversation was that night trip down the Júcar

. . . the deputy, sweating his life out over the oars, and she waking half the country up with her strange songs! . . . And she laughed, but with a hard, harsh laugh of affected gaiety that showed the nervousness underneath, though without a word of complaint.

Rafael remorsefully reflected that she had foreseen all that in first repelling his advances. He admired her resignation. She would have been justified in rebuking him for the harm he had done her. As it was, she was not even telling him all she knew! Ah, the wretches! To harass an innocent woman so! She had loved him, given herself to him, bestowed on him the royal gift of her person. And the deputy began to hate his city, for repaying in insult and scandal the wondrous happiness she had conferred on its "chief"!

On another night Leonora received him with a smile that frightened him. She was affecting a mood of hectic cheerfulness, trying to drown her worries by sheer force, overwhelming her lover with a flood of light, frivolous chatter; but suddenly, at the limit of her endurance, she gave way, and in the middle of a caress, burst into tears and sank to a divan, sobbing as if her heart would break.

"Why what's the matter? What has happened . . .?"

For a time she could not answer, her voice was too choked with weeping. At last, however, between sobs, burying her tear-stained face on Rafael's shoulder, she began to speak, completely crushed, fainting from virtual prostration.

She could stand it no longer! The torture was

becoming unbearable. It was useless for her to pretend. She knew as well as he what people were saying in the city. They were spied upon continuously. On the roads, in the orchard, along the river, there were people constantly on the watch for something new to report. That passion of hers, so sweet, so youthful, so sincere, was a butt of public laughter, a theme for idle tongues, who flayed her as if she were a common street-woman, because she had been good to him, because she had not been cruel enough to watch a young man writhe in the torment of passion, indifferently. . . . But though this persecution from a scandalized public was bad enough, she did not mind it. Why should she care what those stupid people said? But, alas, there were others—the people around Rafael, his friends, his family, . . . his mother!

Leonora sat silent for a moment, as if waiting to see the effect of that last word; unless, indeed, she were hesitating, out of delicacy, to include her lover's family in her complaint. The young man shrank with a terrible presentiment. Doña Bernarda was not the woman to stand by idle and resigned in the face of opposition, even from him!

"I see . . . mother!" he said in a stifled voice. "She has been up to something. Tell me what it is. Don't be afraid. To me you are dearer than anything else in the world."

"Well . . . there is auntie . . ." Leonora resumed; and Rafael remembered that doña Pepa, remarking his assiduous visits to the Blue House, had thought her niece might be contemplating marriage. In the afternoon, Leonora explained, she

had had a scene with her aunt. Doña Pepa had
gone into town to confession, and on coming out
of church had met doña Bernarda. Poor old
woman! Her abject terror on returning home betrayed the intense emotion Rafael's mother had succeeded in wakening in her. Leonora, her niece, her
idol, lay in the dust, stripped of that blind, enthusiastic, affectionate trust her aunt had always had for
her. All the gossip, all the echoes of Leonora's
adventurous life, that had—heretofore but feebly—
come to her ears, the old lady had never believed,
regarding them as the work of envy. But now they
had been repeated to her by doña Bernarda, by a
lady "in good standing," a good Christian, a person
incapable of falsehood. And then after rehearsing
that scandalous biography, Rafael's mother had
come to the shocking effrontery with which her niece
and Rafael were rousing the whole city; flaunting
their wrong-doing in the face of the public; and
turning her home, the respectable, irreproachable
home of doña Pepa, into a den of vice, a brothel!

And the poor woman had wept like a child in
her niece's presence, adjuring her to "abandon the
wicked path of transgression," shuddering with horror at the great responsibility she, doña Pepa, had
unwittingly assumed before God. All her life she
had labored and prayed and fasted to keep her soul
clean. She had thought herself almost in a state
of grace, only to awaken suddenly and find herself
in the very midst of sin through no fault of her own
—all on account of her niece, who had converted her
holy, her pure, her pious home into an ante-chamber
of hell! And it was the poor woman's superstitious
terror, the conviction of damnation that had seized

on doña Pepa's simple soul, that wounded Leonora most deeply.

"They've robbed me of all I had in the world," she murmured desperately, "of the affection of the only dear one left after my father died. I am not the child of former days to auntie; that is apparent from the way she looks at me, the way she shuns me, avoiding all contact with me. . . . And just because of you, because I love you, because I was not cruel to you! Oh, that night! How I shall suffer for it! . . . How clearly I foresaw how it would all end!"

Rafael was humiliated, crushed, filled with shame and remorse at the suffering that had fallen upon this woman, because she had given herself to him. What was he to do? The time had come to prove himself the strong, the resourceful man, able to protect the beloved woman in her moment of danger. But where should he strike first to defend her? . . .

Leonora lifted her head from her lover's shoulder, and withdrew from his embrace. She wiped away her tears and rose to her feet with the determination of irrevocable resolution.

"I have made up my mind. It hurts me very much to say what I am going to say; but I can't help it. It will do you no good to say 'no'—I cannot stay under this roof another day. Everything is over between my aunt and me. Poor old woman! The dream I cherished was to care for her lovingly, tenderly till she died in my arms, be to her what I failed to be to father. . . . But they have opened her eyes. To her I am nothing but a sinner now and my presence upsets everything for her. . . . I must go away. I've already told Beppa to

pack my things. . . . Rafael, my love, this is our
last night together. . . . To-morrow . . . and you
will never see me again."

The youth recoiled as if someone had struck him
in the breast.

"Going? Going . . . ? And you can say that
coolly, simply, just like that? You are leaving me
. . . this way . . . just when we are happiest . . . ?"

But soon he had himself in hand again. This
surely could be nothing more than a passing impulse, a notion arrived at in a flash of anger. Of
course she did not really mean to go! She must
think things over, see things clearly. That was a
crazy idea! Desert her Rafaelito? Absurd!
Impossible!

Leonora smiled sadly. She had expected him to
talk that way. She, too, had suffered much, ever
so much, before deciding to do it! It made her
shudder to think that within two days she would
be off again, alone, wandering through Europe,
caught up again in that wild, tumultuous life of art
and love, after tasting the full sweetness of the most
powerful passion she had ever known—of what she
believed was her "first love." It was like putting
to sea in a tempest with destination unknown. She
loved him, adored him, worshipped him, more than
ever now that she was about to lose him.

"Well, why are you going?" the young man asked.
"If you love me, why are you forsaking me?"

"Just because I love you, Rafael. . . . Because
I want you to be happy."

For her to remain would mean ruin for him: a
long battle with his mother, who was an implacable,
a merciless foe. Doña Bernarda might be killed,

but never conquered! Oh, no! How horrible!
Leonora knew what filial cruelty was! How had
she treated her father? She must not now come
between a son and a mother! Was she, perhaps,
a creature accursed, born forever to corrupt with
her very name the sacredest, purest relations on
earth?

"No, you must be good, my heart. I must go
away. We can't go on loving each other here.
I'll write to you, I'll let you know all I'm doing.
. . . You'll hear from me every day, if I have to
write from the North Pole! But you must stay!
Don't drive your mother to despair! Shut your
eyes to the poor woman's injustice! For after all,
she is doing it all out of her immense love for
you. . . . Do you imagine I am glad to be leaving
you—the greatest happiness I have ever known?"

And she threw her arms about Rafael, kissing
him over and over again, caressing his bowed, pen-
sive head, within which a tempest of conflicting ideas
and resolutions was boiling.

So those bonds which he had come to believe
eternal were to be broken? So he was to lose so
easily that beauty which the world had admired,
the possession of which had made him feel himself
the first among men? She talked of a love from a
distance, of a love persisting through years of separation, travel, all the hazards of a wandering life;
she promised to write to him every day! . . . Write
to him . . . from the arms of another man, perhaps! No! He would never give up such a treasure; never!

"You shall not go," he answered at last decisively.
"A love like ours is not ended so easily. Your

flight would be a disgrace to me—it would look as
if I had affronted you in some way, as if you were
tired of me."

Deep in his soul he felt eager to make some
chivalrous gesture. She was going away because
she had loved him! He should stay behind, sad
and resigned like a maid abandoned by a lover, and
with the sense of having harmed her on his conscience! *Ira de diós!* He, as a man, could not
stand by with folded arms accepting the abnegation
of a woman, to stick tied to his mother's apron-
strings in boobified contentment. Even girls ran
away from home and parents sometimes, in the grip
of a powerful love; and he, a man, a man "in the
public eye" also—was he to let a beautiful girl like
Leonora go away sorrowful and in tears, so that
he could keep the respect of a city that bored him
and the affection of a mother who had never really
loved him? Besides, what sort of a love was it
that stepped aside in a cowardly, listless way like
that, when a woman was at stake, a woman for
whom far richer, far more powerful men than he,
men bound to life by attractions that he had never
dreamed of in his countrified existence, had died or
gone to ruin? . . .

"You shall not go," he repeated, with sullen obstinacy. "I won't give up my happiness so easily.
And if you insist on going, we will go together."

Leonora rose to her feet all quivering. She had
been expecting that; her heart had told her it was
coming. Flee together! Have her appear like an
adventuress, drawing Rafael on, tearing him from
his mother's arms after crazing him with love? Oh,
no! Thanks! She had a conscience! She did

not care to burden it with the execration of a whole
city. Rafael must consider the matter calmly, face
the situation bravely. She must go away alone.
Afterwards, later on, she would see. They might
chance to meet again; perhaps in Madrid, when the
Cortes reassembled! He would be there, and alone;
she could find a place at the *Real*, singing for nothing if that should prove necessary.

But Rafael writhed angrily at her resistance. He
could not live without her! A single night without
seeing her would mean despair. He would end as
Macchia ended! He would shoot himself!

And he seemed to mean it. His eyes were fixed
on the floor as if he were staring at his own corpse,
lying there on the pavement, motionless, covered
with blood, a revolver in its stiffened hand.

"Oh, no! How horrible! Rafael, my Rafael!"
Leonora groaned, clasping him around the neck,
hanging upon him in terror.

Her lover continued to protest. He was free.
Had he been a married man; if, in his flight, he
were leaving a wife behind to cry betrayal, or children calling for his help in vain, it would all be a
different matter. She could properly feel the repug-
nance of a kind heart unwilling that love should
mean a shattered home! But whom was he abandoning? A mother, who, in a short time, would
find consolation in the thought that he was well and
happy, a mother jealous of any rivalry in her son's
affection, and to that jealousy willing to sacrifice
his very happiness! Any harm an elopement would
bring would by no means be irreparable. No, they
must go away together, parade their love through
the whole world!

But Leonora, lowering her head again, repeated feebly:

"No, my mind is made up. I must go alone. I haven't the strength to face a mother's hatred."

Rafael flushed indignantly:

"Why not say outright that you don't love me. You're tired of me, and of this environment. The hankering for your old life has come over you again; your old world is calling!"

The actress fixed her great, luminous, tear-stained eyes upon him. And they were filled with tenderness and pity.

"Tired of you! . . . When I have never felt such desperation as tonight! You say I want my old life back. You don't realize that to leave here seems like entering a den of torture. . . . Oh, dear heart, you'll never know how much I love you."

"Well, then . . . ?"

And to tell everything, to spare no detail of the danger he would face after separation, Rafael spoke of the life he would lead alone with his mother in that dull, unspeakable city. Leonora was assuming that affection played some part in his mother's indignant opposition. Well, doña Bernarda did love him—agreed: he was her only son; but ambition was the decisive thing in her schemes, her passion for the aggrandizement of the House—the controlling motive of her whole life. She was openly, frankly, using him as security in an alliance she was planning with a great fortune. She wanted to marry him to money: and if Leonora were to go, if he were left alone, forsaken, then despair—and time, which can do all things—would break his will; and eventually he would succumb, like a victim at the altar,

who, in his terror and abasement, does not sense
the real significance of the sacrifice forced upon
him.

The words reached a jealous spot in Leonora's
heart. All the scattered rumors that had come to
her ears in former days now echoed in her memory.
She knew that Rafael was telling the truth. The
man she loved, given away by his mother—to another woman! . . . Lost forever if she lost him
now! . . . And her eyes opened wide with horror
and revulsion.

"And I refuse, Leonora, do you understand? I
refuse!" continued her lover with unaffected resolution. "I belong to you, you are the only woman I
love. I shall follow you all over the world, even
against your wishes, to be your servant, see you,
speak to you, and there are not millions enough in
the world to stop me!"

"Oh, my darling! My darling! You love me,
you love me—as I love you!"

And in a frenzy of passion she fell impetuously,
madly upon him, clutching him in her arms like a
fury. In her caresses Rafael felt an intensity that
almost frightened him. The room seemed to be
whirling about him. Trembling, limp and weak,
he sank to the divan, overwhelmed, pounded to
pieces, it seemed, by that vehement adoration, that
caught him up and carried him away like a tumultuous avalanche. His senses left him in that trembling confusion, and he closed his eyes.

When he opened them, the room was dark.
Around his neck he could feel a gentle arm that was
tenderly sustaining him, and Leonora was whispering in his ear.

Agreed! They would go together: to continue their love duet in some charming place, where nobody knew them, where envy and vulgarity would not disturb. Leonora knew every nook in the world. She would have none of Nice and the other cities of the Blue Coast, pretty places, coquettish, bepowdered and rouged like women fresh from their dressing tables! Besides there would be too many people there. Venice was better. They would thread the narrow, solitary silent canals there, stretched out in a gondola, kissing each other between smiles, pitying the poor unfortunate mortals crossing the bridges over them, unaware of how great a love was gliding beneath their feet!

But no, Venice is a sad place after all: when it rains, it rains and rains! Naples rather; Naples! *Viva Napoli!* And Leonora clapped her hands in glee! Live in perpetual sunshine, freedom, freedom, freedom to love openly, as nakedly as the *lazzaroni* walk about the streets! She owned a house in Naples,—at Posilipo, that is—a *villino*, in pink stucco, a dainty little place with fig trees, nopals and parasol pines, that ran in a grove down a steep promontory to the sea! They would fish in the bay there—it was as smooth and blue as a looking-glass! And afternoons he would row her out to sea, and she would sing, looking at the waters ablaze with the sunset, at the plume of smoke curling up from Vesuvius, at the immense white city with its endless rows of windows flaming like plaques of gold in the afterglow. Like gipsies they would wander through the countless towns dotting the shores of the miraculous Bay; kissing on the open sea among the fisherboats, to the accompaniment of passionate Neapolitan boat-songs; spending whole nights in the open air, lying in each other's arms on the sands, hearing the pearly laughter of mandolins in the distance, just as that night on the island, they had heard the nightingale! "Oh, Rafael, my god, my king! How wonderful!"

When day dawned, they were still sitting there weaving fanciful plans for the future, arranging all the details of their elopement. She would leave Alcira as soon as possible. He would join her two days later, when all suspicion had been quieted, when everybody would imagine she was far, far away. Where would they meet? At first they thought of Marseilles, but that was a long way off! Then they thought of Barcelona. But that, too, meant hours of travel, when hours, minutes, counted for so much. It seemed utterly incredible that they could live two days without each other! No, the sooner they met again the better! And, bargaining with time like peasants in a market, at last they chose the nearest city possible, Valencia.

For love—true love—is fond of brazenness!

## VII

They had just finished lunch among the trunks and boxes that occupied a great part of Leonora's room in the *Hôtel de Roma* in Valencia.

For the first time they were at a table in familiar intimacy, with no other witness than Beppa, who was quite accustomed to every sort of surprise in her mistress's adventurous career. The faithful maid was examining Rafael with a respectful kindliness, as if he were a new idol that must share the unswerving devotion she showed for Leonora.

This was the first moment of tranquillity and happiness the young man had tasted for some days. The old hotel, with its spacious rooms, its high ceilings, its darkened corridors, its monastic silence, seemed to him a veritable abode of delight, a grateful place of refuge where for once he would be free of the gossip and the strife that had been oppressing him like a belt of steel. Besides, he could already feel the exotic charm that lingers around harbors and great railroad terminals. Everything about the place, from the macaroni of the lunch, and the Chianti in its straw-covered, heavy-paunched bottle, to the musical, incorrect Spanish of the hotel-proprietors—fleshy, massive men with huge mustaches in Victor Emmanuel style—spoke of flight, of delightful seclusion in that land so glowingly described by Leonora.

She had made an appointment with him in that

hotel, a favorite haunt of artists. Somewhat off the main thoroughfares, the "Roma" occupies one whole side of a sleepy, peaceful, aristocratic square with no noise save the shouting of cab-drivers and the beating of horses' hoofs.

Rafael had arrived on the first morning train—and with no baggage; like a schoolboy playing truant, running off with just the clothes he had on his back. The two days since Leonora left Alcira had been days of torture to him. The singer's flight was the talk of the town. People were scandalized at the amount of luggage she had. Counted over in the imagination of that imaginative city, it eventually came to fill all the carts in the province.

The man who knew the business to the bottom was Cupido, the barber, who had dispatched the trunks and cases for her. He knew where the dangerous woman was bound, and he kept it so secret that everybody found it out before the train started. She was going back to Italy! He himself had checked and labelled the baggage to the Customs' House at the frontier—cases as big as a house, man! Trunks he could have lain down comfortable in, with his two "Chinamen" to boot! And the women, as they listened to his tale, applauded the departure with undissimulated pleasure. They had been liberated from a great danger. Joy go with her!

Rafael kept quite to himself. He was vexed at the curiosity of people, at the scoffing sympathy of his friends who condoled with him that his happiness was ending. For two days he remained indoors, followed by his mother's inquiring glances. Doña Bernarda felt more at ease now that the evil influence of the "chorus girl" promised to be over;

but none the less she did not lose her frown. With a woman's instinct, she still scented the presence of danger.

The young man could hardly wait for the time to come. It seemed unbearable for him to be there at home while "she" was away off somewhere, alone, shut up in a hotel, waiting just as impatiently as he was for the moment of reunion.

What a sunrise it had been that day when he set out! Rafael burned with shame as he crept like a burglar in his stockings and on tip-toe, through the room where his mother received the orchard-folk and adjusted all accounts pertaining to the tilling of the land. He groped his way along guided by the light that came in through the chinks in the closed windows. His mother was sleeping in a room close by; he could hear her breathe—the labored respiration of a deep sleep that spelled recovery from the insomnia of the days of his love trysts. He could still feel the criminal shudder that rippled through him at a slight rattle of the keys, which had been left with the confidence of unlimited authority in the lock of an old chest where doña Bernarda kept her savings. With tremulous hands he had collected all the money she had put away in the small boxes there. A thief, a thief! But, after all, he was taking only what belonged to him. He had never asked for his share of his father's estate. Leonora was rich. With admirable delicacy she had refused to talk of money during their preparations for the journey; but he would refuse to live on her! He did not care to be like Salvatti, who had exploited the singer in her youth! That thought it had been which gave him strength to take the money finally and steal out of the house. But even on the train he felt uneasy; and *su señoria*, the deputy, shivered with an instinctive thrill of fear, every time a tricorne of the Civil Guard appeared at a railroad station. What would his mother say when she got up and found the money gone?

As he entered the hotel his self-confidence returned and his spirits revived. He felt as if he were entering port after a storm. He found Leonora in bed, her hair spread over the pillow in waves of gold, her eyes closed, and a smile on her lips, as if he had surprised her in the middle of a dream, where she had been tasting her memories of love. They ordered lunch in the room early, intending to set out on their journey at once. Circumspection, prudence, until they should be once beyond the Spanish border! They would leave that evening on the Barcelona mail for the frontier. And calmly, tranquilly, like a married couple discussing details of house-keeping in the calm of a quiet home, they ran over the list of things they would need on the train.

Rafael had nothing. He had fled like a fugitive from a fire, with the first clothes he laid hands on as he bounded out of bed. He needed many indispensable articles, and he thought of going out to buy them—a matter of a moment.

"But are you really going out?" asked Leonora with a certain anguish, as if her feminine instinct sensed a danger. "Are you going to leave me alone? . . ."

"Only a moment. I won't keep you waiting long."

They took leave of each other in the corridor

with the noisy, nonchalant joy of passion, indifferent
to the chamber-maids who were walking to and fro
at the other end of the passageway.

"Good-bye, Rafael. . . . Another hug; just one
more."

And as, with the taste of the last kiss still fresh
on his lips, he reached the square, he saw a bejew-
elled hand still waving to him from a balcony.

Anxious to get back as soon as possible, the young
man walked hurriedly along, elbowing his way
among the cab-drivers swarming in front of the
great *Palacio de Dos Aguas*, closed, silent, slumbering, like the two giants that guarded its portals, displaying in the golden downpour of sunlight the
the overdecorated yet graceful sumptuousness of its
roccocò façade.

"Rafael! Rafael! . . ."

The deputy turned around at the sound of his
name, and blanched as if he had seen a ghost. It
was don Andrés, calling to him.

"Rafael! Rafael!"

"You? . . . Here?"

"I came by the Madrid express. For two hours
I've been hunting for you in all the hotels of Valencia. I knew you were here. . . . But come, we
have a great deal to talk over. This is not just
the place to do it."

And the old Mentor glowered hatefully at the
*Hôtel de Roma*, as if he wanted to annihilate the
huge edifice with everybody in it.

They walked off, slowly, without knowing just
where they were going, turning corners, passing several times through the same streets, their nerves
tense and quivering, ready to shout at the top of

their lungs, yet using every effort to speak softly, so as not to attract attention from the passers-by who were rubbing against them on the narrow sidewalks.

Don Andrés, naturally, was the first to speak:

"You approve of what you've done?"

And seeing that Rafael, like a coward, was trying to pretend innocent astonishment, asking "what" he had done, observing that he had come to Valencia on a matter of business, the old man broke into a rage.

"Now, see here, don't you go lying to me: either we're men or we're not men. If you think you've acted properly, you ought to stand up for it and say so. Don't imagine you're going to pull the wool over my eyes and then run off with that woman to God knows where. I've found you and I'm not going to let you go. I want you to know the truth. Your mother is sick abed; she tipped me off and I caught the first train to get here. The whole house is upside down! At first it was thought a robbery had been committed. By this time the whole city must be agog about you. Come now! . . . What do you say to that? Do you want to kill your mother? Well, you're going about it right! Good God! And this is what they call a 'boy of talent,' a 'young man of promise'! How much better it would have been if you were a dunce like me or your father——but a dunce at least who knows how to get a woman if he has to, without making a public ass of himself!"

Then he went into detail. Rafael's mother had gone to the old chest to get some money for one of her laborers. Her cry of horror and alarm had

thrown the whole house into an uproar. Don
Andrés had been hastily summoned. Suspicions
against the servants, a "third degree" for the whole
lot, all of them protesting and weeping, in outrage!
Until finally doña Bernarda sank to a chair in a
swoon, whispering into her adviser's ear:

"Rafael is not in the house. He has gone . . .
perhaps never to return. I am sure of it—he took
the money!"

While the others were getting the sobbing mother
to bed, and sending for the doctor, don Andrés had
made for the station to catch the express. He could
tell from the way people looked at him that everybody knew what had been going on. Gossip had
already connected the excitement in the Brull mansion with Rafael's taking the early train! He had
been seen by several persons, in spite of his precau-
tions.

"Well, is the Hon. don Rafael Brull, member
from Alcira, satisfied with his morning's work?
Don't you think the laugh your enemies have raised
deserves an *encore*?"

For all his bitter sarcasm the old man spoke in
a faltering voice, and seemed on the verge of tears.
The labor of his entire life, the great victories won
with don Ramón, that political power which had
been so carefully built up and sustained over decades,
was about to crumble to ruins; all because of a light-
headed, erratic boy who had handed to the first
skirt who came along everything that belonged to
him and everything that belonged to his friends as
well.

Rafael had gone into the interview in an aggressive mood, ready to answer with plain talk if that

sodden idiot should go too far in his recriminations.
But the sincere grief of the old man touched him
deeply. Don Andrés, who resembled Rafael's
father as the cat resembles the tiger, could think of
nothing but Brull politics; and he was almost sobbing
as he saw the danger which the prestige of the Brull
House was running.

With bowed head, crushed by the realization of
the scene that had followed his flight, Rafael did
not notice where they were going. But soon he
became conscious of the perfume of flowers. They
were crossing a garden; and as he looked up he saw
the figure of Valencia's conqueror on his sinewy
charger glistening in the sun.

They walked on. The old man began in wailing
accents to describe the situation which the Brull
House was facing. That money, which perhaps
Rafael still had in his pocket—more than thirty
thousand *pesetas*—represented the final desperate
efforts of his mother to rescue the family fortune,
which had been endangered by don Ramón's prodi-
gal habits. The money was his, and don Andrés
had nothing to say in that regard. Rafael was at
liberty to squander it, scatter it to the four winds
of heaven; but don Andrés wasn't talking to a child,
he was talking to a man with a heart: so he begged
him, as his childhood preceptor, as his oldest friend,
to consider the sacrifices his mother had been making—the privations she had imposed upon herself,
going without new clothes, quarreling with her help
over a *céntimo*, despite all her airs as a grand lady,
depriving herself of all the dainties and comforts
that are so pleasant to old age—all that her son,
her *señor hijo*, might waste it in gay living on a

woman! Thirty thousand! And don Andrés mentioned the sum with bated breath! It had taken so
much trouble to hoard it! Come, man! The sight
of such things was enough to make a fellow cry like
a baby! . . .

And suppose his father, don Ramón, were to rise
from the grave? Suppose he could see how his
Rafael were destroying at a single stroke what it had
cost him so many years to build up, just because of
a woman! . . .

They were now crossing a bridge. Below, against
the background of white gravel in the river-bed the
red and blue uniforms of a group of soldiers could
be seen; and the drums were beating, sounding in
the distance like the humming of a huge bee-hive—
a worthy accompaniment, Rafael reflected, to the
old man's evocation of the youth's father. Rafael
thought he could almost see in front of him the
massive body, the flourishing mustache, the proud,
arrogant brow of don Ramón, a born fighter, an
adventurer destined from the cradle to lead men
and impose his will upon inferiors.

What would that heroic master of men have said
of this? Don Ramón would give a lot of money
to a woman—granted—but he wouldn't have
swapped all the beauties on earth put together for
a single vote!

But his son, the boy on whom he had grounded
his fondest hopes—the redeemer destined to raise
the House of Brull to its loftiest glory—the future
"personage" in Madrid, the fondled heir-apparent,
who had found his pathway already cleared for him
at birth—was throwing all his father's labors
through the window, the way you toss overboard

something it has cost you nothing to earn! It was easy to see that Rafael had never known what hard times were—those days of the Revolution, when the Brulls were out of power and held their own just because don Ramón was a bad man with a gun— desperate election campaigns, when you marched to victory over somebody's dead body, bold cross-country rides on election night, never knowing when you would meet the *roder* in ambush—the outlaw sharpshooter who had vowed to kill don Ramón; then endless prosecutions for intimidation and violence, which had given doña Bernarda and her husband months and months of anxiety, lest a catastrophe from one moment to the next bring prison and forfeiture of all their property! All that his father had gone through, for his boy's sake; to carve out a pedestal for Rafael, pass on to him a District that would be his own, blazing a path over which he might go to no visible limit of glory! And he was just throwing it all away, relinquishing forever a position that had been built up at the cost of years and years of labor and peril! That is what he would be doing, unless that very night he returned home, refuting by his presence there the rumors his scandalized adherents were circulating.

Rafael shook his head. The mention of his father had touched him, and he was convinced by the old man's arguments; but none the less he was determined to resist. No, and again no; his die was cast: he would continue on his way.

They were now under the trees of the Alameda. The carriages were rolling by, forming an immense wheel in the center of the avenue. The harnesses of the horses and the lamps of the drivers' boxes gleamed in the sunlight. Women's hats and the white lace shawls of children could be seen through the coach windows as they passed.

Don Andrés became impatient with the youth's stubbornness. He pointed to all those happy, peaceful-looking families out for their afternoon drive—wealth, comfort, public esteem, abundance, freedom from struggle and toil! *Cristo,* boy! Was that so bad, after all? Well, that was just the life he could have if he would be good and not turn his back on his plain duty—rich, influential, respected, growing old with a circle of nice children about him. What more could a decent person ask for in this world?

All that bohemian nonsense about pure love, love free from law and restraint, love that scoffs at society and its customs, sufficient unto itself and despising public opinion, that was just bosh, the humbug of poets, musicians and dancers—a set of outcasts like that woman who was taking him away, cutting him off forever from all the ties that bound him to family and country!

The old man seemed to take courage from Rafael's silence. He judged the moment opportune for launching the final attack upon the boy's infatuation.

"And then, what a woman! I have been young, like you, Rafael. It's true I didn't know a stylish woman like this one, but, bah! they're all alike. I have had my weaknesses; but I tell you I wouldn't have lifted a finger for this actress of yours! Any one of the girls we have down home is worth two of her. Clothes, yes, talk, yes, powder and rouge inches deep! . . . I'm not saying she's bad to look at—not that; what I say is . . . well, it doesn't take much to turn your head—you're satisfied with the leavings of half the men in Europe. . . ."

And he came to Leonora's past, the lurid, much exaggerated legend of her journey through life— lovers by the dozens; statues and paintings of her in the nude; the eyes of all Europe centered on her beauty; the public property of a continent! "That was virtue to go crazy about, come now! Quite worth leaving house and home for, no doubt of that!"

The old man winced under the flash of anger that blazed in Rafael's eyes. They had just crossed another bridge, and were entering the city again. Don Andrés, wretched coward that he was, sidled away to be within reach of the customs' office if the fist he could already see cleaving the air should come his way.

Rafael, in fact, stopped in his tracks, glaring. But in a second or two he went on his way again, dejected, with bowed head, ignoring the presence of the old man. Don Andrés resumed his place at the boy's side.

The cursed old fox! He had stuck the knife in the right place! Leonora's past! Her favors distributed with mad lavishness over the four corners of the globe! An army of men of every nation owning her for a moment with the appeal of luxury or the enchantment of art! A palace today and a hotel tomorrow! Her lips repeating in all the languages of Babel the very words of love that had fired him as if he had been the first to hear them! He was going to lose everything for that—that refuse, as don Andrés said—a public scandal, a

ruined reputation; and a murdered mother perhaps,
—for that! Oh, that devil of a don Andrés! How
cunningly he had slashed him, and then plunged his
fingers into the bleeding gash to make the wound
deeper! The old man's plain common-sense had
shattered his dream. That man had been the rustic,
cunning Sancho at the side of the quixotic don
Ramón; and he was playing the same rôle with
Rafael!

Leonora's story came back to the boy in one flash
—the frank confession she had made during the
days of their mere friendship, when she had told
him everything to prevent his continuing to desire
her. However much she might adore him, he would
be nothing after all but a successor to a Russian
count, and a German musician; the latest, simply
among those countless ephemeral lovers, whom she
had barely mentioned but who must none the less
have left some trace in her memory. The last item
in a long inventory! The most recent arrival, coming several years late, and content to nibble at the
soggy over-ripe fruit which they had known when it
was fresh and firm. Her kisses that so deeply disturbed him! What were they but the intoxicating,
unhealthful perfume of a whole career of corruptness and licentiousness, the concentrated essence of
a world madly dashing at her seductive beauty, as a
bird of night breaks its head against the globe of a
lighthouse? Give up everything for that! The
two of them traveling about the world, free, and
proud of their passion! . . . And out in that world
he would encounter many of his predecessors; and
they would look at him with curious, ironic eyes,
knowing of her all that he would know, able to

repeat all the panting phrases she would speak to him in the exaggerations of her insatiable passion! The strange thing about it was that all this had not occurred to him sooner. Blind with happiness, he had never thought an instant of his real place in that woman's life!

How long had they been walking through the streets of Valencia? . . . His legs were sagging under him! He was faint with weariness. He could hardly see. The gables of the houses were still tipped with sunlight, yet he seemed to be groping about in a deep night.

"I'm thirsty, don Andrés. Let's go in somewhere."

The old man headed him toward the Café de España, his favorite resort. He selected the table in the center of the big square salon under the four clocks supported by the angel of Fame. The walls were covered with great mirrors that opened up fantastic perspectives in the dingy room where the gilded ornaments were blackened by the smoke and a crepuscular light filtered in through the lofty skylight as into a sombre crypt.

Rafael drank, without realizing just what his glass contained—a poison, it felt like, that froze his heart. Don Andrés sat looking at the writing articles on the marble table: a letter-case of wrinkled oil-cloth, and a grimy ink-well. He began to rap upon them with the holder of the public pen—rusty and with the points bent—an instrument of torture well fitted for a hand committed to despair!

"We have just an hour to catch our train! Come, Rafael, be a man! There's still time! Come, let's get out of this mess we're in!"

And he held out the pen, though he had not said a word about writing to anybody.

"I can't, don Andrés. I'm a gentleman. I've given my word; and I will not go back upon it, come what may!"

The old man smiled ironically.

"Very well, be as much of a gentleman as you please. She deserves it! But when you break with her, when she leaves you, or you leave her, don't come back to Alcira. Your mother won't be there to welcome you! I shall be—I don't know where; and those who made you deputy will look upon you as a thief who robbed and killed his mother. . . . Oh, get mad if you want to—beat me up even; people at the other tables are already looking at us. . . . Why not top the whole business off with a saloon brawl? But just the same, everything I've been saying to you is gospel truth! . . ."

\* \* \* \* \* \*

In the meantime Leonora was growing impatient in her hotel room. Three hours had gone by. To relieve her nervousness she sat down behind the green curtain at the window watching pedestrians crossing the square.

How like a small piazza of old Florence this place was, with its stately aristocratic residences, shrouded in imposing gloom; it's grass-grown, cobble-stone pavements hot from the sun; its sleepy solitude: an occasional woman, or a priest, or a tourist, —and you could hear their footsteps even when they were far away! Here was a curious corner of the *Palacio de Dos Aguas*—panels of jasper stucco with a leaf design on the mouldings! That talking came from the drivers gathered in the hotel door—the innkeeper and the servants were setting the chairs out on the sidewalk as if they were back at home— in a small Italian town! Behind the roof opposite, the sunlight was gradually fading, growing paler and softer every moment.

She looked at her watch. Six o'clock! Where on earth could that Rafael have gone? They were going to lose the train. In order to waste no time, she ordered Beppa to have everything in readiness for departure. She packed her toilet articles; then closed her trunks, casting an inquiring glance over the room with the uneasiness of a hasty leave-taking. On an armchair near the window she laid her traveling coat, then her hand-bag, and her hat and veil. They would have to run the moment Rafael came in. He would probably be very tired and nervous from returning so late.

But Rafael did not come! . . . She felt an impulse to go out and look for him; but where? She had not been in Valencia since she was a child. She had forgotten the streets. Then she might actually pass Rafael on the way without knowing it, and wander aimlessly about while he would be waiting for her at the hotel. No. It would be better to stay there!

It was now dusk and the hotel-room was virtually dark. She went to the window again, trembling with impatience, filled with all the gloom of the violet light that was falling from the sky with a few red streaks from the sunset. They would surely lose the train now! They would have to wait until the next day. That was a disappointment! They might have trouble in getting away!

She whirled nervously about as she heard some-one calling from the corridor.

"Madame, madame, a letter for you!"

A letter for her! . . . She snatched it feverishly from the bell-boy's hand, while Beppa, seated on a trunk, looked on vacantly, without expression.

She began to tremble violently. The thought of Hans Keller, the ungrateful artist, suddenly rose in her memory. She looked for a candle on the chiffonier. There was none. Finally she went to the balcony and tried to read the letter in the little light there was.

It was his handwriting on the envelope—but tor-tuous, labored, as if it were the product of a pain-ful effort. She felt all her blood rush back upon her heart. Madly she tore the letter open, and read with the haste of a person anxious to drain the cup of bitterness at a single draught, skipping a line here and a line there, taking in only the sig-nificant words.

"My mother very ill. . . . I must go home for a day or two . . . my duty as a son . . . we'll soon meet again." And then all the cowardly, con-ventional excuses that chivalry has created to soften the harshness of desertion—the promise to join her again as soon as possible; passionate protestations that she was the only woman in the world he loved.

Her first thought was to go back to Alcira at once, walk there if necessary, find the scamp some-where, throw the letter into his face, beat him, claw him to pieces!

"Ah, the wretch! The infamous, cowardly, un-speakable wretch!" she cried.

Beppa had found a candle. She lighted it. And

there her mistress was—staggering, deathly pale, her eyes wide open, her lips white with anguish! Leonora began to walk up and down the apartment, taut and strained, as if her feet were not moving at all, as if she were being thrust about by an invisible hand.

"Beppa," she groaned finally, "he has gone. He is deserting me."

The maid did not care about the desertion particularly. She had been through that before. She was thinking about Leonora, waiting for the impending crisis, studying the anguished countenance of her mistress with her own placid, bovine eyes.

"The wretch!" Leonora hissed, pacing back and forth in the chamber. "What a fool, what a complete, unconscionable fool I have been! Giving myself to that man, believing in that man, trusting that man, giving up my peace of mind, the last relative I had in the world for that man! . . . And why would he not let me go off alone? He made me dream of an eternal springtime of love, and now he deserts me. . . . He has tricked me . . . he is laughing at me . . . and I can not hate him. Why did he insist on rousing me when I was there alone, quite peaceful, forgetting everything, sunk in a placid indulgent calm! . . . The cool fraud that he was! . . . But what do I care, after all? . . . It's all over. Come Beppa, cheer up! Hah-hah! Come, Beppa! We're off! We're off! We're going to sing again! Off over the whole globe. Good-bye to this rat-hole forever! I'm through educating children! Now for life again! And we'll drain them dry, the brutes! Kick them about like the selfish donkeys they are! Well, well! I can't believe I've been taken in this way! Isn't it a joke? The best joke you ever heard! Ha, ha, ha! And I thought I knew the world . . . ! Ha, ha! Ha, ha! . . ."

And her laugh was audible distinctly down in the square. It was a wild, shrill, metallic laughter, that seemed to be rending her flesh! The whole hotel was in commotion, while the actress, with foaming lips, fell to the floor and began to writhe in fury, overturning the furniture and bruising her body on the iron trimmings of her trunks.

# PART THREE

## I

"Don Rafael, the gentlemen of the Committee on the Budget are waiting for you in the second section."

"I'll be there directly."

And the deputy bent low over his desk in the writing-room of the Congress, went on with his last letter, adding one more envelope to the heap of correspondence piled up at the end of the table, near his cane and his silk hat.

This was his daily grind, the boresome drudgery of every afternoon; and around him, with similar expressions of disgust on their faces, a large number of the country's representatives were busy at the same task. Rafael was answering petitions and queries, stifling the complaints and acknowledging the wild suggestions that came in from the District —the endless clamor of the voters at home, who never met the slightest annoyance in their various paths of life without at once running to their deputy, the way a pious worshipper appeals to the miracle-working saint.

He gathered up his letters, gave them to an usher to mail, and sauntering off with a counterfeit sprightliness that was more counterfeit as he grew fatter and fatter with the years, walked through to the central corridor, a prolongation of the lobby in front of the *Salón de Conferencias.*

The Honorable señor don Rafael Brull, member from Alcira, felt as much at ease as if he were in his own house when he entered that corridor,—a dark hole, thick with tobacco smoke, and peopled with black suits standing around in groups or laboriously elbowing their way through the crowds.

He had been there eight years; though he had almost lost count of the times he had been "duly elected" in the capricious ups and downs of Spanish politics, which give to Parliaments only a fleeting existence. The ushers, the personnel of the Secretariat, the guards and janitors, treated him with deferential intimacy, as a comrade on a somewhat higher level, but as much of a fixture as they were to the Spanish Congress. He was not one of those men who are miraculously washed into office on the crest of a reform wave, but never succeed in repeating the trick, and spend the rest of their lives idling on the sofas of the Conference Chamber, with wistful memories of lost greatness, waiting to enter Congress afternoons, to preserve their standing as ex-deputies, and forever hoping that their party will some day return to power, so that once again they may sit on the red benches. No, don Rafael Brull was a gentleman with a District all his own: he came with a clean, undisputed and indisputable certificate of election, whether his own party or the Opposition were in the saddle. For lack of other discoverable merit in him, his fellow-partisans would say: "Brull is one of the few who come here on honest returns." His name did not figure brilliantly in the Congressional record, but there was not an employee, not a

journalist, not a member of the "ex-honorables"
who, on noticing the word "Brull" on all the committees, did not at once exclaim: "Ah, yes! Brull
. . . of Alcira."

Eight years of "service to the country." Eight
years of lodging-house life, while yonder lay a sumptuous home adorned with a luxuriousness that had
cost his mother and his father-in-law half a fortune!
Long seasons of separation from his wife and his
children—and without amusements, to avoid spending money lest the folks at home suspect him of dere-
liction in public—and private—duty! What a dog's
life his eight years as deputy had been! Indigestion
from the countless gallons of sugared water drunk
at the Congressional bar; callouses on his feet from
endless promenades along the central corridor, absent-mindedly knocking the varnish off the tiles of
the wainscoating with the tip of his cane; an incal-
culable quantity of *pesetas* spent on carriages,
through fault of his supporters, who sent him trotting every morning from one Ministry to the next,
asking for the earth, and getting a grain of sand!

He had not as yet gotten anywhere in particular;
but according to Chamber gossip he was a "serious"
well-balanced young man, of few words, but good
ones, and sure some day to be rewarded with a Port-
folio. Content with the rôle of safety and sanity
that had been assigned to him, he laughed very sel-
dom, and dressed soberly, with not a dissonant color
to brighten his black attire. He would listen patiently to things that did not concern him in the
least, rather than venture a personal opinion with
the chance of going wrong—satisfied with premature wrinkles, premature corpulency, and premature

baldness, since nothing could be more respectable than a thoughtful face, a conspicuous paunch, and a pate that could shine with venerable brilliancy under the lamps of the Chamber. At thirty-four, he looked more like forty-five. When he spoke he would remove his spectacles with a gesture he had carefully imitated from the deceased leader of "the Party." He would never take the floor without prefacing his remarks with: "My understanding is . . . ," or "I have my own humble opinion on this matter. . . ." And this was what don Rafael Brull had learned in eight years of parliamentary assiduity!

The new Conservative leader, seeing that he could always depend on Brull's vote and that Alcira elections cost "the Party" nothing, had a certain consideration for Rafael. He was a soldier always on hand for roll-call, whenever a new Parliament was formed. He would present himself with his certificate of election, whether his party, with all the insolence of victory, occupied the benches on the Right, or hungry and defiant, and reduced in numbers, was huddled on the Left, determined to find fault with everything the reigning Ministry did. Two sessions as part of the minority had won him a certain intimacy with the leader in that frank comradeship that Oppositions always have, since, from leader down to the most silent member, all the deputies "out of power" are on a level. Besides, in those two seasons of misfortune, to aid in the destructive tactics of his faction, he put little interpellations to the government, at the openings of the sessions when the crowds were small; and more than once he heard from the pale smiling lips of the chief: "Very good,

Brull; that was to the point." And such congratulations were duly echoed in his home city, where rustic imagination did the rest.

In addition, a few parliamentary honors had come his way; the "Grand Cross" had been given him, as it is given to most deputies of a certain length of service—from membership, eventually, on committees charged with representing the legislative branch of the government at formal public functions. If an "Answer to the Message" was to be taken "to the Palace," he was one of those chosen for the purpose; and he trembled with emotion to think of what his mother, his wife, all the people down yonder at home would say if they could see him riding there in the sumptuous carriage of state, preceded by bright-liveried horsemen and saluted by trumpets blaring the royal march! He was also usually among the delegates who came out on the staircase of the Congress to welcome Their Majesties on the opening of a parliament. Finally, for one session, he was on "the Committee for the Interior," an appointment that raised his prestige a thousand percent among the ushers.

"That fellow Brull," they would say in the Chamber, "will be somebody the day his party returns to power."

Well, now "the Party" was in power again. During one of those ordered, calculated "changes of direction" to which Spain lives subject, because of its parliamentary system of party weights and party balances, the Conservatives captured the premiership; and Rafael went on the budget committee. There he would do something more than make interpellations when he opened his mouth to speak. In fact he had to win his spurs, justify his filling one of those posts which, according to report, his chief was holding for him.

The green deputies, the younger set constituting the new majority, elect and triumphant through grace of the Ministry of the Interior, respected him and deferred to what he said, much as students listen to a tutor who they know receives his orders from the master directly—the subordination of freshmen, as it were, to the sophomore who knows the rules.

Whenever a vote was being taken and the Opposition was excited over the chance of putting the government in the minority, the Premier would look about anxiously over the hall for Brull.

"See here, Brull, better bring your people in; we're going to have a close call."

And Brull, proud at being noticed thus, would dash out like a streak of lightning while the bells were ringing and the ushers were running about summoning the deputies to vote. He would make the rounds of the desks in the writing rooms, elbow his way into groups in the corridors; and filling with self-importance because of the authority conferred upon him, he would rudely shoo the ministerial flock off toward the Chamber, grumbling fogeywise and assuring them that "in his time," when he was serving his first term, there was "far better discipline." When the vote was all in and the victory won, he would sigh with satisfaction. He had saved the government! And perhaps the nation!

At times a residue of the sincerity and frankness of his character as a boy would rise to the surface in him. Then cruel doubts would assail his faith in himself. Weren't they all playing a stupid com-

edy there without the slightest wit or sense in it?
Really was what they said and did there of the
slightest importance to the country—to anybody?

Standing in the corridor, he would feel the nervous
flutter of the journalists about him—those poor,
intelligent, attractive, young fellows, who found it
so hard to make a living. From the press-gallery
they would sit and look down on the legislators the
way birds in the treetops must look down on the
wretchedness of the streets below, laughing at the
nonsense those solemn baldpates were talking! Could
a farce on the stage be more amusing?

To Rafael those "intellectuals" seemed to bring
a breeze from out of doors into the close, sordid,
vitiated air of the Chamber. They stood for the
thought of the world outside—the idea fatherless,
unsponsored, the aspiration of the great masses—a
breath of fresh air in the sick-room of a chronic invalid forever dying, forever unburiable.

Their judgment always differed from that of the
country's representatives. His Excellency señor
don What's-his-Name was in their eyes, a mud-eel,
and in their lingo a *congrio*; the illustrious orator
What-do-you-call-him, who took up a sixteen-page
sheet in the Congressional Record every time he
spoke, was a *percebe*, a "barnacle on the keel of
Progress"; every act of parliament struck them as
a bit of balderdash, though, to hold their jobs, they
praised it to the skies in their articles. And why
was it that the country, in some mysterious way,
would always think eventually what those boys
thought, so long, and only so long, as they remained
boys? Would they have to come down from their
seats in the press-gallery to the red benches on the

floor before the real will of the country would make itself felt?

Rafael Brull finally realized that national opinion was present on the floor, among his fellow members, also, but like a mummy in a sarcophagus: bound hand and foot in rhetoric and conventional utterance, spiced, embalmed with proprieties that made any outburst of sincerity, any explosion of real feeling, evidence of "bad taste!"

In reality everything was going well with the Ship of State. The nation had passed from action to talk, and from talk to passivity, and from passivity to resignation. The era of revolutions was gone forever. The infallible system of government had proved to be this mechanism of pre-arranged "crises" and amicable exchanges of patronage between Liberals and Conservatives, each member of the party in power and each member of the party out of power knowing just what he was to say and just what he was to get.

So, in that palace of over-ornate architecture, as pretentious and as showy as the mansion of a millionaire *parvenu*, Rafael was condemned to spend his lifetime, foregoing the blue sky and the flowering fields and orchards of Alcira that a family ambition might be realized.

Nothing noteworthy had occurred during those eight years. His life had been a muddy, monotonous stream, with neither brilliancy nor beauty in its waters, lazily meandering along, like the Jucár in winter. As he looked back over his career as a "personage," he could have summed it up in three words: he had married.

Remedios was his wife. Don Matías was his

father-in-law. He was wealthy. He had control over a vast fortune, for he exercised despotic rule over his wife's peasant father, the most fervent of his admirers. His mother seemed to have put the last of her strength into the arrangement of that "marriage of convenience." She had fallen into a senile decrepitude that bordered on dotage. Her sole evidence of being alive was her habit of staying in church until the doors were closed and she could stay no longer. At home she did nothing but recite the rosary, mumbling away in some corner of the house, and taking no part in the noisy play of her grandchildren. Don Andrés had died, leaving Rafael sole "boss" of "the Party." He had had three children. They had had their teeth, their measles, their whooping-cough. These episodes, with a few escapades of that brother of Remedios, who feared Rafael's paunch and bald head more than the wrath of don Matías, were the only distractions in a thoroughly dull existence.

Every year he bought a new piece of land. He felt a thrill of pride when from the top of San Salvador—that Hermitage, alas, of such desperate and unfading memory!—he looked down upon the vast patches of land with orange-trees in straight rows and fenced in by green walls, that all, all, belonged to him. The joy of ownership, the intoxication of property had gone to his head.

As he entered the old mansion, entirely made over now, he felt the same sense of well-being and power. The old chest in which his mother used to keep her money stood where it had always stood; but it was no longer devoted to savings hoarded slowly at the cost of untold sacrifice and privation to raise mortgages and temporize with creditors. Never again had he tip-toed up in the dark to rifle it. Now it was his own. And at harvest time it became literally crammed with the huge rolls of banknotes his father-in-law paid over in exchange for the oranges of the Brull orchards. And Rafael had a covetous eye on what don Matías had in the banks; for all that, too, would come to him when the old man died. Acquisitiveness—money and land—had become his one, his ruling passion. Monotony, meanwhile, had turned him into an accurate, methodical, meticulous machine; so that every night he would make out a schedule, hour for hour, of all that he would do on the following day. At the bottom of this passion for riches conjugal contagion probably lay. Eight years of unbroken familiarity had finally inoculated him with most of the obsessions and most of the predilections of his wife.

The shrinking, timorous little she-goat that used to gambol about with him in pursuit, the poor child who had been so wistful and downcast during the days of his wantonness, had now become a woman with all the imperious obstinacy, all the domineering superiority of the female of the species as it has evolved in the countries of the South. Cleanliness and frugality in Remedios took the form of unendurable tyranny. She scolded her husband if he brought the slightest speck of dust into the house on his shoes. She would turn the place upside down, flay all the servants alive, if ever a few drops of oil were spilled from a jar, or a crumb of bread were wasted on the table.

"A jewel for the home! And didn't I tell you

so?" her father would whisper, satisfied with his daughter's obtrusive qualities.

Rafael, for his part, found them intolerable. He had tried to love his bride in the early months of their marriage. He made an honest effort to forget, and recall the playful, passionate impulses he had felt on those days when he had chased her around the orchards. But after a first fever of passion had passed, she had proved to be a cold, calculating child-bearer, hostile to expansiveness of love out of religious scruples, viewing it her duty to bring new offsprings into the world to perpetuate the House of Brull and to fill "grandaddy" don Matías with pride at sight of a nursery full of future "personages" destined to the heights of political greatness in the District and in the nation.

Rafael had one of those gentle, temperate, honest, households that, on the afternoon of their walk through Valencia, don Andrés had pointed out to him as a radiant hope, if only he would turn his back on his mad adventure. He had a wife; and he had children; and he was rich. His father-in-law ordered shotguns for him from his correspondents in England. Every year a new horse was added to the stable, and don Matías would see to purchasing the best that could be found in the fairs of Andalusia. He hunted, took long horseback rides over the roads of the district, dispensed justice in the *patio* of the house, just as his father don Ramón had done. His three little ones, finding him somewhat strange after his long absences in Madrid and more at home with their grand-parents than with him, would group themselves with bowed,

bashful heads around his knees, silently waiting for
his paternal kiss. Everything attainable around
him was within his reach for the asking; and yet—
he was not happy.

From time to time the adventure of his youth
would come back to his mind. The eight years that
had passed seemed to have put a century between
him and those ancient days. Leonora's face had
slowly, slowly, faded in his memory, till all he could
remember were her two green eyes, and her blond
hair that crowned her with a crown of gold. Her
aunt, the devout, ingenuous doña Pepa, had died
some time since—leaving her property for the salvation of her soul. The orchard and the Blue House
belonged now to Rafael's father-in-law, who had
transferred to his own home the best of its equip-
ment—all the funiture and decorations that Leonora
had bought during her period of exile, while Rafael
had been in Madrid and she had thought of living
the rest of her life in Alcira.

Rafael carefully avoided revisiting the Blue
House, out of regard for his wife's possible suscepti-
bilities. As it was, the woman's silence sometimes
weighed heavily upon him, a strange circumspection,
which never permitted the slightest allusion to the
past. In the coldness and the uncompromising scorn
with which she abominated any poetic madness in
love, an important part was doubtless played by the
suppressed memory of her husband's adventure with
the actress, which everybody had tried to conceal
from her and which had deeply disturbed the preparations for her wedding.

When the deputy was alone in Madrid, as much at
liberty as before his marriage, he could think of

Leonora freely, without those restraints which seemed to disturb him back at home in the bosom of his family. What could have become of her? To what limits of mad frolic had she gone after that parting which even after years had passed, still brought a blush of shame to Rafael's cheeks? The Spanish papers paid very little attention to matters of foreign art. Only twice in their columns did he discover Leonora's stage name with an account of her new triumphs. She had sung in Paris in French, with as much success as a native *artiste*. The purity of her accent had surprised everyone. In Rome she had played the "lead" in an opera by a young Italian composer, and her coming had been announced by press agents as a great event. The opera had failed to please; not so the singer. Her audience had been moved to tears by her execution of a scene in the last act, where she wept for a lost love.

After that—silence, no news whatever! She had disappeared. A new love affair, Rafael supposed, a new outburst of that vehement passion which made her follow her chosen man like a slave. And Rafael felt a flash of jealousy at the thought, as if he had rights over the woman still, as if he had forgotten the cruelty with which he had bidden her farewell.

That, fundamentally, had been the cause of all the bitterness and remorse in his life. He understood now that Leonora had been his one genuine passion: the love that comes to people once in a lifetime. It had been within reach of his hand, and he had failed to grasp it, had frightened it away forever with a cowardly act of villany, a cruel farewell, the shame of which would go to the grave with him. Garlanded in the orange-blossoms of the orchard, Love had passed before him, singing the hymn of wild Youth that knows neither scruples nor ambition. Love, true love had invited him to follow—and he had answered with a stab—in the back! That love would never return, as he well knew. That mysterious being with its smiles and with its frolics, goes forever when once it goes. It knows no bartering with destiny. It demands blind obedience and bids the lover take the woman who offers her hand, orchard-maid or prima donna as she may be. The man who hesitates is lost.

And Rafael felt that an endless night had closed around him! He found all his efforts to escape from his dullness and depression vain. He could not shake off the senility that was creeping over his spirit. Sadly he bowed to the conviction that another love like the first was impossible.

For two months he had been the lover of Cora, a popular girl of the private rooms of the Fornos, a tall, thin, strong Galician beauty—as strong, alas, as the other. Cora had spent a few months in Paris, and had returned thence with her hair bleached and a distinctly French manner of lifting her skirt as if she were strolling along the *trottoir* of the *boulevards*. She had a sweet way of mixing French words in her conversation, calling everybody *mon cher* and pretending expertness in the organization of a supper. At all events she shone like a great *cocotte* among her competitors, though her real asset was a line of *risqué* stories, and a certain gift for low songs.

Rafael soon wearied of this affair. He did not like her manufactured beauty, nor her tiresome chatter that always turned on fashions. She was always wanting money for herself and for her friends.  Rafael, as a wealthy miser, grew alarmed.  Remorsefully he thought of his children's future, as if he were ruining them; and of what his economical Remedios would say of his considerably augmented expenditures.  Well he knew that Remedios haggled for everything down to the last *céntimo,* and that her one extravagance was an occasional new shawl for the local Virgin, and an annual *fiesta* for the Saint with a large orchestra and hundreds of candles!  He broke off relations with the Galician *boulevardière,* and found the rupture a sweet relief.  It seemed to remove a sully from the memory of his youthful passion.  Moreover, his Party had just returned to power and it was important to have no blemish on his standing as a "serious" person!  He resumed his seat on the Right, and near the Blue Bench this time, as one of the senior deputies.  The moment for work had come!  Now, it was time to see whether he could not make a position for himself with one good boost!

They named him to the Committee on the Budget, and he took it upon himself to refute certain strictures presented by the Opposition to the Government program on Pardon and Justice.  One friend he could count on was the minister: a respectable, solemn marquis who had once been an Absolutist, and who, wearied of platonisms, as he put it, had finally "recognized" the liberal régime, without amending his former ideas, however.

Rafael was as nervous as a schoolboy on the eve of his first examinations.  At the library he studied everything that had been said on the subject by countless deputies in a century of Parliamentary gov-

ernment. His friends in the Conference Chamber
—the legislative bohemia of "ex-honorables" and un-
successful aspirants, who were loyal to him in gratitude for passes to the floor—were encouraging him
and prophesying victory. They no longer approached him to begin: "When I was auditor . . ." to indulge in a veritable intoxication on
the fumes of their past glory; no longer did they
ask him what don Francisco thought of this, that, or
the other thing, to draw their own wild inferences
from his replies and start rumors going based on
"inside information." Now, quite frankly, they "advised" him, giving him hints in accordance with what
they had said or meant to say during that discussion of the budget back in González Brabo's time, to
end by murmuring, with a smile that gave him the
shudders: "Well, anyhow, we'll see! Good luck to
you!"

And that flock of disgruntled spirits who sat
around waiting for an election that would never
come and ran like old war-horses at the scent of
gun-powder to group themselves, as soon as a row
started and the bell began to ring for order, in two
factions on either side of the president's chair, could
never have imagined that the young deputy, on many
a night, broke off his study with a temptation to
throw the thick tomes of records against the wall,
yielding finally, with thrills of intense voluptuous-
ness, to the thought of what might have become of
him had he gone out into life on his own in the trail
of a pair of green eyes whose golden lights he
thought he could still see glittering in front of him
between the lines of clumsy parliamentary prose,
tempting him as they had tempted him of yore!

## II

"Order of the day. Resumption of debate on ecclesiastical appropriations!"

The Chamber suddenly came to life with a wild movement of dispersion, something comparable to the stampede of a herd or the panic of an army. The deputies of quickest motory reactions were on their feet in an instant, followed by dozens and dozens of others, all making for the doors. Whole blocks of seats were emptied.

The Chamber had been packed from the opening of the Session. It was a day of intense excitement: a debate between the leader of the Right and a former comrade who was now in the Opposition. The jealousy between the two old cronies was resulting in a small-sized scandal. Mutual secrets of their ancient intimacy as colleagues were coming to light —many of the intrigues that had settled historic parliamentary contests for the premiership. The galleries were filled with spectators who had come to enjoy the fun. The deputies and ministers occupied every seat on either hand of the presidential chair. But now the incident was closed. Two hours of veiled insult and pungent gossip had passed all too soon. And the phrase "Ecclesiastical Appropriations" had served as a fire-alarm. Run—do not walk—to the nearest exit!

However, the name of the orator who was now

being given the floor served to check the stampede
somewhat, much as routs have been stopped by some
great historic warcry. A few deputies hurried back
to their benches. All eyes turned toward the ex-
treme Left of the Chamber, where, a white head,
rising above the red seats over a pair of spectacles
and a gently ironical smile, was coming into view.

The old man was on his feet, at last. He was
small, so frail of person, that he hardly overtopped
the men still seated. All his vital energies had been
concentrated in that huge, nobly proportioned head
of his, pink at the top, with shocks of white hair
combed back over it. His pale countenance had the
warlike transparency of a sound, vigorous old age.
To it a shining, luminous silvery beard added a majesty like that with which Sacred Art used to picture the Almighty.

The venerable orator folded his arms and waited
for the noise in the Chamber to cease. When the last
determined fugitives had disappeared through the
exit doors, he began to speak. The journalists in
the press-gallery craned their necks toward "the
tribune," hushing for silence in order not to lose a
word.

This man was the patriarch of the Chamber. He
represented "the Revolution"—not only the old-
fashioned, the political, revolution, but the modern,
the social and economic revolution. He was the
enemy of all present systems of government and society. His theories irritated everybody, like a new
and incomprehensible music falling on slumbering
ears. But he was listened to with respect, with
the veneration inspired by his years and his unsullied
career. His voice had the melodious feebleness of

a muffled, silver bell; and his words rolled through the silence of the hall with a certain prophetic stateliness, as if the vision of a better world were passing before his eyes as he spoke, the revelation of a perfect society of the future, where there would be no oppression and no misery, the dream he had so often dreamed in the solitude of his study.

Rafael was sitting at the head of the committee bench, somewhat apart from his companions. They were giving him ample room, as bull-fighters do their *matador*. He had bundles of documents and volumes piled up at his seat, in case he should need to quote authorities in his reply to the venerable orator.

He was studying the old man admiringly and in silence. What a strong, sturdy spirit, as hard and cold and clear as ice! That veteran had doubtless had his passions like other men. At moments, through his calm impassive exterior, a romantic vehemence would seem to burn, a poetic ardor, that politics had smothered, but which smouldered on as volcanic fires lie dormant rumbling from time to time under the mantle of snow on a mountain peak. But he had known how to adjust his life to duty; and without belief in God, with the support of philosophy only, his virtue had been strong enough to disarm his most violent enemies.

And a weakling, a dawdler like himself, must reply to a hero like that! . . . Rafael began to be afraid; and to recover his spirits he swept the hall with his eyes. What the regular hangers-on of the sessions would have called a medium-sized house! A few deputies scattered about the benches! But the public galleries were filled with spectators, workingmen mostly, absolutely quiet, and all ears, as if they were drinking in every word of the old republican! In the reserved seats, just previously packed with curiosity-seekers interested in the set-to scheduled for the opening of the session, only a few foreign tourists were left. They were taking in everything—even the fantastic uniforms of the mace-bearers; and they were determined not to leave until they were put out. A few women of the so-called "parliament set," who came every afternoon when there was a squabble on the program, were munching caramels and staring in wonderment at the old man. There he was, the arch enemy of law and order! The man whose name it was bad form to mention at their afternoon teas! Who would have supposed he had such a kindly, harmless face? How easily, with what naturalness and grace, he wore his frock coat! Incredible! . . . In the diplomatic gallery a solitary lady! She was extravagantly attired in a huge picture hat with black plumes. Almost hidden behind her was a fair haired youth, his hair parted in the middle, his dress the height of correctness and foppery. Some rich tourist-woman probably! She was directly opposite Rafael's bench. He could see that her gloved hand rested on the railing, as she moved her fan to and fro with an almost discourteous noise. The rest of her body was lost in the darkness of the gallery. She bent back from time to time to whisper and laugh with her escort.

Somewhat reassured by the empty appearance of the house, Rafael scarcely paid any further attention to the orator. He had guessed all that the man would say, and he was satisfied. The outline of the long answer he had prepared would not in the least be affected.

The old man was inflexible and unchangeable. For thirty years he had been saying the same thing over and over again. Rafael had read that speech any number of times. The man had made a close study of national evils and abuses, and had formulated a complete and pitiless criticism of them in which the absurdities stood out by force of contrast. With the conviction that truth is forever the same and that there is nothing ever so novel as the truth, he had kept repeating his criticism year after year in a pure, concise, sonorous style that seemed to scatter the ripe perfume of the classics about the muggy Chamber.

He spoke in the name of the future Spain, of a Spain that would have no kings, because it would be governed by itself; that would pay no priests, because, respecting freedom of conscience, it would recognize all cults and give privileges to none. And with a simple, unaffected urbanity, as if he were constructing rhyming verses, he would pair statistics off, underscoring the absurd manner in which the nation was taking leave of a century of revolution during which all peoples had done things while Spain was lying stagnant.

More money, he pointed out, was spent on the maintenance of the Royal House than upon public education. Conclusion: the support of a single family in idleness was worth more than the awakening of an entire people to modern life! In Madrid, in the very capital, within sight of every one of his hearers, the schools remained in filthy hovels, while churches and convents rose overnight on the principal streets like magic palaces. During twenty-odd years of Restoration, more than fifty completely new, religious edifices, girding the capital with a belt of glittering structures, had been built. On the other hand, only a single modern school, at all comparable to the ordinary public schools of any town in England or Switzerland! The young men of the nation were feeble, unenthusiastic, selfish and—pious—in contrast with fathers, who had adored the generous ideals of liberty and democracy and had stood for action, revolt! The son was an old man at majority, his breast laden with medals, with no other intellectual stimulus than the debates of his religious fraternity, trusting his future and his thinking to the Jesuit introduced into the family by the mother, while the father smiled bitterly, realizing that he was a back-number, belonging to a different world, to a dying generation—though to a generation which had galvanized the nation for a moment with the spirit of revolutionary protest!

Here was the Church collecting pay for its services from the faithful, and then over again from the State! Here was the Ministry of the Interior appealing for a reduction in taxes—a program of strict economy—while new bishoprics were being created and ecclesiastical appropriations swelled for the benefit of the upper clergy; and with no advantage at all, meanwhile, to the proletariat of the soutane, to the poor curates who, to make a bare living, had to practice the most impious worldliness and unscrupulously exploit the house of God! And while this was going on public works could wait, towns could go without roads, Districts without railroads, though the wildest savages of Asia and Africa had both! Fields could continue to perish of drought while nearby rivers continued to pour their unutilized waters into the sea!

A thrill of conviction rippled through the Chamber. The silence was absolute. Everybody was holding his breath so as not to lose a syllable from that faint voice, which sounded like a cry from a distant tomb. It was as though Truth in person were passing through those murky precincts; and when the orator ended with an invocation to the future, in which social absurdities and injustice should no longer exist, the silence became deeper still, as if a glacial blast of death were blowing upon those brains that had thought themselves deliberating in the best of all possible worlds.

It was now time for the reply. Rafael arose, pale, pulling at his cuffs, waiting a few minutes for the excitement in the Chamber to subside. The audience had relaxed and was whispering and stirring about, after the sustained attention compelled by the concise style and the barely audible voice of the old man.

If Rafael was depending on the sympathy of an audience to encourage him, things looked promising indeed! The hall began to empty. Why not? Who is interested in a committee's reply to the Opposition? Besides, Brull had a bundle of documents on hand. A long-winded affair! Let's escape! Deputies filed by in line across the semi-circle in front of him; while above, in the galleries, the desertion was general. The caramel-chewers, noting that the display of celebrities was over for the day, rose from their places. Their coaches were ready outside for a ride through the Castellana. That strange woman in the diplomatic gallery had also risen to go. But no: she was giving her hand to her companion, bidding him good-bye. Now she had resumed her seat, continuing the busy movement of her fan that annoyed Rafael so. Thanks for the compliment, my fair one! Though as far as he was concerned, the whole audience might have gone, leaving only the president and the mace-bearers. Then he could speak without any fear at all! The public galleries, especially, unnerved him. Nobody had moved there. Those workingmen were without doubt waiting for the rebuttal of his answer from their venerable spokesman. Rafael felt that the swarthy heads above all those dirty blouses and shirt-fronts without collars or neckties were eyeing him with stony coldness. "Now we'll see what this ninny has got to say!"

Rafael began with a eulogy on the immaculate character, the political importance and the profound learning of that venerable septuagenarian who still had strength to battle consistently and nobly for the lost cause of his youth. An exordium of this nature was the regular procedure. That was how "the Chief" did things. And as he spoke, Rafael's eyes turned anxiously upon the clock. He wanted to be long, very long. If he did not talk for an hour and a half or two hours he would feel disgraced. Two hours was the least to be expected from a man of his promise. He had seen party chiefs and faction leaders go it for a whole afternoon, from four to eight, hoarse and puffing, sweating like diggers in a sewer, with their collars wilted to rags, watching the great hall-clock with the intentness of a man waiting to be hanged. "Still an hour left before closing time!" a speaker's friends would say. And the great orator, like a wearied horse, but a thoroughbred, would find new energy somewhere and start on another lap, round and round, repeating what he had already said a dozen times, summarizing the two ideas he had managed to produce in four hours of sonorous chatter. With duration as the test of quality, no one on the government had yet succeeded in equaling a certain redheaded deputy of the Opposition who was forever heckling the Premier, and could talk, if need be, three days in succession for four hours a day.

Rafael had heard people praise the conciseness and the clarity of new-fangled oratory in the parliaments of Europe. The speeches of party leaders in Paris or in London took up never more than half a column in a newspaper. Even the old man he was answering had adopted, to be original in everything, that selfsame conciseness: every sentence of his contained two or three ideas. But the member from Alcira would not be led astray by such niggardly parsimony. He believed that ponderousness and extension were qualities indispensable to eloquence. He must fill a whole issue of the Congressional Record, to impress his friends back home in the District. So he talked and talked on, trying deliberately to avoid ideas. Those he had he would keep in reserve as long as possible, certain that the longer he held them prisoner the longer and more solemn would his oration be.

He had gained a quarter of an hour without making any reply to the previous speech whatever, and literally burying his illustrious antagonist in flowers.

*Su señoria* was noteworthy firstly, because, secondly, because, fourteenthly, because . . . Nay more, he had accomplished this, performed that, endeavored the other thing—"But"—and with this *but,* alas, Rafael must begin to loosen up on a little of what he had prepared in advance. *Su señoria* was an "ideologue" of immense talent, but ever removed from reality; he would govern peoples in accordance with theories dug out of books, without paying any attention to practical considerations, to the individual and indestructible character possessed by every nation! . . .

And it was worth sitting an afternoon even in that Chamber to hear the slighting tone of scorn with which the member from Alcira emphasized that word *ideologue* and that phrase about "theories dug out of books" and "living removed from reality!"

"Good, fine. That's the way to give it to him," his comrades encouraged, nodding their sleek baldpates in indignation against anybody who tried to live apart from reality. Those *ideologues* needed somebody to tell them what was what!

And the minister, Rafael's friend, the only auditor left on the Blue Bench, pressing his huge paunch against the desk, turned his head—an owlish, hairy head with a sharp beak—to smile indulgently on the young man.

The orator continued, his confidence increasing as he went on, fortified by these signs of approval. He spoke of the patient, deliberate study the committee had made of this matter of the ecclesiastical budgets. He was the most modest, the least among them, but there were his comrades—they were there, in truth, solemn gentlemen in English frock-coats, with their hair parted in the middle, from their foreheads to the napes of their necks—studious young men—who had flattered him with the honor of speaking for them—and if they had not been more economical, it was because greater economy had been impossible.

And the heads of the committee-men nodded as they murmured gratefully:

"Say, this fellow Brull can make quite a speech!"

The government was ready to exercise any economy that should prove prudent and feasible, without prejudice to the dignity of the nation; but Spain was an eminently religious country, favored by God in all her crises; and no government loyal to the national genius could ever touch a *céntimo* of the ecclesiastical appropriation. Never! Never! . . .

On the word *never* his voice resounded with the melancholy echo that rings in empty houses. Rafael looked in anguish at the clock. Half an hour. Half an hour gained, and still he had not really damaged his outline. His talk was going so well that he was sorry the Chamber was far from crowded! . . . Before him, in the shadows of the diplomatic gallery, that fan kept fluttering. Pesky woman! Why couldn't she keep quiet and not spoil his speech!

The president, so restless and vigilant, so ever-ready with watch and bell in hand when any of the Opposition had the floor, was now sitting back in his chair with his eyes shut, dozing away with the confidence of a stage director who is sure the show will go off without a hitch. The panes of the glass dome were glowing under the rays of the sun, but they allowed only a diffuse, green light, a discreet, soft, crypt-like clarity to seep through into the

Chamber that lay below in monastic calm. Through
the windows over the president's chair, Rafael
glimpsed patches of the blue sky, drenched in the
gentle light of an afternoon of Springtime. A white
dove was hovering in the perspective of those blue
squares.

Rafael felt a slackening of his powers of endurance, as if an irresistible languor were stealing over
him. The sweet smile of Nature peering at him
through the transoms of that gloomy, parliamentary
tomb had taken him back to his orange-orchards, and
to his Valencian meadows covered with flowers. He
felt a curious impulse to finish his speech in a few
hasty words, grab his hat and flee, losing himself
out among the groves of the Royal Gardens. With
that sun and those flowers outside, what was he
doing in that hole, talking of things that did not
concern him in the least? . . . But he successfully
passed this fleeting crisis. He ceased rummaging
among the bundles of documents piled up on the
bench, stopped thumbing papers so as to hide his
perturbation, and waving the first sheet that came
to his hand, he went on.

The intention of the gentleman in opposing this
appropriation was not hidden from him. On this
matter he had his own, his private and personal
ideas. "I understand that *su señoria,* in here pro-
posing retrenchment, is really seeking to combat
religious institutions, of which he is a declared
enemy."

And as he reached this point, Rafael dashed
wildly into the fray. He was treading firm and familiar ground. All this part of the speech he had
prepared, paragraph by paragraph: a defense of

Catholicism, an apology *pro fide,* so intimately bound up with the history of Spain. He could now use impassioned outbursts and tremors of lyric enthusiasm, as if he were preaching a new crusade.

On the Opposition benches he caught the ironic glitter of a pair of spectacles, the convulsions of a white chin quivering over two folded arms, as if a kindly, indulgent smile had greeted his parade of so many musty and faded commonplaces. But Rafael was not to be intimidated. He had gotten away with an hour almost! Forward, to "Section Two" of the outline, the part about the great national and Christian epic! And he began to reel off visions of the cave of Covadonga; the fantastic tree of the Reconquest "where the warrior hung up his sword, the poet his harp," and so on and so on, for everybody hung up something there; seven centuries of wars for the cross, a rather long time, believe me, gentlemen, during which Saracen impiety was expelled from Spanish soil! Then came the great triumphs of Catholic unity. Spain mistress of almost the whole world, the sun never allowed to set on Spanish domains; the caravels of Columbus bearing the cross to virgin lands; the light of Christianity blazing forth from the folds of the national banner to shed its illuminating rays throughout the earth.

And as if this hymn to enlightening Christianity, chanted by an orator who could now hardly see across the gloomy hall, had been a signal, the electric lights went on; and the statues, the escutcheons, and the harsh, blatant figures painted on the cupola, sprang forth from obscurity.

Rafael could hardly contain his joy at the facility with which his speech was developing. That wave of light which was shed over the hall, in the middle of the afternoon, while the sun was still shining, seemed to him like the sudden entrance of Glory, approaching to give him the accolade of renown.

Caught up now in the real torrent of his premeditated verbosity, he continued to relieve himself of all that he had learned by cramming during the past few days. "In vain does *su señoria* fatigue his wits. Spain is and will remain a profoundly religious country. Her history is the history of Catholicism: she has survived in all her times of storm and stress by tightly embracing the Cross." And he could now come to the national wars; from the battles in which popular piety saw Saint James, on his white steed, lopping off the heads of the Moors with his golden cutlass, to the uprising of the people against Napoleon, behind the banner of the parish and with their scapularies on their bosoms. He did not have a word to say about the present. He left the pitiless criticism of the old revolutionist intact. Why not? The dream of an ideologue! He was absorbed in his song of the past, affirming for the hundredth time that Spain had been great because she had been Catholic and that when for a moment she had ceased to be Catholic, all the evils of the world had descended upon her. He spoke of the excesses of the Revolution, of the turbulent Republic of '73, (a cruel nightmare to all right-thinking persons) and of the "canton" of Cartagena (the supreme recourse of ministerial oratory),—a veritable cannibal feast, a horror that had never been known even in this land of *pronunciamientos* and civil wars. He tried his best to make his hearers feel the terror of those revolutions, whose chief defect had been that they had revolutionized nothing. . . . And then came a panegyric on the Christian family, on the Catholic home, a nest of virtues and blessings, whereas in nations where Catholicism did not reign all homes were repulsive brothels or horrible bandit caves.

"Fine, Brull, very good," grunted the minister, his elbows stretched forward over his desk, delighted to hear his own ideas echoing from the young man's mouth.

The orator rested for a moment, with his glance sweeping the galleries now bright with the electric lighting. The woman in the diplomatic section had stopped fanning herself. She was following him closely. Her eyes met his.

Of a sudden Rafael nearly fell to his seat. Those eyes! . . . Perhaps an astonishing resemblance! But no; it was she—she was smiling to him with that same jesting, mocking smile of their earlier acquaintance!

He felt like the bird writhing on the tree unable to free itself from the hypnotic stare of the serpent coiled near the trunk. Those sarcastic, mischievous eyes had upset all his train of thought. He tried to finish in some way or other, to end his speech as soon as posible. Every minute was an added torment to him; he imagined he could hear the mute gibes that mouth must be uttering at his expense.

Again he looked at the clock; in fifteen minutes more he would be through. And he spurted on at a mad pace, with a hurried voice, forgetting the devices he had thought of to prolong the peroration, dumping them out all in a heap—anything to get through! "The Concordate . . . sacred obliga-

tions toward the clergy . . . their services of old
. . . promises of close friendship with the Pope
. . . the generous father of Spain . . . in short, we
cannot reduce the budget by a *céntimo* and the committee stands by its proposals without accepting a
single amendment."

As he sat down, perspiring, excited, wiping his con-
gested face energetically, his bench companions
gathered around him congratulating him, shaking his
hands. He was every inch an orator! He should
have gone deeper into the matter and taken even
more time! He shouldn't have been so modest!

And from the bench below came the grunt of the
minister:

"Very good, very good. You said exactly what I
would have said."

The old revolutionist arose to make a short rebuttal, repeating the contentions of his original
speech, of which no denial had been attempted.

"I'm quite tired," sighed Rafael, in reply to the
felicitations.

"You can go out if you wish," said the minister.
"I think I'll answer the rebuttal myself. It's a courtesy due to so old a deputy."

Rafael raised his eyes toward the diplomatic gallery. It was empty. But he imagined he could still
make out the plumes of a woman's hat in the dark
background.

He left his bench hastily and hurried to the corridor, where a number of deputies were waiting with
their congratulations.

Not one of them had heard him, but they were
all profuse in their flattering remarks. They shook
his hand and detained him maddeningly. Once more

he thought he could descry at the end of the corridor, at the foot of the gallery staircase, standing out against the glass exit-door, those black, waving plumes.

He elbowed his way through the crowds, deaf to all congratulations, brushing aside the hands that were proferred to him.

Near the door he stumbled into two of his associates, who were looking out with eyes radiant with admiration.

"What a woman? Eh?"

"She looks like a foreigner. Some diplomat's wife, I guess!"

# III

As he came out of the building he saw her on the sidewalk, about to step into a vehicle. An usher of the Congress was holding the carriage door open, with the demonstrative respect inspired by the goldbraid shining on the driver's hat. It was an embassy coach!

Rafael approached, believing, from the carriage, that it still might prove to be a case of an astonishing resemblance. But no; it was she; the same woman she had always been, as if eight hours and not eight years had passed:

"Leonora! You here! . . ."

She smiled, as if it were the most natural thing in the world to see him again.

"I saw you and heard you. You did very well, Rafael: I enjoyed it."

And grasping his hand in a frank, hearty clasp of friendship, she entered the carriage with a rustle of silk and fine linen.

"Come! Won't you step in too?" she asked, smiling. "Join me for a little drive along the Castellana. It's a magnificent afternoon; a little fresh air won't do any harm after that muggy room."

Rafael, to the astonishment of the usher, who was surprised to see him in such seductive company, got in; and the carriage rolled off. There they were, together again, sitting side by side, swaying gently back and forth with the motion of the soft springs.

Rafael was at a loss for words. The cold, ironic smile of his former lover chilled him. He was flushed with shame at the thought of how he had treated that beautiful creature the last time they had seen each other. He wanted to say something, and yet he could not find a way to begin. The ceremonious, formal *usted* she had employed in inviting him into the carirage embarrassed him. At last he ventured, timidly, also avoiding the intimate *tu!*

"Imagine our meeting here! What a surprise!"

"I got in yesterday; tomorrow I leave for Lisbon. A short stop, isn't it! Just time for a word with the director of the *Real;* perhaps I'll come next winter to sing *Die Walküre* here. But let's talk about you, illustrious orator. . . . But I may say *tu* to you, mayn't I?" she corrected—"for I believe we are still friends."

"Yes, friends, Leonora. . . . I have never been able to forget you."

But the feeling he put into the words vanished before the cold smile with which she answered.

"Friends; that's it," she said, slowly. "Friends, and nothing more. Between us there lies a corpse that prevents us from getting very close to each other again."

"A corpse?" asked Rafael, not catching her meaning.

"Yes; the love you murdered. . . . Friends, nothing more; comrades united by complicity in a crime."

And she laughed with cruel sarcasm, while the carriage turned into one of the avenues of Recoletos. Leonora looked vacantly out upon the central boulevard. The rows of iron benches were filled with people.  Groups of children in charge of governesses were playing gaily about in the soft, golden splendor of the afternoon.

"I read in the papers this morning that don Rafael Brull, 'of the Finance Commission,' if you please, would undertake to speak for the Ministry on the matter of the budget; so I got down on my knees to an old friend of mine, the secretary of the English embassy, and begged him to come and take me to the session.  This coach is his. . . . Poor fellow!  He doesn't know you, but the moment he saw you stand up to speak, he took to his heels. . . . He missed something though; for really, you weren't half bad.  I'm quite impressed.  Say, Rafael, where do you dig up all those things?"

But Rafael looked uneasily at her cruel smile and refused to accept her praise.  Besides, what did he care about his speech?  It seemed to him that he had been for years and years in that coach; that a whole lifetime had gone by since he left the halls of the Congress.  His gaze was fixed on her in admiration, and his astonished eyes were drinking in the beauty of her face, and of her figure.

"How beautiful you are!" he murmured in impulsive enchantment.  "The same as you were then. It seems impossible that eight years can have flown by."

"Yes; I admit that I bear up well.  Time seems not to touch me.  A little longer at the dressing table—that's all.  I'm one of the people who die in harness, so to speak, making no concessions, so far as looks go, to old age.  Rather than surrender, I'd kill myself.  I intend to put Ninon de Lenclos in the shade!"

It was true. Eight years had made not the slightest impression on her. The same freshness, the same robust, energetic slenderness, the identical flames of arrogant vitality in her green eyes. Instead of withering under the incessant parching of passion's flame, she seemed to grow stronger, hardier, in the crucible.

She measured the deputy with sarcastic playfulness.

"Poor Rafael! I'm sorry I can't say as much for you. How you've changed! You look almost like a Knight of the Crown. You're fat! You're bald! And those eyeglasses! Why, I could hardly recognize you in the Chamber. How my romantic Moor has aged! You poor dear! You even have wrinkles! . . ."

And she laughed, as if it filled her with intense joy, the joy of vengeance, to see her former lover so crestfallen at her portrayal of his decrepitude.

"You're not happy, are you! I can see that. And yet, you ought to be. You must have married that girl your mother picked for you. You doubtless have children. . . . Don't try to fib to me, just to seem more . . .what shall I say . . . more interesting! I can see it from the looks of you. You are the *pater familias* all over. I am never mistaken in such things! . . . Well, why aren't you happy? You have all the requisites for a personage of note, and you will shortly be one. I'll bet you wear that sash to hold your paunch in! You are rich, you make speeches in that horrid, gloomy, cave. Your friends back home will go into ecstasies when they read the oration their honorable deputy has delivered; and I imagine they're already preparing fire-

works and music for a reception to you.  What more
could you ask for?"

And with her eyes half-closed, smiling maliciously, she waited for his reply, knowing in advance what
it would be.

"What more can I ask for?  Love; Leonora, the
love I once had . . . with you."

And with the vehemence of other days, as if they
were still among the orange-trees of the old Blue
House, the deputy gave way to his eight years of
longing.

He told her of the image he nourished in his sadness.  Love!  The Love that passes but once in a
lifetime, crowned with flowers, and followed by a
retinue of kisses and laughter.  And whosoever
follows him in obedience, finds happiness at the end
of the joyous pathway; but whosoever, through pride
or selfishness, lags by the wayside, comes to lament
his folly and to expiate his cowardice in an everlast-
ing life of tedium and sorrow!  He had sinned, griev-
ously.  That he would confess!  But could she not
forgive him?  He had paid for his deliquency with
eight long, monotonous, crushing, meaningless
years, one suffocating stifling night that never broke
into morning.  But they had met again!  There was
still time, Leonora!  They could still call back the
Springtime of their lives, make it burgeon anew,
compel Love to retrace his footsteps, pass their way
again, stretching forth his sweet hands of youth to
them!

The actress was listening with a smile upon her
lips, her eyes closed, her head thrown back in the
carriage.  It was an expression of intense pleasure,
as if she were tasting with delight the fire of love

that was still burning in Rafael, and that, to her, meant vengeance.

The horses were proceeding at a walk along la Castellana. Other carriages were going by and the people in them peered back at the coach with that beautiful, unknown woman.

"What is your answer, Leonora? We can still be happy! Forget the past and the wrong I did you! Imagine it was only yesterday that we said good-bye in the orchard, and that we are meeting again today to begin our lives over again from the beginning, to live together always, always."

"No," she replied coldly. "You yourself just said so: Love passes but once in a lifetime. I know that from cruel experience. I have done my best to forget. No, Love has passed us by! It would be sheer folly for us to ask him to hunt us up again. He never comes back! Our most desperate effort could revive barely the shadow of him. You let him escape. Well, you must weep for your loss, just as I had to weep for your baseness . . . Besides, you don't realize the situation we are in now! Don't you remember what we talked about on our first night there in the moonlight? 'The arrogant month of May, the young warrior in an armor of flowers, seeks out his beloved, Youth.' Well, where is our youth now? Quite frankly, you can find mine on my dressing-table! I buy it at the perfumer's; and though that gentleman is quite skilled at disguising me, there's an oldness of the spirit underneath, a terrible thing I don't dare think about, because it frightens me so. And yours, poor Rafael—you just haven't any, not even the kind you can buy! Take a good look at yourself! You're ugly, to put it mildly, my dear boy! You've lost that attractive slimness of your younger days. Your dreams make me laugh! A passion at this late date! The idyll of a middle-aged siren and a bald-headed father of a litter of children, with a paunch, with a paunch, with a paunch! Oh, Rafael! Ha, ha, ha!"

The cruel mocker! How she laughed! How she was avenging herself. Rafael grew angry at this cutting, ironic resistance. He began to flame with a more excited passion. . . . The ravages of time made no difference. Could not Love work miracles! He loved her more than he had ever loved her in the olden days. He felt a mad hunger for her. Passion would give them back the fires of youth. Love was like a springtime that brings new sap to branches grown numb in the winter's cold. Let her say "Yes," and on the instant she would behold the miracle, the resurrection of their slumbering past, the awakening of their souls to the future of love!

"And your wife? And your children?" Leonora asked, brutally, as if she wished to bring him back to realities, with a smarting lash from a whip.

But Rafael was now beside himself, drunk with the nearness of all that beauty, and with the waves of perfume that filled the interior of the carriage.

Wife? Family? He would leave everything for her: family, future, position. It was she he needed to live and be happy!

"I will go with you; everybody is a stranger to me when I think of you. You, you alone, are my life, my love!"

"Many thanks," Leonora answered curtly. "I could not accept such a sacrifice. . . . Besides, all that sanctity of the home you were just talking about a few moments ago in the Chamber? And all that Christian morality, without which civilization would go to the damnation bow wows! How I laughed when I heard you say that. How you were stuffing those poor ninkampoops! . . ."

And again she laughed cruelly, at the contrast between his pious words in Congress and his mad idea of forsaking everything to follow her around the world. Oh, the hypocrite! She had felt, as she sat listening to him, that his speech was a pack of lies, a mess of conventional trumpery and platitudes! The only one there who had spoken with any real sincerity, any real virtue, was that little old man, whom she had listened to with veneration because he had been one of her father's idols!

Rafael was crushed with bitter shame. Leonora's flat refusal, her pitiless mockery of his speech, had brought him to realize the enormity of his baseness. She was avenging herself by bringing him face to face with the abjectness of his mad, hopeless passion, which made him capable of committing the lowest deeds!

Dusk was gathering. Leonora ordered the driver to the Plaza de Oriente. She was stopping in one of the houses near the Opera where many theatrical people lodged. She was in a hurry! She had a dinner engagement with that young man from the Embassy, and two musical critics were to be introduced to her.

"And I, Leonora? Are we not to see each other any longer?"

"As far as my door, if you wish, and then . . . till we meet again!"

"Oh, please, Leonora, stay here a few days! Let

me see you! Let me have the consolation of talking to you, of feeling the bitter pleasure of your ridicule, at least!"

Stay a few days! . . . Her days did not belong to her. She traveled from one end of the world to the other, with her life marked off to the tick of the clock. From Madrid to Lisbon—an engagement at the San Carlos—three performances of Wagner! Then, a jump to Stockholm! After that she was not quite sure where she would go; to Odessa, or to Cairo. She was the Wandering Jew, the Valkyrie galloping along on the clouds of a musical tempest, from frontier to frontier, from pole to pole, arrogant, victorious, suffering not the slightest harm to health or beauty.

"Oh, if you only would! If you would let me follow you! As your friend, nothing more! As your servant, if necessary!"

And he grasped her hand, passionately, thrusting his fingers up her sleeve, fondling the delicate arm underneath her glove. She did not resist.

"There! Do you see, Rafael?" she said, smiling coldly. "You have touched me, and it's useless; not the slightest thrill. You're as good as dead to me. My flesh does not tingle at your fondling. In fact, I find it all decidedly annoying!"

Rafael realized that it was true. She had once trembled madly under his caresses. Now she was quite insensible, quite cold!

"Don't worry, Rafael. It's over, spelled with a capital O. It's not worth wasting a moment's thought on. As I look at you now I feel the way I do when I see one of my old dresses that, in its time, I went mad over. I see nothing but the defects—the absurdities of the fashion that is out of date. Our passion died as it should properly have died. Perhaps your deserting me was for the best. It was better for you to default in the full splendor of our honeymoon than to have broken with me afterwards, when I should have moulded my nature forever to your caresses. We were brought together . . . oh, by the orange perfume, by that cursed Springtime; but you were not meant for me, nor was I ever meant for you. We are of different breeds. You were born a bourgeois. I am an out-and-out bohemian! Love and the novelty of my kind quite dazzled you. You struggled hard, you beat your wings, to follow me, but you fell to earth from the very weight of your inherited traits. You have the appetites and the ambitions of people like you! Now you imagine you are unhappy! But you'll find you're not when you see yourself become a 'personage,' when you count the acreage of your orchards over, when you see your children growing up to inherit papa's power and fortune. This business of love for love's sake, mocking at law and morality, scorning life and peacefulness, that is our privilege, the privilege of us bohemians—the sole blessing left to us mad creatures whom society looks upon—quite properly, I suppose—with disdainful mistrust. Each to his own! The poultry to their quiet roost, where they can fatten in the sun; the birds of passage to their wandering life of song, sometimes in a flowering garden, sometimes in the cold and storm!"

And smiling again, as if those words, uttered with such gravity and conviction, had been too cruel in

their effective summary of the whole story of their
love, she added in a jesting tone:

"That was a fine little paragraph, wasn't it?
What a pity you didn't hear it in time to tack it
on at the end of your speech!"

The carriage had entered the *Plaza de Oriente*,
and was drawing up in front of Leonora's house.

"May I go in with you?" the deputy asked anxiously, much as a child might beg for a toy.

"Why? You'll only be bored. It will be the
same as here. Upstairs there is no moon, and there
are no orange-trees in bloom. You can't expect two
nights like that in a life like yours. Besides, I don't
want Beppa to see you. She has a vivid recollection
of that afternoon in the Hôtel de Roma when I got
your note. I'd lose prestige with her if she saw
me in your company."

With a commanding gesture she motioned him to
the sidewalk. When the carriage had gone they
stood there together for a moment looking at each
other for the last time.

"Farewell, Rafael. Take good care of yourself,
and try not to grow old so rapidly. I believe it's
been a real pleasure, though, to see you again. I
needed just this to convince myself it was really all
over!"

"But are you going like this! . . . Is this the
way you let a passion end that still fills my life!
. . . When shall we see each other again?"

"I don't know: never . . . perhaps when you
least expect it. The world is large, but when a person gads about it the way I do, you never can tell
whom you are going to meet."

Rafael pointed to the Opera nearby.

"And if you should come to sing . . . here?
. . . If I were actually to see you again? . . .

Leonora smiled haughtily, guessing what he
meant.

"In that case, you will be one of my countless
friends, I suppose, but nothing more. Don't imagine that I'm a saint even now. I'm just as I was
before you knew me. The property of everybody—
understand—and of nobody! But of the janitor of
the opera, if necessary, sooner than of you. You are
a corpse, in my eyes, Rafael. . . . Farewell!"

He saw her vanish through the doorway; and he
stood for a long time there on the sidewalk, completely crushed, staring vacantly into the last glow
of twilight that was growing pale beyond the gables
of the Royal Palace.

Some birds were twittering on the trees of the
garden, shaking the leaves with their mischievous
playfulness, as if the fires of Springtime were cours-
ing in their veins. For Spring had come again, faithful and punctual, as every year.

He staggered off toward the center of the city,
slowly, dejectedly, with the thought of death in his
mind, bidding farewell to all his dreams, which that
woman seemed to have destroyed forever in turning
her back implacably upon him. Yes! A corpse, indeed! He was a dead man dragging a soulless
body along under the sad glimmering of the first
street-lamps. Farewell! Farewell to Love! Farewell to Youth! For him Springtime would never return again. Joyous Folly repelled him as an unworthy deserter. His future was to grow a fatter
and fatter paunch under the frock coat of a "personage"!

At the corner of the Calle del Arenal he heard his name called. It was a deputy, a comrade of "the Party" who had just come from the session.

"Let me congratulate you, Brull; you were simply monumental! The Chief spoke enthusiastically of your speech to the Prime Minister! It's a foregone conclusion. At the first new deal you'll be made director-general or undersecretary at least! Again, my congratulations, old fellow!"

THE END